Praise for *Songs for the Missing*

"This is a novel about loss and healing; a novel that acknowledges the depth of loss and the limits of healing. . . . You could call this novel many things. You could call it a mystery. You could call it a thriller. You could even call it a self-help book, for reading it slowly and carefully causes one to consider love and sorrow in a much larger context than simply that of this well-paced tale. O'Nan has a remarkable ability to pinpoint the ways in which hope and suffering are intertwined. . . . This is a fine, absorbing book. It's easy to imagine that O'Nan is on a kind of mission to restore a simple, true sense of humanity to the novel; a worthy goal, indeed."
—*The New York Times Book Review*

"Some books should come with warnings. That's not a complaint, at least in the case of Stewart O'Nan's haunting novel *Songs for the Missing*, which kept me up most of the night. . . . O'Nan, a former aviation engineer, describes emotional roller coasters in prose that's remarkably taut and precise."
—Bob Minzesheimer, *USA Today*

"*Songs for the Missing* has a plot that is deceptively easy to summarize, but the book has a mood so subtle that only first-rate fiction can evoke it. . . . As we read, we, too, are changed, and in ways we cannot even understand. . . . It's the sort of experience that reveals why we read in the first place, knowing that the sadness we find inside a book mirrors the sadness always within reach."
—*San Francisco Chronicle*

"Art, like athletics, is all about making it look easy. That's the special magic behind the work of Stewart O'Nan, a novelist who brings his uncommon gifts to the task of rendering the common world. He writes with quiet precision about people we all know, people in regular jobs with lives we can all recognize, and the result is work that shimmers with versimilitude. You can forget, for long stretches, that you're reading fiction, because it feels as if you're eavesdropping on somebody's cell phone conversation on the bus. His writing is that true."
—Julia Keller, *Chicago Tribune*

"Too often the face on the milk carton becomes a dimensionless symbol, but by allowing his cast of characters to grow and change and to find their real selves, O'Nan restores humanity even among those whose fate remains in suspended animation."
—*Los Angeles Times*

"Stewart O'Nan is a daredevil. . . . In scene after scene, these spare descriptions will make you catch your breath. . . . The world that O'Nan captures thwarts our expectations for cathartic tragedy or gleeful celebration, which makes the story even more devastating."
—*The Washington Post*

"The book's emotional power is undeniable, as each character grieves for Kim, wanting her disappearance to mean something beyond 'the world's incoherence.' In the midst of the search, they elegiacally discover a little of what has been missing among themselves."
—Don Lee, *The Boston Globe*

"O'Nan also sensitively observes the fraying and deepening of relationships during trauma and the unexpected ways it can change people."
—*The Seattle Times*

"At the heart of Stewart O'Nan's powerful fiction is his compassion for ordinary people. . . . With his characteristic spare prose style and his impressively precise use of detail, O'Nan reflects and illuminates life in Kingsville. His major achievement, however, is the intensity of the empathy he conveys to readers for all who knew Kim Larsen."
—*Star Tribune* (Minneapolis)

"*Songs for the Missing* is anything but an easy read, but it's a spectacular one. And, like most of O'Nan's work, one that resolutely draws the reader in and refuses to let go."
—*The Denver Post*

"Chilling and honest . . . Like all great writers, O'Nan possesses the ability to place the reader squarely inside the thoughts of his characters. In *Songs for the Missing* it may be an ultimately nightmarish place no parent, sibling or friend ever wants to be. But you won't regret that O'Nan put you there."
—*St. Louis Post-Dispatch*

"O'Nan's novel is an elegant elegy: He has plumbed the depth of the horror no one ever wants to experience, and done it with sympathy, honesty and respect."
—*The Times-Picayune* (New Orleans)

"Choosing to avoid the what, who and why of Kim's disappearance, Mr. O'Nan instead paints a nuanced portrait of how people are changed by tragic events and the far-reaching effect a person's disappearance has on their family and community. *Songs for the Missing* is an elegantly crafted, memorable book that resonates with sadness."
—*The Economist*

"O'Nan writes with great sympathy and perceptiveness, and he really captures the texture of working-class American lives."   —*Newsday*

"Riveting . . . *Songs for the Missing* is an engaging and often excruciating read; it makes vivid our most dreadful thoughts, forcing us to contemplate the kind of thing we like to believe only happens elsewhere. O'Nan uses the filter of fiction along with his razor sharp, unerring eye for local detail to render our darkest and most disturbing nightmares all too real."
—*The Cleveland Plain Dealer*

"Taut prose and matter-of-fact detail enrich this compelling portrait of teenage life in small-town Ohio. . . . Though the author sustains narrative momentum through the conventions of the police procedural, ultimately the novel is less about a possible crime than about the interconnections of small-town life. 'The problem was that everything was connected,' thinks one of Kim's friends. 'One lie covered another, which covered a third, which rested against a fourth. It all went back to Kingsville being so goddamn small.' A novel in which every word rings true."
—*Kirkus Reviews* (starred review)

"O'Nan proves that uncertainty can be the worst punishment of all in this unflinching look at an unraveling family. Through shifting points of view . . . O'Nan raises the suspense while conveying the sheer torture of what it's like not to know what has happened to a loved one. When—if ever—do you stop looking?"   —*Publishers Weekly* (starred review)

"What begins as a procedural turns into something more interesting: a mosaic-mirror reflection of the small town that mourns her loss."
—*Vogue*

"A page-turner that illustrates the unsettling idea that sometimes answers only raise more questions."   —*Marie Claire*

"*Songs for the Missing* is the kind of book that makes you wish your flight were longer. . . . After hooking readers with the fact-paced opening, Mr. O'Nan edges away from the easy payoffs of the thriller genre. He resists the clichés of closure and triumph over adversity. Instead, he gives the reader more ordinary satisfaction of characters who confront tragedy and doggedly endure."   —*The Dallas Morning News*

"It's a story as familiar as a photo on a milk carton, as unimaginable as death. It's also a situation that has been the basis for countless tearjerking and predictable movies and TV episodes. Not in this novel; *Songs for the Missing* has an emotional austerity and courage that make it far more moving. . . . One of the great strengths is that very little of what happens then is what you might expect—and yet it rings entirely, heartbreakingly true."
—*St. Petersburg Times*

"O'Nan's use of details . . . give a believable, behind-the-scenes glimpse of what a grieving family must endure. . . . A nuanced portrait."
—*Pittsburgh Post-Gazette*

"The characters he creates are so lifelike that one tends to forget they are fictional. . . . Many of O'Nan's books contain a dark element, and *Songs for the Missing* is one of the most haunting. The writing, as always, is consistently beautiful."
—*The Free Lance-Star* (Fredericksburg)

"O'Nan shifts his point of view . . . and hits each with pointillist accuracy, creating complex portraits of each individual as well as the shifting mood of the town itself. Most impressive, however, is the precision with which O'Nan conveys the transformation of a family's fresh terror into a kind of quotidian torture. . . . O'Nan creates his narrative tension out of the relationships between his multilayered characters. There is none of the easy sensationalism here that his subject might suggest and not a single wasted sentence. Powerful, honest and at times elegiac, this absorbing and masterfully written novel is not to be missed."
—*Shelf Awareness*

"Both profound and profoundly beautiful. A haunting meditation on the power of those we lose, its emotional resonance defies description. Like most of Stewart O'Nan's work, my ultimate response was the highest praise one writer can pay another: envy. I so dearly wish I'd written it."
—Dennis Lehane

"Stewart O'Nan has done the seemingly impossible—taken a story with tabloid potential and not just avoided the pitfalls of melodrama and unearned grace but written a novel that is singularly insightful, beautifully modulated, and genuinely moving. It's also very suspenseful. I read it quickly but will remember it for a very long time."
—Ann Packer

PENGUIN BOOKS

SONGS FOR THE MISSING

Stewart O'Nan is the author of eleven novels, including *Snow Angels* and *A Prayer for the Dying*, a story collection, and two works of nonfiction. His previous novel, *Last Night at the Lobster*, a national bestseller, was nominated for the *Los Angeles Times* Book Prize and was named one of the New York Public Library's Books to Remember. Additionally, *Granta* named him one of the twenty Best Young American Novelists. O'Nan lives with his family in Avon, Connecticut.

SONGS FOR THE MISSING

· · ·

Stewart O'Nan

PENGUIN BOOKS

PENGUIN BOOKS
Published by the Penguin Group
Penguin Group (USA) Inc., 375 Hudson Street, New York, New York 10014, U.S.A. • Penguin Group
(Canada), 90 Eglinton Avenue East, Suite 700, Toronto, Ontario, Canada M4P 2Y3 (a division of Pearson Penguin
Canada Inc.) • Penguin Books Ltd, 80 Strand, London WC2R 0RL, England • Penguin Ireland, 25 St
Stephen's Green, Dublin 2, Ireland (a division of Penguin Books Ltd) • Penguin Group (Australia), 250
Camberwell Road, Camberwell, Victoria 3124, Australia (a division of Pearson Australia Group Pty
Ltd) • Penguin Books India Pvt Ltd, 11 Community Centre, Panchsheel Park, New Delhi – 110 017,
India • Penguin Group (NZ), 67 Apollo Drive, Rosedale, North Shore 0632, New Zealand (a division of
Pearson New Zealand Ltd) • Penguin Books (South Africa) (Pty) Ltd, 24 Sturdee Avenue, Rosebank,
Johannesburg 2196, South Africa

Penguin Books Ltd, Registered Offices: 80 Strand, London WC2R 0RL, England

First published in the United States of America by Viking Penguin,
a member of Penguin Group (USA) Inc. 2008
Published in Penguin Books 2009

10 9 8 7 6 5 4 3 2 1

THE LIBRARY OF CONGRESS HAS CATALOGED THE HARDCOVER EDITION AS FOLLOWS:
O'Nan, Stewart.
Songs for the missing / Stewart O'Nan.
p. cm.
ISBN 978-0-670-02032-4 (hc.)
ISBN 978-0-14-311602-8 (pbk.)
1. Teenage girls—Fiction. 2. Missing persons—Fiction. 3. Ohio—Fiction. 4. Domestic fiction. I. Title.
PS3565.N316S66 2008
813'.54—dc22   2008022274

Printed in the United States of America
Designed by Carla Bolte • Set in Granjon

For Trudy and Caitlin and Stephen

Someday I'll wish upon a star
and wake up where the clouds are far
behind me
Where troubles melt like lemon drops
away above the chimney tops
that's where you'll find me

Songs for the Missing

Description of the Person, When Last Seen

July, 2005. It was the summer of her Chevette, of J.P. and letting her hair grow. The last summer, the best summer, the summer they'd dreamed of since eighth grade, the high and pride of being seniors lingering, an extension of their best year. She and Nina and Elise, the Three Amigos. In the fall they were gone, off to college, where she hoped, by a long and steady effort, she might become someone else, a private, independent person, someone not from Kingsville at all.

The sins of the Midwest: flatness, emptiness, a necessary acceptance of the familiar. Where is the romance in being buried alive? In growing old?

She did not hate the town, as, years later, her sister would tell one lover. Not Kim, not the good daughter. She loved the lake, how on a clear day you could see all the way to Canada from the bluffs. She loved the river, winding hidden in its mossy gorge of shale down to the harbor. She even loved the slumping Victorian mansions along Grandview her father was always trying to sell, and the sandstone churches downtown, and the stainless steel diner across from the post office. She was just eighteen.

At the Conoco, on break, she liked to cross the lot and then the on-ramp and stand at the low rail of the overpass, French-inhaling menthols in the dark as traffic whipped past below, taillights shooting west into the future. Toledo was three hours away, on the far side of Cleveland, far enough to be another country. Trucks lit like spaceships shuddered under her feet, dragging their own hot wind, their trailers full of unknown cargo. Slowly, night by night, the dream of leaving was coming true—with her family's blessing, their very highest hopes. She could not regret it. She could only be grateful.

Inside, the a/c was cranked so high she wore a T-shirt under her uniform. They poached old nametags they found in the junk drawer under the register. She was Angie, Nina was Sam. They spun on their stools and watched the monitors, punching in the pump numbers and making change. They read heavy, insane fashion magazines and called around to see what was going on later—even though they were on camera too—and fought over whose turn it was to refill the nacho pot. Her timecard was in its slot, the clock beside it chunking with every minute, a record of her steadiness. She'd worked seven days a week since graduation and hadn't missed a shift. Later the police would call this strict pattern a contributing factor. Secretly she was proud of it. She'd never been so determined. She'd never had a reason before.

The Conoco was an oasis of light, drawing cars off the highway like the muffleheads that fluttered against the windows. Drivers came in squinting and rubbing their necks, stopping on the mat inside the door as if this was all new to them, and too much, the bright aisles of candies and chips overloading their brains so they couldn't read the sign directly in front of them.

They blinked at her, apologetic. "Where are the—?"

"Straight back."

Fifty, a hundred times a night. She pointed her whole arm like a ghost.

"It's true," Nina said. "The more you drive, the dumber you get."

"Thank you, thank you, Sam I Am."

The living dead had bad breath. They bought coffee and soda and water, cigarettes and gum, Tootsie Pops and jerky, anything to get them to the next stop. In line they nodded their heads and mouthed the lyrics to the dinosaur pop that played endlessly inside and out, a fiendish commercial-free satellite feed pieced together, it seemed, by U2 and the Doobie Brothers. They paid double what they would at the Giant Eagle and were grateful when she took a penny from the little dish to cover them.

"Thanks a lot, Angie."

"Thanks a lot, Angie," Nina mocked, acting retarded, nuzzling her and flicking her tongue near her ear.

"Eww. Did you *smell* him?"

"He wanted to pet you and hug you and love you."

"No, that's you."

"Don't tell Hinch."

"Too late."

The creepiest were the old guys who bought condoms and wanted to joke about it like they were on the same team. There was a regular from down the county Nina christened Fat Joe-Bob who must have weighed three hundred pounds and wore a chunky gold chain and the same black Steeler sweatpants year-round.

"I don't think he actually uses them," Nina said. "You know, the normal way?"

"Maybe he's married."

"Ow, my eyes!" Nina said, covering them. "I'm not supposed to get fatfuck in them."

Eight hours in a freezing glass box. Even Nina couldn't make it go fast enough.

Their customers weren't all strangers. Friends and classmates visited, sliding their fake IDs across the counter for them to inspect. Nina thought it was funny that Kim felt guilty, since they both had their own. For Kim it wasn't the fear of getting busted so much as the feeling she was being taken advantage of, but hours later, when they caught up with their friends again, she drank her fair share of beers and was thankful she didn't have to pay for them.

Every night they fought a war against boredom and lost. She thought their bodies should have adapted to swing shift after a whole month. Nina thought it had something to do with the fluorescents, the flat, shadowless wash of light that brought out the veins in their hands, their palms splotchy as raw hamburger. It was like living under water, two captured mermaids displayed in a tank.

And then, with half an hour left, they rallied, as if the day nearly done, they were just now waking up. They wiped down the counters by the Icee machine and the microwave and restocked the coffee station, getting the place ready to hand over to Doug-o and Kevin. Whose turn was it to do the men's room?

From there it was like a countdown. They took turns fixing their makeup and brushing their hair in the dinged steel mirror of the women's room while the other manned the front. When graveyard punched in they hung up their tops—"'night, Angie" "'night, Sam"—then headed for their getaway cars, parked side by side.

Everyone's schedule was different. In town Elise had already tipped out at Pape's while J.P. was helping close the Giant Eagle. Hinch and Marnie still had another hour to go at the DQ, so they met there. It was convenient. They could leave their cars in the lot, backed up against the cemetery. The sheriff lived right across the road; no one would bother them.

Her new curfew was two o'clock, a compromise neither side liked. Her mother worked in the emergency room and thought everyone was going to die in a car crash. Her father was calmer, framing his argument in terms of insurance premiums. She needed to remember (as if she could forget), she was still living under their roof.

Part of it was J.P., who was new, and laid-back, into frisbee and hanging out, not her usual confident jock. His mother had raised him by herself, another mark against him. It didn't help that they lived back behind the harbor in the same neighborhood her parents had fled a dozen years ago, and that he drove a crappy Cavalier and had hair down to his shoulders. Her mother blamed J.P. for Kim's tattoo, even though he was the one squeamish about needles. Her parents didn't believe her when she said he was harmless, and actually very sweet. If anything, she was a bad influence on him, but all they saw was the loser who might ruin her future.

"Just let us know where you're going to be," her mother said, as if that was the least she could do. What she meant was, stay out of the police log in the *Star-Beacon* so you don't hurt your father's business. It could have been the family motto: All a realtor has is his good name.

"We'll probably go to the beach if it's nice," Kim said, and it wasn't a lie. They might hit a couple of dives on the way, but by the end of the night they would be sitting in the cold sand around a driftwood fire, listening to the soft wash of the waves. If it rained they'd probably go to Elise's and play pool in her basement.

"Let us know if you go anywhere else. You've got your phone."

Her mother didn't really mean this. She needed to be in bed by ten at the latest to get up for work. Her father was the one who waited up for Kim, though that had changed since graduation. Weekends she used to find him asleep on the couch with the TV on mute and the clicker in his lap; now that she was out every night he turned off all the lights but the ones in the back hall and the stairwell, making a path to her room.

Her parents' door was closed. So was Lindsay's. Closing hers just completed the set.

Alone in bed she read Madeleine L'Engle and Lloyd Alexander—otherworldly fantasies she'd loved as a girl, as if trying to call back that lost time. Even if J.P. and Nina had had to drive her home, she could convince herself she wasn't tired. There was nothing to get up for, and in the quiet warmth of the covers she fought the spins by concentrating on the sentences snaking down the page and in the morning woke up with a killer headache, the room too bright. She pulled her pillow over her head and made it all go away.

That day she got up around eleven, to Cooper licking. He'd butted the door open and was beached with his head under her dresser. "Stop," she said, "Cooper, stop," and then couldn't get back to sleep. To make up for it she took a leisurely shower, closing her eyes beneath the spray.

On her dry-erase board her mother had left a message to please take Lindsay out driving, and a little cartoon car with two heads in it. Lindsay had her permit but needed someone with a license to go with her, and her mother conveniently didn't have time.

"Fuck me," Kim said, because everyone was going swimming at the river. If she'd known she would have gotten up earlier.

Lindsay was downstairs, lying on the couch, watching *Bubble Boy* for the millionth time, laughing before the actors could deliver their lines. They were three years apart, just close enough so they overlapped her last year at the high school. Lindsay was the baby, and the brain. She still had braces, and painful-looking zits she tried to cover with foundation. She hung around with the other nerdy girls in the wind ensemble and the robotics club. Last spring she and her friends had camped out overnight to be first in line for the new *Star Wars*. Since then Nina called her Obi Wan Ke-No-Boobs. Kim didn't like to think of her alone here with their parents, as if she was abandoning her to an infinite limbo.

Today, though, she was a pain. Kim knew she was being selfish—exactly what her mother had trumped her with in their most recent battle—but that only made it worse.

"Let's go," she told her. "Put your shoes on."

"It's almost over."

"Just pause it. I've got shit to do."

"Okay, you don't have to be a jerk about it."

"I'm not the one crying to Mom every five seconds."

"I didn't!" Lindsay said. "It was Dad who said—"

"Whatever, just come on. I need to be back by one."

Lindsay brushed past her and ran upstairs.

"Where are you going?"

"I need my glasses."

Her answer made Kim shake her head. Who wore glasses anymore?

In the driveway she watched Lindsay squinting at the idiot lights of the dash, trying to remember the steps in the right order. Her hand paused over the shifter like a novice trying to defuse a bomb. She'd brought her manual, like that might help.

"Emergency brake," Kim said.

"I know."

"Then do it."

She was tentative backing up, leaning to peer in her side mirror, drifting toward the mailbox. Kim turned off the radio so she could concentrate.

"Straighten it out. Good. Now give it some gas."

They shadowed the railroad tracks, practicing right-hand turns in the rundown blocks off Buffalo. The streets back here were still the original red brick, frost-heaved and dotted with ugly patches of asphalt. The houses were rentals, sagging Italianates and vinyl-sided duplexes with rusty wire fences threatening tetanus. Her father saw them as the enemy in the endless struggle to keep up Kingsville's property values, blaming the landlords more than the tenants, as if ownership somehow made them more responsible. She and Nina had waited outside late one night before graduation while J.P. and Hinch went in. Everybody knew where to go.

Now, in the middle of the day, husky mothers in shorts sat smoking and drinking sodas on their stoops while their kids chased one another around the sun-browned yards. They marked the Chevette each time it swung wide and then corrected, followed it like cops, and Kim told Lindsay to take the underpass to the high school.

She was surprised to find so many cars in the lot. Like idiots, the football team was out practicing in the heat. One mother had brought a lawn chair to watch them, an umbrella attached to make her own personal shade. Down at the empty end, Lindsay parked and parked. Kim had done the same drills with her father, and imitated his patience, praising her when she fitted the car between the lines (though she'd done it in the company wagon, nearly twice the size of the Chevette), calmly calling for the brake when she seemed headed for the curb.

"You been going out with Dad a lot?"

"Not a lot. Why?"

"You're doing really good."

"Thanks." Lindsay was puzzled, as if this might be a set-up. Kim hadn't been very nice to her lately. She'd complained about it to her mother, who as usual did nothing.

"Let's go do the drive-thru at the DQ." Only after the offer was out did Kim realize what she was saying. The lane that wrapped around the Dairy Queen was narrow, and two cement-filled steel posts guarded the window.

"I thought you had 'shit' to do."

"I do, but it's lunchtime. My treat."

It took forever to get there, and then there was a line.

"I can't do this," Lindsay said.

"Let the brake off and inch up behind this guy. You've got room on my side if you need it."

Once, when Kim was just beginning, she veered too close to some parked cars and without a word her father grabbed the wheel with one hand and tugged it till they were going straight. She resisted the urge now. Lindsay craned her chin toward the windshield, trying to see over the hood.

"Just follow him," Kim said. "He's bigger than you are."

At the order board she braked too hard, jerking them forward.

"Sorry."

"You have to roll your window down."

"What the hell do *you* want?" the speaker blurted—Marnie, pointing at them from the cockpit of the pick-up window. She didn't see it was Lindsay driving till they pulled up. They were so far away that Lindsay had to open her door to grab the bag.

"Nice job there," Marnie said.

"Don't take that shit from her," Kim said, and stuck out her tongue.

"Don't die in a terrible fiery accident," Marnie said.

"You too."

Eating fries while driving was too advanced, so they found a shady spot at the back of the lot and turned on the radio. The trees inside the spiked iron fence were old, their roots poking through the dry grass like knucklebones. Sparrows hopped among the faded decorations, wreaths on green wire stands and flags left over from Memorial Day. Lindsay squeezed ketchup into the top of her clamshell so they could share. They sat side-by-side, dipping and chewing. They didn't spend time together like this, and she was self-conscious, not wanting to ruin it.

"Got a game tonight?"

"Yeah," Lindsay said, downcast, as if she didn't want to be reminded.

"Who you playing?"

"D'know. We suck anyway."

"That's not what Dad says."

"You've never seen us." Kim had played for him too, enduring his relentless overcoaching as Edgewater Properties sank to its proper spot at the bottom of the league. But Kim could actually play. Lindsay had inherited her cleats but that was it. With her knobby knees and braces she was terrified of the ball, and dreaded every game.

"I thought you were supposed to be going to the playoffs."

"Everybody goes to the playoffs now. It's like the Special Olympics."

"How many more games you got?"

"Five and then the playoffs. So six."

"Good luck."

"Yeah, thanks."

They ate to Weezer and Franz Ferdinand, pinching the soggy ends of their burgers, trying not to drip on anything. Kim finished first, and though she was afraid it would sound lame and melodramatic, she also knew this might be the perfect opportunity, while Lindsay's mouth was full.

"You know, dude," she said, "I'm really going to miss you."

"No you won't," Lindsay said, tipping her chin up so she didn't spew lettuce everywhere.

"You don't think so."

"You'll be too busy with your new friends and everything."

She didn't have to say "Just like now." Okay, that was fair, but she would miss Linds too. Couldn't both things be true?

"You can come visit me."

"I don't think Mom'll let me."

"Maybe not this year but next year. You're going to have to start looking at schools then anyway. Not that you'll be looking at Bowling Green."

"God, I hope not," Lindsay said—a joke, or it was supposed to be, so she was relieved when Kim laughed. Deep down Lindsay knew Kim was disappointed with Bowling Green—as were her parents, though they never said anything. Case Western had been her first choice, but she didn't even make the waiting list. Nina was going to Denison, Elise had been early decision at Kenyon. While Lindsay felt bad for Kim, she vowed to herself she would do better than any of them.

They were both finished and it was nearly one. Kim turned off the radio. "Ready?"

Lindsay nodded, serious, sitting upright like a test pilot. She had to use both hands to depress the button of the emergency brake.

"Come on, Muscles," Kim said.

They drove back past the hospital with its helipad off in the corner of the lot. Her mother's Subaru was in its usual spot, a fold-out silver reflector protecting the dash from the sun. In the ER, she would be sitting at her window, patiently taking down someone's information, checking off boxes, the queen of clipboards. By the time she got home Kim would be at work. The only time they saw each other now was on weekends. Lindsay thought it was easier. Since the end of school they'd been fighting over J.P. and her drinking and breaking curfew. Her mother was just freaked out about her leaving.

They all were, maybe Kim more than any of them. Every day she felt strangely charged, knowing that in another month all of this would vanish. She liked driving around, imagining it happening, like now, the stucco doctors' offices and low, motel-like nursing homes fading behind her, the box factory and the company park with its backstop facing the railroad tracks wavering like a mirage, growing fainter and fainter until it was all just fog taken away by a lake breeze. But underpinning that fantasy was a queasy panic, a fear of the unknown and the confusing realization that by leaving she might be losing everything. She tried to ignore it the same way she blew off her mother. The fact was that she had thirty-nine days to go. Nothing was going to change that.

Lindsay was afraid of the mailbox and turned early, the rear tire on her side four-wheeling over the curb.

"Sorry."

"It's okay," Kim said. "Mom does it all the time. You did good. Plus you got lunch out of it."

Inside, they split. Lindsay flopped on the couch and unpaused *Bubble Boy* while Kim went upstairs and changed into her swimsuit and some cutoffs, pulling her hair back with a rubber band. Cooper knew what the suit meant and followed her down the stairs like she might take him. She didn't have time today, and felt bad.

"Call him," she asked Lindsay, and she did.

Back in the car she was pissed off again. It was almost one thirty, and she'd just noticed she was low on gas. It wasn't worth going all the way out there when she had to be back to get ready for work in an hour. She wondered if Nina would be mad if she called in sick. Probably, though Nina did it all the time. She rumbled over the train tracks, cut left and flew down the long, empty straightaway beside the old grain elevators instead of dealing with the lights on Main. She was so focused on the road that she almost didn't see the cop.

"Ah *shit*."

It was the sheriff, staked out in the dirt turnoff of the substation, waiting for someone like her. Instead of braking she lifted her foot off the gas and let the car float past him, still going way over the limit. She glanced at her mirror hopefully. He was pulling out, turning her way, but so far hadn't thrown his lights on, and she signaled right for the stop sign ahead, thinking she'd crawl into the side streets and hide.

Here came the lights, and a single whoop of his siren as he tucked in behind her. It was just that kind of day.

Her mother's lectures had worked. Waiting for him to get out of his car, she was terribly aware that she was Ed Larsen's daughter.

The sheriff had to bend at the waist to see in her window. He was a regular at the Conoco, and recognized her without her uniform. "Afternoon," he said. "You know how fast you were going?"

"Around thirty?"

"I had you at forty-eight. You know the limit here's twenty-five."

She had to dig in the glovebox for her registration and then wait while he sat in his car writing on a clipboard, which he brought back with him. He carefully tore off the top sheet.

"Miss Larsen, because this is your first time, I'm only giving you a written warning. You think you can keep it in check from now on?"

"Yessir. Thank you." Did he say her name that way because of her father? Her instinct was to shred the ticket and bury the pieces in the nearest garbage can, except she had the feeling he'd hear about it some-how—at the monthly Rotary meeting or the fire department car wash.

"There's no need to be going fifty miles an hour here."

"Yessir."

"You take it easy now."

She did for a while, babying it through town. She was so late it didn't matter, and for now her relief outweighed her irritation. When she was out on the flats of Route 7 and there was no one around she gunned it up to eighty. "That's right," she shouted, "you can't catch me! No one can catch me!"

At the river J.P. kissed her and gave her shit, asking what took her so long, and she made a joke of it.

"Forty-eight," he said, smirking. "You know what would happen to me if I got stopped doing forty-eight?"

"Your car doesn't go forty-eight."

"But if it did."

The river was low, rocks sitting high and white in midstream. In the big hole below the falls Nina and Hinch floated in yellow tubes, splash-ing each other. Elise and Sam sat farther down on a giant boulder with their backs turned, conferring seriously (Elise had told Nina she was breaking up with him, but that was weeks ago). She had just enough time to get wet and then dry off on the ledge, lying beside J.P., her head resting on her crossed arms. The smell reminded her of her mother tak-ing her to the town pool when she was little, the wet mark her body left on the hot concrete slowly evaporating. The stone was warm on her front, the sun beating against her back, reaching deep into her skin. She could sleep like this all day, just listening to the rush of the water.

J.P. couldn't resist messing with her straps.

"Good luck. The hook's in the front."

"No fair."

With a finger he wrote his name on her shoulder blade.

"I don't want to go to work," she said with her eyes closed.

"So? Blow it off."

"I wish."

Nina climbed out and wrung her wet hair over them. "Rise and shine, campers."

"Actually that feels good," Kim said. "You know what? We should both call in and make the Wiener work."

"He'd just get Kevin and Doug-o to cover. Come on, quit stalling."

"I really don't feel like going in."

"Waa waa waa. If I'm going, you're going. I'm not going to sit there all night listening to Kevin's war stories."

"How long's he been back now?" Hinch asked from below.

"I know, it's been like two years. He was only over there five months."

"Wooze did a whole year and never talks about it," J.P. said.

"That's cause Wooze has a life," Hinch said.

Nina grabbed her ankle, and Kim kicked free. "Come on, get your ass up." She poked her in the butt with her big toe.

"Stop. Stop, I'm getting up."

She pulled on her cutoffs but Nina was right, it was too nice for a top.

Hinch's brother's friend Evan was working the door at the Three Ls, so that was the plan for later.

"Bring your big cash money," J.P. said, kissing her.

"Yeah right," Kim said, and pushed him over the edge. He tucked into a cannonball and took the other tube.

"Don't miss us too much," she called.

"We won't."

"Bye, Elise!" she yelled downstream, waving her towel. Elise waved back. Sam didn't.

"I don't get it," Nina said as they crossed the rocks. "If she didn't want to be with him this summer she should have just cut him off after prom."

"It's typical Elise. She's got to have some kind of drama."

"This way she gets to be the center of attention."

"I feel bad for Sam. He's a nice guy."

"Hinch wouldn't put up with that shit."

"Neither would J.P." But J.P. wasn't in love with her. J.P. knew this summer was it and it didn't bother him. In the fall he'd be in Columbus with half of their class. They were both just being realistic.

"How much you want to bet he's there tonight?"

"Too easy."

They climbed the winding path through the trees and up to the road, scissoring over the wire guardrail. "All right," she said. "See you there, Squinky Square."

They left together, headed for town on 7.

It was a race, Nina explained later. They had forty-five minutes to drive home, shower, change and make it back to the Conoco by three. By now they'd gotten it down to a routine. Nina lived closer. On a good day she could do it in thirty-two, and today was a good day. She easily beat Kim in, taking over from Dave and Leah right on time.

When Kim still hadn't shown up at a quarter past, Nina called her cell and got her voicemail. She'd probably turned it off.

"You suck," she said. "I already punched you in. I'm kidding. Enjoy your night off, bitch. I'll say hi to Kevin for you."

When Lindsay returned home from the Hedricks' just before dinner, Kim's suit and towel were draped neatly over the shower curtain in their bathroom as usual.

J.P. tried her around midnight from outside the DQ. In the dark corner of the lot, the open phone made his ear glow. He was semi-annoyed that she hadn't told him, but didn't want anyone to know. "I guess you're asleep or just not answering. We'll be at the Three Ls if you're interested. I'm buying. Call me if you get this."

They closed the place and ended up down at the beach, drinking

Coronas they bought at the Conoco. The torn cardboard from the 12-packs curled, the coating burning blue. Smoke rose through the moon over the rocky arms of the breakwater. Far out on the lake an ore boat hung silent and motionless, starting its long haul back to Superior or Duluth.

"It's weird," Sam said, "Kim not being here."

"I know," Nina said. "It's like I'm missing my twin."

"Yeah," Hinch said, "your good twin," and she hit him and then snuggled back into his chest.

It was growing cold, sweatshirt weather, and the stars were out. In town, across from the cemetery, the sheriff's cruiser sat facing the street to discourage speeders. The DQ was dark, as were the houses along Main, the streetlights shedding a dim silver tint, as if underpowered. At the corner of Euclid and Harbor, the prerecorded chimes of Lakeview United Methodist sounded two o'clock, her curfew.

Kim's mother was asleep. Her father was asleep. Lindsay, who'd struck out twice and made a key error at second base, was asleep, Cooper snoring next to her on the bed.

In the middle of the night her father woke up to go to the bathroom and noticed the line of light under their closed door. In the morning the light was still on. Her door was open, her bed untouched. The light in the downstairs hall was on, and the outside light by the back door, invisible during the day. Her car wasn't in the driveway.

The first person her mother called was Nina.

The second was J.P.

The third was Connie at the hospital.

The fourth was the police.

Known Whereabouts

He knew she thought he was being macho and foolish, going out alone, just as she knew he would go anyway, despite anything she might say. At this point in their marriage, negotiation was a tone of voice, a warning glance if the girls were in the room. "Don't be an ass," she would say when Ed was being unreasonable, and he would go quiet, removing himself. Hours later she'd find him at his tool bench in the garage or in his office, still tending an ember of resentment like a child, and though nothing was settled, she'd try to apologize.

They were both aware of the deal. While she didn't believe for a minute that he'd succeed, she would allow him to go look, for his own sake (and somewhere beyond logic, hers). Now, quickly, while Lindsay was still asleep. The police were sending someone to take a report, and she didn't think she could handle them by herself.

"I'll have my phone on," he said, kissed her and ran out the door.

He stabbed at the ignition as if he were being pursued, cranked his wrist and revved the Taurus to life, racking the shift into reverse. The rear window was frosted with condensation, and he had to hop out and slop it off with his forearm. From the kitchen she watched him slalom down the drive, thinking that if he hurt himself or someone else it would be her fault.

He hadn't showered or shaved and felt sour and wild-haired, and was grateful none of their neighbors were out to see him take off. He tore down Lakewood, hunched over the wheel, daring anyone to cut in on him. The air in the car was chilled from sitting out all night, and he used it to wake up, charging himself the way his high school coach had pumped up the dugout, the same way he still tried to fire up his girls: "Come on now, let's get some!"

In town he had to force himself not to pass the slow-asses in front of him. He took Buffalo to Main, her usual route, eyes flicking over the cars and pickups parked in the driveways. The Chevette was practically an antique, impossible to miss, but it was also small, and as he poked along he imagined it sitting inside every darkened garage, tucked under a tarp.

"Jesus," he said, "drive your car!" and then missed the light at Geneva.

Maybe J.P. was lying and she'd just had too much last night and crashed at his place. Nina and Elise would back her up on principle, feigning ignorance. She wasn't as honest with them as Fran liked to believe, and maybe that came from him. As a teenager he'd told his share of lies to stay out of trouble.

The lot of the DQ was empty, the sheriff's cruiser gone, meaning Perry was on duty, a relief. Ed had sold Perry's mother's place after she died, and could count on him to be discreet.

A public person, Ed Larsen valued, above all, privacy. Like a priest or a doctor, part of his job was to keep his clients' secrets, and know the town's. Like right up here: a registered sex offender lived on Sandusky— a married man named Greene who'd drugged a girl Kim's age he'd met at a bar. Ed had had problems moving a three-bedroom on the next block because of the disclosure forms. It wasn't on his way, but for his own peace of mind he detoured into the leafy side streets, pausing at a couple of stop signs before creeping by a brown cape with a trailered bass boat in the drive. Two-car garage, fancy arrow weathervane. The lawn had recently been sodded, and a swath of dew glistened in the sun. It was a trick, and unnerving. In the pale morning light, nothing looked sinister.

He couldn't take the time to check downtown or the strip of bars above the harbor. He was already behind schedule.

He followed 7 south out of town toward the interstate, the road splitting around the prow of a concrete island and then a grassy median before dropping down and crossing the river. Below, off to one side, stood the twin arches of the old stone bridge the new one had replaced, crumbling and tagged with bad graffiti. In the movies killers weighted their victims and dropped them into the surging current, but here the water was rusty and ankle-deep, a shopping cart capsized in midstream.

Ahead stretched the long grade to the flats, where the kids liked to drag race. As he crested the rise, the sun was just peeking over the trees, and he flipped his visor down. The shoulders on both sides were empty. He stayed in the right lane, peering at the fenced, overgrown farmland with its tumbledown barns and marshy stands of weed trees. Dirt roads edged the cornfields, then wormed back into the hills. Doorless trailers and open tractor sheds, silos and slurries, corncribs and chicken coops and pond after pond. The farther off the road, the more hiding places there were.

He was beginning to think Fran was right. He'd seized on the problem of Kim being missing and in his panic he'd jumped at the easiest solution.

It had been eighteen hours. She could be in Iowa by now. She could be in New York, or Chicago.

The zoning changed near the interstate. He slowed to scope the whitewashed Arco, pumpless and abandoned since the late '80s, twisting in his seat as if he could see behind it. The lot of the Days Inn was dotted with semis and Harleys, a pair of power company cherrypickers backed into a corner. He signaled and turned off for a quick recon, circling the building, then gunned the Taurus up the exit and across the oncoming lanes.

He was stalling. Logically she wouldn't be at the Conoco.

He was nearly there when a state trooper passed him coming the other way, clipping along, in no hurry. For a second he was tempted to jerk the Taurus across the median and run him down, enlist him in the search, the two of them cruising the interstate, setting up roadblocks, checking every car.

He wanted to blame J.P. and Kim's friends. She spent more time with them than she did at home. That was exactly how it happened. Too much freedom, too much free time. He'd been a latchkey kid himself, and done things as a teenager he could only shake his head at now, stupid, dangerous shit his mother never suspected, and he worried that

maybe through some poetic stroke of fate Kim was paying for his reck-
lessness. She was more like him than Fran would ever know. He should
have kept a better eye on her.

The Conoco was busy with commuters filling up for the trek to Erie.
He pulled in, confirmed with a glance that the Chevette wasn't there, then
rolled around to the far corner by the air hose, where he could see trucks
highballing along the interstate side by side. Across the overpass, its stem
rising from the bottom of a cow pasture, a shimmering red billboard en-
ticed eastbound drivers to try ADULT PARADISE just over the PA line. He
left the car running, stepped out and stood at the guardrail, a hand over
his eyes like a sailor, scanning both ways. Traffic bombed along, the gaps
between filled with music from the pumps. He watched the lanes, chewing his lip, mesmerized, as if at any second she might come driving by.

"Come on, Kimba," he said to break the spell, and even then he was
slow to pull away.

He checked his phone to make sure it was on. It was almost eight—
frustrating. He needed to get home, but at the same time he thought it
was wrong to give up. Going down to the next exit and coming in the
back way might take longer, but at least he'd be covering new ground,
and before Fran could call and talk him out of it he ducked into the
Taurus and got back on 7.

A sign at the top of the on-ramp prohibited pedestrians, farm equipment and animals. He blew past it and then the yield at the bottom, ac-
celerating away from a lumbering dump truck. He drove close-mouthed
and frowning, blinking away a twitch in his right eye. They would all
laugh at him later, he imagined, Dad freaking out, driving around like
a maniac. That was fine with him, as long as she was all right.

He didn't expect to see anything, but kept a generous following distance so he could look, fastening on random objects as if they were clues.
A scrap of truck tire. A tuft of roadkill. A garbage bag broken open, its
contents scattered in the grass. In the median two identical tractors sat
nestled against each other, their mower bars raised for the night. He
couldn't make sense of the world, and clung to the idea of a mission,
forgetting everything else. Just cover this last leg and get home.

When he saw the car far ahead on the shoulder he automatically slowed.

The size was right, a tiny box. He thumbed on his hazards and braked, veering off as traffic behind him shot by. He could see how it happened. The car was his mother's, ancient and temperamental, a bad match for her, except that she loved it. It had broken down halfway between exits—walkable even in the heat, but instead of waiting for triple-A she'd accepted a ride from someone, and like that she was gone.

Except, as he rolled up, it was obviously not hers. This car was squatter, and the wrong color, an old beater of a Toyota. He stopped behind it, noting the Pennsylvania plates. He decided to take down the number just in case, jotting it on the pad suction-cupped to his dash. While he was there he figured he might as well take a look, and got out and walked around the Corolla, peeking in the windows as traffic shuddered past, analyzing it like a crime scene. There was a black scrunchy twisted around the base of the stick shift and a pack of sugarless gum in the dish beneath the emergency brake—both items he associated with Kim, and for an instant he imagined she'd been driving the car. He saw her struggling, arms raised, both wrists gripped in a man's fist, then shook his head to banish the vision.

Fran was right, he had no idea what he was doing. He was a good salesman, despite the beating the market had been handing him lately, an okay coach, a decent husband and father, not a bad or incompetent man at all (he hoped), but he was not going to find her, not this way. He'd felt helpless at times in his life, over money troubles most recently, or, more often, the unhappiness of a loved one. This was different. His usually reliable talents of hustle and attention to detail were worthless against the unknown, and he was frightened.

Why wasn't Perry out here? Where were all the state cops?

He was still picturing Kim when his ringtone knocked him out of his brooding. Traffic was loud, and he stuck a finger in his ear.

"Lindsay's up," Fran said. "Where are you?"

"I'm just heading back."

"Find anything?"

"Nothing," he said, then had to add, "I think that's good though."

"Come home," she said. "I need you here."

He promised he'd be there as fast as he could, and for the tenth time today she asked him to be careful. He would, he said, thinking at least he could do this for her. As he was telling her he loved her, he noticed that the people whooshing past were staring at him. Truckers, a woman his mother's age, a school bus full of kids. "I love you too," she said. Even as he closed the phone and started for the Taurus, he felt watched and weighed, on display for the whole world. Another pack of traffic was coming. He could make it if he ran, but kept the same determined pace. Their faces turned to him, suspicious and concerned, as if he were either a criminal or some poor bastard who was stranded.

Victimology

The detective interviewed them separately, as if they were suspects. He was older than Fran expected, paunchy and olive-skinned, with fragile-looking moles on his eyelids and a black toupee that rode high and didn't match his sideburns. He took Ed into the den and closed the door, leaving her and Lindsay to fill out forms in the kitchen. A blond deputy not much older than Kim stood by the fridge like a proctor. He'd only spoken once, politely turning down her offer of coffee, and Fran thought his silence was a bad sign.

Full name, date of birth, height, weight, hair, eyes—these were easy. She'd been at work when Kim left, and couldn't have guessed what she was wearing. Lindsay was the one who came up with her light blue Old Navy T and Levis. Fran had gone through Kim's dresser and hamper to make sure. Likewise, Lindsay knew Kim's sneakers were Asics, showing her the box in the top of her closet.

"Thank you," Fran said, abject, wondering why she'd wanted to keep her out of this. It was just like Lindsay to have all the answers.

She'd already interrogated her in private, asking if Kim had said anything about leaving, anything about J.P., anything at all strange lately. This wasn't like the drinking and drugs, she knew about those. She didn't want to scare Lindsay, but she needed her to be honest, and she was. Fran was fairly sure of that.

List any distinguishing features (birthmarks, scars, tattoos, piercings):

Her tattoo, obviously, but she'd forgotten her jewelry—Ed's mother's cameo ring, and the butterfly pendant Fran had picked out for her Sweet Sixteen, but which earrings, and did she have on her bracelets? She thought she should know. She was almost relieved that Lindsay didn't. They'd have to look upstairs.

When Fran stood, the deputy held out a hand and patted the air, waving her down again. "That's okay, ma'am. We're going to have a look around right after this."

Health concerns. Did allergies count, or did they have to be serious? And then, waffling, she realized this was for people with Alzheimer's who wandered away from home.

At work she'd filled out these forms from the other side of the desk, documenting the unconscious and unidentified, translating the painful and life-changing into the bloodless acronyms of emergency medicine. As a professional she honored calmness above all, trusting efficiency over emotion. She didn't want to be the hysterical mother, demanding her child be seen immediately, but it felt like they were wasting time. They should be out searching for her.

Special interests she left blank, just to be done. Lindsay was still writing, and Fran couldn't help but peek.

Horses, she'd written, *softball, iceskating, drawing*—all the talents Lindsay envied, and Fran wanted to stop her, to tell her that was enough for the police.

The deputy said they should hold on to their papers, so they waited. With no radio or TV to distract her, she ran through the possibilities again, as she'd done every few minutes since Ed had told her Kim hadn't come home, quickly tripping over the worst before settling on the less dire, like an accident, a head injury. She'd seen people brought in who didn't wake up for days. Her car could be down a ravine. She could be in the woods somewhere, hurt and disoriented, and here they were sitting around.

Lindsay was watching her, so she gave her a pinched buck-up smile—unconvincing, she thought, yet Lindsay returned it, and again Fran wanted to protect her from this.

"Your turn," Ed said when he finally came out. He was trying to be businesslike but looked clenched, and she took his hand and squeezed it as they passed. As she followed the detective in she wondered if they needed a lawyer.

The detective barely glanced at her completed sheet before sliding it into a folder. His name was Ronald Holloway, and he was the detective with the County Sheriff's Department. From his delivery Fran understood that he was the only one, so they should get used to him. He shook her hand and listed his credentials to reassure her, stressing that he'd worked several successful missing persons cases in Erie County. She didn't ask how long ago or what he meant by "successful."

They were lucky, he said. Because Kim was an adult and there were no signs of foul play, up until last year they would have had to wait twenty-four hours to file a report. Now, with Suzanne's Law, they could get this information out right away. Fran didn't have to ask what had happened to Suzanne.

"Mrs. Larsen, I told your husband, and I'm going to tell you the same thing. Ninety-nine percent of missing adults that want to be found *are* found, okay? That's the main thing to keep in mind."

But, she wanted to say, she's not an adult.

He flipped his yellow pad to a blank page and wrote her name. "First time anything like this has happened with your daughter?"

"Yes."

"Responsible girl."

"Yes."

"Usually good about keeping in touch?"

"Most of the time."

"Not all the time."

"Sometimes she's not so good when she's out with her friends. Like any teenager."

He took a different sheet from the folder and spun it toward her on the coffee table, pointing to a list of names with a pen. "Anyone I'm missing here?"

"No, that's them." She was surprised Ed had gotten them all, he paid so little attention.

"You've got phone numbers and addresses for all of them."

"I think so, yes."

"How about her place of work?"

"I've got the number by the phone." Which magically rang out in the kitchen, making her turn her head as Ed picked up.

"How well do you know her coworkers?"

"We know Nina very well. I've never met any of the others."

"Places she hangs out at. Friends' places. Her boyfriend's."

This was so obvious that she didn't know why she didn't want to admit it. Was she resisting out of pride, or just because she didn't like the man presuming? "They mainly hang out at Elise's."

"Any public places—bars, party spots?"

"They go to the beach a lot."

"The river?"

"That's during the day."

"They ever go there at night?"

"Not that I know of."

"They drink?"

"Yes."

"Heavily?"

"Just beer, mostly."

"She ever come home drunk?"

Wouldn't Ed have already answered this? "Yes."

"Did she ever drink and drive that you know of?"

"No." Though she suspected.

"How about drugs?"

"Not that I know of for sure. My guess is she's probably smoked pot."

"Any problems with the boyfriend, far as you know?"

"No."

"They're serious."

"I don't think I'd go that far. She just started seeing him around Easter."

"Exclusive."

"I believe so."

"No one else you know of."

"No." Not that Kim would have told her.

"She on birth control?" He didn't look up when he asked it.

"Yes," Fran said. At least in that respect she'd been responsible.

"How long?"

"Since she was sixteen."

"Are her pills here?"

"Yes."

"Has she ever been pregnant?"

"No."

"Any health problems?"

"Nothing major."

"Broken bones, unexplained bruises, anything like that?"

"No."

"History of depression, suicide attempts."

"No."

"Any enemies or rivals?"

The idea made her laugh—as if Kim were part of a gang. In her whole life she'd gotten into one fight. That was in middle school, and the girl ended up becoming her friend.

"Does the boyfriend have any enemies you know of?"

"Not that I know of."

"Any ex-boyfriends who might give her trouble?"

"No." Adam Vozza coming to the door drunk one night, but he wasn't really a boyfriend.

"Things all right at home?"

The change of pace threw her. Was it an accusation? Because that's how it sounded. For the last four years she and Kim had fought each other to a draw, but that was over now. Fran was heartbroken that Kim was leaving, but relieved too. No one had ever made her unhappier, or more unsure of herself. Hateful. Helpless.

She wanted to be honest, and was aware of him waiting. He had to know how complicated these questions were. "We have our differences, like any mother and daughter."

"Any big issues the last couple of weeks?"

"No."

"When was the last time you talked with her?"

"Sunday." He wrote it down, and she hurried to explain about their work schedules. They'd gone to church as a family that morning, that had to count for something.

"What did you talk about?"

She turned her head, trying to remember, pinching her lips in one hand. They were eating lunch on the back deck; Ed and Kim were laughing at some punchline from the Simpsons. Lindsay was being Ralph Wiggum.

"If you can't remember, that's fine."

"I don't know, just normal conversation. She was laughing."

"Would you say your relationship with your daughter is good?"

"It's not perfect by any means, but it's good."

"And your husband's?"

"Good. He's the good cop, I'm the bad one."

"And things between you two, how are they?"

She shrugged as if there was no reason to think of it. "Fine."

"Family finances?"

Ed had sold one of their mutual funds to cover their June estimated taxes, but that had nothing to do with this. "Okay, as far as I know. We're not starving."

He stopped to write something at the very bottom of the page, then flipped it over.

"Your daughters get along?"

"Most of the time."

"Usual sibling stuff."

"Yes."

"Any extended family she's especially close to?"

"Her grandmother—Ed's mother."

"Where does she live?"

"Erie, in an assisted living place. Ed's already talked to her."

"Anyone else she might turn to in a tight spot?"

"Nina and Elise, that's really it."

"Neighbors?"

"The Hedricks next door. They haven't seen her."

"Good neighborhood."

"Very good."

"How long have you lived here?"

She had to subtract. "Thirteen years."

"Know everybody."

"Yes."

"Any suspicious characters?"

"No."

"Anyone move in or out in the last few years?"

"No."

He asked about traffic, and what kind of service workers came around during the day—landscapers, delivery vans, meter readers. He asked about Kim's cellphone bills and e-mail accounts, who was on her buddy list for instant messaging. He asked if she knew when Kim had gotten paid last, and whether she'd made any big purchases lately. Any clothes or bags missing? What kind of driver was she? How many miles were on the car? Had it been in the shop recently, even for an oil change? On and on, with the same bureaucratic coolness, skipping from one leading topic to the next, pretending to be utterly noncommittal. He never badgered her, but it was relentless, and tiring for her, having to strain for answers. There was so much she didn't know.

Finally he set the pad aside. "Okay, next to last question. Would you be willing to take a polygraph test, if it's necessary?"

"Yes."

"Thank you. Now I'm going to ask you the single most important question I'm going to ask you today. I don't want you to think about it, just say the first thing that pops into your head, no matter what it is, okay? Ready?" He paused like a talkshow host. "What do *you* think happened to Kim?"

The answer came to her, complete and irreducible, not at all new, but she naturally balked at it. Now she understood why Ed had looked sick coming out of the room, and the mother in her rose up, adamant. There was no way she was going to let him do this to Lindsay.

"Mrs. Larsen?" he prompted, and she resented him for making her say it, as if she were betraying Kim.

"I think someone took her."

BOLO

Not knowing any better, they did what he told them. The first thing they needed to do was call around and let everyone know they were looking for her. This would let her know they were on her trail if she really was a runaway. None of them believed she was, though Lindsay remembered with a twinge how Kim said she'd miss her (she hadn't told the detective, and now she thought she should have). Was that why she'd taken her to lunch, to secretly say good-bye?

They waited in the upstairs hall while the detective poked through Kim's room, the deputy shining his flashlight under the bed and dresser and around the bottom of her closet. He was interested in the Sea Wolves tickets fringing her mirror, and one from a Cake concert at the Agora Ballroom, trying to imply that she knew her way around Eric and Cleveland. Her father explained that they all went to those games with her grandmother, it was a tradition, and that the concert had been three years ago, before Kim had gotten her license. They'd driven her and Nina and Elise to Cleveland and celebrated their anniversary with a nice dinner before picking the girls up after the show. But the man did find something right off that had taken Lindsay herself a while to notice and then delivered to Kim like news: In the collage of pictures she'd stuck to the wall above her headboard, there wasn't a single one of her and J.P.

He turned up nothing except a butane torch in a shoebox packed with Newports that Lindsay already knew about. Since there were no signs of foul play, they'd be going forward with a missing persons investigation rather than a suspicious disappearance.

"Isn't the fact that she disappeared suspicious enough?" her father asked.

No. Without specific evidence they couldn't consider Kim at-risk.

"That's idiotic," her mother said. "She's a child out there by herself. That's as at-risk as it gets."

"I understand," the detective said. "I'm not a fan of the policy myself. On the other hand, I'm glad I didn't find anything to make me think otherwise. I very well may find something when I talk to her friends that changes my mind."

He asked for a recent picture, preferably a head-on shot of her smiling. Lindsay thought this was a sentimental way of getting people's attention—help find the pretty girl. Later she'd read online that it let forensics superimpose a skull over her face and directly compare the teeth.

Her mother had her favorite shot of Kim from graduation propped beside the stereo. Kim was cradling a dozen roses in one arm and her diploma in the other, smiling in too much lipstick like Miss America. Her mother had sent copies of it to all their relatives. She was always showing it off for company, picking it up with a glass of wine in her other hand, saying Kim could have been a model if she wanted. Lindsay's boring school portrait sat next to it, an unfair comparison. Her mother slipped the whole mat out, leaving the empty frame flat on the sideboard.

In the kitchen the detective called in an APB on the car and a Be On the Lookout bulletin for her. As they waited for him to finish, her mother laid an arm over Lindsay's shoulders, something she never did. Instead of comforting her it set off a whole chain of inner alarms, and she stood there paralyzed, feeling its weight.

"Make those calls," the detective said. In the meantime he'd interview her friends while another unit canvassed the neighborhood.

"How long is that going to take?" her father asked.

"You want to start searching on your own, feel free. It's probably not the most efficient use of your time, but I understand some people have to. Just make sure you have someone here to take down any information that comes in. You have caller ID?"

"Yes," her mother volunteered.

"Take a cellphone," he told her father. "If I can't get anything out of the friends, most likely we're going to go public, so don't go too far, okay?"

He backed the unmarked car out of the driveway, leaving them with the deputy, whose presence stifled any real discussion.

"Help me make a list of people to call," her mother asked her. They sat at the kitchen table while her father hovered, pacing to the window as if Kim's car might come rolling down the block.

"Go," her mother said. "I know you want to."

"Where am I supposed to go?"

"Then help us call."

It was the kind of stressed-out exchange between them that Lindsay hated, made worse by the deputy pretending not to hear. Like always, her father did what her mother told him, sitting on the other side of Lindsay so she was sandwiched between them.

They started with her closest friends, using their cellphones so they didn't tie up the line. They tried Nina again, first getting Nina's mother, who was surprised they hadn't found her, as if they just hadn't looked hard enough. Nina offered to call around, and her mother gratefully accepted—too quickly for her father, who wanted to keep some control over the situation.

"Why?" her mother asked.

"I just think it would be better if we did it ourselves."

"What's the difference? We're going to call the same people anyway."

"I'd like to know who she's calling that we're not."

"It doesn't matter," she said.

"It would be nice to have a record of it."

"You want me to call her back and tell her not to?"

"No," he said, but upset, as if that wasn't the point.

They called J.P. and Elise and Hinch and Sam and Marnie while Lindsay flipped through the Kingsville High Caller, writing down the numbers of people she'd heard Kim talk about. As she pushed deeper into the alphabet, skimming the seniors, she passed over her own classmates, struck by how few she could call friends. What if she were the one missing, what kind of list would she have?

Dana, Micah, Jen, the Hedricks... Father John and the families at church she babysat for, but they knew nothing about her, the same for her teammates—remembering Shelly's throw tipping off her glove and rolling into right field while the runners wheeled around, and Shelly turning away from her. She'd wanted to disappear then, and when her father squeezed her shoulder as they came off. "It's okay," he said, "we'll get 'em back," except they didn't, and when she went around collecting the bats and bases after, no one helped her.

If she disappeared, besides her parents, who would really miss her?

"I'm completely serious," her mother was saying beside her. "I wouldn't joke about something like this."

"Who's next?" her father asked, and Lindsay turned the pad toward him.

Her mother was done, and tipped it her way. "I swear, that woman's on the wrong medication."

"Who's that?" her father asked.

"Jeannie McKenna."

"I wouldn't be surprised." He ducked his head, a finger in his ear, and broke into his phone voice, bright and excited, as if he were trying to sell something. "Hello, is this Tim Means? Ed Larsen here—Kim's dad, yeah, hey. I was hoping you could do us a favor."

They worked outward from the center of her life to the edges. On his computer her father still had the roster from her last season with the team, three years ago. Her mother dug through the church caller for members of her youth group. Kim didn't see those people anymore, but Lindsay took down the names anyway, leaving room for comments. A lot of them weren't home—probably on vacation, her father thought; it was that time of year.

"Hi," her mother said, "this is Fran Larsen. We're looking for our daughter Kim—she used to be in the bell choir?"

She didn't say "runaway" or "kidnapped." She just said Kim didn't show up for work, and that her car was missing, and that they were asking people who knew her to keep an eye out for her. The way she said it, it almost sounded normal.

When the house phone began ringing, Lindsay started a log. One by one the neighbors checked in. Everyone was confused and sorry for them. Everyone wanted to help. Lindsay wasn't allowed to handle these calls, just to document them. The deputy came around the table to look over her shoulder. "That's good," he said like a teacher, and she was way too proud of herself. Her grandmother always said she had nice handwriting.

When they were done with Kim's friends her mother called Connie at the hospital and wandered into the living room as if she didn't want them to hear. Lindsay expected the deputy to follow her but he just stood there. Her father called Peggy, the receptionist at his office, and canceled a house showing he had that afternoon. Lindsay figured they didn't need her anymore, but as soon as he hung up he turned to her, puzzled. "She wouldn't have taken the boat out, would she?"

"I don't think so," she said slowly, unsure, since she knew Kim and J.P. had taken it out several times, once with her onboard. The people at the marina didn't care as long as you had the code to the gate. She pictured Kim standing at the wheel with her back to shore, slowly motoring out through the gap in the breakwater.

The marina took a few minutes to get back to them. The boat was in its slip with the cover on.

Her mother was still talking to Connie. Her father went over the lists with a pen as if he was correcting them.

"Did you want to try the Landrys again?" Lindsay asked.

"No, I think we're done for now." He thanked her for helping.

"Sure," Lindsay said, like it was easy, and went straight upstairs, afraid he might ask her something else.

Away from them, she could breathe. She could think. She'd just woken up when her mother told her, and it still didn't seem real. She needed time alone to figure out exactly what it all meant, the way she barricaded herself in her room with an impossible problem set from geometry and emerged hours later with not just the right answers but an understanding of the relations behind the equations. When people said she was smart (she'd heard it used as an insult too), she didn't believe them, because at first she didn't get anything. She was slow to pick up on jokes, and often found herself rewinding conversations to see where she'd lost hold of the meaning. People thought she was weird, and shy, but really she was just dense and self-centered. Like now, with Kim, she knew she should be feeling more than this. Things were different—her parents working as a team was proof that this was serious—yet after so long she couldn't stop being jealous of Kim and wondered, crazily, if she was playing a trick on them.

The detective had asked them not to touch anything in Kim's room. Lindsay saw her father close the door; now it stood wide open. Cooper was sacked out with his head under her dresser, as if that made him invisible. She used him as an excuse, aware they could hear her downstairs. "Come on, Goob," she said, "I don't think they want you in here," but not hard enough to budge him.

She stood at the foot of Kim's bed, still as a ninja, taking in the pictures and dressage ribbons on the wall, the hand-carved African mask and the cross made of a single twisted palm frond, the pennant from Camp Conestoga, where they'd both gone. She knew the room intimately; she'd been snooping through it since she could walk. She'd lifted each skating trophy high above her head like they did in the Olympics, and tried on every new hairclip and headband. She could feel Kim here, and smell her. Every piece of furniture, every object, the paint, the carpeting, even the dust motes floating through the sun connected them. Beside her nightstand Barry Bear sprawled atop a jumble of stuffed animals, staring back with amber eyes. On her desktop sat the wire cup of colored pencils Lindsay had always coveted, and a vial of black sand from Hawaii, and the dancing hip-hop hamster from her grandmother Kim would leave on just to annoy her. The top of her dresser held the real treasure: her jewelry box, maroon velvet with a dozen little drawer-pulls like gold BBs, on one side of it a flotilla of ornate porcelain jars and imported candy tins and lidded raffia baskets, on the other, arranged by height, a half-dozen bottles of perfume that Kim refused to share and

Lindsay had secretly tested. Her bookcase was alphabetized, neat rows of paperbacks interrupted by a block of Harry Potters, the bottom shelf filled with complete sets of Tolkien and C. S. Lewis and SAT manuals thick as phone books. Nothing, Lindsay thought, that she would really need.

What was missing? Her purse. Her red hoodie. Her CD holders were all there, but her iPod wasn't, and she wondered if they knew that.

Sometimes Kim kept money in her two-toned Chinese puzzle box. Lindsay had never taken any, but right after Kim's graduation she'd stood in this same spot holding a remote-control-sized wad of twenties as thrilling as a gun in her hand, wondering where Kim had gotten it all. A week later it was gone.

Downstairs, the phone rang. Her father answered, his voice a murmur.

She crept a step closer to the dresser, worrying that she would leave fingerprints. Cooper watched her, confused. The box was easy once you knew the sequence, but the quiet made her nervous and she almost dropped it. She held it against herself, lining up the slots until the spring pushed the top free.

She half-expected the note she found—a torn sheet of looseleaf paper folded over and over until it was the size of a pill. As she opened it, she was wishing. She wanted Kim to tell her not to worry, to let everyone know she was okay. She could trust Lindsay to be her messenger. Her parents would hold her and cry as if she were Kim, grateful and devastated at the same time. Somehow the three of them would go on.

The paper was blank—or no, the writing was just tiny, two words nearly hidden in the very center. In her cutesy, rounded script, itty bitty, Kim had written: YOU SUCK.

Another Kind of Lie

Nina called him right after the detective left. "He's probably on his way over there."

"What did you tell him?" J.P. asked.

"About what?"

"What do you think?"

"I didn't tell him anything."

"Sorry, I'm just super paranoid right now."

"He asked a lot about you," Nina said.

"Like what?"

"Like did I ever see you get physical with her."

"Jesus."

"I told him you were a good guy."

"I don't know about that," J.P. said.

"You are."

Would Kim's parents think so when they found out about the speed? Because they would. For a second he could feel the whole mess rising inside him, looking for a way out.

"This is so fucked up."

"I know," she said. "Me and Hinch are going over there later if you want to come."

"Yeah," he said.

"They'll find her."

He wasn't that positive, but agreed.

When he was talking with Nina he was okay, but when he got off the fear set in again. He sat on the edge of his bed with his head in his hands and his eyes closed, as if he could block out everything, and still he could see his whole future crumbling—his job, college, all of it destroyed. He was so stupid. Why did he ever listen to Hinch?

On top of that, he knew that the secret they were keeping was nothing compared to Kim being missing, and felt selfish and small for protecting it. He'd told her mom the truth—he didn't know of any reason she'd just take off—but she was so desperate that he wanted to be completely honest with her, as if that would suddenly make her like him.

"Brass monkey," his phone chimed, *"that funky monkey,"* and he flipped it open.

It was a local cellphone by the area code, and he sat up straight before answering.

It was Kim's dad again, warning him about the detective.

"Nina already told me."

"Do me a favor," Kim's dad said. "If there's anything you can think of that's suspicious, tell him, because right now it's pretty clear he thinks she's a runaway, and they're not going to look for her the way they'd look for someone who's been kidnapped. It's a huge difference. If you can think of anything at all, let him know, okay?"

"Yes, sir."

"Can you think of anything?"

He could only think of the secret, how it wasn't connected to Kim but sat off to one side, lurking. He wanted to tell him there was something, but that would just be another kind of lie.

Since he'd been going out with Kim he'd only spoken seriously with her dad once, at four in the morning after he brought her home late and shit-faced from the spring formal. Her dad was waiting in the dark kitchen and ambushed them, flicking the switch. Kim was swearing and incoherent under the bright lights, and they had to help her up to bed. Her dad gave him credit for driving, then asked him what he was doing while Kim was getting ripped. "If you really cared for her," he said, "you wouldn't let her do this to herself." Kim always made fun of her mom, calling her a lush, drinking her bottle of wine every night, but J.P. stayed silent, not wanting to make things worse. Somewhere deep down her dad must have known there was no way they could stop either of them, all they could do was hold on and limit the damage. But her dad was right too. J.P. didn't love her enough, and certainly not enough to sacrifice himself. The shame was, he would have if Kim had let him.

"No," he said, "but I know she wouldn't run away."

"We told him that. It didn't seem to do any good."

"She was leaving in another month anyway."

"That's what we told him. She just bought all this stuff for college. There's a whole bag of shampoo in her bathroom."

J.P. didn't know what to say to this.

"I think the problem is that he doesn't know her. He thinks she's some messed up teenager. He's got to be in his sixties—you'll see. I really think he just doesn't get it."

"Doesn't sound like it."

"We need to make him understand. Otherwise the cops are just going to sit on their asses when they should be out looking for her."

"I'm going to come over later with Nina and Hinch."

"Good. We're going to need everybody we can get. Okay, I've got a call on the other line. You tell him whatever you have to."

"I will," J.P. said.

Nonfamily Abduction Sample

Connie told her to go online. "Right now, come on. If they're not help-ing you, you've got to help yourself. What do we tell our people?"

"Information—"

"—is education. So get educated."

Live Smarter was the hospital's name for its patient outreach pro-gram. In their sillier, more cynical moments they called it Die Smarter, but Connie was right. The detective hadn't gotten back to them, and Fran needed this pep talk. Connie gave her a direction, guiding her through sites dedicated to the missing.

Fran was amazed at how many there were for children. It was a kind of heavenly netherworld decorated with hearts and cherubs, yellow rib-bons and white roses and scrolls of poetry. The Hope Network, 18-Wheel Angels, BringJoHome. In between the 800 numbers and links for national clearinghouses and private eyes, the lost smiled for the cam-era. Some of them had been missing for years.

She lagged behind Connie, her eye caught on a teenaged boy with Down syndrome from Indianapolis who disappeared after applying for a job at a Wendy's. In the picture he wore a Colts hat and his mouth was slightly open, as if he'd forgotten what he was going to say. The forum had archived the news stories on him in order. The last headline read: KY. MAN ADMITS '04 KILLING.

"Doubleclick on 'Resources.'"

"Hang on," Fran said. She hated this computer; it was so slow. At work she could bounce from screen to screen, but Kim and Lindsay's music downloads and the attached spyware had choked their hard drive.

The page that came up was a manual, *Finding Your Child.* The corny clip art on the cover made it look out of date.

"They're calling her an adult," Fran said.

"Keep reading."

The first section was titled "The First 24 Hours." Step-by-step it described what they needed to do. There were links to pages where they could design their own flyers, with checklists of information. She wouldn't have thought to include a second picture from a different angle, but it made sense. She was dazed and grateful.

Clear all released information with Law Enforcement.

Do not use your own phone number.

Review and proofread several times before reproducing.

Ask local printers to copy for free or at a discount rate.

"This is really good."

"Good," Connie said. "Bookmark it."

It had tips on the best way to organize volunteers, and where to post flyers, how to get pizza places and video stores to tape them to their boxes. She printed out the whole section for Ed, drawing the deputy's attention. Let him look, she thought.

Connie was ahead of her, on an entirely different site. "From what this lady's saying, you want to bring in dogs as soon as possible. That's what she wishes they'd done."

"We'll ask for them." She was still trying to learn the rules about the different types of flyers—who could use NONFAMILY ABDUCTION instead of ENDANGERED MISSING, or worse, VOLUNTARY MISSING.

"The police have to request them. In this case they waited two months—"

"Two months?" She couldn't imagine Kim being gone that long. She couldn't really imagine what was happening now.

"That's what she says—don't wait, make a stink about it."

She added the manual to her favorites before joining her at the Ohio K-9 site with its pictures of German shepherds in blaze orange halters. Along with search-and-rescue teams they offered cadaver dogs. Their homepage ran on and on, and she felt queasy from all the coffee, her mind spinning out ahead of her.

"I can't read it. What does it say?"

"They're nonprofit," Connie said. "All the police have to do is call them."

She printed it out and went back to the manual while Connie forged ahead.

Do not disturb or remove anything from your child's room or bathroom, even and especially trash. Preserve all worn clothing as is. Pillowcases, sheets and towels may contain evidence. Secure your child's comb, brush and toothbrush for fingerprinting and DNA testing.

The detective hadn't said anything about this, and Fran made a note to save Kim's towels, and the washcloth hanging in the shower, and the shower curtain, and the bath mat, and the garbage can. From what this said they should have closed off both rooms. Instead, she'd let Lindsay take her shower.

"Looks like Erie has a good horse team," Connie said. "They're supposed to be faster than dogs."

"Can we do both?"

"I don't see why not."

"What's the link?"

Find videotapes or movies of your child and make copies for law enforcement and the media.

Ask your child's doctor and dentist for copies of recent X-rays.

Record a daily update on your answering machine to keep family members informed of your progress.

There were too many things to do, and the further she read, the more overwhelmed she felt.

"It says here the state police have helicopters that can see body heat," Connie said.

"Do me a favor and print that out. And anything else you think we can use. I've got to get working on this flyer."

"I'll be there in fifteen minutes, if you can wait."

"It looks pretty simple."

"You're going to need an alpha geek anyway."

She loved Connie for trying to keep things light, even if she didn't feel it. She wished Ed would joke with her, but she knew him too. He was so focused that he might misinterpret any attempt at humor on her part as distracting and inappropriate.

He hadn't left the kitchen table. He sat with the phone directly in front of him, his cellphone to his ear. She clipped the printed pages of *The First 24 Hours* together and set them next to him. He looked up in acknowledgment, still talking to someone—his brother in Minnesota, it sounded like. Before she could leave he reached his free arm around her waist and she leaned into him, his head pressed against her rib cage. "We don't know yet," he said. "We don't know anything." His hair was thin and graying, his part growing wider by the month. When she'd met him his hair was blond and longer than hers, with a natural curl she envied. She smoothed what was left with a hand. He squeezed her once and patted her hip to release her, and though she wanted them to stay like that, she let him go.

Upstairs, Kim's door was closed. So was Lindsay's. She knocked, and when she didn't get an answer she opened the door a foot and stuck her head in. Lindsay was on her bed, reading and listening to her iPod, Cooper half across her lap. She plucked out one earbud.

"Hey," Fran said. "Don't use your bathroom, okay? Use ours or the downstairs."

"Okay."

"Did you want to invite Dana or Micah over?"

"No, I'm good."

"I'm not," Fran said. "I don't like this. We're just going to have to deal with it, I guess. I've got to go make a flyer, I just wanted to see how you were doing."

"Okay." She held the earbud up to stick it back in.

"Okay," Fran said, and shut the door.

On the stairs she felt herself frowning and tried to relax her face. She didn't expect Lindsay to accept the invitation, but she wanted more out of her. The way she'd closed herself off lately reminded her of Kim, turning distant and dismissive. Maybe it was the age. Her own mother had accused Fran of being moody. "Smile," she was always telling her, "you have such a nice smile," as if she were withholding it out of spite.

Ed was still on the phone. The deputy was standing at the window over the sink and barely turned his head to see her sit down at the computer.

She went to the blank flyer and filled out the information line by line, stopping only to spellcheck Caucasian. When she was done the computer asked her to rename the file.

The first name that came to mind was Kim.

FLYER1, she typed.

In the folder with her pictures from graduation were a couple dozen shots from the party at Elise's, none of them useful. Fran lingered briefly over each, reading her face, and the crowd around her. Beneath that file was the Fourth of July they'd spent on the lake, more recent, except Kim hadn't gone with them. Fran had to go back to Easter to find a good one of her from the waist up. Kim's hair was shorter and darker, but the dress showed off her neck and shoulders and gave a better sense of her presence. The gold chain with her butterfly was just a bonus.

She pulled them up side by side, trying them one way and then the other. She couldn't wait until Ed was off, and waved him over. He leaned toward the screen and gave her the okay sign.

When he left she flipped them again, and then again, unsure. She opened the flyer and dragged the pair over to the waiting empty space. A click and she'd be done. They didn't have time to waste, yet she balked as if she were making a mistake. The twin Kims smiled out at her, cheeky and bright-eyed, ripe. The right flyer might save her life, Fran knew—the manual said so—but all she could think of was the boy in the Colts hat, the badly animated flickering candles and glowing rainbows. She wanted to stop and close the folder, turn off the computer, afraid that once she sent Kim into that other world, she'd never get her back.

The Right to Disappear

His gut said they were screwed, and nothing he could do would change that. The old guy was clueless. He'd been gone almost two hours now while they sat here cooped up, doing nothing.

At the same time Ed knew they couldn't afford to piss off the cops. Yes, he was frustrated, but Fran was so stuck on what was right that she didn't understand their position was weak. Always deal from strength, that was one fundamental law of his business. (Another was, you can't bargain with an idiot.) They could only hope the detective had turned up something, and that's what was taking him so long.

He knew Kim's friends well enough by now that he could read them like clients, Nina and Elise especially. Elise seemed normal, calm but concerned, asking how they were, if there was anything she could do. Nina, as usual, was all over the place, impossible to stop, but J.P. hardly said anything. He didn't seem surprised, and talked dully, as if he'd just woken up. Maybe it was shock, but it bothered Ed. If he was eighteen and his girlfriend was missing he'd be tear-assing around town looking for her.

There was a lot about Kim and J.P. he didn't get. They were sleeping together, Fran assured him, yet when they were deciding on colleges Kim had scoffed at the idea of going to Ohio State. When he and Fran had faced the same choice they'd battled their parents to stay together. While he sensed that sex had returned to the semicasual status it held in the seventies, he was confused by their lack of romance. As a father, he was at times grateful for that missing intensity, but as a man who liked to surprise his wife with flowers, it baffled him. Maybe he was old-fashioned, but to him a couple meant a strong bond, with positive and negative charges constantly arcing between them. He'd never seen Kim and J.P. kiss, let alone argue.

Outside, the sun flashed off a passing car—not the detective's. It was already hot, a good day to be on the lake. According to the thing Fran had printed off the internet, they needed to be out searching with bloodhounds, beating the bushes from here to the interstate.

He offered the deputy a soda, then, pouring himself one, asked when they should expect the detective.

"I'm really not sure."

"Can you call and find out? Tell him we're getting a little antsy here."

"Sure," he said, then went outside to do it.

Ed watched him from the window. His nametag said Oester, but Ed couldn't put an address to it.

"This is bullshit," Fran said, holding aside the curtain. "I think you should call Perry."

"I want to wait and see what this guy says."

"Maybe Perry can talk to him."

"I'm hoping he won't have to."

"God help me, if they screw this up we're going to sue them for everything they've got."

It was a reckless statement, tempting fate, yet he'd had the same thought. "I know," he said, and held her.

"Connie's coming over."

"Good." Exactly what they didn't need—another cook.

The deputy headed back up the drive, and they broke, Fran taking her place at the computer.

"He's on his way," the deputy said.

"Did he find anything?"

"That's what he's going to talk to you about."

"So you don't know."

"Sorry."

"That's all right," Ed said. "Thanks for checking."

While they waited he went over his pitch. Forget the family—her friends agreed she had no reason to leave. She wasn't in trouble, she hadn't broken up with her boyfriend, she hadn't met anyone new, she wasn't pregnant or depressed or on drugs. She hadn't taken any favorite clothes or jewelry, she hadn't taken her glasses or even a box of her contacts. She hadn't mentioned leaving to anyone, hadn't left a note. Altogether, the facts pointed to her not being a runaway, and yet, with no other evidence, the police were assuming she was. He was hoping that that, along with some honest parental hysteria, would shame the man into action. If not, he'd call Perry.

If he'd known how hard convincing them was going to be, he would have sliced open his own arm and dripped blood across the backyard.

At the computer Fran ran out of paper and fought with the feed tray. He was afraid she'd break it, but didn't look, just stood there watching the street, and soon she had it going again.

He had practice at waiting, his livelihood depended on it: waiting for buyers, waiting for counteroffers, waiting for contracts. This was different. This was like waiting for the market to pick up. For over a year he'd been riding it down, liquidating their savings to pay the bills. The feeling he had now was the same, and even the sight of the unmarked car pulling in didn't change that, unless the passenger door opened and Kim got out, head bowed in apology, her hair hanging limp and dirty.

No, only the driver's side opened. The detective tottered as if he had bad knees, stopping once to adjust the fat stack of folders under his arm. Beside Ed the deputy left his post at the window to get the door. Fran took advantage of this, stealing over.

"We've got to have dogs," she said.

"I'll try."

"You get them."

They sat on one side of the kitchen table with the detective across from them, shuffling his papers like a lawyer at a closing. He folded his hands and hunched over them.

"First, I want you to understand that because this is an open investigation I can't share every piece of information we uncover with you. For the good of the case sometimes we have to withhold things, okay? I know that's not what you want to hear, but believe me, it's in your daughter's best interest."

Ed didn't believe this one bit, but nodded.

"Second, I think it's important to remember that as an adult your daughter has a right to privacy. If we locate her and she requests that right, legally we're prevented from telling you where she is."

"That can't be right," Fran said.

"Third, Mr. Larsen, I know this is a difficult time, but I'm going to have to ask you to please refrain from contacting any further persons of interest."

It didn't have to be J.P. He'd talked to all of them. "I was just calling around to see if anyone knew anything."

"I appreciate that, I'd just rather we didn't muddy the waters."

"Are you saying we can't talk to her friends?" Fran asked.

"I'm not saying that. You can talk to her friends, you can talk to your neighbors all you like, but please let us talk to them first. It makes our job that much easier."

"Got it," Ed said.

The two uniforms were still going door-to-door, the detective said, but he was finished with his preliminary interviews. He'd talked with her coworkers, and by phone with Ed's mother—a surprise that made Ed like the guy even less.

"Did you find out anything useful?" Fran asked.

"Everyone seems to like your daughter—"

"I think we told you that," she said, and Ed patted her arm.

"No one believes she'd just run away."

They nodded at each other in confirmation.

"At the same time, I'm finding some low-level involvement with drugs among her circle."

It wasn't entirely a shock, though Ed found himself grimacing. Was this good or bad for them? They had so little to negotiate with.

"At this point I can't say much more. I'm applying for a warrant to get access to her bank account, hoping that might tell us something."

"But so far," Ed said, "you're not finding any evidence that she planned on running away."

"In most cases there wouldn't be any. Whereas in a forcible abduction you generally have some sort of trail—if not witnesses then some kind of physical evidence: a car, a purse, signs of a struggle."

"But not always," Ed said.

"Not in all cases, but in a significant majority. The bottom line in either case is that we need to get word out and start looking for her as soon as possible. The deputy says you've put together a flyer."

Fran pushed a copy across the table.

"Outstanding, except technically we still have to go with 'missing' at this point. I know it's hard, but try to think of it as a good thing."

Behind him the back door opened with a swish. The deputy took a step toward the back hall and met Connie, lugging a plastic bag from Staples, a ream of paper inside weighting it like a brick.

"Hey," she said.

"I'm going to ask you to wait outside if that's all right," the detective said, and motioned for the deputy to accompany her.

"What I'm worried about," Ed said reasonably, "is that we're coming up on twenty-four hours, and no one's really looking for her."

"I know it doesn't feel like it, but we're looking for her as we speak. Right now we've got two units checking every inch of Route 7. Every patrol car in the county's got her on their screens—Conneaut, Ashtabula, *and* the state police. We're tied in with Erie, same for Cleveland and Akron. She's out on the wire with the car. That's national, plus she's registered on every major website, including the FBI's."

"What about dogs?" he said.

"Dogs are great if you've got a clear idea of where you're looking, but they're not much help finding cars at long distances, and that's what we're looking at here, I'm afraid."

"It wouldn't help if we brought a team in," Fran asked.

"Here in the house, you mean. They'd get her scent but I'm not sure what they'd do with it. There's no sign that anything happened here, and even if it did, you've still got the car as a mode of transport."

"They could search for her along 7," Ed said, "or down by the river."

"I know it sounds logical, but you're talking a needle in a haystack. When we find the car, that's when we want the dogs. What we need right now is leads, and the way to get leads is to get her face out there. That's why the flyer's so important."

The technique was familiar to Ed—burying the client's naive question beneath an avalanche of shoptalk. As in any business, flashing a little knowledge with nothing to back it up was a red flag to a professional. He had thought the guy was doddering and incompetent; now he realized how truly screwed they were. As the detective went on lecturing them, Ed remembered standing by the side of 90 with the girl's abandoned Toyota, the sense of the road going on forever in both directions, impossible to follow, and beyond its narrow shoulders, the land and the rivers and the oceans, the whole world. A person could be anywhere.

Fran looked at him, lips pinched, and shook her head. This guy wasn't interested in helping them. He'd have to call Perry, but even that—his gut told him—wouldn't work.

"All right," Ed said, to stop him. "So what do we do now?"

Answers to Name

Everyone had secrets, that was life. Driving over with Hinch, Nina thought it wasn't just her. They'd all lied to the detective. Kim would have too if it had been one of them. She'd always been better than Nina at keeping her secrets, ever since they were little. Kim would get a kick out of the irony: They really needed her now.

The secret they were protecting was nothing compared to Kim being missing, and separate from it, as far as Hinch and J.P. knew. They were guys, interested only in what affected them directly. Being Kim's best friend, Nina had an endless stock of confidences to draw on, many of them connected, or at least overlapping at the edges. She'd never had a problem carrying them before—it was a privilege to be chosen over Elise, and Nina had reciprocated, holding back almost nothing (drunkenly kissing J.P. that one time in the bathroom was an exception, an honest slip she could barely admit to herself)—but now, faced with the question of what might have happened to Kim, Nina, more than anyone, had to decide what was important for the police to know and what wasn't.

So far she hadn't decided or divulged anything, stonewalled the guy, as if the code of silence was absolute. She could tell he didn't believe her, asking if she'd take a lie detector test, then saying, "I might just take you up on that." She almost wanted to. Having the truth forced out of you was somehow more honorable than squealing.

They had to pass the DQ on their way to Kim's house. Normally as they cruised by, Hinch would click his heels together and give a rigid *sieg heil*, but like Nina he had his eyes on the side streets, as if the cops could have possibly overlooked Kim's little car. They rode in silence, out of respect, and still Hinch bobbed his head to some inner jam band. Earlier he'd complained—to make a joke—that it was his day off, except Nina could see he'd shaved and was wearing hiking boots instead of his Tevas in case they needed to search the woods.

Kingsville was still and bright around them, black shadows under the heavy trees, flags hanging limp. As they jounced over the tracks by the box plant, looking both ways, the baked air shimmered like water in the distance, and Nina wondered if anyone had checked the right-of-way out of town. As girls they'd walked the ties for hours, the Three Amigos, imagining their dream lives in mythical cities like Rome and Paris, spying on line workers taking smoke breaks and mothers sunning in their backyards. They'd make peanut-butter-and-banana sandwiches and fill a canteen with ice cubes and Kool-Aid and hike to the bridge over the river and dare one another to jump, until one day, the summer before eighth grade, Kim stood up from where they were sitting high above the sluggish current, smiled at them and stepped off. Nina didn't even think. Still wearing her sneakers, she launched herself after her, hollering all the way down. "Don't be a chicken, Elise!" They taunted, treading water, until, with a shriek they imitated for years, she leapt, arms flapping.

See, she thought, most of their secrets were happy like that.

"What?" Hinch asked, turning from his window.

"What?"

"You sighed."

"Thinking too much."

"You need to be more like me," he said.

"Yeah—no thanks."

She took the turn on to Lakewood like she had a million times before. Any normal day they'd be at the river, and she wished herself there, floating on the cold water with her eyes closed and the sun flooding her skin.

"Look at this shit," Hinch said.

A block from Kim's house, cars lined both sides of the road. Mr. Hedrick from next door was talking with a cop in the driveway, and there was a crowd on the porch. Nina overshot, grabbed the first spot she saw, nudging the curb, and they hustled back as if they were late.

At the bottom of the porch stairs, a woman she didn't know gave them each a nametag. Mrs. Lavery who taught art was there, and Ashley Bisbee, and Jen Gaither's mom, and Mr. Riggio who umpired their softball games. She didn't recognize everyone; they were probably neighbors and people Kim's mom and dad worked with. Kim's mom sat at the far end of the porch behind a folding table, handing out posters and rolls of tape. Since the moment Nina had found out, she'd been irrationally afraid that Kim's mom would blame her, but now Nina went directly to her, brushing past strangers, and Kim's mom stood and took her in her arms.

"Where is she?" Kim's mom asked, squeezing and rocking her side to side.

"I don't know" was all Nina could say.

Kim's mom let go of her to hold Hinch, then dabbed at her eyes and nose. Without makeup her face was gray, an age spot like a water stain on her cheek, and Nina wanted to tell her not to worry, everything would be all right, they'd find her.

"Kim's dad's out putting up flyers." She motioned to a stack. They'd used the picture Kim hated, the one that made her face look fat, and another glam shot Nina had never seen. It seemed like bad luck just to look at it, and Nina's eyes skipped off, trying to find a neutral spot to rest on. Taped to the table was a map of the county crosshatched with magic marker, a perfectly plotted grid that made her think of old war movies. "I guess I should sign you guys in. You both have your cellphones?"

J.P. had beaten them by nearly an hour. The sheet said he was assigned to section D–4, right downtown. Elise and her mom were up by him, covering Lake Road from the township park out past the golf course.

"I'm so glad you could make it," Kim's mom said, like they might not have. She waved to someone behind them, smiling like a hostess, making Hinch twist around, then excused herself, saying she'd see them later. "Frank," she said, "I'm so glad you could make it." Hinch popped his eyes like this was creepy, but Nina thought it was a skill, flying on autopilot. All morning, between calls, she'd felt herself drifting that way and had to snap awake. All she had to do was think of Kim walking up from the river with her, the two of them climbing single file up the path, the flaming sun on the small of Kim's back peeking out of her cutoffs. What did she say to her—"See you there, Squinky Square." It sounded like something from SpongeBob. That could not be the last thing they said to each other.

They joined a group from the Larsens' church as a heavy woman named Connie with brightly dyed hair and a clipboard briefed them on the procedure. The idea was to saturate every square on the map, moving from the center of town outward. The Copycat had donated the flyers, so they shouldn't be shy with them. The most effective approach was to ask people who worked at gas stations or fast food places to post them on their doors. Banks, grocery stores, laundromats, pharmacies, the post office—anywhere people gathered. After that, hit utility poles on corners where cars had to stop. And no trees—this was very important. The town could fine them for any flyers on trees.

"Questions?"

"What if we run out?" an older lady asked.

"We'll give you enough so you won't."

Connie split them into teams of two, making Nina wonder who was with J.P. They drew F–5, the neighborhood off State behind the Railroad Museum. It was mostly ratty back streets sloping down to Conneaut Creek. Nina couldn't think of anything there except the old firehouse and Monroe Park and was disappointed. They wouldn't find anything there.

The church had provided a van, but the woman encouraged anyone with a car to drive and save those open seats for people who needed them. Heading over, Nina was just as glad; Hinch was more than enough company for her. He'd grabbed a free water and was reading the flyer out loud. He was surprised that Kim was five foot eight.

"She's not," Nina said. "She's five seven."

"Is this bracelet the one you gave her?"

"Yeah." Nina had given it to her for her twelfth birthday, and Kim still wore it for luck.

"What would you call your complexion?" Hinch asked.

"Olive."

"What about mine?"

"Annoying."

There was no way around the Dairy Queen and the cemetery. They repeated like the background in a cheap cartoon. The sidewalks were empty, only the occasional car nosing in, windows closed against the heat. Even in the summer, Nina thought, this town was so dead. If Kim had run away (and she didn't, she wouldn't), the only thing Nina would blame her for was not taking her with her.

At the Railroad Museum they had their choice of parking spots. A yearly field trip when they were in grade school, it was closed and for sale. Inside the chained gate massive black locomotives and coal cars sat marooned in thigh-high weeds. She held a flyer at eye level between the barred ticket windows while Hinch taped the top and bottom. Immediately she wanted to rip it down, as if it weren't true.

"Which way?" Hinch said, wearing the tape on his wrist like a bracelet.

They zigzagged down the street, hitting every telephone pole, then at the end cut left on Sandusky. The blocks back here were shady and quiet. The farther in they went, the smaller and shabbier the houses were, bungalows and saltboxes with short driveways and carports sheltering derelict cars. A felt banner announcing JESUS IS THE LIGHT hung from a porch covered in astroturf.

They'd just started on Rockledge when they came across a competing flyer. REWARD, it said, above a grainy black-and-white picture of what was supposed to be an orange cat. His name was Tuffy, and his family missed him very much. It didn't say how long he'd been gone, but the paper was stained and wrinkled, and it hadn't rained in at least a week. Down the block, his owners had stapled one to a tree; someone had torn it off, leaving the four corners. Another clung to the rounded top of a mailbox.

"That can't be legal," Hinch said.

Nina took a new flyer and fixed it next to the old one, and he didn't argue with her.

They matched Tuffy all the way into the park, wrapping one around the pole of each basketball hoop, taping another to the side of the dry water fountain. Where she could, Nina put Kim above the cat, as if to reestablish the natural order, but as they passed from the glare into shadow again she noticed she was glancing down driveways and peering under cars, checking along hedges, ready to dial the number on the flyer. Sometimes her father left the back gate open and their dogs wandered out—dangerous, considering how fast their road was—but they weren't adventurous. When Nina opened the front door they'd be waiting there. Cats were different, but still, especially now, she couldn't help but sympathize. Her first reaction—that she would trade a million Tuffys to have Kim back—turned into a grudging acceptance that other people were hurting too, and then, out of desperation more than anything, bloomed into a childish equation: Maybe if she found Tuffy, someone would find Kim.

On Laurel a jungle of ivy had taken over one place, swamping tree trunks, a coachlight, the whole yard.

Hinch made kissing sounds. "Here, Tuffy. Here, kitty kitty kitty."

She gave him a skeptical look.

"It says he knows his name."

Spring Street, Willow, Townsend down at the bottom of the hill. Holding the flyer up again and again, she couldn't avoid memorizing it. IF YOU HAVE ANY INFORMATION CONCERNING THIS CASE, PLEASE CALL THE ASHTABULA COUNTY SHERIFF'S DEPARTMENT.

The information she had might be useless, since it was at least three months old. She hoped so. Kim had said it was a one-time thing, and seemed more embarrassed than concerned, as if she was sorry she hadn't thought of the consequences. Nina told her not to worry, and that was the last they spoke of it. If she'd continued to see him, Nina didn't know. She and Nina had practically spent the last month together, and she didn't think so.

J.P. didn't know, she knew that much.

The problem was that everything was connected. One lie covered another, which covered a third, which rested against a fourth. It all went back to Kingsville being so goddamn small.

They'd reached the last street, half a block long. On the far side shotgun shacks with rusty mailboxes and gardens for front yards backed up to the creek. There were only two poles. Both had a Tuffy poster.

It was hot and the walk up the hill was long.

"How many we got left?" Hinch asked.

She showed him the inch-thick stack. On top, looking up at her, Kim's face was a question. What had Kim said? "It was *definitely* a mistake." That could have meant anything, or nothing. It wasn't the first time she'd picked the wrong guy.

Nina could see herself calling from the pay phone at the edge of the lot of the Conoco, the way she'd seen hundreds of people do, leaning out of their cars to punch the buttons.

"How do you spell that?" the cop would say.

She wouldn't even guess, because she'd be wrong. She had his address and his phone, but they could look that up. "Everyone just calls him Wooze."

Or not, she thought. Just because it was true didn't mean it was useful, and when it came to him Nina had her own secrets to keep. They all did. The detective would find out in time, she was as sure of that as Hinch was convinced he wouldn't. Could telling him now help, or would it just fuck things up worse? As with any big decision, she needed to discuss it with Kim.

Baby Steps

There was a logical order to their panic, Fran thought. Every failure led to the next step.

The police weren't doing anything, so they appealed to the media. She was lunch buddies with Jocelyn, who handled the hospital's PR. Together they fashioned a cover letter, saying Fran would be available for interviews, and faxed it with the flyer to every TV and radio station and newspaper from Erie to Cleveland. Within minutes the *Star-Beacon* called. As she answered their questions—"Tell me a little bit about Kim as a person"—she wondered if Ed would be angry with her when he got back.

He wasn't. He was still angry with the detective. He'd finally gotten through to Perry and discovered, after all this time, that Perry himself had actually stopped Kim for speeding yesterday around two o'clock and written her a warning. Fran didn't know what to make of this clue, if that's what it was.

"You'd think they'd check those records first," she said.

"You'd think. He said she seemed fine, just a little nervous, which is normal since it's the first time she's been stopped, as far as I know. Anyway, we talked. He said he'd do what he could."

"What does that mean?"

"He's the sheriff," Ed said. "It's his department."

"He's got to follow the rules like everyone else."

"I'd say this is more of a judgment call."

"So we should be hopeful."

"I think so."

They'd retreated upstairs to their room for privacy, leaving Connie in charge, and for a moment, holding him, she could believe they were making progress.

He sweated when he was nervous, and the bill of his Sea Wolves cap was soaked through. He peeled off his T-shirt, swabbing his armpits with it, then reapplied deodorant before tugging on a new one.

"Give me the hat, I'll wash it."

"No," he said, "it's lucky."

He sat on a corner of the bed, trading his sneakers for his seldom-used hiking boots. He was taking J.P. and a team of volunteers to search along the river. Technically it was the last place she was seen, and though Fran doubted she'd go back there, she wanted to stay positive for him.

"Did you get lunch? Giant Eagle sent stuff over."

"I'm not hungry. D'you get something?"

"I tried," she said.

"What about Lindsay?"

"I took her a sandwich. I wish she'd come out of there. I've got tons of things she can do."

Ed thought Lindsay's reaction made perfect sense, but he also knew this cue was nonnegotiable. Fran rarely asked for help with the girls. The house was overrun, and he'd been gone for more than an hour, and now he was taking off again. It didn't matter that his mind was miles away. In the basic emotional math of their marriage, he owed her.

He waited for her to go downstairs before knocking on Lindsay's door.

She was reading with a half-eaten sandwich in her lap, and didn't look up. Cooper sniffed at the paper plate. She shooed him with a backhand.

"How's it going?" he asked.

"I'm ten pages from the end." It was *Julius Caesar*, part of her summer reading.

"It's a little crazy down there."

"I know, I can hear it." She saved her place with a finger and gave him her full attention.

"When you're done your mom could use a hand."

"Okay," she said, and he thought it was too easy, as if she was just agreeing to get rid of him.

"I know everyone's worried about Kim. Your mother and I are worried about you."

"Why?"

"If you were missing, do you think Kim would just be sitting in her room?"

"No—"

"I'm sorry."

"—she'd be out rescuing me, but I can't because I can't do anything. I can't drive, I can't even answer the phone."

"I don't know what driving has to do with anything. We all need each other right now, so finish your book, then come down and help—please. Okay?"

"Can I go with you?"

Out of habit he was going to tell her to ask her mother, because the answer was no. He wouldn't risk both of them. "I'd really rather you didn't."

"What does Mom want me to do?"

"You'll have to ask her."

"Fine," she said with a sigh. "I'll be down."

"Thank you," he said, but when he closed her door he thought he'd only made things worse.

On the porch Fran was briefing another team, two middle-aged women he didn't recognize wearing fanny packs. One of the websites Connie had found said that abductors sometimes signed up as volunteers as a way of gloating or prolonging the thrill. The new rule was they had to take everyone's picture and scan his or her driver's license. They'd already started filling milk crates with files: A to L, M to Z.

"She's coming down," Ed said, amending the good news with a grimace. "She wanted to go look with me."

"What did you tell her?"

"No."

"Good."

So at least he'd done that right.

His team gathered in the yard for a group picture, in case one of them got lost. He had a roll sheet, like a teacher. Most were Kim's friends and teammates, dressed for heavy bushwhacking. Grant Hedrick was the other token oldster. He was ex-Merchant Marine and could handle a map and a compass. Ed planned on making him a squad leader. He'd take one side of the river, Grant could take the other.

Connie was still hung up on dogs, afraid the searchers would trample Kim's scent, as if she'd suddenly become an expert. Ed listened to her with the proper concern, nodding. She was Fran's best friend, and incredibly helpful, except she didn't understand. This wasn't Recordkeeping. She wasn't in charge here.

"I appreciate what you're saying," he said, "but until we actually get some dogs we just have to work with what we've got."

"Be careful," Fran said as they filed onto the short bus, into the blasting air-conditioning. As their leader he was the last one in, and patted the driver on the shoulder to get going.

Kim's teammates filled the back rows while her friends paired up in couples, leaving J.P. alone at the very front. Ed wanted to read shock and heartbreak in his posture. He slouched against the window with his head bowed so his bangs covered one eye, his arms crossed over his chest. In his third-generation Ramones T-shirt, he seemed skinny and defenseless, the ghost of the reckless kid Ed had been. Despite all of Connie's paranoid warnings, he'd been relieved to see J.P.'s name at the top of the sign-in sheet. They'd both been out posting flyers and hadn't talked face-to-face yet, and as if to physically apologize for his earlier opinion, Ed took the seat beside him.

J.P. had hoped he'd keep going down the aisle, but somehow knew he wouldn't. It felt like a trap, as if he would turn and interrogate him the whole way there. He sat up straight to make room, aware of Nina and Hinch behind them.

"You going to be all right in those sneakers?" Kim's dad asked.

"The only boots I have are for winter."

"What size are you? I might have an old pair you can borrow."

"That's okay."

"Seriously, you're going to need a pair. I mean, I hope we don't have to, but we could be doing this a lot, in a lot worse places."

J.P. couldn't tell if this was a trick. "Eleven-and-a-half?"

"Close enough. I'm a twelve. I'll check when we get back."

As they rolled onto Buffalo, Kim's dad shifted sideways with his feet in the aisle and raised a hand for quiet. There was sunscreen and bug spray if people needed it, he announced. Everyone should take a bottle of water. They were going to search till they ran out of daylight. If they found anything that looked like evidence—this was critical—they shouldn't touch it. He or Mr. Hedrick would document it for the police. He reminded them of what Kim had been wearing. Her blue shirt had been one of J.P.'s favorites, the ribbed sleeves snug about her muscled upper arms, and he looked out the window, latching on to a tree, a street sign, a fire hydrant.

All day his imagination had been coughing up snatches of slasher flicks, flashes of bloody floors and basement torture chambers, chains and gags and leather masks. He knew they were fake, just bad stage-craft. What lay beneath the clichés was worse: Kim's skin.

He'd worshipped it gratefully, greedily, amazed each time that she would give herself to him. He felt like he was stealing from her. He really didn't see what she was getting in return. The first time they made love she cried, and he didn't understand. She was just happy, she said. He'd been flattered, as if it had something to do with him. It didn't, just as, later, when she raged at him, he was merely the object of her anger, not the source. That she could treat him both ways confused him. Only slowly did he come to realize that in certain cases her emotions were so strong that, temporarily at least, she didn't care how he felt. The next day she might apologize, but she'd also joke that he should have seen it coming, as if it was somehow his fault, so that occasionally he hated her, and himself for taking it. And then in his room she would slip off her clothes and totally overwhelm him, and they would start the cycle all over again. Even now he couldn't stop himself from seeing her in bed, rising above him, and had to erase it.

The detective had asked him if he loved Kim. Immediately J.P said yes, on the strength of his feelings, but was that love? It was more like addiction, trading his self-respect for a temporary ecstasy.

His thoughts had gone too far, and he focused on a cloud about to cover the sun. The window tattooed the gray reflection of his face on the yards of passing houses. She was on every telephone pole, and people were driving down Main Street like nothing had happened.

Beside him Kim's dad was marking a laminated map with a grease pencil. The topographic lines curved with the river, gathering in bands where the gorge narrowed. J.P. found the island and the turn below the boulder and worked his way back up to the hole.

"Are you looking for where we were?" J.P. asked.

"This isn't it?"

J.P. pointed, leaning in. "Here's where we usually go. There's a path on the other side that runs down this way. It stops when it reaches this wall. People fish that pool there. The water's not high enough right now."

"Is there any way out on that side?"

"No, it's too steep."

Nina peeked her head between them. "Sometimes when she wanted to be alone she'd go sit on the boulder."

"Is it possible she could have fallen off it and hurt herself?"

"I don't think so," Nina said.

J.P. had thought of her slipping on the rocks, hitting her head and drowning, but there was still the car to be accounted for, though he supposed if she'd left it overnight someone might have taken it. He'd skipped lunch and the air-conditioning smelled of burnt rubber. He couldn't rely on things making sense, he just wanted to get out there and see what they could find. He was glad Kim's dad was in charge. He knew he wouldn't be able to do it.

At Route 7 the driver waited for the light instead of taking a right on red, then went the speed limit. They crossed the new bridge and dieseled up the long hill, angling off before they reached the top, then dipping down again in shadow, the bad road jolting the whole cabin. On their right, beyond the guardrail, the gorge fell away, giving them glimpses of the river between the trees. Kim's dad leaned across him to see. J.P. looked with him, and became aware of the silence. As they descended, no one spoke, as if they were riding into battle.

They parked where Kim had last been seen, the team filing out and standing on the shoulder like new recruits. The bus left and they were surrounded by birdsong and the insistent buzzing of locusts. Kim's dad split them into two groups. J.P. and Elise and Sam would go with him while Nina and Hinch would help guide Mr. Hedrick. The idea was to line up about ten feet apart and slowly sweep downstream. Once they got down there they should all find a good walking stick to probe the bushes. They needed to remember, they weren't necessarily looking for Kim, they were looking for evidence. The littlest thing might be important.

After the pep talk, as J.P. was leading them down the path, he heard some girl in the back laugh, and a friend echo her. He understood they were nervous, maybe afraid, but the giggly brightness in their voices mystified him.

They came down out of the woods into the sun. Along the far shore, halfway up the cliffs, a brown swath of groundwater dripped, but the river was just as low as it had been yesterday. The current murmured as they crunched across the rocks. Farther down, where the channel narrowed, the surface glinted golden and hazy between dark walls of pines, the glare describing the tangled flights of bugs and dive-bombing swallows. They stopped to choose their walking staffs from a pile of old wrack and deadfall. The branches were bleached and dried light as bones, smoothed and seasoned, impossible to break. A cloud sailed over, cooling them for a second, turning the far wall dark. It passed, but the sky was flocked with them now. If it rained, would they keep looking?

J.P. didn't believe they'd find anything, but now that they were here he was grasping at any excuse not to start, as if searching like this was admitting she was lying dead somewhere and it was just a matter of covering enough ground. While that was probably true, he didn't want to believe it, yet at the same time he wanted—he thought he needed—to be the one who found her, alive or dead. Not to be a hero, or to prove to her parents he was innocent and that he really loved her, but for the simpler, more selfish reason that she'd left him and he wanted her back.

Out of habit he led them to the shelf above the swimming hole, where Kim's dad gave them their final instructions. Keep your neighbors in sight. Take baby steps. Read the ground like you're reading a newspaper. Elise and Sam were holding hands, Nina and Hinch standing side by side, and J.P. thought that just yesterday they were all here with Kim, and that that must mean something, but he couldn't say what. Behind him a cellphone chimed, and Kim's dad asked everyone to please turn theirs off for now.

"Remember," he said, "it's not a race. Do it right, and we only have to do it once."

With the water so low, getting across was easy. Kim's dad spread them out, giving J.P. the river's edge and Elise and Sam the base of the wall while taking the middle himself. He raised his arm to show Mr. Hedrick they were ready, then brought it down and they all started forward.

They pushed through the weedy brush, snapping stalks, tromping the brittle grasses. The girl beside J.P., Ashley something, lagged behind him, looking over as if for help. Out of impatience as much as chivalry he cheated toward her, his staff sweeping half of her lane. He had to force himself to go slow, shuffling to stay even with Kim's dad. He read the ground, noting an eyeless, dried-out sunfish, a scratched-up Gatorade bottle, a snarl of nylon line. His eyes skimmed from side to side, stopping just long enough to register an object before flitting off again. He was trying not to see a curled hand sticking out from under a bush, the purple toenails of a bare foot. He was trying not to see her shirt.

A few minutes in, a girl by Elise called out that she'd found something. Kim's dad went to her and knelt down.

The line on the far side of the river kept moving. A breeze stirred the leaves, releasing a flurry of cottonwood fluff.

Word spread down the line: It was just a cigarette butt.

What kind? It could have been his or Nina's or Elise's. It probably meant nothing, yet he pictured someone spying on them yesterday, watching Kim lying on her towel. Guys were always checking her out, even when he was right there. After they'd taken her in, they'd do the same to J.P., measuring him. When he complained about it, she thought it was cute that he was jealous. She was right, but only partly. Though it hurt, he wasn't tortured by the thought of her with someone else. What bothered him was the idea that it was obvious to everyone that he didn't deserve her.

They moved on. A plastic bag, a bottle cap, the wrapper from someone's Combos. The search took on a jerky rhythm that prevented them from getting anywhere. J.P. saw a bent Genesee Cream Ale can in the rocks, but it was so faded that he didn't bother to call out.

The river hid nothing. A tire, a broom that looked like it had been gnawed on, a rusted, flaking paint can. What looked like a drowned cat resolved into a sopping paper bag. He wished he were in the middle with Kim's dad. He could hear him thrashing the heavy brush with his stick as if it were the enemy.

Ashley was happy to trade spots, as was the girl beside her. They were wading through a buggy stand of brambles and stunted willows. J.P. hacked at the jungle on both sides. Again and again he parted the leaves and stuck his face into the humid tent of branches. He was sweating freely, and thorns had scratched bloody lines on his arms. Across the river someone called out. He listened for a second to make sure it was nothing, then went on. When he checked Kim's dad's progress, he saw that his hat was dotted with burs.

After the second hour they took a water break. After the third his water was gone, and Kim's dad passed him his bottle. He should have eaten something earlier. It was muggy and his sinuses hurt. The biggest thing they'd found was an anklet with a blue pom-pom—definitely not hers. High above them a hawk turned, its wingtips defined against a gray sky. The cloud cover was solid now, with dark patches. The trees were flashing the undersides of their leaves. Kim's dad called Mr. Hedrick. They agreed. This was probably not the spot they wanted to be in if a storm kicked up. To J.P., it felt like they were quitting.

He wasn't alone—everyone wanted to go on.

"I appreciate that more than anyone," Kim's dad said, "but I'm also responsible for your safety."

"We should at least check the boulder," J.P. said.

"How far is it?"

"Two minutes."

He didn't have to convince him, and took this as proof that they were cool.

Elise and Sam headed the others back while he led Kim's dad along the path, walking fast. Rain pattered around them, drops falling on his bare arms. On their left the cliff rose sheer, the wall amplifying the rush of the river. Without his stick he felt light and excited, as if they might actually find something.

Through the years people had worn a staircase into the rock, marking their territory with graffiti. J.P. stepped aside to let Kim's dad by, then climbed up after him.

On the bald top Kim's dad squatted as if he'd discovered a clue. He straightened, shaking a cigarette butt at him. "Marlboro."

"Probably Elise's. She was down here yesterday."

Before J.P. could protest he tossed it over the side. It floated on the surface, turning with the pool's slow swirl as raindrops pocked the water. They stood looking downstream, where the rapids dropped into a frothing chute before the bend. Seagulls were flying up the gorge, taking shelter on the wet ledges.

"We should keep going," J.P. said.

"No," Kim's dad said, but didn't move, as if he was still deciding. "I don't think she's here." He looked to J.P. for his opinion—openly, not at all a trick.

"I don't either."

"That doesn't mean we're going to stop looking."

"No," J.P. said.

"Just not today." He reached over and patted his shoulder, just a cuff from a teammate, and J.P. felt the same flush that seized him the first time Kim slid her fingers between his. "Remind me, we've got to get you some boots."

"I will," he promised, marking the moment, pledging that somehow he would prove himself worthy of this trust.

Upstream, across the river, Nina watched them talking. She was as sure of Hinch as she was of herself, maybe more so. Of the three of them (four, if she included Kim), J.P. was the weakest link, and seeing him alone with Kim's dad bothered her.

On the bus they took the same seats. She nosed in to be part of their conversation and almost gagged at the overpowering tang of Kim's dad. A scratch above J.P.'s eye had scabbed over in a raspberry line, and his chin was dirty like a little kid's. She felt guilty for being so clean.

The plan for tomorrow was to get going early and do as much of Route 7 as they could, rain or shine. With the flyers and the publicity they could expect more volunteers. That was worst case, Kim's dad said. He was hoping the police would take over the search. Nina couldn't tell if this was directed at her or not.

"What time should we come over?" she asked.

"I'll be up at five-thirty. I don't know, seven?"

"What time's sunrise?" J.P. asked.

"Good question."

The ride back was louder, with the rain banging the roof and everyone gabbing on their cellphones. Hinch listened to his iPod with his eyes closed, leaving Nina to monitor J.P. Kim's dad fished in his backpack and offered him the dregs of a water bottle before finishing it himself. It was more than just politeness.

"Where is she?" Kim's mom had asked, holding her close, because of all the people in the world, Nina would know best. Kim's dad was trying the same thing with J.P., just coming at him casually. J.P. had to know that.

When the bus dropped them off she figured he'd sign out like everyone else, but he went inside with Kim's dad. Nina waited for him on the porch, and then when that was too obvious, sat in her car with Hinch, checking the rearview mirror. After a few long minutes of fogging the windows, she wondered where the cop who belonged to the car in the driveway was, and decided it made better sense to take off.

Upstairs, while J.P. tried on his old boots, Ed checked with Fran. So far there was no word from Perry. The detective said the hotline was fielding calls and that he'd assigned people to track down any possible leads.

"Does that mean they have leads?"

"It didn't sound like it."

"When did he call?" he asked, then caught himself. Out of frustration he was building a case for the man's incompetence. That wasn't helpful now.

There should have been a good hour of daylight left, but the sky was already so dark that the streetlights were on. The rain fell steadily, spattering off the asphalt, bubbling along gutters, pouring into storm drains. Only Connie's black Pontiac and J.P.'s Cavalier were still parked out front. The rest of the searchers had dispersed, the phones were quiet. The deputy asked if they wanted someone for tonight. They said no. It was a relief to close the house against the world.

It was eight before they got dinner, though no one was hungry. Fran had planned on making chicken salad. Their neighbors made it unnecessary. The basement fridge was stocked with casseroles, hot and cold. She asked J.P. if he could stay—the least they could do was feed him—but he said he should be getting home.

"Lindsay!" she called up the stairs. "Dinner!"

Cooper came bounding down, growling and prancing wild-eyed around her legs. Fran had completely forgotten about him. She gave him an extra half-scoop of kibble, which he finished before Lindsay reached the kitchen.

They set the dishes on the counter like a pot-luck supper, then sat around the dining room table, strategizing. Channel 12 from Erie was coming to interview her in the morning. Connie thought it would be a good idea to show the viewers a picture of Kim's car with the license plate number. Ed surprised her by agreeing. They should release a picture of the car to the media at large, and maybe redo the flyer. If they didn't have a good shot they could probably find an old magazine ad online.

What about a reward? While the detective warned that it might attract psychics and con artists, it would buy them attention and maybe motivate people who otherwise would keep quiet.

CrimeStoppers had a toll-free tipline they could use. The faster they went national, the better. All the sites said they should try to get on *America's Most Wanted*. The cable shows were okay, but *AMW* had a dedicated following. It was on Saturday, and tomorrow was Friday. They should have Jocelyn call the producers.

Fran had allowed herself a glass of wine, and sipped as she bulleted each idea on a yellow pad beside her untouched plate. All day she'd been documenting their efforts, and couldn't stop, as if distilling their thoughts on paper gave them more power.

Across from her Lindsay finished and pushed back from the table. She was the only one who'd eaten, too quickly. Other than remembering John Walsh's name, she'd hardly said a word.

"Did you get enough?" Fran asked. "Mrs. Schoyer made brownies."

"I'm good." She rinsed and racked her dishes and came out through the hallway, headed for the stairs.

"You can watch TV if you want."

"No, I'm going to read."

Honestly Lindsay would have rather watched TV, but thought her mother wouldn't like that, and now she was committed. It was the safe move. Downstairs one of them would sit next to her and want to talk. Upstairs she could stare at her bedspread and no one cared.

"Right, Goob?" she asked Cooper, who'd followed her up. "Goober knows."

The problem with reading was that it left too much room to think. The last book she had for English was *Betsey Brown*. It was about a little black girl who loved her family and whose family loved her. As far as Lindsay could tell, that was the whole story. After a chapter and a half she gave up and got online, killing time playing Text Twist. The jumbled letters took all of her attention. Racking up a high score didn't matter. That satisfying instant when her brain relaxed and the hidden word magically snapped into place was her reward.

She was still undefeated when the IM box popped up. It was Dana next door. If Lindsay looked out her window she'd see the square of light from Dana's room on her backyard.

sup

sup, Lindsay wrote back.

ne news?

nope

i just heard a rumor she was kidnapped by bikers

says who?

mike s.

dont tell me shit like that

sry

r there bikers around here?

theres a big rally at geneva-on-the-lake this weekend

the cops know that, right?

they should

Mike had also heard they'd found Kim's bra during the search, which Lindsay knew was untrue. After she signed off and went back to Text Twist she tried to think of bikers but kept getting stuck on the gang in *Bubble Boy* that helped Jake Gyllenhaal run away. Kim being kidnapped seemed just as unreal, but so did everything today. Part of that was her fault. While she was sure the world was full of evil people, she couldn't imagine Kim with anyone but her friends, or anywhere but here, at home. If right now Lindsay did their secret knock on the wall, she wouldn't be surprised if Kim answered.

APE, she typed. TAPE, PATE, PEAT, TEAT, but the big one escaped her. POTATE? TAPTOE?

"Shit," she said when time expired. How could she not get TEAPOT? Stupid compound words.

Downstairs, chairs shifted and became footsteps, making Cooper raise his head. Voices congregated in the front hall. Connie was finally leaving. Lindsay listened for the shudder of the door closing, then her car door and the car starting. Her parents moved to the kitchen, one of them rumbling down the basement stairs before the dishwasher kicked in. Her mother would be up soon, so Lindsay turned off her computer, changed into her nightshirt, and got under the covers with *Betsey Brown*. In response, Cooper circled and flopped down in a new spot.

The rain knocked on the roof above her, plinking against the gutters. Betsey wanted a chocolate bar. Betsey wanted to go to the barber shop. After the endless speeches of *Julius Caesar* it should have been easy, but it was the stupidest book in the world. She wished she was watching TV or back online. She could IM all night with Dana and Micah about school and movies and guys and never get bored. Everything was different now. If she thought about anything except Kim—if that was possible—she was a terrible sister. What was she supposed to do? She wanted to go find her, but she wasn't allowed out of the house.

She was still battling *Betsey Brown* and her stupid candy bar when she heard her mother on the stairs, and right behind her, a heavier set of footsteps. Her father never went to bed before the news at eleven. Tonight he had a reason to watch, but here he was in the doorway, looking in with her mother, telling her not to stay up too late.

"Tomorrow's going to be another long day," her mother warned. "Don't forget, your bathroom's—" She did a kind of hiccup, sucking in a breath, then covered her mouth. Her father squeezed her shoulder as if to say it was okay.

"I'll go downstairs."

"Thank you." Her mother's lips trembled, and as Lindsay feared, she left her father at the door and staggered toward her, already crumbling. She fell against her, weeping, smelling sourly of wine, a hot tear landing on her cheek. Lindsay held her place in her book with one hand and patted her mother's back with the other. She looked over her shoulder and saw her father coming to rescue her, but instead of prying her mother off and consoling her, he piled on, sobbing along with her, burying Lindsay in a group hug.

"We just have to pray she's all right," her mother said, sniffling. "That's all we can do."

Deep down, Lindsay wanted to agree with her, and hated herself for just patting her back and waiting.

Her mother recovered first, telling her it was okay, they were all in shock. Lindsay had never seen her father like this, and watched him turn away, swiping at his eyes. He couldn't stop, and steadied himself against her dresser, his back heaving until her mother told him to go take his shower.

"We were talking," her mother said when they were alone. "If you want to go with Dad tomorrow, that's your call."

"Can Dana come?"

"She'll have to ask her folks."

After she'd left, Lindsay wanted to know what had changed. They didn't need her today. Did they think they weren't going to find her, so it was safe now?

In her parents' bath the toilet flushed. The shower curtain racked back and water thundered into the tub, then sprayed from the nozzle. She used the noise to cover her escape, closing the door so Cooper wouldn't follow her.

The change in the bathroom was obvious as soon as she turned on the light. The towel racks were empty, as if her mother was doing laundry. Her toothbrush stood alone in the pink holder. Kim's hairbrush was gone, and the razor they shared. The trash had been emptied, a new plastic bag from Giant Eagle in its place. Ignoring her reflection in the mirror, she grabbed the lime green plastic caddy she used at camp and filled it with everything she needed, turned out the light and closed the door behind her.

Downstairs, all the milk crates and boxes of flyers stacked in the darkened living room made it look like they were moving. The light in the back hall was on. When she investigated, creeping toward the back door, she saw the outside light shining on the wet driveway like any other night. It made sense, she guessed, and didn't turn them off.

Her parents' bathroom was directly above the one downstairs. As she brushed her teeth, she could hear water rushing through the pipes, and then, when she was on the pot, the abrupt, wrenching stop. She finished and packed everything back in the caddy. Carrying it up reminded her of camp, tramping down the cabin line right before lights-out to the kybo in her flip-flops, the cold grass tickling her feet. Kim had the same caddy, in purple. Sometimes Lindsay would see it sitting on a bench or on the long counter of sinks and feel both a familiar comfort and a bitter jealousy in knowing she was so close. Just like at school, at camp they moved in different circles, but in such a limited, informal setting, Kim's popularity swamped her. She was Little Larsen, and after the first morning competition, no team captain made the mistake of choosing her just for her name. The flip side was that being Kim's sister protected her from the nastier pranks, most of which involved bug spray or wiping bodily fluids on the victim's pillowcase. It was always the problem: without Kim she would be free to be her own person, but she would also be picked on or ignored because that person was weak.

In bed, with the light out, she resolved to be strong tomorrow, as if she could pay her back that way. "If it was you," her father had said, "do you think Kim would just be sitting in her room?" From now on she would do whatever she had to, whatever she could. For once, Lindsay would save her.

Outside, a car splashed by. Cooper twitched and whimpered, running in a dream, then subsided. She held her breath, straining to make out the faintest noise from her parents' room. There was only the constant, rhythmless drumming overhead. She'd thought the rain would help her sleep. Now she was aware of it falling on the backyard and the woods, on the fields and farms and creeks that fed the river. She imagined the water in the gorge rising slowly in total blackness, a smudge of a pale body drifting downstream, caught in the rocks. On one rubbery hand would be her grandmother's cameo ring. She opened her eyes, rolled on her side and squeezed them shut again. A minute later she sighed loudly and rolled the other way. She could see Kim naked and lying in the mud, her dark hair tangled like seaweed, part of her face neatly buried like a rock uncovered by the tide. She smacked her pillow flat, then flipped it. The rain pattered, maddening. Stop it, she thought. Just stop.

Talent

Jocelyn came over early to help Fran prepare. She'd never been on TV before, and was terrified. Jocelyn was a pro. The hospital owned a portable lectern with its new logo on the front that she rolled out for groundbreaking ceremonies and Coast Guard rescues. She was slender and dressed well, and when she answered questions she sounded like a doctor. Fran wanted her to be their spokesperson, but understood a mother would evoke more sympathy.

The first thing she had to do was change. Even on a cloudy day a white blouse would turn into a blob of light. She had Sunny Hedrick mind the sign-in table while they went through her closet, looking for a dark solid. Nothing too fancy. She should look like she was going to work. They chose three and had her model them, circling her like a bride. After they picked the winner, Jocelyn redid her makeup, drawing on eyeliner and powdering her cheeks till they were beige. To Fran it looked garish. Jocelyn assured her it would translate.

She should stand up straight and look serious without frowning. And be careful not to laugh. A lot of people laughed out of reflex because it felt strange to be on-camera.

"If you have to cry," Jocelyn said, "stop talking and take a step back off your mark. It's not live. They're going to edit you for space anyway, so you want to control what they have to choose from."

"Crying's not good."

"You don't want to come off as hysterical."

"Even if I am."

"Even if you are. That's private, this is public. Big difference. Think about what you're doing. You're asking people who don't know you to help you. You don't want to make them uncomfortable. You want them to think: What would I do in her shoes? So they'll be rooting for you *not* to fall apart, because they're afraid they would. They want you to be braver than they think they are. Do that and they'll like you."

"Now I know I'm going to cry."

"That's okay," Jocelyn said. "Just take a step back and they'll have to stop rolling. Make sure you have a tissue with you. You don't want to be too cool either. Remember Meryl Streep."

"I don't think that's going to be a problem," Fran said.

"Tears are fine. You just don't want them to have you breaking down on tape, because they'll use that, and then that's who you are. Trust me, you don't want to be that person."

Why not? Fran wanted to ask. She already was that person.

Connie had blown up a shot of the car and mounted it side-by-side with Kim's picture on foam board. That was okay, Jocelyn said, but fly-ers were like wanted posters, too cold. It would be better if Fran held a small framed picture of Kim, something intimate and precious. The idea was to make the viewers think of their own pictures of loved ones and imagine what else they had in common. For the same reason, they wanted to do the shoot in the driveway to show they were a regular family with a garage and a lawn and a front door.

"There but for the grace of God," Fran said, and immediately wanted to take it back.

"Exactly."

It would have been better if Ed and Lindsay could have stood behind her, but they couldn't wait. They were out along Route 7, sweeping the woods with three full busloads of volunteers. Father John was coming over to be by her side and to serve as a visual reminder that starting to-morrow the parish hall at Lakeview would serve as their command cen-ter. Connie had a placard with the address and a phone number for donations. Fran worried that all this information was too much at once.

"Break it down into your three points," Jocelyn said. "This is Kim. This is her car. This is how you can help. That's all you're here to do. Anything they ask, you bring it back to those three. Say her name, say the name of the car, say the name of the church. It's like advertising, you're just looking for awareness."

What were they going to ask?

"Easy stuff," Jocelyn said, and ticked them off on her fingers. "What kind of progress are you making. How's the family holding up. Do you have a message for Kim."

"None, not well, and 'Come home.'"

"Wrong. The support's been incredible. The whole community's turned out to help with the search and the police are busy tracking down leads."

"They haven't done jack-shit!" Fran said.

"Whoa, whoa."

"They haven't."

"You can't badmouth the cops on the air. You'll come off as angry, and you don't want that. Everyone's been so helpful, the family's really pulled together, and you want to tell Kim that you love her. That's all you have to say."

"How about if I don't say anything about the police?"

"Don't get hung up on this," Jocelyn said, but as Connie and Father John and then the news van arrived, the idea of lying grew, pushing what she was supposed to be focusing on to the edges. She had to consciously list her three points, going over and over them, afraid she'd blank once she got on-camera. It couldn't be more simple: Kim, the car, the church. The cops weren't important.

The reporter was young and pretty but sickly thin in her red Channel 12 polo shirt, with sticks for arms and frightening cheekbones. Her head was too large for her body, like a marionette's, and she was made up so her eyes and lips were huge. Her textbook posture was impressive at first and then, as she helped the cameraman unload his light stands, looked stiff and exaggerated. She shook Fran's hand and said she was sorry with refreshing directness, not the halting helplessness Fran had become used to from their neighbors. She had to remember, this woman didn't know Kim at all. To her she was just another assignment. Tomorrow she'd be covering a fishing tournament or demolition derby.

"I'm a little nervous," Fran confessed.

"Don't worry, Benny will make you look good."

The cameraman, fussing with some cables in the grass, just smiled and cracked his gum.

They set up not in the driveway but on the front walk, with the reporter and Fran sitting on the porch stairs, one-on-one. There was no-where to step back. They might take a shot of Fran with Kim's picture at the end, but for now they just wanted her. They moved the whole sign-in table so it was in the background, with Father John and Connie pretending to register Jocelyn. A crowd of neighbors gathered on the sidewalk to watch. The cameraman waved for quiet.

This was for Kim. Someone somewhere might see it and provide the clue they needed. Fran held on to that thought.

"Speed," he said, and the reporter drew herself upright and put on a concerned face before reciting her lead-in. Fran had thought she was silly, but under the lights she took on force, nailing her lines in character. Now she understood. It was an act, and the reporter was an actress. All Fran had to do was play herself.

The reporter turned to her and asked how the search was going.

Fran was supposed to look at her, not the camera, but was aware of it running, recording her every word and gesture. She nodded. "It's going. Everyone's been so supportive, all of Kim's friends, and our neigh-bors, and the church. It's really been heartwarming to know so many people care about Kim."

She'd almost finished her last remark when, a few houses down, a lawnmower started up. The cameraman sent Jason Bonner to ask who-ever it was to hold off.

On the second take she tried to remember what she'd said the first time and stumbled over her words.

"That's okay," the reporter said, "just let it come," but now her an swers felt canned and unnatural, like she was reading from a script— like the reporter sneaking a peek at her questions while Fran was talking. Heartwarming sounded corny. How were people at home going to believe it if she didn't? As she grew more frustrated, she worried that she might seem angry, and overcompensated, nearly smiling.

The reporter asked her what kind of person Kim was, which was easy, and how the family was holding up. They talked about the time frame, and Kim's job, the possibility of someone coming in off the interstate and taking her. Fran feared she was rambling and clipped off her answers, sticking to the facts. She didn't want to speculate.

"The police are treating Kim's disappearance as a missing persons case rather than a criminal investigation. How does the family feel about that?"

It wasn't Fran's fault. She'd plucked this nugget from the *Star-Beacon* article. "The police are following every lead they can. Right now the most important lead is her car. It was her grandmother's and it's very rare, so we're hoping someone out there will see it and call in."

"Has there been any input from the FBI yet, with Kingsville being so close to the state line?"

"Not yet, but I know the police are talking with Erie."

"At this point, how involved are the police in the search for Kim?"

"They're doing everything they can, legally."

"But right now you're relying almost solely on volunteers, is that right?"

"That's right, and we're hoping folks will come out and help us this weekend." She gestured behind herself at the sign-in table and gave the information for the church, feeling like a huckster.

She was surprised when the reporter lowered the mic and asked if there was anything she'd like to add. Was that it? It seemed too fast. She hadn't asked if she had a message for Kim, and while it seemed obvious, Fran took this chance to tell the audience that she loved and missed her daughter very much and wanted to thank all of the volunteers.

They waited a few seconds in silence.

"And we're clear," the cameraman said.

"You did great," the reporter said, patting her knee.

"Yeah, you sounded really good," Connie said, setting up the poster so they could shoot it.

"I don't know why you wanted me to do it," Jocelyn said. "That was perfect."

Fran accepted their praise for what it was. She'd felt tight the entire time, her face a rigid mask, and was sure that would come across on TV. They hadn't used the little picture, and as they packed up she took it inside and set it by the stereo with the others. She should have been relieved that the filming was done, but instead she felt a sense of letdown, of an opportunity squandered, and wanted to apologize to Kim. She thought it was absurd that she should cry now. "Stupid," she said. On the porch they were moving the sign-in table back, and she gathered herself and went out to help.

The reporter said the segment would air at six and then again at eleven, and that they'd love to come back and talk to her as the story developed. Jocelyn made sure to get one of her cards.

When they were gone Fran went upstairs and washed the makeup off her face. In the mirror the lines around her mouth were pronounced. She looked tired, even though it was only ten thirty. That would come through too, she thought.

In the afternoon she did two newspaper interviews, and one by phone for the radio. After each she felt the same useless emptiness, and had to remind herself that they could only do good. The hotline had been busier since the *Star-Beacon* article; the website was getting more hits. This was progress.

By six only one busload had returned. Ed wanted to use every second of daylight, and she couldn't blame him. The searchers sat in groups on the porch steps and on the lawn, drinking bottled water and eating donated Kentucky Fried Chicken. Connie called them into the living room to watch the news.

Fran didn't want to see herself on TV. She even hated the cameras inside the door at Wal-Mart that showed her walking in. As their spokesperson, she had no choice. They were the second story, right behind a private plane crashing out by the raceway. She sat on the couch and endured their cheers when she appeared.

Whether it was the makeup, the lighting, some magical lens of Benny's, or the combination of all three, her skin seemed rosy, and the blouse they'd chosen worked perfectly. The crowd went quiet to hear her words, then murmured approvingly. What she said actually made sense, and while she hadn't been aware of it while the camera was rolling, the reporter nodded along in sympathy. She was composed, mostly, though during the long question about someone possibly coming in off the interstate, Fran caught herself gnawing her lower lip.

"Jesus," someone behind her said, "why would she ask that?"

The editor had done a good job of fitting it together. Connie's graphics popped up in just the right places—Kim, the Chevette, the church. At the end they clapped. They were rooting for her, and at once she was grateful and hopeful and proud. She thought Ed would want to see it, but by eleven, with the house emptied out and the curtains drawn against the darkness, there was no reason to celebrate. They'd searched all day and found nothing, and Ed had turned his ankle. Perry hadn't bothered to call. As the detective said when he checked in, nothing had significantly changed. They were on their own, Kim was still missing and another day was gone.

Crime Stoppers

The night she disappeared she was seen arguing with a dark-haired man in a red pickup in the lot of Lake Shore Park. The next day she was spotted wandering along the commercial strip in Ashtabula, not far from the on-ramp of Route 11. Friday evening she materialized in Fairport Harbor, buying a pack of cigarettes at a convenience store. Her face was swollen and she seemed dazed.

A cult had taken her to use as a human sacrifice.

The crew of an ore boat had kidnapped her to service them.

A ring of Asian slave traders based in Toledo had auctioned her off to the highest bidder.

"I ate her liver with fava beans and a nice chianti," a teenaged boy said, and slurped, making his friends in the background crack up.

Look for a trucker who drove for J. B. Hunt and called himself the General.

In town there was a man named Green who'd done time for statutory rape.

The boyfriend did it.

The father did it.

A friend of a friend was wasted the other night and bragging about how he killed this girl. He figured the guy was lying, but thought he should call anyway.

She'd probably met someone on the internet, all they had to do was check her computer.

She was pregnant and had gone to Cleveland for an abortion that went wrong.

She was being held underground against her will. The caller could see a white house, near running water. The name of the road started with the letter M, or N.

"Help…me," another teenager croaked.

Then there were the hang-ups, dozens of them, some in the middle of the night. They leaned close to the machine, listening through the layer of tape hiss for any hint that it might be Kim.

Competing with the tipline were the rumors volunteers felt obligated to share, as if to protect them from the latest gossip by keeping them up to date. Saturday there'd been whispers of a cloth doll stuffed with hair hung from a tree. Sunday's favorite was a bloody sneaker, supposedly recovered in a search of the neighborhood. In later variations the shoe was a man's, found stuck in the mud of a creekbed deep in the woods. Out of a sense of completeness more than anything, they kept a log of these.

The website had its own guestbook in which visitors left messages. A few well-wishers they knew, but a surprising number were from out-of-state or even overseas. There was serious interest in Finland and India. Most of the entries were outpourings of support, welcome prayers and inspirational homilies. *With God's help, miracles can happen.* More upsetting were posts that began *In 1987 I lost my son in a hunting accident* or *My two golden retrievers were missing for three days a few years ago* or *I've never met Kim, but after reading your site I feel like I know her.* Predictably, their appeal for help had drawn a large audience of armchair detectives, playing at solving the case as if it were a game. One lengthy string debated the problems with Kim driving her car off a bridge. Another connected her to three other disappearances near I-90 over the last decade, all involving young women with dark hair.

They kept as much of this speculation from Lindsay as they could, knowing what their own imaginations had done with it. Ever since Fran had appeared on TV the sheer volume was confusing.

Not all the tips were anonymous or far-fetched. A Geneva woman named Anna Fyfield thought she'd seen Kim's car ahead of her at a Wendy's drive-thru late Wednesday night. It fit the timeline. The detective said they were following up on it, but like so many of his promises, it was impossible to verify.

A doctor from down the county treated a man who claimed his dog had nipped him, though the bite marks on his wrist were clearly human.

A man driving north on Route 7 Wednesday afternoon saw a blue car traveling southbound pick up a hitchhiker carrying an army-style duffel bag.

It was hard not to attach some hope to these scraps, especially after the weekend's searches turned up nothing. Even tougher to gauge were the detective's assurances that the police were pursuing several persons of interest he couldn't discuss. They didn't have enough faith in him to buy this outright, yet they desperately wanted to, and hedged and second-guessed themselves until they didn't know what to believe.

Hello, My Name Is

His cell went off in the dark—*Brass monkey, that funky monkey*—hauling J.P. up from sleep, making him slap at his nightstand.

She'd never returned his last call. Now every time his phone rang he thought it was her, so that he was continually disappointed. He'd come to hate his ringtone, but was too superstitious to change it, as if he'd be deleting her.

He flipped the cover open and for a second the blue light blinded him. It was Nina. What time was it?

"One thirty," she said.

"I just got to sleep."

"Sorry. Listen, I need to ask you something."

"What?" He was tired of this shit. He knew what she was doing, and while he agreed that it was too late to say anything, it still bothered him. He wanted her to stop. He wanted to tell her to worry about herself.

"I'm serious," she said. "I need to know if you're ready in case what I think is going to happen happens."

"What's up?"

"The cops just talked to Kevin and Doug-o. They were asking about Wooze."

"Fuck."

"I figured I'd better tell you."

"Thanks." A part of him should have been relieved, but his mind was following the logical branches.

"Are you ready?"

"Yes," he said.

"Okay," she said, "I'll see you tomorrow," and left him holding the phone.

He was tempted to speed-dial Kim, as he had every night since she'd disappeared, just to hear her outgoing message, but closed the cover and lay back, wide awake. He didn't blame Nina. He'd known from the beginning what the right decision was, and out of fear or selfishness he hadn't been able to make it. Now he was done. He'd tell them the truth and take his punishment.

The problem with this solution was that it only worked when he was alone in the dark. Eating breakfast with his mother or helping Kim's dad stack flats of bottled water, he understood why he lied. Even now he hoped his mistakes would go away and not harm them. He could bear his own self-loathing. To confess would be to lose everything.

He'd gotten time off so he could devote himself to the search. He and Kim's dad and Lindsay were the first ones at the church besides Father John, their cars parked side-by-side on the newly lined tarmac. The stone facade with its square belltower and lancet windows had recently been sandblasted; without its weeping coat of soot it looked less intimidating. Landscapers had shaved the hedges by the front entrance into smooth lobes. The doors were so heavy he had to help Lindsay open one. Inside, the stairs were marble, the banisters polished brass. The air smelled of candles and old books and dust. His mother wasn't religious but had friends who went to Lakeview. "Respectable folk," she joked. The few times he'd been inside as a child were for carnivals and pancake suppers in the same high-windowed parish hall they were using as a command center. When Kim's dad left them to go downstairs and get the weather, he felt like an intruder.

The first thing they had to do was fill a cooler for each team with bottled water and ice. Like everything else, the coolers were donated, identical except the numbers magic-markered on the lids.

"How many do we need?" Lindsay asked.

Saturday they'd had over two hundred volunteers and ran out of water. Sunday they had a hundred and fifty. Each team was made up of ten volunteers plus a leader, usually one of Kim's dad's fellow coaches or Kim's old teachers. It was Monday and a lot of people would probably go back to work.

"I don't know," he said, "ten?"

It was his call—she refused to make decisions. She skidded a cooler over to the flats while he lifted a fifty-pound bag of ice out of the freezer and dropped it on the floor—once, twice—then tore it open and poured the jagged chunks over the bottles. By the time he lugged the cooler around the counter to Team One's table, she had another ready.

Though there was an old boom box on the shelf above the deep double sink, they worked in silence. "Shit," Lindsay said when a water got away from her. "Come on," he said when a bag was being stubborn. Short of conversation, these stray words were a way of acknowledging each other, offering the possibility that they might talk.

Like Kim's dad, she was a mystery to J.P. He knew only Kim's view of her—nerdy and immature, the snotty kid sister. She was slim and plain, and her ponytail made her look younger than she was. For the middle of July she was strikingly pale, as if she never left the house. She was quiet but attacked each job with the same intense concentration, and when she had nothing to do she folded her arms and watched people across the room, her head panning like a camera, lingering then moving off again to find new subjects. He thought it must be hard on her, not having her friends there. She'd mentioned once that they weren't old enough—not to complain, just to explain why she was by herself, as if she was afraid he'd think she didn't have any.

They were both slowing down.

"How many's that?" she asked.

"This'll be eight." He picked up a bag, dropped it and squatted there, thinking this might be his best chance. Once they broke into teams she'd go off with her dad. He waited until she scraped the cooler across the floor to him, then froze. He'd never studied her so closely, and was surprised to find her eyes were the same gray green as Kim's.

"What?" she said.

"I was going to ask if you heard anything new."

"Good luck. They don't tell me anything."

"Maybe there's nothing to tell." Could he open his mouth without lying?

"That's even better," she said. "Thanks for cheering me up."

"No problem."

They finished the coolers and got the big coffee urn going, setting out the cups and stirrers and baskets of sugar packets and individually sealed creamers on the counter. The kitchen was cramped, and they juked to avoid each other, twisted sideways to brush by. On the surface it felt like work, but the hall and the empty tables wouldn't let him forget why they were there.

Kim's dad returned with Father John, who waved to them. J.P. waved back with Lindsay as if he were a regular member of the congregation.

The early birds were already drinking their coffees when Nina arrived with an armload of doughnut boxes. There were a few more in the car, she said—a cue for J.P. to come outside and help her.

"Where's Hinch?" he asked in the stairwell.

"He has to work lunch. His boss is being a dick."

"What about Marnie?"

"She said she'd come by later."

Outside, the day was bright and cloudless, the lake a deep blue, the horizon a sharp dividing line.

A car was turning into the lot. Compared to the weekend it was empty. In the far corner the buses and vans waited in the shade.

Nina lifted the hatchback. There were only four more boxes. They'd slid around while she was driving and wrecked against the seats. They both leaned in, reaching.

"Hear anything else?" he asked.

"No."

"Did Hinch try calling him?" Because he should be warned, at least. Not that it would save them.

"Probably not the smartest idea right now."

"Right."

They'd given up any pretense of working and stood hunched over the boxes, looking at each other. She'd kissed him once at a party and he'd kissed her back, leaving him confused and guilty. This was another secret bond he didn't want.

"Forget all the little shit, okay?" she said. "Think about Kim."

"I am," he said defensively, because she was right. He'd spent his whole life thinking of himself. No matter what happened, that had to change. He just didn't see how.

Back inside he manned the sign-in desk with Lindsay, checking driver's licenses and making nametags for people like Mr. Hedrick who'd been searching beside them all weekend. During a lull they played tic-tac-toe until they acknowledged the other wasn't going to make a mistake. Lindsay sniffed her Sharpie, crossed her eyes and pretended to fall over. She made him show her his license before she signed him in, then did his nametag, blowing on the wet ink. She peeled the sticker from the backing and held it out to him on a fingertip.

Slowly the volunteers rolled in. There was no line. "Mornin'," they said, and handed over their IDs like it was normal. He understood that organization was important, but so much of it was redundant. By now the regulars were familiar. It was silly to take pictures of the teams before they went out, as if someone might disappear and not be missed.

It would be hard to lose anyone from today's group. By eight forty only the first three tables were filled, and most of them were seniors—a problem, since Kim's dad and Mr. Hedrick had targeted the hills on the far side of the interstate. They held off starting the briefing, highlighting a different set of maps. J.P. couldn't see what part of the county they'd shaded. He figured they'd keep sweeping south along 7, filling in the grid block by block, hopscotching their way to Wooze's place.

Around nine Elise finally showed up, lamely apologizing for Sam. "Where is everybody?"

"I don't know," J.P. said. "Maybe they're out looking for Sam."

The total turnout was thirty-seven. Kim's dad rolled over the dry-erase board with the master map and split them into three teams, hand-picking one so all the younger volunteers would be together.

Teams One and Two would concentrate on the farms along the west-bound lanes of the interstate. The land was private, and while the owners had granted them permission to search, they still needed to be careful. If they ran into any trouble they should immediately advise their team leaders, who should immediately advise the command center. He held up one walkie-talkie and gave it to Mr. Hedrick, held up another and gave it to Mr. Riggio.

Team Three, which included J.P., Nina, Elise and Lindsay, would do the hills by Route 7 as planned. The same guidelines applied. They might want to search these areas again, so if there was a problem, play it safe and call. He held up the last walkie-talkie and came over to their table as if to take charge, and then, before J.P. could protest, slid the walkie-talkie across the map so he had to catch it.

He'd been there every day, and knew the routine. Kim's dad stood beside him while he checked off the roster, assigning everyone their numbers. He passed a flyer around and reminded them not to touch or move any evidence. The terrain was moderate to difficult, the high would be in the mid-eighties, so they needed to stay hydrated. Lunch was at one, sandwiches, chips and cookies from Subway. They'd search until sunset. Dinner would be available here afterward. Any questions?

No, they were all veterans. They stood so Kim's dad could take their picture.

Before they left to get on the buses, Father John led them in prayer. Holding hands with Kim's dad on one side and Lindsay on the other, J.P. wondered why he'd been surprised. From the beginning he'd been trying to make himself indispensable—something he'd failed to do with Kim. Now that he'd succeeded, he thought it was a mistake, and too late to take back. While his pride told him this responsibility was an honor, he was afraid the more they relied on him, the more, eventually, they would hate him, whether any of it was his fault or not.

"Amen," they all said.

Stop, Look & Listen

At night the trains came through. The woods behind her house ran unbroken, crisscrossed with creeks and ATV trails before backing up to the Conrail tracks. A half mile inland the Norfolk Southern's lines shadowed them like rivals. All day the trains barreled east- and westbound, blaring their horns before every crossing, but after dark, when the clamor of work died down and the moon hung low over the trees, they filled the deepening sky with sound, their mournful warnings growing louder as they approached, peaking in a furious thrumming of diesels and clatter of trucks as if they were passing right behind her mother's fenced-off compost heap, then fading again, long-drawn chords calling ever softer, moving away through town and into the distance until there was nothing but the sawing of locusts surrounding the house.

Like everyone in their subdivision, Nina knew the schedule intimately. As a girl she stayed up to hear the ten o'clock freight before giving herself to sleep, and was disappointed when she missed it. Since eighth grade she no longer considered catching the one o'clock an achievement. This last week she'd become reacquainted with the three-oh-five and the four thirty—trains she might hear once a month while drowsily using the bathroom.

Now when she padded to the toilet she was perfectly, frustratingly awake. Her feet were tender and her legs were jumpy from walking all day, and through a combination of exhaustion and being around too many people, she'd picked up a summer cold, which the central air that kept the house bearable made worse. Her mother suggested Nyquil, and while it knocked her out it also gave her terrible nightmares and made it harder to wake up. She decided to go without, with the predictable result that for hours while the rest of the house slept she lay chilly and alert and ready for tomorrow to start, picturing Kim and her at work, Kim in her bikini that last day, and then, when she'd resigned herself to counting the trains, fell unknowingly into a dreamless void that was over before she could appreciate it.

At breakfast her mother listened to the news. The war in Iraq had knocked Kim from the top spot. *The search continues for a local woman,* the anchorman read, professionally detached. It had been five days since she'd called the tipline. Every morning Nina waited to hear that the police were questioning a suspect, but there was nothing. She finished her orange juice and dressed for the woods, rubbing Skin So Soft into her neck and arms, pocketing a travel pack of tissues.

Hinch was being a dick. He only came when he didn't have to work. He said he'd tried to switch shifts, but she questioned his effort. She didn't see why he couldn't quit. It was just the fucking Dairy Queen.

"I would if I thought it would do any good," he said, meaning it had been eight days. The second weekend was coming up. They'd posted new flyers around town to rally support.

"So you're just going to give up."

"I'm not giving up, I just can't do it 24-7 like you."

"What if it was me?" Nina asked.

"Come on, Ni-ni."

"No. How long would you look for me?"

"Forever."

"Bullshit. You can't even take one day off for Kim."

"I already took three. I've been out every day except Monday and yesterday."

"You're not getting it," she said.

What made her angrier was that he was just being realistic. Friday the turnout was barely enough for three teams, and though they were getting nothing done she was still pissed when he had to leave early.

"I'll see you later," he said.

"That's okay," she said. "I'm going to try and get some sleep tonight."

"Are you guys all right?" Elise asked on the way home, and Nina shrugged like she didn't care.

She didn't, she decided sometime between the one o'clock and the three-oh-five. If Hinch didn't understand how important Kim was to her, he didn't understand anything. J.P. and Elise knew they weren't going to find anything out there. That wasn't the point.

Saturday he had to work. She was too busy to miss him. The flyers brought in a flood of volunteers, and they covered more ground than they had all week. It was only on the bus back to church that she turned on her phone and saw she had three messages.

He'd left two, in the middle of the afternoon, during the long lull between lunch and dinner, probably on break. She could see him smoking in the shade by the cemetery fence, rethinking his decision. As always, too late, he would try to apologize, saying they both knew he was a jerk. As always, she would confirm that fact and forgive him, but only after exacting serious concessions. The idea of the world returning to normal appealed to her. Outside, dusk was falling, softening the hills. The scale of today's search had been gratifying, and she was too tired to fight. She would say she wasn't angry with him, just frustrated, clearing the way for them to make up. It was Saturday night. Maybe they could go to the movies or down to the harbor. It had been too long since they'd been together. She suspected that was one reason why she couldn't sleep.

The first message said he was at the sheriff's department and needed a ride.

The second, a minute later, said to forget it, Marnie was going to pick him up.

He knew she couldn't stop searching and come get him. They were warnings, but what was she supposed to do with them?

Her mother had left the other one. The police stopped by and said they wanted to talk to her. "I told them you were out searching for Kim."

Neither of them sounded upset. Nina had to remind herself that this step was inevitable, and necessary. She was surprised it had taken this long.

She called Hinch but couldn't really talk, with people all around and the racket of the engine blowing through the windows in stereo. He was paranoid about his phone being tapped. In the background, drawers rolled open and thumped shut.

"Are you okay?"

"My mom's the one who's going nuts. There's clothes and shit all over the place. They said they could arrest me for having a scale. That was their excuse."

"What did you say?"

"I just told them the truth."

How she interpreted this would determine her strategy. She spent several questions nailing down what happened, and realized she needn't have. She could count on Hinch to stick with the plan. His allegiances were simple.

"So I guess I won't be seeing you later," she said.

"Oh yeah."

"What about tomorrow?"

"I seriously doubt it."

By the time she got off they were on the bridge, the river invisible beneath them. Across the aisle, J.P. and Lindsay were curled over the Sudoku from today's paper. Nina reached out and tapped him on the arm, crooking a finger so he leaned closer.

"It's happening," she whispered. "What I said."

He pulled away and appraised her, then nodded. She thought he would dig out his phone, but he just went back to watching Lindsay fill in the squares.

She wanted to be that calm. From the minute she decided to call the tipline, she knew what would happen, yet now she felt the urge to run. Her chance was coming up. The bus had to stop for the Norfolk Southern tracks. She could ask the driver to drop her off and walk a mile along the ties, then cut through the woods—impossible in this light, and where could she go but home? She was overreacting. If they hadn't arrested Hinch she had to believe she'd be okay.

The driver slowed and came to an exaggerated stop. Far up the line a single headlamp shone, but it was impossible to tell if it was moving. Foolishly she was rooting for anything that might postpone their arrival. The driver waited a full three seconds before inching them over the hump. He did the same at the Conrail tracks, the bus lurching when he let out the clutch. Nina held on to the seatback in front of her as they lumbered across, swaying. He found second gear and the first street-lights of town floated by, the dark houses and parked cars. They made the light at Main and Harbor, dashing her last hope.

The facade of the church was floodlit, the belltower rising into the night. As they turned into the lot she could see a pair of news vans and an unmarked car in front, and standing on the curb as if to greet them, the detective and his deputy. Behind them a door opened and a figure with a clipboard descended the stairs, favoring one leg—Kim's dad.

J.P. and Lindsay were watching him too. As the bus swung through the circle, braking, he hobbled straight for them, the cops falling in be-hind him, all three converging on the door as it folded open.

Kim's dad pulled himself up the steps. Nina and J.P. were sitting near the front, and she imagined him striding down the aisle and dragging them off. Instead, he stood beside the driver and held up his arms for quiet. For a sickening instant she was certain he was going to tell them Kim was dead.

The detective watched from the top step, taking note of her and J.P. She stayed still, afraid of betraying herself.

"Lindsay," Kim's dad said, holding out a hand, and J.P. got up to let her by.

Kim's dad hugged her with the clipboard and kept that arm over her shoulder as he addressed them.

"I just wanted to thank you all for coming out today, and to let you know that starting tomorrow we'll be working out of Firehouse Num-ber Four." He was subdued, as if he didn't agree with the move. Nina wanted him to look at her, but he was focused somewhere above her head. "That's the one on Erie right across from the park. So don't show up here, because we're going to be over there. And please tell anyone you know who couldn't make it today. Thank you." He gave the front row a batch of flyers to pass back, waved and ducked down the stairs with Lindsay.

Nina watched them go. Instead of heading for the doors they walked arm-in-arm toward their station wagon, Lindsay propping him up on one side.

"Thanks for your patience," the detective said. "I won't keep you long." He had a single sheet of paper, and paused, looking over the rows as if he might read a list of names. Outside, first one and then another silvery spotlight popped on, blinding them, etching the interior with shadows. "The reason for shifting the command center is that the state police are taking over the case. Earlier today they found Kim's car outside of Sandusky."

As the bus erupted Nina turned to J.P., who was just as confused as she was.

All she knew about Sandusky was that Cedar Point was there.

"That doesn't mean we stop looking here," the detective said loudly, to quiet them.

It was good news, but now she doubted everything they'd done so far. The flyers, the searches. They'd wasted ten days looking in the wrong place. She'd snitched on Wooze for nothing.

"We've got some media people who are going to want to talk to you, so please, think before you speak, okay? Remember that what you say could have an effect on Kim. Finding the car is definitely a positive, but it's not the end of anything, it's just a starting point."

After he dismissed them she and J.P. shuffled up the aisle and down the steps together, careful of the curb. The reporters had grabbed the first people off and were grilling them on the walk, using the bus as a backdrop. Nina didn't want to talk with anyone. She wanted to skip the debriefing and go straight home, but followed J.P. toward the doors. The lights were so distracting that she didn't see the deputy until he was right beside her.

"If you'd come with me," he said discreetly. "You too, sir."

The Motorist's Prayer

He drove out the same way she'd been taken, passing the same exits and rest areas and billboards, navigating the same insane curve to skirt downtown Cleveland, wondering if she was still in the car then. I-90 sliced clear across the top of the state, a straight shot popular with long-haul truckers. He recalled the serial killer theories left in the guestbook and found he could no longer dismiss them, if only because he was following the road. He kept the radio on as a distraction, a call-in show about the Indians' second-half chances after a disappointing beginning—not good, he agreed. It was a gray Sunday and the Winnebagos were rolling, the lacquered muscle cars being trailered back from shows. At home Fran and Lindsay would be at church, and he wished he was sitting between them, listening to Father John calmly untangle the knot of his sermon.

The state police had told him the car was clean, they just needed him to identify her personal effects—as if she was already dead. Though all the evidence was against him, he'd done his best to suspend judgment, and refused to draw any conclusions.

In the back of the Taurus he had a thousand new flyers, a couple hundred buttons and a whole box of office supplies donated by the Copycat. He had extra pictures of Kim if the media needed them, and a dozen copies of the DVD Fran had put together. For the dogs he had Kim's bikini bottom and a pair of underpants from her hamper, sealed in a freezer bag.

On the far side of Avon he hit the drive-thru at Roy Rogers for lunch, balancing a Gold Rush sandwich on his thigh, chewing with his eyes on the road. Worried that he was dripping, he wolfed it and had to release the pressure with several gurgling, flavored burps. He balled up the wrapper and tossed it into the passenger footwell, slapped the crumbs off his shirtfront and took a cleansing suck of soda.

"Well that was a mistake," he said.

"Why are you in my lane?" he asked a camper, and miles later caught himself arguing with a perky shill for a discount furniture store.

As a realtor he was accustomed to being his only company—the car was his office—but after being so besieged these last weeks it was strange to be alone, and dangerous, on the heels of such ugly news. Though he was on a quest, speeding toward a destination where he was urgently needed, he felt disconnected and empty, and couldn't rid himself of the notion, as in a bad dream, that he was going the wrong way.

What Kim sleeping with this Wooze character meant, Ed didn't know, but he held it against him as if he'd raped her. Dennis Wozniak, twenty-two, a decorated Marine, as if that made any difference. A drug dealer. Perry promised they were keeping a close eye on him while they secured a warrant. He lived out in the hills, so he might be cooking up the stuff. If they came across anything that gave them probable cause they'd go back to the judge for another warrant. Ed didn't understand why they were giving the guy time to hide everything. They might as well call him and tell him they were coming.

The interstate was dangerous this way—too many unbroken miles letting his thoughts wander. He was glad to leave 90 for a two-lane blacktop, dipping through rolling vineyards, slowing for crossroads towns not much smaller than Kingsville. Their main streets were a mix of white Greek Revivals and brick Victorians partitioned for business, their suburbs a sprawl of well-spaced ranches and, farther out, new construction and dormant farmland for sale, including several apple orchards—always a selling point. He could imagine life here, and the idea soothed him.

When he reached the Sandusky city limits, the zoning totally collapsed. The road in was a gauntlet of muffler shops, fast food chains and used car lots. A stranded caboose maintained by the chamber of commerce hawked the local attractions, though the only one of note, Cedar Point, needed no advertising. As he neared the address of his motel, he passed, in quick succession, a Super 8, a Ramada, a Travelodge, a

Comfort Inn, a Rodeway Inn, a LaQuinta, a Quality Suites, a Budget Suites, a Red Roof Inn, an Econo Lodge, a Best Western, a Hampton Inn, a Holiday Inn and a Howard Johnson's, as well as several raw job sites. He was looking for the Country Inn, and had to fight the signage to figure out which driveway was his.

Yesterday Fran had spent hours online trying to find him a room. With the amusement park, the weekends were impossible. His reservation was for five nights, ending Friday, but, faced with writing the departure date, he told the desk clerk he might want to stay longer.

"That could be a problem," the clerk said, checking.

Ed leaned against the counter, bowing his head, and guiltily wished he was wearing a button. He couldn't fault the kid for being thorough, but after driving for so long, standing still made him feel like he was wasting time.

Yep, the clerk said, they were full up. August was their busy month. They got a lot of visitors from Europe, and cancellations were rare. He could leave a note for the manager if he wanted.

"That would be great," Ed said, and went back out to drive around to his room.

It was a musty cinderblock box with a knee-high dresser along one wall, on which sat a dusty TV crowned by a laminated ad for Pizza Hut. There was no refrigerator, just an ice bucket with a filmy plastic bag. He dropped his duffel on the round table in the corner and used the bathroom, then hung up his shirts, turned the a/c to lo cool and left, making sure the door was locked. Before starting off he called the barracks to let them know he was coming, and promptly got lost, finally stopping at a Sohio to ask.

An officer was waiting for him—Sergeant McKnight, a squat brunette with ramrod posture who introduced herself as the troop's media liaison. Her hair was pulled back under her hat, making her face look bare. She was thin-lipped, with stark mascara and a plain engagement ring. She handed him her card and offered the family their collective sympathy, nodding to make it stick. On the way to her office she apologized for Lieutenant Solari, the incident commander, who was coordi-

nating from a command post on site. They had tracker dogs out, and
the county search-and-rescue. She didn't give her opinion on how it was
going, as if that wasn't her place, and he wondered what she was withholding from him. He imagined she knew about Wooze and J.P. and
the speed, and figured Kim for some rotten-toothed meth-head.

She had a file of pictures for him to look at—the interior of the Chevette and then, item by item, against a white background, the contents.
There was no broken glass, no slashed seats, no blood that he could see.
The translucent blue dolphin air freshener still hung from the rearview
mirror, the paisley box of Kleenex still sat in the backseat. The contents
were presented like evidence, flat and shadowless. He identified a CD
case with a pink and yellow daisy sticker, an ice scraper with a blue
brush on one end. He couldn't be sure of the Altoids, but the crushed
pack of Newports was hers. There was a picture of nothing but cigarette
butts, another of used tissues and foil cocoons of chewed gum. Her registration and insurance, and the warning for excessive speed that Perry
had written her. The photographer had emptied out the glove com-
partment, down to the tiny metal box of fuses that had resided there
since he'd fixed the bubble light for his mother, back when she still had
her sight. Here was the tire gauge he'd bought for Kim, and the screw-
driver and the adjustable wrench for emergencies, and the Motorist's
Prayer Fran had found at a card shop. Pens and pencils, a film canister
full of quarters for the car wash, a plastic spoon still in its cellophane
wrapper, a mint-flavored toothpick, a straw and several wet wipes from
the Dairy Queen, a tiny packet of salt. All of it belonged.

"Anything that should be here that isn't," the sergeant prompted.

He pictured Kim leaving for work, sweeping through the kitchen
and out the back door. "Her cellphone. Her purse. Sunglasses. Keys."

She took out a second file and leafed through another set of photos,
shielding them from him until she found the one she wanted and slid it
across the blotter. "This isn't information we're releasing."

The shot was a close-up of the old-style chrome door handle on the
driver's side. Poking from the keyhole was the jagged shank of a key, the
dirty brass bright gold where it had sheared off.

More than anything he'd seen today this hurt him, but what did it mean?

"The car was locked when they found it."

He still didn't understand.

"It suggests someone continued to use the car after they parked it. Again, this isn't something we're making public."

"I understand." Did they think she'd willingly gone with someone?

"Also, the driver's seat was pushed all the way back."

"That's normal. She's tall."

He asked to see the car, if that was possible.

"Of course," she said.

He expected it would be housed in a spotless garage, attended by technicians in labcoats. She led him out back, across a hot parking lot full of idle cruisers and then a weedy patch of grass to a long, shedlike carport with open stalls, some empty, some occupied by wrecks. The Chevette sat in its dim pen, facing out. Beside the sleek Crown Victorias it looked like a toy. The front bumper on the passenger side was mashed like a fat lip. While he'd had doubts after finding out about Wooze, he knew absolutely that she wouldn't treat her car like this.

"It wasn't like that before," he told the sergeant, and entered the dirt-floored shed, circling to check for further damage, careful not to touch anything.

Soot mottled the window frame and door's edge down to the handle as if it had been burned—they'd dusted for prints and not cleaned it off. Below the handle was a hole; the missing lock rested in a baggie on the driver's seat, along with a pink invoice. The hatch had been dusted, and they'd pulled up the rear deck to get at the spare and then left it open so the back looked ransacked.

The sergeant said they hoped to release it to him this week.

"That's fast," Ed said. He'd just assumed they'd keep it until they solved the case. Up until yesterday he thought he might never see it again, and now its presence was disorienting. The idea that he would take it back with him—without Kim—seemed wrong.

Before they headed over to the site he gave the sergeant Kim's clothes. She accepted them without ceremony, tucking the bag under one arm.

He showed her everything else he'd brought with him, dishing it out of the backseat like a traveling salesman. She liked the DVDs. They could hand them out at the press conference tomorrow. He pinned on a button and offered her one. They weren't allowed to wear anything on their uniforms, but she took a couple for her nieces.

Her car had a laptop mounted between the seats, separating them like a wall. As they drove over to the command post he pointed to her ring. "When's the big day?"

"We haven't set a date."

"Is he in law enforcement?"

"Thank God, no. He's a bank manager."

"So you're both in security."

"What do you do?" she asked, though she must have known.

He was happy to tell her about himself, baiting his answers with interests they might have in common. Boating was the first, an instant bond. She'd grown up on the water; her father was a serious fisherman. "That's what I'd be doing today," he said. She lived in Bayview, a small town not much different from Kingsville. She'd gone to Kent State— Fran too, though she'd only taken a few night classes at the Ashtabula satellite. She'd served a tour in Iraq, as had several of Kim's friends (he flashed on the faceless Wooze, their white limbs tangled in the dark). "Let's just say it's good to be back," she said, and he realized there was no need to stretch for connections. It was her job to make him feel welcome.

The detective said they'd found the car in a hospital parking lot outside the city, but the neighborhood the sergeant drove him through was urban—redbrick rowhouses with adjoining porches abutting vacant lots and old funeral homes, shuttered drug stores and abandoned gas stations on the corners. He thought he shouldn't be alarmed that there was trash everywhere and all the people on the streets were black, but as the blocks wore on he found himself hoping she'd keep going until they were out of this part of town.

She turned onto a boulevard edged on one side by an endless park behind a spiked wrought-iron fence and on the other by a massive bus yard defended by razor wire. A half mile down the road she signaled and turned into the park—Mercy Hospital, according to the brass plaque. It wasn't a place you'd just stumble on, he thought; you'd have to know it was there.

The drive wound uphill past a looming crucifix through landscaped grounds to a complex of ivied buildings with slate roofs that reminded him of a small college, an aqua water tower and banded smokestack topped with lightning rods rising to the sky. At the far end of the cordoned-off visitors' lot sat a huge RV painted battleship gray and bristling with satellite dishes and mast antennas like a TV truck. An awning off the side shaded a long counter where a pair of troopers wearing headphones manned built-in workstations. They were so focused they barely noticed him, nodding to the sergeant as they directed people in the field.

Inside it was bright and spare as a space capsule, and the air smelled of coffee. The floors were gray nonslip rubber, the white walls massed with cabinets. Lieutenant Solari stopped tapping at a monitor, spun around in his chair and stood to shake Ed's hand. Like the sergeant, he was squared away and military. On receiving Kim's clothes he immediately excused himself and gave them to one of the men outside, who doubletimed it to a cruiser and charged off.

The dogs were all working, so the lieutenant showed Ed around the ERV, or Emergency Response Vehicle. The idea was to take the specialized technology that was out there—GPS, wireless, IT—and combine it with the dogs and their handlers. A single dog could cover the same ground as twenty-four searchers, and much more thoroughly. Nature had simply equipped them better. And the handlers weren't weekend warriors; they were all law enforcement, trained in specific types of terrain.

There was a flatness to his delivery, a rote recitation of facts that told Ed he'd done this before. Even his little joke, calling the ERV their 9/11-mobile, was rushed. No, Ed wanted to tell him, this is not how you sell a client.

Still, compared to their command center at Lakeview it was

impressive. The forward bay was dedicated to communications, with a phone bank, three flat-screen monitors and rack upon rack of scanners. In the aft conference room, beside a pull-down topo map, hung an aerial photo divided into sectors. Ed found the gate and the drive and the O of the smokestack. Behind the hospital, surrounded by woods, sat a black tadpole of a reservoir. On the far side of the spillway was a high school with two tan baseball diamonds and an oval track ringing a football field. Across the street the city continued, tightly packed blocks repeating to the photo's upper edge. He had no idea Sandusky was so big.

"Here's where we're at right now," the lieutenant said, pointing to a dry-erase board with a menu of checked-off action items. The first thing they did once they identified the vehicle was to initiate a reverse 911, the system automatically sending a recorded message to every residence and business in a one-mile radius. Since yesterday, tracker K9s had performed searches of all four quadrants. Air scent K9s covered the unpopulated areas, two water-certified dogs checking the reservoir. Last night a helicopter ran infrared scans of the area, looking for any strange heat signatures. They'd be going up again tonight. Today there was a dive team working the reservoir, and they were rotating the trackers clockwise through the quadrants for triple redundancy. That's where the officer was taking Kim's clothing. With a better scent article the teams could work the blocks beyond the grounds that much harder.

The whole scene made perverse sense to Ed. Now that it was too late they had everything they needed.

"What have you found so far?" he asked, hoping it didn't sound like a challenge.

The lieutenant reached up above the map and pulled down a rattling mylar transparency that featured three grease pencil Xs and a short dotted line. The line led from the X in the center of the parking lot, around the power plant and a couple hundred feet downhill toward the reservoir. The second X, in the woods between the reservoir and the football field, represented a single latex glove that was now at their forensics lab. The third, a half mile west of the high school, was a torn shirt found in a dumpster behind a 7-Eleven. It didn't fit the description of what Kim had been wearing, but a tracker had alerted on it, so they were making sure. Yesterday two cars had been reported stolen within a mile of the hospital—not uncommon for the neighborhood. "There may be no connection," the lieutenant said. "Hopefully we'll be able to determine that when we locate those vehicles. At this point we're not assuming anything."

"Sounds like you guys are on top of it," Ed said, though for all the technology involved they hadn't turned up much. Already he was discounting the shirt out of hand and creating explanations for the glove (it was a hospital, dogs loved garbage). The sheer abundance of resources guaranteed nothing. He needed to watch his optimism.

"What can I do?" he asked.

"We're going to have you working with Sergeant McKnight," the lieutenant said, and deferred to her as if they'd practiced it, a tag team.

"We've gotten so much interest from the media, we'd like to use that to our advantage. Depending on how comfortable you are with it."

That wasn't what Ed meant, but she used the opportunity to go over Monday's schedule—a local wake-up show, drive-time radio, a daily status report at ten thirty that could be used for the noon news, then an hour before lunch for print interviews. He'd never had to think about deadlines, and wished Fran were there. All he wanted was a simple physical job that made him feel like he was doing something.

As they walked him outside and showed him the exact spot where the car had been parked, he wondered if his sense of letdown was from a loss of control. At Lakeview he'd been in charge. Here he had no place in their chain of command. To them he was the clueless, distraught father, a role he'd resisted so far. They probably thought he was in shock— a suspicion he fought off constantly.

The feeling of uselessness nagged at him. The lieutenant was busy, and handed him off to the sergeant, shaking his hand and telling him he was welcome to visit the ERV anytime, an invitation that served to further exclude him. Ed left him a handful of buttons, aware that he was using her as currency.

The sergeant took him to see the dive team and the two black labs that were searching the reservoir. The divers worked out of a zodiac in the center while the dogs rode in their own separate boats, barely moving, heads hung over the gunwales. Both the handlers and the dogs wore blaze orange vests. One of the handlers waved to them. Naturally they waved back.

She was giving him the tour. In the car she pointed out landmarks he struggled to remember, thinking he would come back by himself and put up flyers before dark. There was the 7-Eleven, like any other. In the trash-strewn lot a little girl on a bike turned one-handed circles, eating a popsicle. Behind the high school he met a handler named Tammy with a white shepherd named Blizzard he was encouraged to pet. He couldn't help but wonder if the dog had smelled Kim's things and now held her scent in its memory. More teams rotated in, setting out bowls of water in the buggy shade. The sergeant introduced them as if they were couples—Pete and Duke, Helen and Lucy, Scott and Jager. To them he was a civilian, a lesser breed. He thanked them for giving up their weekends.

"They've got a lot of experience," the sergeant assured him.

"I could tell," he said.

On their way back through the bombed-out blocks he glimpsed street names he knew from Kingsville. Huron, Erie, Superior. He memorized them like a hostage, repeating the sequence as the sergeant finalized their plans for tomorrow. The first stop he made after saying good-bye to her was at a gas station, to fill up and buy a map. He persuaded the girl behind the counter to let him put up a flyer. Smoothing the tape against the glass was a relief.

On paper the city wasn't that big. He took a minute beside the pump to highlight his route and carefully made his way back. He parked at the 7-Eleven, locking the Taurus, and walked along the boulevard with a tape gun and an armful of flyers, drawing stares from passing cars. The sun was low and the heat of the day had settled, the air freighted and thick. In minutes he was sopping. He put her face on every pole and bus shelter around the grounds, then did the other side of the street until he ran out of flyers. His ankle hadn't bothered him driving, but now, coming back, he limped as if he had blisters. Two teenagers in front of the 7-Eleven watched him get into the Taurus as if he were covered in blood.

For the second time today he hit the drive-thru, taking the fragrant bag of Wendy's back to his room. Dusk was falling over the motels, signs sparking on. In the lot the shuttle from Cedar Point was letting off exhausted families—moms with backpacks and souvenir cups, dads lugging plush SpongeBobs and Scooby Doos. He and Fran had made the trip when Lindsay was finally tall enough for the coasters. It seemed impossible that it had only been six years ago, and as he ate, watching the Indians game to fend off the silence, he remembered all of them getting off the Gemini and scampering down the exit ramp to get back on, vowing revenge. It was the smallest coaster, and the oldest, a rattling wooden racer he'd ridden as a kid. On the curves you could lean out and slap hands with your friends in the other train, taunting them as you pulled away. Later Fran confessed she was envious that both of the girls wanted to sit with him. For three nights the four of them had lived in a room this size—an idea that seemed equally impossible.

The game was his companion, talking to him as he explored the drawers and arranged his toiletries by the sink. Even for one person the bathroom was small. He pocketed his keycard and hobbled barefoot to the ice machine under the stairs and filled his bucket. With the door locked and chained, he knotted the bag around his ankle, spread a hand-towel over a pillow and lay back with his leg elevated. When the Indians failed to score with the bases loaded and no outs, he turned off the sound and called Fran.

It was cheaper for her to call him right back.

"Did you see it?" she asked, meaning the car, as if by some fluke it might not be Kim's.

"I saw it."

He told her about the bumper and the key and the dotted line. He described the hospital grounds, but left out the ghetto, as if it were unimportant. The ERV impressed her, and the dogs and divers, the helicopter, and he worried that he was selling her the same flashy package the police had tried to sell him. So far all they really had was the car, and it had been discovered by a security guard.

"They sound very professional," she said.

"You'd like them. They're all about lists."

"There's nothing wrong with a little organization."

"What's going on there?"

After church she and Lindsay and some volunteers from coffee hour broke down the command center. She didn't know where to put all the boxes so they were in the living room in their own corner. She and Connie spent the afternoon calling possible sponsors for the walk-a-thon. His brother called, and some kid spammed the guestbook, but she'd backed it up so they only lost a few messages.

"You'll never guess who we got an e-mail from. Terry Benjamin."

"Wow." She was the mother of a girl in California who'd been kidnapped and murdered by a paroled rapist. She was famous for her crusade to change the state's sex-offender laws. Call-in shows tapped her as an expert.

"She was very nice. She said she talked to some TV people about Kim. She's going to add a link to our site."

"I'm going to be on TV tomorrow at six a.m.," he said, just to hear her laugh. "Any pointers?"

"Don't yawn. And don't smile—you always smile too much. Did you bring something decent to wear?"

"I've got my blue shirt." The action on-screen distracted him—a Tiger wheeling around second, sliding headfirst into third. "How's Lindsay doing?"

"Okay. Cooper pooped in her room."

"He *is* a super duper pooper."

"I don't know if you noticed, but he's been super duper weird lately."

"He probably misses Kim."

"So do I, but I'm not pooping on the rug. It's not like we don't let him out. She was good about cleaning it up though."

"Did she cut the grass?"

"Not yet. I'll bug her about it tomorrow. How's your ankle?"

"It's okay."

"What about you," she asked, "are you okay?"

"I'm just tired."

"Go to bed."

"I'm going to." Lying there with her voice in his ear, he thought he could fall asleep like this. They hadn't made love in weeks, and the distance and the blank room only sharpened his longing. "I miss you, Franny."

"I miss you too."

"You know," she said after a while, as if she'd been building up to it, "I can understand why they lied, but it doesn't help."

"I know."

"It could have made a difference those first couple of days."

"It might have just confused things."

"I guess."

"It doesn't matter now," he said, but he didn't believe that. Everything mattered.

After they hung up he lay there a while in silence as if paralyzed, watching the Indians lose as the TV in the next room nattered through the wall. It was an effort to lift the remote. His ankle was still swollen, the skin blanched with cold. He didn't know what he was doing here, or what he could possibly accomplish. If he left now he could be home by two, except the sergeant had scheduled all those interviews. He padded to the bathroom and brushed his teeth, leaning over the sink to avoid himself in the mirror. Sitting on the edge of the bed, he set the alarm, knowing he wouldn't sleep. At home he had Fran to hold on to, her breathing and the reassuring scent of her skin. Here he was alone with Kim and the dwindling odds. All day his thoughts had been circling. In the dark they would gather and attack him, breaking down his rationalizations. Every night it grew harder, yet even now, on the verge of surrender, he could fool himself into believing again. The trick was simple. Before he pulled off his shirt he unpinned his button, angling it on the nightstand so that the last thing he saw as he reached for the light was her face.

The Loser's Bracket

The game was scheduled for seven, and all day she prayed for rain. Weather.com had gone back on its promise of scattered showers, the cartoon drops holding off until midnight—too late. The hours ahead were solidly partly cloudy. The evidence was right outside her window. Hanging from the back of her door was her uniform, freshly ironed by her mother and delivered to her room like a costume, a new loop of yellow ribbon sewn to the front. In the bottom of her closet were Kim's beat-up cleats. She would put them on and be an inspiration to her team—to the whole community.

She wasn't even supposed to be here. According to the calendar on the fridge she was at camp. It was her last year. She was signed up to be a CIT, meaning next year she could apply for staff. That had been the plan, but her mother had called and canceled her reservation. It was more important for her to be here, and Lindsay understood. With her father gone, her mother didn't want to be alone, though Connie came every day, as well as Father John. The neighbors were still bringing them meals. After having the house to herself it was like an invasion. Now when she wanted to go across the yard to Dana's, her mother made her take her phone and watched from the back door as if she might get lost. Forget riding her bike to Micah's. If her mother was free she'd drive her the half mile; if she was busy she'd tell her to invite Micah over— pointless, since her friends shunned the place as if it was haunted. Most of the time she stayed in her room, her mother clumping upstairs and checking on her, peeking over her shoulder to see who she was chatting with. She wasn't allowed to talk to J.P. or Nina anymore. It was like being grounded, except she hadn't done anything.

Then there were the public functions like tonight, where she was supposed to smile and shake everyone's hand. She was sick of people she didn't know asking her how she was doing and telling her how wonderful Kim was, or, worse, saying they were praying for her. At church it made sense—tomorrow she would stand up and say Kim's name during the Prayers for the People—but at the bottle-return at Safeway it was creepy. Stooped old ladies with papery hands gazed into her eyes. All she could do was thank them.

Lindsay didn't pray for Kim, not officially. She didn't fit her palms together or get down on her knees beside her bed. She didn't ask God why this was happening. She asked Kim.

It was like talking to herself, or talking to the screen while she was IMing someone. "I can't believe you're so stupid," she'd say, responding to a snarl of thoughts. It wasn't that she heard Kim's voice in her head. They weren't long conversations. She just found herself muttering things out loud.

"Who were you on the phone with just now?" her mother would ask, sticking her head in, and Lindsay would have to say Dana and then wait till she retreated downstairs.

Lindsay eavesdropped just as much, reconstructing calls from her mother's side of the conversation, sifting through them for clues. When Connie was over they kept the stereo tuned to NPR and she had to battle the classical music and endlessly repeating news to hear what they were saying. Occasionally her mother would laugh, an abrupt, shocking bark that made Lindsay frown and wonder what Connie had said. Her mother never laughed with her father, but that was at night, when the house was quiet.

He was supposed to be coming home tomorrow, but then he was supposed to already be home yesterday. She wished he were back, if only to absorb some of her mother's attention and restore the balance in the house. It was already too empty without Kim.

She played Text Twist to kill the time. By five the sky hadn't changed. A little later her mother came up and said they needed to be there early to help set up. Besides the ribbons, they were selling pink sport bracelets that said KIM'S KREW. Everyone on the team would be wearing them. Thursday when the box came her mother gave her the first one as if it was an honor. Lindsay thanked her and went to set the unopened package on her dresser, but her mother wanted her to model it. Now it sat in the heart-shaped twig basket with the glitter-filled jellies she never wore.

ill buy 1 but im not wearing it, Dana wrote. *way 2 gay.*

On-screen she agreed, but that wasn't her problem with the bracelet. The idea was that it would remind not just the wearer but anyone who saw it of Kim. Lindsay already did that.

"We're leaving in fifteen minutes," her mother said, looking in, because she hadn't moved from her computer.

"Fifteen minutes."

Standing at her dresser with her head bowed, she buttoned her top deliberately, a gladiator preparing for the arena—for the last time, she reminded herself. All she had to do was get through tonight.

She tucked in her shirt all around and cinched the built-in belt, then sat in her chair, bent double, and tugged on the silly stirrup socks, twisting them straight. She took off her watch and replaced it with the bracelet, self-conscious of the one's absence and the other's presence. In her closet, on the shelf, her hat sat atop her glove, the two untouched since her last game, before Kim. Taking them down, she felt like she was disturbing a shrine.

"Is Cooper's steak in your room?" her mother called.

"No," Lindsay called, just as she saw the googly-eyed toy by the bookcase. "Yes."

"Can you bring it down with you?"

Lindsay hated that he had to go in his cage, and kissed him on the nose. He turned a circle and folded down on his bed, resting his muzzle on the steak.

"Go to sleep," she said.

In the back hall she added her glove and hat to the Sea Wolves gym bag with Kim's cleats. The bag was cheap, a freebie from a few summers ago. The vinyl was ripped along the zipper, and no matter how much

Lysol they sprayed, the inside smelled like feet. Lindsay had been look-ing forward to throwing it away after the season, except now it was a relic, sentimental and precious. Even she could feel it.

Her mother circled the downstairs, making sure the doors were locked and the answering machine was on. She was wearing jeans and a brand new T-shirt silkscreened with Kim's face. Lindsay supposed she was lucky she didn't have to wear one.

"Got an extra hand?" her mother asked, and gave her a box to take to the car.

The air felt heavy, but the clouds above the woods were white.

"Did you want to drive?" her mother asked, holding out the keys as if they'd discussed it.

"I'm good."

"Come on, you need the practice."

It was true, just as it was true—though no one had mentioned it for weeks—that her test was in less than a month, but she'd become at-tuned to any special treatment, and something about her mother's offer seemed false. For a moment they stood rooted at the hatchback, parry-ing wordlessly, until, with a grimace, Lindsay relented and reached for the keys and they crossed to the opposite doors.

She wasn't being oversensitive or paranoid. Her mother never let her drive the Subaru. They'd been out a few times in the Chevette when she'd first gotten her permit, but that was in the parking lot of the high school. Even at those low speeds her mother shied back from the dash, her foot searching the floor for an imaginary pedal. Her father was calmer, hardly saying anything. Kim might make fun of her, but she never made her nervous.

"You can adjust the seat," her mother said as Lindsay fixed the mirrors.

"I'm all right."

No matter how casual they both acted, it was going to be a lesson. Lindsay wondered if her mother understood it was also an anniversary. The last time she'd driven had been with Kim. Since she'd disappeared there hadn't been time for anything else.

At the end of the driveway she just touched the brake and the car jerked to a stop, toppling a box in the back.

"I should have warned you," her mother said. "They're a little stiff."

Lindsay didn't see why she had to do this. Today was already hard enough.

She babied it out into the street, then goosed it, and the front end lunged. Her mother looked out her window as if fascinated by the neighbors. "That's it," she said when Lindsay had reached a steady speed, and an odd thought occurred to her. If they crashed, she wouldn't have to play.

Her mother navigated as if Lindsay didn't know where they were going. They took State Street downtown, then turned left onto Harbor. Lindsay swung wide, straying into the other lane before straightening out.

"Sorry."

"That's okay. Better wide than tight there."

They followed Harbor all the way down like they were going to the marina. She hunched over the wheel, keeping the hood between the lines, looking up every so often to check her mirrors. She had a habit, as she concentrated, of compressing her lips and breathing shallowly through her nose, which, after a time, gave her a headache. She relaxed her jaw and drew in a deep breath like at the doctor's.

"You're doing great," her mother said.

"Thanks."

"You should be driving every day. Maybe when Dad gets back we can figure out a schedule. What do you think? Would you like that?"

"Sure."

"You must be getting bored up there in your room. I don't know. Would you rather be at camp?"

"No, it would be too weird."

"This whole thing is too weird," her mother said.

They coasted down the long hill toward the park, the harbor and the lake spread before them. The sky was darker over the water, and a line of pickups hauling empty trailers waited at the boat ramp. Beyond the jetty, wind dashed the waves into whitecaps. If Lindsay didn't know better she would have thought it was going to pour. She couldn't let herself believe it.

The softball diamonds with their stalky light towers were at the far end, by the inlet. Dustdevils twisted across the infields. At the nearest backstop people were battling a flapping pink banner. A van from WKGO was already there, playing music, and Connie's Pontiac and a few other cars Lindsay didn't recognize. She overshot them, choosing an empty stretch, then missed the spot she wanted, her side well over the line. She had to back up and head it in again.

"Good enough," her mother said, and reminded her to put it in park.

"Stupid," Lindsay accused herself.

"No 'stupid.' You just need practice."

They were downwind from the concession stand, and the air smelled of popcorn and hot dogs. Lindsay let her go first, tagging along as they lugged the boxes over to the table where Connie was taping a flyer to a wheeled tank of helium. The Kim that never existed smiled out at Lindsay. The flat black-and-white combined with her ridiculous updo made the picture look dated, as if she'd been kidnapped from 1985. Above the flyer was a price list. Balloons were two dollars, ribbons three, bracelets five.

It was like a carnival. The police had their own table where they'd fingerprint and take digital pictures of little kids for free, and WKGO would be broadcasting live from a tent pitched next to their van. A continuous feed of studio patter and bad commercials blasted from the speakers. Her mother cut across the grass to hug a slender woman with long dark hair who was talking with some technicians. At first Lindsay thought she must be the DJ, and wondered how her mother knew her. When the woman turned it was Jocelyn. Lindsay had never seen her in jeans.

None of the other players had shown up yet, and she felt dorky in her uniform. They put her to work filling pink balloons printed with an inkblot of Kim's face above the Crime Stoppers number. Connie showed her how to use the tank. She didn't have to tie them; there was a plastic clip that pinched the neck. She had to knot a string around that and then fasten it to the backstop. After she almost lost the first one to the wind, she learned to tuck each under her arm like a football and wrap the string around her wrist. With every gust Kim's face kissed the fence.

Her mother relieved her when Mr. Pallantino arrived with the equipment. He'd taken over as coach, giving the team the chance to lose two more games.

Like all the adults, he said he was sorry and asked how she was doing.

"I'm okay," she said wearily, because she didn't want it to be a big deal.

He shouldered the bat bag while she carried the box with the helmets and the balls—the opposite of her routine with her father. It felt wrong, like she was getting off easy. The bag was heavy and dusty, one touch ruining a clean uniform. Her father made her carry it for a reason. "I'm not hitting today," he'd say when she complained, "you are." As much as Lindsay hated playing, at the end of the game she'd collect and then count the bats and haul them to the car as if they were her personal burden, dumping the bag in the back of the wagon as if it held a body. Early on she understood why she took such grim satisfaction in completing the task. It wasn't just that for now the torture was over. The truth was more pathetic: It was the one thing she could actually do.

They were at home, meaning they were in the first-base dugout. She tucked her sneakers into the Sea Wolves bag and laced up Kim's cleats. Even after two seasons they didn't fit right, as if the leather kept the memory of their original owner. She double-knotted the laces and tucked the tips under the way her father had taught her.

Mr. Pallantino sat on the far end of the bench, going over the scorebook. They were playing the number one seed, Pizzi's Café, a team that had destroyed them both times this season.

"Who's pitching for us?" Lindsay asked, as if it mattered.

"Beanie."

"Not Tessa?"

"She's on vacation."

They only had twelve people on the roster—a sore spot with her father—and it came to her that they might not have enough players and would have to forfeit. They'd play the game anyway, but it wouldn't count, so it wouldn't matter if she struck out or made an error.

As she warmed up, tossing with Mr. Pallantino on the sidelines, her teammates trickled in and joined them, saying hey as they trotted past. Shelly and Amanda made seven, and Beanie wasn't there yet. Pizzi's gathered down the left-field line to stretch in the grass. Beyond them, boats chugged up the inlet, headed home. They had eight, then nine. Officially you were supposed to have ten, but there was still half an hour till game time. Connie deputized Amanda's little sisters Evie and Edie; they went along the outfield fence with a bunch of balloons, attaching one to every post. A TV truck rolled in—Channel 12 from Erie, she knew it from a distance. The music was loud and the stands were filling, the crowd speckled pink. The wind had died down, and far over the lake the clouds parted, letting through a single sunbeam that fell on the water like a spotlight. They were going to play, she needed to resign herself to that fact, yet, numbly, she resisted. Only when Beanie took the field—to cheers from their side of the bleachers—did Lindsay give up.

In the end they had exactly ten. They sat hip-to-hip on the bench while Mr. Pallantino paced the fence, reading off the lineup. For a dizzy instant she was afraid—since it was Kim's day—that he would have her leading off, but it was a copy of her father's. She'd be playing second base and batting last, an insult she was used to.

Halfway between home plate and the mound a tech was setting up a mic stand for the pregame ceremonies. All week her mother had been practicing her speech on Connie, asking an imaginary crowd for "a moment not of silence, but of hope." She tried the line different ways, like it was part of a play. Any way she said it, it was lame. Then they'd play the song and everyone would release their balloons. The symbolism didn't make sense to Lindsay, or maybe it was her own guilt that made her reject the metaphor of letting go. She'd thought she was being a chicken, but she'd known that first night when they hadn't heard anything that Kim was dead. The rest was just not wanting to believe it. The balloons wouldn't do anything. The whole thing was stupid.

The third-base bleachers were a sea of pink, and it wasn't just Pizzi's fans. The stands behind her were jammed with families from church. They'd been to the playoffs last year, but the crowd was nothing compared to this. She craned around for Dana and the rest of the Hedricks. It was hard with all the balloons. She'd almost given up, searching the fence down the right-field line, when she spotted J.P.

Her first reaction was that she had to warn him. He wasn't supposed to be here.

He was standing just past first base, holding a balloon like everyone else. Beside him, half hidden by her own balloon, was Nina. She said something, and as J.P. bent his head to listen, he pushed his hair out of his eyes. The way Nina tipped her lips to his ear, Lindsay couldn't help seeing them as a couple. She thought she had no reason to be jealous, even if it was true. He'd been nice to her because she was Kim's sister, that was all. It was another case of being Little Larsen. She'd built the rest herself out of private jokes and quiet words of encouragement, those long days he'd asked her to save him a seat on the bus and they rode with the sun setting and their arms and legs touching. When they were alone together she didn't have to act. Unlike everyone else, he didn't ask her how she felt. He already knew.

He turned toward her and she looked away as if slapped.

The speakers crackled. "Hello, Kingsville," the MC said, as Mr. Riggio waddled over in his blue umpire's shirt and motioned for them to take the field. A cameraman knelt by home plate, waiting.

"Come on now," Mr. Pallantino said, "let's see some smart defense out there. Outfield, get the ball in. Infield, take the easy base."

Connie was guarding the opening with a bunch of balloons. Everyone was supposed to take one, even Ashley, who had to carry her catcher's mask in her glove. Beanie led them out, and the crowd cheered politely.

"Come on, let's see some hustle!" Mr. Pallantino said, just like her father, and they ran to their positions, the balloons jerking behind them.

At deep second Lindsay was even with J.P. and Nina, and suspected it wasn't a coincidence. She considered casually waving to them, but couldn't make herself look over. Beside the backstop as if she was up next, her mother stood at attention, a balloon in one hand, a ribbon pinned to her shirt. The MC was telling Kim's story as if they all didn't know it by heart. Standing there alone and exposed, she imagined people in the bleachers pointing and whispering—that's her sister.

"Ladies and gentlemen, boys and girls," the MC said, "please help us welcome Kim's mom, Mrs. Fran Larsen." The crowd rose and applauded as she walked to the mic. Lindsay patted her mitt soundlessly.

Her mother wasn't nervous. Her speech was short, just a thank you to everyone for coming, for being so generous and keeping Kim in their hearts. They'd timed it to the music, a lilting, syncopated plinking of a ukelele and then a man moaning soulfully—*Somewhere Over the Rainbow*, by the big Hawaiian guy. The idea was to choose a song people could request and dedicate to Kim, reminding listeners that she was still missing. When Lindsay first heard the song they picked she'd shaken her head. It was from a commercial, this little kid and his grandfather chasing fireflies. It had been in movies, it had even been on *ER*. It was the kind of mushy, overplayed song Kim hated. Lindsay just assumed that knowing it was cheesy made her immune to its emotional pull, yet now that it was playing and she had no choice but to stand still and listen, the singer's high voice and the spare strumming seemed lonely and haunting (he was dead, a kind of saint in Hawaii), and despite herself she felt her throat closing.

Not here, she thought. Not now.

Rigid as a Marine, she fought back the idiotic Disney tears, but the song wouldn't stop. The intro was just long enough for her mother to finish her speech—"in a moment not of silence, but of hope"—and turn to find her.

This they hadn't practiced, and a twinge of disbelief made Lindsay's face flush. The music was plinking, the singer moaning like the wind. Her mother reached out a hand for her to join her.

The cameraman panned to Lindsay, his lens trained on her face. She hesitated, thinking crazily of running away, of racing over to the fence and kissing J.P. It wasn't fair. She wasn't the one who died. She hadn't done anything.

With her first step her cleats caught in the dirt and she stumbled, nearly losing her balloon. In the stands behind her a little kid laughed. She recovered and crossed the infield, her cheeks burning, her vision blurred, with every step struggling to remember the intricate mechanics of walking. Her mother intercepted her halfway, taking her in her arms. Lindsay held on to her, wishing she could hide there.

"It's okay, babe," her mother said, rubbing her back, because—for no reason except the dumb song—she was sobbing.

"I'm sorry," Lindsay said, and she meant about everything.

"It's okay."

Someday I'll wish upon a star, the singer sang, like it wouldn't work, and Connie and Jocelyn gave the bleachers the signal to release their balloons.

"Hang on to yours," her mother said as, with a communal *oooh,* everyone watched them slowly ascend, climbing above the treetops into the sky, swirling, forming patterns as they rose to the music, drifting with the competing winds over the harbor and out over the open water, dwindling to dots against the clouds.

When they were almost gone her mother raised hers high. The crowd watched solemnly as the song went on—*there's a land that I heard of*—and standing there beside her, Lindsay realized that this was the real point of the ceremony. For all of their best wishes, in the end her mother would be left alone. When everyone else had stopped, she would still be thinking of Kim, and searching for her, and hoping, because she had no choice. She was different now, separate from them, and always would be. That was why they clapped for her. Looking at her Statue of Liberty pose, Lindsay understood that she was fully aware of it—and that it didn't matter. The song wound down, the singer cooing softly: *Why, oh why, can't I?* Lindsay raised her balloon, and then, together, they let them go.

Follow Me

The police had released the Chevette, so he needed her to FedEx him the spare set of keys. She'd just poured her third glass of wine when he called (her last, she'd promised, then filled it to the brim), and for a moment she was confused. It wasn't that complicated. They needed two people to drive the cars back.

Honestly, Connie wouldn't mind driving her out. It would give them a chance to replace the flyers at all the rest stops.

His plan was to drive the Chevette himself, then take the bus back to Sandusky. As he explained his logic the unthinkable dawned on her: He wasn't coming home.

"Just how long are you going to stay there?"

"We've got the Pennsearch people coming this weekend."

"So you'll be home Sunday night."

"Probably."

"Just like last week."

He ignored the dig. "If there's no change."

"Ed," she tried. "You don't want to take the bus."

"It's just easier if you send them."

"How is it easier?"

"This way we don't have to figure out what to do with Lindsay."

It was true, Fran didn't want to leave her, but that wasn't what they were talking about. He'd been gone for nine days now, and she felt tricked, and disloyal for bringing it up. She stayed silent, letting her disappointment sink in. Drinking could make her picky and bitchy—needlessly, she thought, and relented. "So what's going on with Cedar Point? Is that going to happen?"

She wandered the downstairs, tidying up the kitchen while he filled her in. There was still no trace of the stolen cars, and the T-shirt was so contaminated from the dumpster that the lab results were useless. The glove, as they'd both suspected, had come from the hospital. He relayed this dully, as if he'd already explained it to someone else. In a tone only slightly brighter, she told him about their plans for the fun run, ending up lying on the couch with her eyes closed while the news played mutely. Like every night, she waited for the moment when they set aside the exhausting topic and spoke directly to each other.

Their questions were elemental then. How did she sleep? Did the pills help? Did he want some for himself? What did he eat today? What was she doing tomorrow? They hadn't talked like this since they were dating, and a girlish part of her was tempted to see it as romantic, the two of them separated by fate, surrounded by night, a pair of voices connected by invisible waves traveling the cold air between remote towers—a furtive, unearned bond that dissolved at the thought of Kim out there by herself. She would give up any happiness of theirs to have her back. Short of that she resolved, impossibly, to protect him.

Later it came to her—after another glass—that maybe he didn't think she was strong enough to drive the Chevette. Whether he was being chivalrous or chauvinist, he was wrong. Being here alone was harder than driving the damn car.

The next morning when she sealed the keys in the unyielding FedEx envelope, the idea of him dropping in and taking off again like a soldier on leave bothered her. Some of that was frustration at having to follow the investigation at a distance, and some, she could admit, was jealousy. For all his grumbling about the tedium of motel life, she wanted to be there. Though she believed in him, he wasn't a practical person. As an administrator she had years of experience massaging an unresponsive bureaucracy. She was pushier and more organized, and thanks to Connie and Jocelyn she'd done her research. She wasn't being unfair in thinking she knew the territory better. Because she did, she also knew that three weeks was too long.

The day was taken up with business—the detective's morning

briefing, a conference call with the bank and their accountant Sal about the legalities of the reward, the search for free T-shirts for the fun run. In the end several places promised deep discounts, but no one would donate them outright, not for an order that large. She was up against a deadline, and grudgingly put the deposit on plastic, reading the number over the phone, while right in front of her on the counter were bills they couldn't pay.

She felt bound to the house, and after weeks of neglect it was a wreck. Lindsay hadn't vacuumed as she'd promised, and Cooper's hair was everywhere. Even if she felt like cooking, there was nothing to eat. In the basement there were precarious stacks of other people's Tupperware. Ed coming home wouldn't solve any of this, yet she felt she was getting no help, and after Lindsay had picked at someone's spinach lasagna and slipped back to her room, Fran allowed herself a good cry while she did the dishes.

Afterward, fortified by a glass of pinot grigio, she felt stronger. She wasn't angry with him, he had to know that. He could stay there as long as he wanted.

She wasn't sure he believed her when she told him. As if to make up for it, he promised he'd be home for dinner tomorrow, as long as the keys got there by two o'clock.

"What do you want?" she asked.

"Anything."

"I can do chicken on the grill."

"That sounds good."

It became her mission to make his visit a success. The simplicity of it inspired her. She would give him what she knew he missed, what he counted on—the same dream he'd sold his whole life—but unselfishly. A welcoming house, a home-cooked meal. In bed, as the Ambien lowered her into sleep, she was still choosing a menu.

In the morning she rousted Lindsay and attacked the downstairs, the vacuum racketing, broadcasting the scent of mothballs. The living room had gradually become her office. She emptied it box by box, storing the obsolete records from their first searches in the corner behind the furnace with all of their holiday decorations. The green Rubbermaid containers were treasure chests of ornaments Kim and Lindsay had made in grade school—cotton ball angels and stars made of popsicle sticks dusted with glitter. Here were the Halloween costumes she'd sewn for them, and the pastel Easter baskets with their plastic eggs—saved because she couldn't bear to throw them away. She saw how easily the past could trap her and fled upstairs. She had to keep moving if she was going to do this.

Lindsay humored her, grimly wielding the feather duster from room to room. Fran wished she was more enthusiastic, and more thorough, but it was enough that she was helping. As a reward, after lunch, on her way to the store, Fran dropped her off at Jen's.

She hadn't been shopping since Kim disappeared, and the process of rolling a cart along the aisles felt beside the point, an unearned diversion or indulgence. The Foodland was set up backwards, which made it even stranger. Normally she went to the Giant Eagle, since it was closer, but she didn't want to risk running into J.P. He'd stopped calling, finally, after she'd told him she was sorry it had to be this way but they really didn't need this on top of everything else. Please, she said, because she was trying to be kind, and still he went on apologizing, as if that counted for anything now. Ed thought she was being hard on him, while she was amazed at her restraint. Her first impression of him had been correct, and she scourged herself for not trusting her instincts.

This was just a hit-and-run. She didn't need to go down every aisle. She picked up some brown sugar and vinegar for her barbecue sauce, a half gallon of chocolate ice cream and a premade crushed Oreo crust, a bunch of broccoli, a package of chicken thighs, a pound of bacon, a gallon of milk and a half gallon of OJ, a carton of eggs, a loaf of bread. There was no line at the express lane, so she nosed in and unloaded her cart. It wasn't until she'd dug out her wallet that she saw the cashier was wearing a button, and Fran realized that in her rush to get everything done she'd forgotten hers.

The girl was Kim's age, small and dark and pretty, with two silver rings through one eyebrow. Fran didn't recognize her, and she didn't seem to recognize Fran, just asked if she had her card. When she said no the girl took mercy on her, passing a spare over the scanner.

In the car she promised to never forget her like that again, and when she got home, as if in penance, she pinned a button to her shirt. A few hours later when she left to pick up Lindsay, she patted herself the way she did in the morning before work to make sure she was wearing her ID.

As she was pulling into Jen's driveway her phone rang. It was Ed.

"Just wanted to warn you," he said. "I'm on my way."

"Yay."

"You'll probably be able to track my progress by the calls to the hotline."

She hadn't even thought of it, and for the second time today she wondered where her mind was.

It was on him, and no wonder. In their entire married life they'd never been apart this long. As the afternoon passed she found herself counting the hours and then the minutes. When she'd put together the mudpie and was satisfied with the barbecue sauce, she went upstairs and took a shower, shaving for the first time in weeks. Her hair was dry, like when she was pregnant, and her eyes were baggy. Cover-up only covered so much. She went through her closet as if this was a date, modeling and discarding three blouses before deciding on a sleeveless white one that set off her tan. At the mirror she debated wearing the button. In the end she persuaded herself there was no need, since they wouldn't be leaving the house, and set Kim and her rainbow on the dresser.

At five thirty she called their answering service. There were two messages. The first was a hang-up. The second was from a trucker who'd seen the Chevette on I-90 near Cleveland about an hour ago; he even confirmed the license number. She thought of the thousands of flyers they'd posted, and the millions of people who'd seen them. Even though the man's information wouldn't lead to anything, she was grateful to him. It was the rest of the world she didn't understand.

If he was in Cleveland an hour ago he'd be home soon, so she started the charcoal. Cooper was afraid of the flames, and rumbled upstairs.

He'd learned that Kim's door was locked and no longer tried to butt it open. She listened for him to try Lindsay's. Fran had told her she wanted her to be there to greet her father, but so far she hadn't budged. There was no subtle way to dislodge her. When the fire subsided and the edges of the coals turned gray, Fran slowly climbed the stairs and knocked on her door.

"I know, Dad's coming," Lindsay said, as if she'd been harping on it.

They waited on the front porch, Cooper sacked and panting at her feet. Lindsay took a rocker and read her book—one of Kim's, Fran noticed, but said nothing. Like Lindsay, she'd visited Kim's room. The Hedricks' sprinkler chattered, wetting the edge of the street. The sun was still high, but the locusts had started their sawing. It was August. In three weeks Kim was supposed to leave for college. She and Ed had worried that Lindsay would miss her, though they both knew Fran was the one who would moon over her absence. She was already dreading Lindsay's departure—less than three years away now. When Ed mentioned it he made it sound like a natural passage, and joked about renting out their rooms. His grand plan had been for them to buy a smaller place with a view of the lake—a winterized cottage or a widow's little fifties ranch on the bluffs with a Florida room and picture windows—but lately he'd been saying it might make more sense to stay put.

She didn't like the drift of her thoughts and went and checked the grill, not quite ready yet. The table was set, the house picked up and neat. Back on the porch she stood with arms crossed and watched the street, feeling lightheaded and queasy—distracted, like right before a test. Each passing car was a false alarm. She needed a drink, but had promised to hold off until dinner. She paced at the top of the stairs, turning between the columns, biting the inside of her cheek, thinking he should be here already.

"Why don't you just call him?" Lindsay said.

Sensible advice, but not helpful. Even if it was true, the last thing she wanted was to come across as needy. There was no romance in bugging him when he was almost home.

Five minutes stretched to seven, then ten. She had to stop looking at her watch.

For an instant the fear pierced her that he'd been in an accident. She dismissed it not because it was far-fetched—they happened every day— but because the odds were so long. She statistically denied the idea, aware of the flimsiness of her defense. She knew better than anyone that life was random, that lightning did strike twice, but, hurt and stubborn, she couldn't imagine having to bear any more than she already was. It was the kind of wishful thinking she'd seen at work, and again she felt stuck on the wrong side of the window.

As she tracked an ant zigzagging along the floorboards, Cooper lifted his head and perked up his ears, making her turn. The block was empty. She didn't hear anything, but he stood and joined her. He panted and then stopped with his mouth closed, intent, as if holding his breath.

"Who is it?" she asked, and he broke down the stairs and across the yard, barking, only the invisible fence keeping him out of the street.

"I can hear it," Lindsay said.

Fran strained, and then she could too.

While it was gone she couldn't have described what the Chevette sounded like. Now she knew the burble of its exhaust instantly. The purring resonated from a distance, hidden in the trees, slowly growing until the car emerged from the green halo of the oak in front of the Nai-smiths. It was him, puttering up the street. He'd told her about the bumper, but as he swung into the drive, she saw the damage.

"Oh God, Kim," she said, and looked to Lindsay.

Cooper ran alongside the car, clamoring. Fran thought Ed would stop at the walk, but he kept going around back. The garage door clanked and rattled, retracting. As she and Lindsay turned the corner of the porch, he eased the Chevette into the empty bay, the door already sliding down behind it, sealing him in, and she felt cheated. She didn't want the neighbors to gawk, but he could at least give her a chance to see it.

He came out the side door with his bag. In his T-shirt and jeans and hiking boots he looked thin as a teenager, and his limp was gone.

"You're so tan," she said, holding him.

"Careful, I stink. I think the air conditioner's out of freon."

She let Lindsay take her place and saw that she still had her book. Cooper yapped, jealous. It reminded her of a game they played—just a thing they used to do, a little in-joke. Ed probably started it. Whenever all of them were clumped together in a small space like the kitchen, the first person to notice would call "Whole family in one room." She hadn't thought about it in those terms—it was probably bad luck—but this was their whole family now.

Lindsay took his bag and led them toward the back door.

"Sorry I'm late. Cleveland was crazy."

"I haven't put the chicken on yet. You've got time to take a shower if you want."

"That sounds good."

"I'm glad you're home," she said, and took his hand like they were in high school.

"So am I."

She escorted him upstairs as if he didn't know the way, then sat on their bed as he undressed. She wasn't mistaken, he'd lost his paunch, his hip bones poking out. "Are you eating?"

"I'm eating fine, I'm just not sleeping."

"You look thin."

"It's probably all the walking. It's got to be ten degrees hotter in the city."

He stepped out of his boxers and leaned across the tub to turn on the water. When he got in and pulled the curtain she pictured herself joining him, lathering his chest, and like so many other thoughts she'd had lately, immediately vetoed it.

"Dinner'll be ready in twenty minutes," she said.

"Great," he called over the spray. "I'm starving."

Out on the deck the coals were glowing a volcanic red. She set the chicken around the edges and closed the cover, then went inside and poured herself a glass of wine, congratulating herself for making it till seven. The potato salad was done, the broccoli would take ten minutes tops. She stepped out again and stood at the rail, sipping and following a jet silently chalking a line across the sky. From beyond the garage came splashing and the sing-song—"Marco," "Polo!"—from the Finnegans' pool. The roses along the garage were full-blown and starting to drop their petals, but what caught her eye was the side door. She still wanted to see the car. She had time, and she craved it now, as if she'd been deprived.

She flipped the chicken so it wouldn't burn, set her wine on the rail and then, as if she were running away, crept down the stairs and across the lawn.

It was dim inside, suffocating, the air smelling of hot tarpaper and burnt oil. In the bare rafters there were wasps' nests; one buzzed against the far window. As she looped around the Subaru and circled the Chevette the engine gave off a staggered metallic ticking. Besides the bumper the outside looked like it always did. She couldn't resist gingerly placing her palm on the hood, as if taking its temperature. She trailed her hand up the slanted windshield and along the roof and dipped to peer through the driver's side, naturally grasping the door handle to let herself in, only to discover it was locked.

Why would Ed do that?

She hadn't asked him how the drive was. Not traffic, but being in the same seat as the person who'd taken Kim, if that's what happened. As much as they wished things were different, it wasn't just her car anymore.

On her way in she turned the chicken. It was almost ready for the sauce. She needed to be careful. Too early and the sugar would burn, too late and the coating would be goopy.

The spare keys to the Chevette were hanging in the back hall like always, but she could hear Ed moving around upstairs. She would have all kinds of opportunities tomorrow when he was gone. There was no rush. He was home. That was enough.

She got the broccoli going and stuck a toothpick in the mudpie to make sure it was setting. He came down in a golf shirt and cargo shorts, his hair slicked back, still wet. He wanted to help, but she told him to get a beer and go sit on the deck. It was too nice to be inside.

He arranged two chairs facing each other so he could put his feet up. While she brushed the sauce on he tipped his head back, basking with his eyes closed, one hand absently scratching Cooper behind the ear.

"Feels like Saturday," he said.

"I was thinking Sunday."

"Poke me with your fork if I snore."

As she tended the grill she stole glances at him. With his stubble and his tan he had the same rugged look that came from spending all his free time at the ballfield or on the water. Summer had always been their favorite season. They'd met at camp, teaching kids to swim during the day and taking each other a little further every night on the musty mattresses of the rifle range. She'd been seventeen, and though she knew it wasn't true, she felt like they'd leapt all the years in between and landed here, middle-aged and gray. They'd had a good life until now. She'd been proud of how long they'd been together, as if they'd weathered a test. She wondered if he had any private regrets, or did such mundane heartaches no longer apply to them?

"I talked to my mother," he said.

"What did she have to say?"

"We're supposed to see her next week."

She felt bad for Grace—this was their time with her—but it wasn't realistic. "What did you tell her?"

"I said maybe we could all come for Labor Day."

"Maybe."

Inside, the timer beeped, and they left the question at a stalemate.

The broccoli was just right, a little underdone. She poured herself a second glass of wine before calling Lindsay to help bring out the serving bowls. Though it was almost eight, Ed was still nursing his first beer. After so many nights alone she needed to pace herself.

As they sat down and reached across the table to join hands she became aware, as she did every meal, of the empty chair. It was so common now, after a month, that they no longer remarked on the obvious. Every table they owned came with four, and to banish one would be even more glaring, as if they were no longer saving a place for Kim. Instead, they included her in their prayers, asking God to bless her and watch over her. Because he was a guest, Ed did the honors.

"Looks good," he said, giving Lindsay first choice.

"Go ahead," Fran said. "I've been testing the sauce all afternoon."

"Homemade?"

"This ho made it."

Lindsay gave her a cross-eyed look.

"Well I did!"

It had been so long since she'd cooked that she'd nearly forgotten the pleasure of watching them eat. She wasn't hungry, and sat back after her first piece, offering her second to Ed. Lindsay picked hers up and gnawed on it, kissing the sauce off her fingertips.

"This is exactly what I needed," he said.

"Yeah, Mom, it's really good."

"A round of applause," he said, and clapped in a circle.

This was the silly Ed she loved, and the quiet life she wanted for her family, down to the soft light of evening and the mellow buzz from her second glass, and because she could see how perfect the moment was, she did what she promised herself she wouldn't do. There was no quicker way to ruin the mood. She could feel the tears building like a sneeze, hot and ticklish, and pressed her napkin to her face, jumping up and groping blindly for the sliding door, already sobbing.

He caught her in the kitchen and cradled her head against his chest.

"I know," he murmured, "I know."

"I'm so stupid," she said, sniffling. "I wanted everything to be perfect, and then it was, and it just hit me."

"Don't apologize."

"How's Lindsay? She freaks out when I get emotional."

"She's probably afraid it's contagious."

The screen was open. "The bugs are getting in."

"Fuck the bugs," he said, to make her laugh, and she cried some more.

"I'm such a mess."

"You're my mess."

"Lucky you, huh?"

Later, after she apologized to Lindsay and cut the mudpie and he helped her clean up, she wondered if that was all she wanted, for him to say they were in this together.

Having him home calmed her, yet she already dreaded him leaving. By the time they finally got the dishwasher going, it was dark out. Cooper stuck close to him, and unlike the nights they were home alone, Lindsay didn't hole up in her room but stayed downstairs to watch the Indians game. They were winning, but the innings dragged.

They didn't talk about Kim or discuss visiting his mother. He told stories about the motel. Last night there was a wedding party from England staying there. The couple had gotten married on the Millennium Force after-hours, saying "I do" on the lift hill and kissing down the long first drop. The story prompted Lindsay to remember the time she almost lost her glasses.

It was a legend, all she had to do was mention it and the scene appeared, their roles frozen forever. The girls were in the car right in front of them when the coaster leapt a hump and the glasses rose off her face. For a second they floated in zero gravity as if time had stopped, then slowly drifted backwards, caught in the slipstream. Kim turned and snatched at them but missed. Fran was holding on tight to the lap bar (she hated roller coasters, but went out of solidarity) and couldn't let go. The glasses had actually swum past them when Ed reached back over the headrest and plucked them from the air. The freakish physics and heroic last-second rescue still amazed them, and yet, as they recapped the rest of their visit (eventful and expensive, never to be repeated), Fran thought: It was just a pair of glasses.

The Indians were threatening again.

"Come on, Pronk," he said, as if he were urging on one of his own players, and clapped when the batter knocked in another run. They didn't need it. The game was already out of reach.

As ordinary and relaxing as the evening was, she was afraid they were wasting what little time they had. Lindsay was curled on the far end of the couch with her book, Cooper dozing on the cool tiles of the fireplace—whole family in one room. They had to get up early so Ed could make the eight o'clock bus. Fran wanted to give in to the inertia, but even with him sitting right beside her, his hand on her knee, she felt like she was waiting, and was relieved when the game finally ended.

The TV clicking off brought Cooper to his feet. When she stood she bounded into the hall and spun around, wagging his tail and yipping as if she wasn't going fast enough. Usually his frantic demands amused her—he knew he was going to go out and then get his treat and go to bed—but tonight she understood how routine could breed impatience. "Yes," she said, "I hear you."

Ed went around checking the windows and taking care of the lights. Since he'd been gone it was her job to batten down the house. She gladly ceded it to him. There was no way Lindsay would be up when he left, so they hugged good-bye at the bottom of the stairs. She took Cooper with her, closing her door, making Fran feel like she'd run her off.

They rarely prepared for bed together. She was used to having the bathroom to herself and some quiet time to read while he watched the news. Now she had to make the delicate decision of what to wear with him right there—not that she had much to choose from. Black was not an option, or red. She waited until he was brushing his teeth to get undressed, and settled on her white silk nightshirt, a conservative pick but a step up from her pajamas.

He was done with the bathroom, and by the time she moisturized her face and brushed her hair he was in bed. He lifted the covers for her. She'd changed the sheets, she said. She could feel the difference.

"After the Country Inn, this is paradise. Remind me to take my pillow tomorrow."

"Did you want to try one of my pills?"

"No," he said, "I think I'll sleep tonight."

In the hall, Lindsay's door opened and the bathroom door closed.

"You're not going to read?" he asked.

"No."

He raised up to turn out the light, and as he lowered himself he leaned in, pressing against her shoulder. She twisted so he could kiss her.

"Sweet dreams," he said, and lay back.

"Sweet dreams," she said, letting her head fall.

All along she'd worried that it was too soon. Now, faced with proof, she thought she'd been foolish, and greedy, wanting him all for herself. She couldn't expect him to set Kim aside, not after the drive. It was like her outburst at dinner, the base truth breaking through, overwhelming everything else. She understood if he needed time.

They lay side-by-side in the dark, listening to Lindsay finish and pad back to her room. Faintly, like the gnawing of termites, came the chatter of a keyboard, making Ed lift his head.

"Who's she talking to?"

"Probably Dana."

"How's she been?"

"Better, I guess," she said. "You know her, she doesn't say a whole lot."

"Yeah."

"You've been pretty quiet tonight."

"Me?" He shifted, throwing an arm over her stomach, the contact almost casual. "It's probably living in that room with no one to talk to."

"I wish you didn't have to go back."

"I wish I didn't either."

He stroked her side as if to soothe her. She stilled his hand, then rolled and reached for him, kissing him the way she wanted him to kiss her. He responded as if he'd been waiting for her.

"We have to be quiet," she said.

"I can be quiet."

He couldn't entirely keep his promise, but by then Lindsay was far away, the world narrowed to a tentative edge. He was still hers, that had never been in question. She thought she shouldn't have been surprised at how easily they surrendered their helplessness to each other. They always had before. Her mind was empty with the effort, at rest. It was only well afterward that the fear returned that this hunger—trivial now, having been slaked—was unnatural, but soon the Ambien took hold of her, mingling with the night's wine, smoothing away any misgivings, a blurry softening like sinking into a hot bath, dissolving her thoughts, spiriting her into a dense, dreamless sleep.

In the morning she made him French toast and drove him to the diner downtown and sat in the car with him until the bus rolled up. She kissed him hard in the bright sunlight as if she might never see him again.

"I'll be back Sunday."

"You don't have to," she said.

On the way home she imagined him riding west along Lake Road, passing the neat summer camps along the bluffs, and caught herself biting her cheek.

"Shit," she said, and thumped the wheel. She'd forgotten his pillow.

It was Friday and the street was quiet, motionless except for a crew resealing the Naismiths' driveway. The house was clean, Lindsay was still asleep. The day spread before her like a desert. She had a list of possible sponsors to call, and details to nail down with Sal for the reward, but messed around on the internet instead, visiting Cedar Point's website before checking the guestbook. *You are about to receive a blessing from the Lord,* a woman from Joplin, Missouri, assured her.

Good, she thought. I'm ready for one.

Instead she received their Cingular bill listing all of Kim's calls from last month. They stopped on the fourteenth. The last was to Nina, at ten to three. Fran went over the list, trying to identify the other numbers—Elise, J.P.—upset that she knew so few. KINGSV OH, most of them said, but several showed just their area code and FOLLOW ME. She checked the rate key. DFMR meant call delivery service, some sort of automatic forwarding, she guessed. There were three of them on the fourteenth, including the next to last one, two minutes before she called Nina.

The police had to know this, yet she'd never heard a word about it.

She went through the list backwards, calling every number she didn't recognize. "This is Kim Larsen's mom," she said. "Who's this?"

Marnie, Hinch, Covered Bridge Pizza. She used the fun run as an excuse, as if she were fishing for volunteers. She'd become an expert at asking for things, and at expecting nothing.

Only one person hung up on her, a young guy. She underlined the number. When she was done she called the detective, getting his voicemail.

That first day she'd called Kim until her voicemail was full. Panicked, she clung to the least painful solution, hoping she'd just lost her phone. She wondered where it was now.

It took him twenty minutes to get back to her, and then he sounded impatient, as if she'd interrupted something important. He couldn't tell her what FOLLOW ME meant, but they'd run the numbers weeks ago. The hang-up was Dennis Wozniak. He warned her not to call Wozniak again. "Just give us a chance to do our job, okay?"

There was no point arguing. She spoke with the detective every day, and each time she came away disheartened. Today it only seemed worse because Ed had left, and because she thought she'd actually discovered something. Why did she think there had to be a clue, one improbable piece of evidence that would break the case?

She had a thousand things to do, but wandered the downstairs, gazing out the windows at the leafy street and the Hedricks' yard. Robins hopped in the grass, bees zigzagged—another perfect day. All afternoon she'd have to endure the Finnegans splashing and laughing.

In the back hall the spare keys shared a hook with his coach's whistle, hanging by a lanyard Lindsay had made at camp. She passed them twice before giving in. Outside, crossing the yard, she felt watched, and glanced up at Lindsay's window—filled with her curtains.

She slipped inside the garage, closing the door behind her like a thief, though she wasn't even sure what she was there to steal. After her mother had died she spent a week clearing out her house, saving the fraying afghans and the Time-Life books of the states and the hokey salt-and-pepper shakers she collected, but what meant the most to her was sitting in her mother's ladder-back chair in the kitchen where she'd sat every morning, sipping her coffee properly with a cup and saucer, listening to the radio. When Fran grew tired of bagging her clothes for

Goodwill, she retreated to the kitchen and sat in her mother's chair (the radio was still there, faithfully tuned to the same station, the white plastic cabinet yellowed like old ivory from her cigarette smoke) and the past would settle around her, comforting.

Here there was no chance of that, and yet she didn't hesitate, approaching the car head-on, the key ready. Somehow a wasp had gotten inside, bumping against the windshield, its wings beating. Ordinarily she was terrified of wasps, but today it only provoked her. Inevitably, she was going to be in the car. She would not be run off by some insect.

When she turned the key, the clonk of the lock echoed in the rafters. She opened the door and the wasp bounced away from her, nosing the glass. For a few seconds she waited for it to fly out on its own, then went around and opened the other door. It serpentined between the headrests and into the empty hatchback, exploring a corner of the rear window.

"For God's sake," she said, and popped the hatch, waving a backhand at the wasp until it took off.

Quickly, as if she was in a hurry to leave, she slammed the hatch and the passenger door and curled around the hood. As she did she saw herself as if from above and realized that maybe this was a bad idea.

It was too late. She was already lowering herself into the bucket seat. The vinyl was cool through her shirt, as if the whole car had been refrigerated.

She closed the door, sealing herself in, facing the knotty back wall of the garage. The interior smelled of cigarettes and the chemical perfume of the blue dolphin that hung from the mirror. She resisted the urge to tap it and send it swinging. The wheel seemed far away. Ed had adjusted the seat to fit his big frame, and she ducked down to lift the lever, then bucked forward until she could reach the pedals.

Could she have made the drive by herself? The motel was something else, but she thought she could handle I-90 in the daylight. To test the idea she wrapped her hands around the wheel, gripping it at ten and two. There was no shock, no flood of visions. Maybe after a few hours on the highway her mind would fix on Kim. Still, she wished Ed had let her help.

She bent her head to one side of the steering column and slid the key into the ignition. She twisted the key partway and the red dash lights blinked on. Ed must have changed the station, because it was on some talk show. She switched to FM and spun the old-fashioned chrome knob until she found WERG, Kim's favorite.

She'd called them dozens of times, requesting her song, explaining the dedication, and while it wasn't a rock song they'd made an exception. It was only by luck that it wasn't playing now. What was was boring noise, a whiny British guy singing about a distant, untouchable love. She didn't know the bands anymore, and it made her feel old.

The Killers, they were called—a stupid name.

Three hours was a long time, but some days now she never left the house. She imagined driving, the wide-open road, traffic blasting the other way. Billboards and truckstops, hawks and bikers. She thought just being in the car would spark a connection with Kim, a fleeting memory that might sustain her for this next hard stretch, the way it had with her mother, but as the DJ introduced the next song and then the next, nothing came. She blamed herself for letting the wasp distract her. She told herself she'd stay until they played a group she knew—Pearl Jam or U2, Nirvana. The mood was ruined, but maybe if she was patient it would change. She wanted to believe that, and for a long time she sat there in the dimness with both hands on the wheel, as if she was actually going somewhere.

The Last Time

He went back to work for the routine as much as the money. The search had moved out of town and he had nothing to do. The baking streets, the DQ, the beach—no place was safe. The Larsens refused to talk to him, all but Lindsay, who e-mailed him five, six times a day, a complication he hadn't foreseen. Nina said he was being dense. She'd known all along.

"You never had a crush on anyone?"

"No one ever had a crush on me."

"Honestly," she said.

"Not that I know of."

"It sucks. You kind of feel sorry for them but you don't because they're stalking you. Everywhere you go they just happen to be there."

"That hasn't happened."

"That's because you don't go anywhere," she said.

His room was dark except for the phone. He wanted to go to sleep, but he liked her voice and the way she jabbed him back to life. During the day he hardly talked with anyone.

"How do you stop it?" he asked.

"You have to squash them. It's no fun."

"You've got a lot of practice at this."

"That's the danger of having boobs in the sixth grade. You're a target for every twelve-year-old boy."

"Like you're not anymore."

"I wish I could just cut them off."

"You don't mean that."

"Seriously, you don't want to know what a pain they are."

"You're right, I probably don't."

"So are you coming out with us tomorrow or what?"

He'd been staying in nights, using his mom as an excuse, when really it was Kim. It didn't seem right to go to the beach without her. He even felt guilty for being at work. He'd confessed everything to the police, expecting them to arrest him. They let him go, leaving him to devise his own punishment. Wooze had been working on it: Someone keyed his car right in his driveway, pouring acid on the scratched hood, burning big patches down to the bare metal. His mom was shocked, threatening to call the cops. J.P. was surprised it had taken so long, and knew the cops wouldn't do anything. This was about paying your debts. He kept expecting to punch out and find three or four guys waiting for him in the lot.

"I don't know," he said.

"It's Elise's last night," she said. "I'll be pissed if you don't."

The trouble with talking to her so late was that when they hung up he couldn't get back to sleep. He went over their conversation like an actor studying a role, combing it for hidden meanings.

The terrible thing was that he would have said yes if he knew Hinch wasn't going to be there. It wasn't sudden. Nina had always confused him, broadcasting her flirty mix of signals. He still remembered their kiss as if it was more than an accident. The memory, like any deep desire, had the ability to thrill and shame him at the same time. Already overloaded, he wanted to think it was temporary, a perverse side-effect of losing Kim and then learning she'd been with someone else. In three days he'd be gone and wouldn't have to worry about it anymore.

The fact that he was leaving should have been a relief. He'd already registered for classes and drawn a roommate in the housing lottery, a communications major from Indonesia named Talman, except he couldn't see himself on campus, living day to day surrounded by thousands of strangers. He was having a hard enough time here.

In the morning his mom let him sleep in, weighting a note on the kitchen table with cash for him to replace his lost winter jacket—an argument they'd been having since he'd been accepted, as if Columbus was part of the Arctic. He pocketed the money not to please her but because he was tired of fighting. It was ninety outside. No one was selling winter stuff yet.

Lindsay had sent him two e-mails late last night that he hadn't answered. He knew he shouldn't now, but she was his only way of keeping up with the investigation. He was brief and impersonal, ignoring her questions about Nina and college, asking why her dad was still in Sandusky.

They'd gotten the car back weeks ago. It was sitting in their garage, and though he wouldn't be able to see it, and their place wasn't on the way, he'd made it a ritual to cruise by before work. He was so used to the route now, when six months ago he had no idea where she lived. Her porch was empty, and he imagined walking up the stairs, ringing the bell and apologizing in person, this time finding the right words to soothe her mom, whose Subaru sat blocking the driveway. He slowed, looking beyond it to the garage as if he might feel her presence. He didn't, and by the time he reflected that he was a fool for expecting anything, he was past the house and moving away.

He could turn left at the next street, but went to the end of Lakewood and swung around in the cul de sac. On his way back he thought he saw her mom in the front window, still and forbidding as a ghost, and kept going.

At work he concentrated on the smallest tasks, stocking the shelves as if he was being graded, and still she came to him. They all did—her mom and dad, Lindsay, Nina, the volunteers and the long days they spent searching the gorge. Kneeling in the aisles, he replayed those lost weeks as if he could go back and change the past. That last day, if only he'd convinced her to stay and blow off work. He'd even said it, but not strong enough, just a joke—except she never called in sick. She was like him that way, it was one of the things he liked about her. She was dependable, which only made the Wooze thing stranger. Obviously he thought he knew her better than he actually did. So he could sympathize with the Larsens. He knew how it felt to be lied to.

Since she'd been gone he'd probably thought about her more—and sometimes thought he loved her more—than when they were together. He wasn't angry about Wooze. All he wanted was to talk to her and clear things up, even if that meant just saying good-bye.

In the same spirit he'd go to the beach tonight and say good-bye to Elise, another friend he should have appreciated more. If Hinch was there he'd clink beers with him and do his best not to think of Nina— which was crazy anyway. When he got home he'd e-mail Lindsay and tell her they had to stop. None of these resolutions seemed impossible, and after they closed the doors and pulled the canvas covers down over the coolers, he left work with a sense of purpose, even thinking he could look for a coat tomorrow.

He'd parked far out like he was supposed to, and as he walked across the lot he could see there was another car behind his. Someone was sitting in it, just the silhouette of a head.

All at once the high spotlights atop their stanchions died, darkness filling the empty space. The only sound was the wash of traffic on Route 7. He kept walking, using his car as a shield. He didn't know Wooze that well, but he didn't think the fucker would shoot him. He clenched his fists, ready to defend himself, and discovered that he wanted this to happen. It wasn't Kim's honor he'd be fighting for. It was his.

He was almost there when the door opened. It was Nina.

"What's up?" he said, as if this was normal.

"I'm stalking you."

"You're doing a pretty good job of it."

"When'd that happen?" She pointed to his car.

"Couple nights ago." He shrugged like he didn't remember.

"They got Hinch too."

"Not you."

"Not yet—knock wood." She rapped her head twice.

They faced each other across the hood. He didn't know why she was there, and didn't know what to say. In the lull Benny passed them in his truck, waving out the open window, the radio blaring bad country, then gunned across the lot.

"We still on for the beach?" he asked.

"I need to talk to you first." She came around the hood until she was right beside him, setting a hand on the fender. She looked up at him, her face half in shadow, and he was ready to confess everything.

"Promise you won't be mad at me." She wasn't flirting, she was totally serious, a side of her he'd rarely seen. He felt privileged that she needed something from him.

"Why would I be mad at you?"

"I told the cops about Wooze."

"So did I."

"No," she said. "Before that. I called the hotline. That's how I knew things were going to happen the way they did."

So she'd known Kim had been playing him all along. It made sense—she was her best friend, closer to her than he would ever be. She probably felt sorry for him. He wondered who else knew, and whether it had any-thing to do with their kiss, one secret unconsciously spawning another.

"I thought it would help," she said.

"It could've."

"No, it just fucked things up." She gestured to the hood.

"It's not your fault."

"So you don't hate me?"

No, he wanted to say, I love you. "You were just trying to help."

"Thank you." She took hold of his hand and squeezed it, then let go. "I had to tell you or I was going to go crazy."

"I know how that feels."

"All this shit is crazy. Elise is lucky. I can't wait to get the fuck out of here."

"Me too."

"Okay"—she patted the hood and started walking away—"so I'll see you down there."

"Yep."

She opened her door. "Thanks."

He gave her a wave like it was no problem, then got in and sat an extra few seconds, flexing the hand she'd touched, letting her reach the exit before he started across the lot. He'd grown so accustomed to being alone that he needed solitude to think, though in this case there was no reason. He didn't see any real option but to follow her.

They gathered at the DQ. Everyone was happy to see him, welcoming him back as if he'd been away on vacation. Hinch showed him his car as if it was a joke—treated to the same acid bath, the windshield cracked, the driver's door kicked in. The peepers in the cemetery pond were shrilling. Across the street the sheriff's cruiser sat in the darkened drive. They huddled, collecting money for a beer run, and J.P. thought it could be June. Nothing had changed except for Kim.

He drove his own car to the beach so he could leave early. It was chilly, the wind whipping his hair into his eyes. Far out over the lake a plane blinked between the stars. Nina was wearing Hinch's hoodie, while Elise and Sam snuggled under a blanket. Everyone was coupled up except him and Marnie. She sat beside him on the log, peeling her label and flicking ashes into the fire. He thought she was bored because he had nothing to say to her, and he wanted to apologize. It wasn't her.

The talk was all about college. Kenyon and Denison weren't that far apart, and Nina and Elise promised they'd visit each other. J.P. should come too—Columbus was right there. They'd make it a Kingsville reunion weekend.

"Sure," he said.

He nursed his beer, the cold and his own inwardness keeping him sober. When he was finished with it he stood and told them he had to get going. He didn't want to worry his mom.

"One more," Hinch said.

"I can't."

"Dude. When's the next time we're all going to be together?"

"Stop," Nina said.

Elise got up to hug him, squashing the argument.

"I'll miss you," he said, and meant it, though he hadn't talked to her in weeks. He'd see the rest of them before he left.

"You better," Nina said.

In the car he thought he'd done what he'd come to do. Then why, all the way home, did he feel like he'd lost something?

His mom had left the lights on for him. He went through the house, turning them off. He was too tired to deal with Lindsay's e-mails, and lay in the dark replaying his conversation with Nina. She was standing there looking up at him, asking him not to be mad. If he'd just taken her by the arms and kissed her. He couldn't believe he was still thinking this way, and shook his head. Idiot. She was just worried about him, and all he could think of was the two of them together, as if that would make everything better.

He'd been so flat all day that he thought he'd sleep. It took him hours, and then in the middle of a dream of a huge, busy airport he woke to his phone buzzing on the nightstand.

"Are you okay?" Nina asked, way too loud. "You just took off."

"I was tired."

"You should've stayed. We got Elise to go skinny-dipping."

"Wasn't it a little cold?"

"Not after a couple shots of Jaeger. You should've seen her, she was hilarious."

She sounded spacy and goofy like she was still drunk. Did she think she was being kind, calling him? Because it was torture. All he could do was play along and wait for her to say good night.

"Listen," she said, "I'm sorry I didn't tell you about Wooze. Hones'ly."

"It's okay."

"Kim didn't even like him. I don't know what she was thinking. She really liked you."

"That's good."

"She could be such a fucking bitch sometimes. You're a good guy, you know that?"

"I don't know about that."

"You are. I told her that too. I said you're a nice guy and she should be nice to you."

"Thanks," he said. "I think you should probably go to sleep now."

"You're probably right. I just wanted to tell you that, that's all."

He thanked her again and shuffled her off, finally. It was his own fault for leaving his phone on, and he wondered if he'd wanted her to call, if somehow he'd counted on it the way he expected a couple of e-mails from Lindsay every time he opened his inbox. Again, he resolved to stop thinking of her and take care of his business. He only had two days left and he still had to pack.

The Long Weekend

He knew it was time to leave when the search teams switched to cadaver dogs, priming them with jars of death scent. The lieutenant warned him in advance, as if apologizing for the department's lack of faith. Ed understood: It had been too long. If she was here they would have found her by now.

He gave them two days, following their progress in the chilled and windowless conference room of the ERV with Sergeant McKnight, praying it was a waste of time. She monitored the radio through a headset and calmly checked off the sectors with a dry-erase marker. At the end of the second day he thanked everyone, shaking their hands as they signed out, then went back to the Country Inn and emptied the drawers into his suitcase. He left the bill on his credit card, afraid of what their monthly statement would look like. Halfway to Cleveland he realized he was giving up on the only real lead they had. With every exit he passed he was leaving her behind.

While he was away, as if to make up for dragging his heels, Perry had personally overseen the search of Wozniak's property and come up with nothing. Ed was angry that they'd done it without him. He didn't care about the drugs, he wanted them to look for Kim. He wanted them to use dogs and the new ground sonar the lieutenant had shown him. He wanted them to drain ponds.

Wozniak was cooperative, Perry said, as if Ed was wasting his time.

"Then he won't mind us looking again."

After a pointed silence, Perry said, "I can ask."

"Thank you," Ed said.

In his absence Fran had cobbled together the reward—thirty thousand dollars, ten of which came from his brother. You couldn't buy a rusting singlewide for that kind of money, but he understood, it was about publicity. They sent out a new flyer to the papers, Fran went on TV, and the tipline lit up. Along with the usual psychics, several private detectives offered their services—a temptation, since they were getting nowhere through official channels. He seriously considered it until he went to a few websites and saw what it would cost.

They could have used the money themselves. Among the bills on his desk was the invoice for Kim's tuition, two weeks past due. For months he'd privately worried that they wouldn't be able to cover both her and Lindsay's education without resorting to a second mortgage. Now he wished he could just write the check and forget it. Instead, he took care of the smaller bills, waiting till the last possible day on their credit cards and then paying the minimum.

On top of everything else, he needed to see his mother. Summer was ending, and he'd promised. She was so close. They could take a day and visit her.

"You don't have to convince me," Fran said, because he was the one who couldn't bear the hospital-like limbo of the retirement home. Besides her failing eyesight, his mother didn't belong there, or hadn't at first, when they could have taken her in (should have, his brother thought, an open rift between them). A series of strokes had left her frail but lucid, and while she insisted that she'd made friends and would hate to leave them, he'd been thinking of moving her somewhere closer.

"I'd like to see Grandma," Lindsay said.

"What day were you thinking of?" Fran asked.

It seemed too easy, and he wondered if they were going along with it for his sake. After dinner Lindsay did the dishes without being asked. When he commented on it before bed, Fran said she'd been very helpful lately. She was worried that she was being too quiet.

More worrisome to him was the way Fran slept. In Sandusky he'd become used to staying up past midnight and then fighting the stiff pillows. Here his sleep was still fitful, while she lay motionless beside him, knocked out. He could turn on the light and she wouldn't stir. He could nudge her—it was like a coma. In the morning he was achy and weak, lingering in the shower; by midafternoon he was ready to crash. She had enough pills for him, but every night he turned down her offer. She thought he was being macho. "The soldiers in Iraq take them, *because they need their sleep.*"

"I'm good," he said, and then lay awake beside her.

Compared to Sandusky the days were long and empty. Part of it was the time of year. Normally they would have just come back from vacation and he'd have this last week to putter around on the boat, maybe drop by the office and scare up a partner for golf. This was his real vacation, the stressless solitude of fishing or walking to his drive replenishing him. Even if he had the time now, he was afraid these reliable pastimes wouldn't save him, that, on the contrary, he'd ruin them forever.

He went to town hall and pulled the tax map for Wozniak's property as if he were preparing to sell it. Like so much of the county, it was a derelict farm bought at auction for pennies on the dollar back in the eighties. The deed was in the name of Regina Holub, Wozniak's grand-mother, who apparently still lived there. Though he'd specifically been warned to stay away, Ed drove by the peeling Greek Revival, noting the pond and the vine-wrapped silo and blackened, leaning outbuildings, the fields running back to the woodline. The gravel drive was rutted, and held puddles. In an open shed a backhoe hunched like a spider. He was wrong, probably, but he had nothing else to go on.

Visiting his mother gave him something to look forward to. Other-wise the days were the same. Every morning he spoke with the detective and left messages for Perry. He copied flyers and ran errands and helped Fran with the details of the Kare-a-Van for Kim, a road rally two week-ends away. Around five, Sergeant McKnight e-mailed him to say they'd found nothing new today. After supper he took Lindsay out driving, quizzing her from the manual as she practiced her turns. If the Indians were on, he watched them. They were winning, but it was too late, they'd never catch the White Sox. And then it was time for bed again, and the question of whether to take the pill or toss all night.

He dreamed of the motel and the hospital, complicated, incomplete scenes. He was the one who was lost, wandering the boxed-in hallways. The desk clerk—a rat-faced actor he'd seen in something recently—said there were no rooms, and Ed walked the blazing strip by the 7-Eleven, vintage seventies cars flashing past, all gaudy whitewalls and chrome, black teenagers taunting him from their windows.

One reason he didn't take the pill was that he longed for a dream of Kim. He didn't expect her to tell him what had happened, he just wanted to see her again, to be in her presence as if she were alive and none of this had happened. Every night he went to bed hoping she'd come to him. Every morning he was disappointed.

The biggest change was his sudden inability to concentrate. Reading the paper, logging entries from the tipline, watching the game—he couldn't stick with anything for more than a few minutes without getting up and pacing around the house, plowing his fingers through his hair and massaging the meat of his temples as if his head hurt. He blamed it on the lack of sleep but feared it was something more drastic, like a panic attack. The smallest sounds distracted him—the kitchen faucet dripping two rooms away, the dryer tumbling in the basement. His skin itched, his leg jiggled and he couldn't think. It reminded him of when he quit smoking, his own impatience crippling him. He not only felt useless, he *was* useless, while Fran was efficient as ever, organizing a month's worth of events between doing interviews and cooking meals.

He wondered if he was clinically depressed, and who he needed to see if he was. They'd probably just give him pills. He thought he could talk to Father John, but put off making the call. He was home, finally. It should have been easier. If he could just get a decent night's sleep.

Fran encouraged him to get out of the house, and Friday when he ran out of errands he ventured to the marina to check on the boat. Downtown the stores were celebrating the three-day weekend with a sidewalk sale, the diner grilling chicken over a cinderblock firepit in the parking lot. On every telephone pole Kim shared space with posters for the leukemia fair and the county rodeo. A banner spanning Main Street announced that tomorrow the chamber of commerce was sponsoring fireworks over the harbor. He pictured the crowd gathered at the park and worried that they were missing an opportunity. At dusk they'd just be getting back from his mother's.

"Already thought of it," Fran said over the phone. "Jocelyn's got an in at KGO. Anytime they do a remote they hand stuff out."

"How about the leukemia fair?"

"Connie's got people on it."

"What about the rodeo?"

"We've got it covered, trust me. Go play with your boat."

In the backseat he had a box of flyers. Instead of wasting his time washing down the boat, he spent the afternoon plastering them to every light pole and drinking fountain and public restroom, always remembering which way the crowd would be facing. He didn't think the park was that big, but to cover both sides of the inlet on foot took hours. Pilings, benches, trashcans, fenceposts. He taped some to the plinth of the tarnished bronze of the slickered mariner at his wheel, and would have stuck a pair on the huge flukes of the anchor commemorating Admiral Perry's victory if he thought he could get away with it. By the end he was drenched in sweat as if he'd gone jogging. He felt good, like he'd done something. He'd sleep tonight.

"Someone's ripe," Fran said when he walked in. "How were the seagulls?"

"Shitty," he said, finishing the old joke.

Sergeant McKnight e-mailed to say this weekend five teams from downstate were joining the search, and though he knew it wouldn't make a difference, he thought he should be there.

After dinner he helped with the dishes, then watched the Indians stuff the Royals. Lindsay took the other arm of the couch, her legs tucked under a blanket. She was too thin, and couldn't bear their airconditioning. She read, paying attention when the game got interesting. He didn't mind that she was quiet. He liked that they could share the same room without having to say anything.

Fran was in the living room, printing something out. From time to time she came in to check on them as if they were kids.

In the seventh Lindsay left and returned with a Fudgsicle.

"Shoot," he said, "I didn't know we had those."

They were his favorite, but he didn't dare. He'd already cut out alcohol and coffee and caffeinated soda. Now all he allowed himself after eight o'clock was ice water, just a single big Indians cup or he'd be back and forth to the bathroom all night.

Fran went up at her regular time. He watched the game to the end, then turned off the lights and let Cooper out, waiting for him at the back door. She'd left her car out again, as if she didn't want to park it next to the Chevette—an observation he knew better than to mention.

Lindsay was in her room, tapping away at her computer. After everything, he didn't like her being online so much, and poked his head in to tell her not to stay up too late.

Their room was dark, just the nightlight on by the sink. He brushed his teeth and slid into bed next to Fran, plumping his pillow and fitting his knees behind hers.

"Hey," he said, because he wanted to thank her for going tomorrow.

She didn't answer, so he tried again, gently—"Hey."

No, she was out.

"Must be nice," he said.

It was like fighting himself. He was too hot, and struggled to find the right position, his limbs caught at awkward angles. On the insides of his eyelids a montage of the day's accumulated negatives flickered, the shifting shapes like Rohrshach blots. He was talking to a man in a pulpit that was actually a Segway. He didn't recall falling asleep; he only realized he must be, since he was dreaming. When he woke, the curtains were still dark, and he thought it was close to daybreak. The clock said it was ten past two.

In the morning his eyes burned as if he'd gotten soap in them, and he took three Advil. Fran was already working, packing a picnic basket with curried chicken salad and cucumber sandwiches. She'd even bought mint Milanos for his mother. While Lindsay showered, they drank coffee out on the deck. The day was bright and perfect, a male cardinal tweeting his two-toned call from the peak of the garage. In the lull, he thanked her; she dismissed it with a wave. She'd asked Dana to watch Cooper, a detail he hadn't thought of. At least one of them was capable.

Lindsay came down with wet hair, already wearing her iPod. Fran made her take a Nutrigrain bar and some orange juice. He'd moved the box of flyers so she wouldn't have to sit with them, but as they pulled out he caught her glancing into the way back, and the look on her face. He should have just stuck them in the garage.

To get on 90 they had to drive out 7, past the gorge and the Conoco—the pumps packed with holiday traffic. Fran watched the doors as they passed, as if Kim might be inside working. Nina was off to school, as were J.P. and Elise. He never expected them to stay, but he didn't understand how they could just leave her behind. While he was away, Fran had seen J.P. drive by the house a few times. If he tried anything, forget calling the cops, she said, she was ready for him. Ed thought he knew J.P. better than she did, and didn't see him as a bad kid, just immature, but didn't blame her for being angry.

At the far end of the bridge he turned and sped down the ramp, merging into the stream of trucks powering east, and soon they were cruising along with everyone else. On their right the massive, shimmering red and gold billboard for Adult Paradise rose above the caved-in remains of a barn. They crossed the state line, an elaborate sign welcoming them to Pennsylvania. Even with Fran right beside him, and the prospect of seeing his mother, he felt the same sense of letdown that gripped him when he'd left Sandusky, the nagging fear that he was going the wrong way.

"We should stop and get some of those mints she likes," Fran said.

"Good idea."

His mother was at the point where dessert appealed to her more than meals, but she'd always had a sweet tooth, a weakness she'd passed on to him. As a child he sneaked the pastel green butter mints from a cut-glass dish on the dining room sideboard, retreating to his room to eat them one at a time, letting them dissolve on his tongue, the chalky solid magically turning sweet and creamy. Like visiting his mother, just the thought of them sparked a mix of comfort and guilt. The new ones didn't taste the same, though it was possible they were cut-rate imitations and not the real thing.

There was a CVS just off her exit where they'd stopped before. He left the car running for the air-conditioning and headed across the lot. They weren't that far from Kingsville, so he was surprised there was no flyer on the door, and weighed going back and getting one.

Why did he have to think? There was no such thing as a holiday for them anymore.

Fran watched him as he backtracked and opened the door, dipping down to trip the latch.

"What's up?"

"No flyer."

It didn't take long. He'd become practiced at explaining the situation, and the cashier was the mother of two teenagers, and glad to help. She gave him a discount on the mints, shook his hand and held it an extra second. "God is good."

"I hope so."

"He is," she said, as if she knew Him personally.

Outside in the heat he wondered what had happened to her that she was so certain, and thought of his mother raising him by herself, his father dead at thirty-seven of a heart attack. Would she have said God was good?

"Well?" Fran asked when he handed her the bag.

"Mission accomplished."

The home was another ten miles through the suburbs of Erie. When he was a boy there'd been nothing out here but Christmas tree farms and hunt clubs, a speculator's dream. Now it was overrun by pricey developments with names like Northglen and Devonwood, switchbacked tiers of McMansions winding up terraced hillsides to sunset views along the ridges. From all the deer crossing signs, he imagined they were a problem, not used to commuters.

He hoped it wouldn't be crowded. Saturday was a big visiting day, but he expected most families had their own plans for the weekend. The weather was ideal. As they closed in on the home, he pictured himself a mile out on the lake, the water sparkling, nothing but blue sky to the horizon, the Indians game on his old transistor, a pair of sandwiches and a couple of cold Buds in the cooler. The hardest thing he'd have to do was wrestle an empty out of a foam cozy. That was the whole idea behind the holiday—a rest from one's labors. When the girls were younger, they'd barbecue at the park, then motor out around dusk with everyone else to the middle of the harbor and wait for the fireworks. Kim loved the big booms, clapping in the gap between the flash and the concussion, while Lindsay covered her ears. It hadn't been that long ago—six or seven years. His mother was still living in the old house then, drinking secretly, her sight just beginning to fade, and again it seemed to him that everything around him had changed drastically while he'd stayed the same. It wasn't true, of course, though his decline, being financial, had taken place privately, hidden in debt refinancing and title transfers, a sudden shift of a balance sheet. That was the market—it fluctuated. If he didn't think it would rebound, he'd have quit years ago and moved them to Florida. No matter how bad it got, he had to believe the lake would always bring people back.

His last thoughts before seeing her were generally this desperate, as if he might better understand his life in relation to hers and somehow justify leaving her there. He didn't need Rich—the success, who never visited—to tell him he should be taking care of her. It was just that with Kim missing, he already felt stretched thin.

"Quit biting your lips," Fran said, and patted his thigh.

"Sorry."

They turned the last curve and the complex spread on their left, commanding a slight rise, its low white wings radiating from a cupolaed rotunda, efficient as a chickenhouse. BRIGHTVIEW HOME, read the ranch-style arch above the entrance. On both sides of the drive, almost choreographed, two uniformed workmen rode identical mowers over the lush, sprawling lawn, and by the flagpole near the front doors a gardener was weeding a thriving bed of geraniums. Initially the home's attention to buildings and grounds had been a selling point, but now the institutional neatness depressed him, so much window dressing. The real life was inside.

To his surprise the visitor's lot was almost full. He imagined these other families were like them, taking this last opportunity to see their loved ones before the regimen of work and school kicked in.

"It's going to be a zoo," he said.

"I've seen it worse," Fran said, and motioned for Lindsay to remove her earbuds.

He carried the basket, grateful to have something to hide behind. Walking in, he always felt exposed, his mere presence an admission, as if he was the only son to leave a parent here. The receptionist at the front desk asked for his mother's room number and called ahead to the nurses' station to make sure she was ready. No one accompanied them down the long hallway—carpeted and uncomfortably quiet—and he was aware of Lindsay sticking close, as if they might ditch her. The walls were a pleasing shade of coffee, with cream chair rails, and between every other door stood a tripod table with a bonsai tree or African violet, yet as much effort as the designers had put into the place they couldn't disguise that in essence it was a hospital. The beds gave it away—fitted with protective rails and wired with call buttons.

His mother's door was open, an aide he recognized from last time helping her stow her tape player and the book she was listening to. She seemed thinner, wasted, the curve of her scalp visible beneath a teased puff of hair. Though it was easily seventy-five degrees, she had a blanket over her lap. Before he said a word, she cocked her head as if sensing some inaudible vibration, then reached her good hand toward him. "Eddie."

Fran took the basket so he could hold her.

She could only raise one arm, the other lay limp in her lap. "I'm so sorry, Eddie," she said, her breath in his ear. She smelled strongly of alcohol—no, butterscotch. She kept his hand as he straightened up, as if afraid he'd run away. "I told Betty here, all we can do is hope."

"How are *you* doing, Grace?" Fran asked loudly, bending to kiss her cheek and present her with the mints.

"Fran, really, you didn't have to do that. Goodness. Thank you. As for me, I'm afraid the news isn't good. Dr. Ray says he wants to test my…my…oh gosh, what do you call it? You know." She appealed to Betty, who didn't know. "My thing. My liver. He wants to check my liver function. Did I tell you, we saw you on TV the other night. Everyone was very impressed."

Fran stepped aside and Lindsay bowed down and hugged her grandmother.

"How tall are you now?" she asked, patting her shoulders. "My God, she's an Amazon."

There weren't enough chairs for them to sit so they stood around her, catching up. The room was furnished with pieces from the old house— the cherrywood secretary where his mother kept her checkbook and stamps, the marble-topped table from the front hall, the hutch from the dining room, complete with dishes he'd eaten off as a boy. On top of his father's dresser, beside a black-and-white photo of his parents cutting their wedding cake, stood a framed portrait of Kim and Lindsay in matching bumblebee dance outfits, springy heart-topped antennae poking from their heads. There were other shots of Kim on the walls, alone or with Lindsay, even a few with all the grandchildren, pictures of himself and Rich as kids, and one of his mother as a little girl in a belted winter coat and a muff, standing on the running board of a long touring car. Normally her gallery didn't bother him, but now instead of a comfort the past was just loss, and he suggested they go outside and find a spot by the pond before they were all taken.

"I'm afraid you're going to have to help your old mother up. I've been having trouble with my legs."

As Betty set the folded blanket on the bed and helped him lift her, he was surprised by how light she was. Her ankles were thick with fluid, but her upper body was a husk.

"Did you want a chair?" Betty asked.

"We're okay," he said automatically. His mother could walk, she was just slow and a bit unsteady, and had been since her sight had deteriorated.

"If you need me for anything, just buzz the desk."

"Thank you," Fran said, and took her place, giving his mother her elbow to hold.

Suspended between them, his mother bent forward at the waist, as if looking down at her feet as she lifted one and then, with effort, the other. She was wearing brand-new white Nike trainers, which they encouraged here for safety, but which looked utterly foreign on her, a woman who considered jogging silly.

"I don't know," she said after a few tentative steps. "A chair might be easier."

"Would you rather have the chair?" he asked.

"If it's no bother. This thing with my legs has been getting worse. It has to do with the . . ." Her good hand fluttered, searching for the word. "With the blood getting down there. I can't think of it now. I have to wear these socks all the time."

"Compression hose," Fran said.

"Even when I'm sleeping."

"It could be phlebitis."

"That's not it."

"They're probably worried about blood clots."

"You'd know better than I would," his mother said, as if the condition was temporary. "I swear it's something new every week around here."

Betty helped them get her into the chair, kneeling to set her shoes on the footrests, and he rolled her down the hall, Lindsay walking ahead to press the oversized button that activated the door. He had to hunch to push the chair, and couldn't avoid the pink, mottled patches on his mother's scalp, the blue veins encased in waxen, almost translucent skin. He recalled his grandmother Biggs the last time he saw her, at his grandfather's funeral, shriveled in a wheelchair, her face a lumpy net of wrinkles behind her veil, but powdered, her cheeks and lips artificially red. He and Rich stood before her in their church clothes—white shirts and clip-on ties, hard shoes. She reached out for them to each take a hand, then pulled them close. Her voice was a raspy whisper. "You need to be good for your mother," she said, as if it was a secret. "You're all she has now." At the time and for years afterward he wanted to think it wasn't true, but honestly it always was. Since his father died they were all she had, just as she was all they had, like it or not. He hadn't always been good, though that was a long time ago. Surely by now he'd paid for his sins against her.

Outside, families strolled the paths, the grandchildren conspicuous, at the periphery. Mostly there were couples, a single child visiting a parent, and he was glad Fran and Lindsay were there.

The koi pond was the centerpiece of the grounds, spring-fed and murky green, the thick orange and white fish rising to kiss the surface. The path snaked through stands of bamboo and cherry trees along the manicured banks. As he'd thought, their favorite spot was taken, but after a short walk they found a bench in the shade of a Japanese maple and Fran spread a blanket on the grass.

"Delicious," his mother said of the chicken salad, though she managed only a few bites. Lindsay opened the mints and poured her a handful. "Oh, that's too many," she said, and, sucking each one until it was gone, proceeded to eat them all.

Somehow—as if she subscribed to a satellite radio station dedicated to their old lives—she had news of neighbors and childhood friends he could no longer recall. Daniel Shostak's father had passed away. The Normans' youngest daughter, who went to Case for astrophysics, was interning with NASA in Cleveland this summer. Her interest in others reassured him, though she regularly groped for what she wanted to say. The gaps were noticeable, and she prolonged them by circling the missing word until they were all stumped.

"That's what happens when you get old," she joked, but it seemed clear that she was foggier than usual, and he racked his memory of his last visit for signs he might have missed.

The afternoon was long, and as hard as they all tried to avoid it, ultimately they had to talk about Kim. While he'd kept his mother informed, he hadn't gone into any real detail regarding the investigation, not merely because he didn't want to upset her, but because he knew she would have her own ideas on how it should be handled—as if the police actually listened to them. Now when she brought up the possibility of her paying for a private detective, Lindsay asked if she could go get a water from the machine inside, and with a finger Fran signaled that she'd go with her.

"Do you think it's too late?" his mother asked when they were gone.

Though he was sure it wasn't her intention, the question hurt him. It was unfair of her to lay the matter out so plainly.

"I'm not sure what bringing in someone from outside would accomplish at this point."

"That's just it, you don't know. Someone from outside might see things differently."

He wanted to tell her this wasn't TV, but said he'd consider it, and thanked her for the offer.

"If you're worried about the money—"

"I'm not worried about the money."

"Because you and your brother are going to get it all anyway. You might as well use it when it can make a difference."

"I'll think about it."

"Please do," she said. "I may not be of much use anymore, but I can at least do this for her."

Her offer was sincere and not the ultimatum he might have seen it as in the past. As the oldest grandchild, Kim had been her favorite. From the beginning she'd seen herself in her, taking credit for her facility with numbers and love of drawing, even her good skin, and while Fran chafed at her claims, he could see some merit to them. The two were at once headstrong and defensive, at the mercy of their own showy emotions yet intensely private, blowing up and then retreating into themselves. Like Kim, his mother would always be a mystery to him.

While they were alone they talked about the tests Dr. Ray wanted her to take. So far the doctor was dumbfounded (her word). Her symptoms were consistent with someone exposed to benzene or some other industrial solvent over a long period. She made it sound like a riddle, her case one of a kind. He didn't ask if she'd told the doctor about her drinking, as if those years had no effect on her liver, and then, in midthought, realized how cold he was being. Directly across the pond a father and son were playing chess on a bench, their legs crossed, jaws propped on fists like twins, and he wondered what they weren't saying to each other. Every family here, he thought, somehow they were all trying to keep the illusion of normal life going. At this point what couldn't be forgiven?

He held tight to the idea through the rest of the afternoon and then dinner in the ballroom-like dining hall, using it to soothe his impatience to get back to Kingsville and Kim. Visiting his mother wasn't an inconvenience, it was a privilege, and he needed to be grateful. After dessert Fran and Lindsay were ready to go, but followed along as he took her outside a last time to watch the fireflies rise from the garden.

"Are there many of them?" she asked, peering into the twilight.

"Lots."

"All we can do is hope," she said. "Isn't that right?"

They said good-bye in her room. He was the last, bending down so she could kiss him, her wrinkled palm soft on his cheek.

"Bless you, dear," she said.

"I'll talk to you this week," he promised.

In the car, headed down the drive, he thought this was the one unpardonable thing—leaving her there, the same way J.P. and Nina and Elise had abandoned Kim. He imagined bringing her home to live with them. They could convert the den. Fran could recommend a nurse.

They turned onto the highway, swooped around the first curve, and the home vanished. It was dark in the hollows, and the longer they drove the more far-fetched his plan seemed.

"Thanks for coming," he told the car at-large.

"You're welcome," Fran said.

Lindsay was already lost in her iPod, and he took advantage of the privacy.

"How did she seem to you?"

"Okay," Fran said. "A little hazy, but that's normal."

"Is it?"

"For what she's been through."

"I don't remember her being that bad."

"Maybe she was having a bad day."

"Maybe," he said vaguely, as if he didn't believe it. He tried to picture a world without her, and without Kim. It didn't seem possible.

They passed the entrance for Devonwood and he flicked on his high-beams. The hills were black on both sides, the sky deepening. He wondered when the fireworks were starting.

"When are the fireworks supposed to start?" Fran asked.

"Don't do that!" he said, laughing. "I was just thinking that."

"Great minds."

"Freaky minds is more like it."

It was fully night by the time they reached the CVS and got on 90. The high lights threw shadows over Fran—silent beside him, absorbed in thought. They'd driven the route too many times with the girls in back, coming home from the old place or a Sea Wolves game, the two of them fighting, or when they were small, slumped against each other, snoring. At home he would carry Kim inside while Fran shouldered Lindsay, waiting until they were safely asleep to go out and close the doors.

A local unit must have just gotten back from Iraq—the overpasses were lined with signs. They crossed into Ohio (THE HEART OF IT ALL, the billboard said) and took the first exit, stopping at the top of the ramp, facing the Conoco. A truck was coming so they had to wait, the turn signal tinking. In the bright strip of the window, half-obscured by signs, a heavy guy in a red shirt was working the register—Kevin.

Minutes later as they sped along the dark flats of Route 7, headed north toward the lake, a green spider of light blossomed just above the horizon, then faded, followed by a burst of silver half lost in the trees.

"Look," Fran encouraged Lindsay, though from this distance they were no more than blotches of color.

He imagined the crowd down by the harbor, their faces tipped toward the sky, mouths open in anticipation, each new explosion tinting the surface of the water, and he wished they were there and part of it.

Impossible. That belonged to the past too, when their greatest cares had been braces and grades and makeup. They dipped down to cross the bridge and all they could see were faint traces of color edging the clouds like heat lightning, but as they crested the hill a single shell corkscrewed up, leaving a skimpy trail of sparks, and a huge orange chrysanthemum bloomed at eye level right in front of them, glittering, its center a delayed white flash that reached them seconds later as a muffled thump. Along Harbor families had turned off their porch lights and set up lawn chairs on their walks. There were no other cars, and cruising through with the rockets floating up beyond the end of the street, flaring and resolving into separate embers and then just smoke drifting on the wind, he thought he should be enjoying the show more. It was something they'd remember.

"Anyone want to stop?" he asked before the turn onto State.

Lindsay didn't answer.

"I think we've had enough excitement for one day," Fran said.

At home Lindsay put Cooper out, then disappeared upstairs. It wasn't that late, but Fran was tired.

"You must be too."

"A little," he admitted.

Like every night, she offered him a pill. This time he surprised her by accepting it. As he washed it down at the sink, he silently apologized to Kim. In bed, in the dark, with Fran asleep beside him, he thought it wasn't working and wondered if he needed another. He replayed the day from the beginning, a reflexive form of torture, sinking into his newest memories as if they were a dream. Now that it was over and he was alone, the whole thing seemed strange. The morning came back vividly, minute by minute, like scenes from an unsettling film. Coffee on the deck, the woman at the CVS, the geraniums by the flagpole. He was just bending down to kiss his mother's sunken cheek when, mercifully, he was gone.

Head Check

The first day of school, everyone stared at her like she was an alien. She verified it with Micah to make sure she wasn't being paranoid.

"What did you expect?" Micah said. "You're like a celebrity."

In the halls faces turned to follow her. People seemed surprised to see her, as if she should have stayed home—as if she should still be out looking. Mrs. Buterbaugh, her guidance counselor, caught her on the stairs and said she could come by her office anytime, never once mentioning Kim. Mr. Czepiel, her chemistry teacher, wore a ribbon on his pocket. In her new homeroom more than half of the girls had pink bracelets. She knew maybe four of them.

Harder to deal with were classmates who were almost but not quite friends—people she sat next to or whose lockers were beside hers, old lab partners and fellow flutists from the wind ensemble, kids from middle or even grade school. She knew them and they knew her enough to say hey as they passed in the halls, but now out of pity they felt obliged to stop and say they were sorry, and to prove it, that they'd volunteered at their church or been at the softball game or raised money in the fun run. She thanked them, aware that, like her parents, they were all trying to read her face for the slightest hint of a crack.

In the morning she drove the Subaru, her mother encouraging her from the passenger seat, but after school she took the bus, waiting in line and then sharing a bench with Dana. They got off at the same stop just before Thornwood and walked back toward her house. It wasn't until the bus pulled around the corner that she felt free, and then only for the minute they were alone together, unobserved, kicking the rotten crabapples into the middle of the street and making fun of the Bonners' new mailbox shaped like a goose ("That won't last long," Dana said). She wanted to hang out with Dana in her basement, watching Maury Povich and avoiding doing their homework while above them Mrs. Hedrick watched her soaps and talked on the phone, except her parents were both at home, waiting for her. If she was a minute late, they'd call out the National Guard.

"You gonna be online later?" Dana asked, peeling off.

"Probably," she said, and kept walking.

From the street her house looked uninhabited, the sun picking out individual shingles, underlining the white siding. The porch was shadowed, the windows dark. In the drive by itself sat the Subaru, meaning her father was out somewhere. She·crossed the lawn at a diagonal so only someone standing at the living room window could see her, then tiptoed up the side of the porch stairs as if she might sneak in undetected.

The screen door squeaked, setting off Cooper. He came charging through the front hall and stopped short, mussing the Oriental rug. He looked right at her, legs braced, and barked a warning.

"Who is it, Goober?" she asked, letting herself in. "Oh, that's right— it's *me*."

"Hey," her mother called from the rear of the house, then intercepted her as she dumped her backpack on the couch. "I hope you know that's not staying there. So? How did it go?"

"Okay."

"Is Micah in your French class?"

"Yeah."

"That's good, right? C'est bon, n'est-ce pas?"

"Oui," Lindsay said, deadpan.

"Any homework?"

"Just my driving stuff."

"Want something to eat?"

"No, we had these disgusting quesadillas for lunch."

"Maybe we can go driving later, if you're up for it."

She wasn't used to her mother being home this time of day. Normally these lazy hours were hers to waste in peace. Even before she disappeared, Kim was never around, though after what the paper said about the drugs, those absences, like the money in her puzzle box, had taken on new meaning. All by herself Lindsay might sing nonsense songs to Cooper the way her father did, or mutter over her homework, or heckle whatever dumb show was on TV, but the demands of actual two-way conversation were too much after dealing with the world, and she was relieved when her mother went back to whatever she was doing.

She dragged her backpack into the den, broke out her driver's manual and spent a half-hour not watching an awful *Deep Space Nine* and memorizing the chart of stopping distances. The written test was supposed to be easy, twelve multiple-guess questions. You could get three wrong and still pass. Kim had missed one, and Lindsay wanted to be perfect—or had before everything happened. Now it didn't matter.

There was no car for her to drive anyway. When Kim left for college the Chevette was supposed to be hers. Now it sat in the garage gathering dust. Whenever she thought of it, she remembered going to the Dairy Queen with her that last day, eating their burgers in the shade of the cemetery and wondering if Kim would really miss her. It seemed so long ago, not just this summer. Even if she could get past the memory, she couldn't ask her parents. She felt guilty just thinking about it.

She had the couch to herself, and spread out, lying longways with her arms crossed above her head and the clicker balanced on her stomach. After *Deep Space Nine* Spike showed three straight episodes of *The Next Generation*. She was in the middle of the second, a holo-deck adventure with Data as Sherlock Holmes, when her mother came in and asked if she was ready to drive.

"Come on, you need the practice."

Her road test was scheduled for Friday, so there was no excuse. She was planning on using the Subaru since it was smaller than the Taurus, easier to park and make three-point turns.

"Can we leave Cooper out?" she asked.

"Oh please," her mother said. "He loves his cage."

As she drove, her mother quizzed her from the manual, trying to trip her up with stopping distances. Lindsay could still picture the chart and rattled them off.

"Okay," her mother said, "here's one that's relevant: What do you do if your vehicle stalls on a railroad track?"

It was one of her favorites. "Get out, get off the tracks and run as far as you can in the direction of the train—*because*, if you run the other way, you could get hit with debris from your car when the train hits it."

"I don't think I've ever heard of that happening. What if your hood pops up while you're driving?"

"Roll down your window and use it to look out of, put on your flashers and pull off as soon as you can."

As long as her mother was asking her questions, she was safe, but the car was a trap. Eventually her mother would ask how she was feeling—a different kind of test—and she'd say she was okay, just worried about Kim, and her mother would say she was too. Lindsay wished they could stop there, the two of them balanced in agreement, but since the police had found Kim's car, her mother had changed. Instead of keeping up a front like her father, she would reach over and hold Lindsay and cry, which would make her cry, which wouldn't help anyone.

For some reason, her mother needed her tears. Sometimes she apologized afterwards, and sometimes, dabbing at her face with a tissue, she said she felt better, but Lindsay always felt used. She never cried by herself, only when her mother provoked her, as if she wanted her to be sad. Lindsay already was. She was sad for Kim and for J.P., for her mother and father, and for herself, but in her own way, unconnected to everyone else. Her sadness was hers, an inner temple where she worshipped alone, untouchable. She did her best to protect it, but each time she fended off one of her mother's break-in attempts, she felt contaminated and ungrateful.

They drove down through the park to the inlet and the far end of the marina where there was an empty stretch of curb. The only part of the road test she was worried about was parallel parking. She was okay with the Chevette, not great, and the Subaru was almost four feet longer. She had a habit of cutting the wheel too early when she was backing up, leaving the car a yard from the curb. The minimum to pass was eighteen inches.

"Okay," her mother said, "give me five good ones and we're done," as if it was that easy.

Her first two tries she didn't come close, and then she was up on the curb.

"Crud."

"It's okay," her mother said, pointing for her to go forward.

"I'm never going to get this."

"Yes you will. It's just a matter of practice."

"I only have three more days."

"Then we'll be out here for the next three days. Come on—five good ones. So far you've got zero."

She had two—and one sucked—when, offhand, her mother said, "I bet school was tough today, huh?"

She was concentrating on tucking the front of the car in and didn't respond.

"That's three," her mother said. "So, how bad was it? I can't go anywhere without people looking at me like I have three heads, and you have to deal with the whole school."

"It wasn't too bad."

"What does that mean?"

"It was okay. Everyone was trying to be nice."

"Don't you hate that?" her mother said. "You're angry and confused and everyone wants to be nice."

Lindsay sensed that she was fishing and just shrugged. "They don't know what to say. I mean, what do you say?"

"I'm sorry," her mother said, which was what Lindsay hated the most, since it wasn't her fault and she didn't know anything about it anyway, but on the way home, and later, watching TV with her father, Lindsay wondered if her mother was right, and if so, how she knew.

She might be angry. She wasn't confused.

It was a guess, she decided, another stab at cracking her open. From now on she'd have to be more careful.

She no longer had to worry about deleting her e-mails. Since J.P. had left for college, she'd written him every day. He hadn't written back. Dana said she could probably find his new address through the school directory, but Lindsay didn't want him to think she was stalking him. If he wanted to write her, he knew where she was.

Every night, syncing songs onto her iPod, she made herself invisible and IMd with Dana and Micah. Sometimes after they signed off she stayed on, seeing who else on her buddy list was still up. In the beginning, she used to end the day by checking Kim's website to see how many hits it had gotten. Now with the counter creeping toward a quarter million, she went to bed and imagined the site floating in space like an asteroid.

School didn't get any better, but her mother and father alternated days taking her out. Her father stood in the marina lot, in her blind spot, pretending to be a parked car, calling "Cut it," while Lindsay twisted her neck and curled the Subaru around him. "Don't think," he said. "See it and be it." It was the same advice he gave about hitting, yet here it seemed to work. She forgot about having to turn the wheel the opposite direction from the one she was looking and just followed the rear of the car as it slid into place. At dinner—because the test had become their main topic of conversation—he took credit for her improvement, making her shake her head. Thursday she went out with her mother after her flute lesson and was five-for-seven—so good that there was no time for prying questions.

"I'm impressed," her mother said.

"So am I," Lindsay said.

Friday at breakfast they asked if she was nervous. "I'll be taking you," her mother announced, as if they'd drawn lots. Her father had a meeting to go to, so Lindsay couldn't protest.

"You'll do great," he said, and squeezed her shoulder like she was up next.

At school she got ten-out-of-ten on her vocabulary in French, and then in Algebra 2 a hundred on her first quiz. She was used to doing well, but still took a neatnik's satisfaction in getting everything right.

She loved the little puzzles her math teachers gave for extra credit, and the chance that they were trick questions. She wasn't a grub, though Dana was partly right when she called her a show-off. She liked being smart, and for people to think she was. It was her one superpower. When Kim was messing up, Lindsay would leave her homeworks and tests on the kitchen table. Now she stuck them in her folder, but as the day passed, a notion took hold—crazy, maybe impossible, but one that appealed to the crossword lover in her.

So far, through her first week, she hadn't missed a single question. The written test was a cinch—she knew the manual by heart. If she could just nail the parking she'd be fine. Still she balked at issuing the challenge to herself. A year was a long time, and as her mother said once to soothe her, an A⁻ was a very respectable grade.

It didn't have to be the whole year. It could be a week, or a month. It could just be tomorrow. All she had to do was work hard every day—and that was what finally convinced her. Until they found Kim, she would be perfect.

"Hey, Rex Racer," Dana said as she split off for home. "Don't fuck up."

"I won't," Lindsay said. "Not that they'll ever let me drive anywhere by myself."

Inside, her mother was ready. As they crossed the back walk to the Subaru she tossed Lindsay the keys. "Last practice, babe. From now on it all counts."

The DMV was in a failing strip mall on Route 20, next to a carpet outlet that used to be a supermarket. The lot was dotted with potholes and loose patches. She turned in her forms and then waited among the short rows of attached fiberglass chairs, assessing the two guys her age as if they were her competition. Her mother had thought to bring a book. All Lindsay had was her manual.

Eventually an older woman with bronze hair and cat's-eye glasses on a chain called them into the next room.

"Break a leg," her mother said.

The written test was a single sheet. She assumed it would be standardized, with little footballs to fill in. Instead it was a spotty, cockeyed photocopy; they were supposed to just circle the letter. They could take as long as they wanted. When they were done they should bring their papers up to her desk. It was all insultingly casual.

The questions were right out of the manual—so easy that she doubted herself and had to retrace her steps, mentally flipping pages. Legally you could park within 15 feet of a fire hydrant, 20 of a crosswalk and 30 of a stop sign. She went over her answers three times and still she was the first one done. The woman looked up from her magazine and gestured to a chair beside the desk. Lindsay watched her grade her test, the tip of her pen zigzagging as it followed the answers down the page. When she reached the bottom she went back up to the top and wrote a zero.

"Have a seat," the woman said.

It was another half hour before a round, red-faced man in a polo shirt and khakis came in and took her paperwork from the woman, clipped it to his clipboard and called her name. He was shorter than her, with a buzzcut that didn't hide the island of his bald spot, and he was visibly sweating, as if he'd run there. He walked her through the waiting room past her mother, who gave her a thumbs-up.

He held the door open for her with the clipboard, then followed her out.

"Which one are you?" he asked.

Lindsay pointed as if she were afraid to speak.

She followed his lead, fastening her seatbelt before she started the car. As she let off the parking brake he marked something on his clipboard.

"This is the road test," he said, still writing. "What that means, Lindsay, is that we're going to take you out on the road and see how you drive in everyday situations. How you feeling there?"

"Good."

"Do me a favor, okay? Take a deep breath."

She tried and discovered her chest was tight.

"Give me one more, I didn't hear that one. Good. Now what we're going to do is go to the store. Mom's run out of ketchup, and she's send-ing you to get some. You know where the Wal-Mart is?"

"Yes."

"We'll head that way to start."

Route 20 was busier than any of the streets she'd practiced on, and faster. She stayed in the right lane, keeping to the speed limit while cars shot past.

"We'll take a right here at the light," he said, pointing with his pen, though the Wal-Mart was straight ahead.

The light was green. She signaled and slowed and fed the top arc of the steering wheel from hand to hand instead of crossing her arms, roll-ing smoothly through the turn, making sure she didn't swing wide.

"And a left up here."

He took her through a section of Ashtabula she'd never seen before, a shady maze of back streets with neat lawns and cars parked on both sides. For a while they went in circles. Over and over she waited her turn at four-way stop signs. He made her zip down her window and show him the hand signals.

"Okay, Lindsay," he said in a cul de sac she imagined he'd used be-fore, "give me your best three-point turn." When she was done he asked her to explain the proper way to park on a hill. As they cruised through the narrow blocks she kept expecting him to pick a tight spot and order her to parallel park, but he guided her out of the neighborhood and back onto 20 West.

"Mom needs ketchup," he said.

At the Wal-Mart, in a far corner of the lot, he had her park the car head-in—too simple. He didn't bother to open the door to see if she was between the lines.

"Take us home," he said.

On the way back she thought he would have her pull into the drive of Edgewood High or the new Home Depot, but he was busy writing.

As they came up on the plaza, he told her to get in the left lane. When she did, he said, "Head check. When you change lanes you need to check your blind spot. You want to look out for that."

She could have sworn that she had. She'd checked her rearview mirror and then her side mirror and there was no one there.

She had to wait for a wave of oncoming traffic before she turned, and then, with another group bearing down on them, gave it too much gas, the engine revving as they lunged across and into the lot.

"Sorry," she said.

"It's okay. We made it back in one piece."

He had her park the car in the same spot and turn it off. While she waited, wondering why she ever thought she could do anything, he silently went over the sheet, finally signing it and handing it to her. "Congratulations, Lindsay."

"Thank you," she said, and shook his hand.

The form had nothing but checkmarks on it. He hadn't taken off for either of her mistakes, and she felt cheated. He probably thought he was being nice. He *was* nice. The problem was all hers, and perverse.

Her mother was waiting for her inside.

"Well?"

"I passed."

"Hooray!" her mother said.

Where She Was

Right outside Geneva, two kids taking a shortcut through the woods behind a rundown motel found the body.

The land was boggy, a dumping ground for broken toilets and rusted hot-water heaters and rotten box springs. They were walking along when one of them noticed a sneaker lying in the mud with a gray sock sticking from it. When they looked closer they saw the sock was a flap of skin.

Apparently the body had been buried but animals had dug it up, scattering the pieces. It was badly decomposed, barely identifiable as female. The Geneva police needed someone to send them Kim's dental records.

Fran was home to take the call, and got Ed on his cell.

"Do the clothes match?" he asked.

"They didn't say anything about clothes."

"What about the sneakers?"

"They didn't say."

"Do they have the flyer?"

"I don't know. They called me and I called you."

"Fax them the flyer."

"I'm going to." For an instant she was annoyed that he felt he had to tell her. He was just afraid.

"I'll be right home."

Though it wouldn't make any difference, she said, "Good."

They'd prepared for this day. Early on she'd put together an ID kit. Now she pulled it out, setting aside the baggie with Kim's hairbrush, and found the copy of her X-rays from Dr. Knowles. The action attracted

Cooper, who watched from the doorway, unsure, then retreated to his usual spot under the dining room table.

After the fax went through and she was boxing everything up, she was tempted to pluck a strand from the brush and rub it between her fingers, to string it between her lips like floss and taste it—anything to bring Kim closer. As a mother she thought she should be able to feel it if one of her children was lost or in pain, a kind of psychic link, but she felt only the same disorienting panic she'd borne the last two months. This couldn't be the end. Like Ed, she wanted to believe they'd made a mistake, when she knew from experience that sometimes the worst did happen, and, most cruelly, for no reason.

She called them to make sure they got the fax.

They had.

"Did you get the flyer?"

"Yes, ma'am," the sergeant said.

"Can you tell me if the sneakers she was wearing were Asics?"

"I'm sorry, we can't release any details until the medical examiner finishes his investigation."

"When will that be?"

"I can't speak for his office, ma'am."

"Do you have a number where I can reach him?"

Like every bureaucracy, they protected their own from those they were supposed to serve. He transferred her to the officer in charge, whose robotic voicemail immediately picked up. She controlled herself, trying to sound reasonable, asking him to please call them and slowly enunciating their phone number, closing with a professional thank you.

She waited for Ed at the living room window the way, years ago, she used to watch for the school bus. Framed by the porch, a squirrel tight-roped across the telephone wire and stopped, its tail flicking. Though it was just past lunch, she was tired, and her mind circled the inert fact of the body, unable to reduce it to an abstract. When he pulled in she rushed out to meet him, flinging the screen wide, making Cooper bark as if he were an intruder.

He quizzed her again, and though he nodded along and said she'd done exactly what he would have, he still had to call them himself—as if he might get a different answer. He hung up without saying a word.

There was nothing they could do but wait—a position she knew too well.

"What should we tell Lindsay?" she asked, because she'd be home soon.

"We'll tell her when we actually know something."

It was at once fair and dishonest. She was a terrible liar (she often joked that she'd never make it as a realtor), and didn't see how she could keep this from her, yet there was no sense upsetting her if it wasn't Kim.

In the lull before the bus, she went back to the new post she was writing for the website, thanking their sponsors for supporting the Kare-a-Van. The sentence she'd left off working on gushed about "the wonderful event," though it had rained and the turnout had been disappointing, and she realized that without intending to she'd become a politician. Her gratitude was genuine, but so was her grief, yet she showed the public only her bright side, always conscious of Jocelyn's warning that people wanted her to be strong. She was tired of being the brave mother. The fundraising mother. And anyway, nothing anyone had done had actually helped (not true, she knew, even before she completed the thought).

If this was Kim, she would have to go on. They would all have to go on, somehow.

If this wasn't her, they would go on hoping.

There was no choice, only those two possibilities, and she feared that at some point she would no longer see the second as preferable. It had been two months and already she was crumbling. What would she be like after two years, or ten?

Her own father had died when she was just four, and while she could see how his absence had shaped her, and she had mourned him her entire life, she didn't know him. In a way, the damage was imaginary. Her mother fed her memories and displayed his picture on the mantel, and sometimes when Fran was alone in the house she stood on the hearth and peered into his eyes (she didn't dare touch the frame), trying to conjure his voice. Kim came to her unbidden, at any age. She recalled her as a newborn, just home from the hospital, when they were living in the little rental on Mitchell Place with the train tracks in the backyard, and Grace, still strong then, bathing her in the sink, trickling palmfuls of water onto her wispy cap of hair. In the basement their old photo albums waited in the dark, and in the den, on obsolete tapes, dozens of birthday parties and dance recitals and family vacations (Kim and Lindsay playing *Titanic* on the bow of the Put-in-Bay ferry). Maybe someday she would need them, but for now her memory was mercilessly sharp, and when a favorite image of Kim bubbled up she was careful not to hold on to it too long. The past was as fraught as the future. *One Day at a Time,* Terry Benjamin had counseled, *just like AA,* and it was true; at her best she inched along like someone in recovery, working on small things while recognizing the enormity of her problems. It was just hard.

She was still fixing the post when she heard the bus go by. A few minutes later Cooper barked and charged for the front door. The screen squeaked and she heard Lindsay telling him to get down. For a second Fran froze with her head turned, her fingers poised over the keyboard, then pushed herself up. It would be easier not to talk to her, but she didn't want to seem suspicious.

She intercepted her as she sloughed her backpack onto the couch.

"I'm going to move it," Lindsay said.

"How was work?"

"Boring."

"Got a lot of homework?"

"Not a lot."

She was glum to the point of rudeness, and Fran didn't know how much of it was merely her being sixteen. Her arms were so thin Fran worried that she might be anorexic, but bugging her to eat would only provoke the opposite reaction. Kim was just as stubborn.

"Look who it is," Ed said, coming through the dining room. He held his arms straight out in a parody of greeting, enveloping Lindsay in a hug she tolerated without returning. "D'you have a good day?"

"No."

"Okay, glad I asked," he said, releasing her and holding up both hands as if he'd been burned. "How was your Chem test?"

"Easy."

"That's good," he said, as if it proved his point. Fran hadn't known about the test, and, stung, wondered how he did.

Lindsay looked from him to her as if they were purposely annoying her. "I'm going to watch TV, if that's okay."

"Knock yourself out," Ed said.

"It wouldn't be on the news, would it?" Fran asked him in the kitchen.

"I don't think she's watching the news."

"It could be on a newsbreak."

"Check online. If it's there it'll be on the news."

It wasn't—"Yet," she said.

If the police had released it to the press, he reasoned, there'd be reporters crawling all over the place.

Without any real information they had to fall back on probability. The latest the lab would operate was likely five. As the hour approached, the phone rang. Ed hustled in from his office to be with her as she picked up.

It was Connie. Fran was supposed to call her earlier to set up lunch tomorrow.

"Sorry."

"What's up?" Connie asked. "You sound stressed."

"Nothing," she said. "The usual."

Connie understood. At this point Fran didn't need an excuse to cancel their plans.

After five it was time to make dinner. She allowed herself a glass of pinot grigio, sipping as Rachel Ray fixed something much nicer than she was cobbling together. When the rice was done, she turned off the TV and called them in, setting out napkins and silverware on the counter.

They ate on the deck. Lindsay hardly talked. Fran wondered if she knew, and—swayed by her second glass—if it wouldn't be better to just tell her.

"You know what tonight is?" Ed said, excited.

No one answered, the shtick was so old.

"That's right: Garbage night!"

"Great," Lindsay said, but after they did the dishes she rolled the big-wheeled can down to the curb while Ed lugged the recycle bin. Fran took the chance to doublecheck the internet. They were safe for now.

Like every night, she was ready to go to bed by eight, her body antici-pating the drop into unconsciousness. While she couldn't imagine sleep-ing without them, she understood the pills were an evasion—a crutch, her mother would say—but after facing her worst fears all day, she'd be damned if she'd wrestle them all night. She waited until nine thirty to go up, wishing Lindsay good night, and then, on the stairs, reflected that only a few years ago Lindsay would have demanded a kiss.

She took her pill and got ready for bed, frowning at the drift of her thoughts as she sat on the john. The room was stifling, and she closed the windows and switched on the air conditioner. In minutes she was cold, and had to pull a blanket over her side of the bed. Lying there wait-ing for the drug to take effect, she thought of the dark lab with its tables and scales and gurneys. She'd never been afraid of the morgue in the basement of the hospital—tiled and bright, with brushed steel sinks and a boom box tuned to KGO—but she'd never had anyone in it. Geneva was two towns down the lake; they could have been there twenty min-utes after she got the call. Did the police really think they wouldn't rec-ognize their own child? (Kim had a strawberry mole just inside her left hipbone, and a small white scar below her knee where she'd fallen on a broken pop bottle on the sledding hill behind the middle school.) She remembered the woman who saw her car in line at the drive-thru at Wendy's and wondered how far it was from where they found the body. She thought of Wozniak's farm. She wanted to close off the possibility that it was Kim, but couldn't with so little evidence, and so she went round and round with the air blowing on her and the covers tucked to her chin until, finally, sleep descended like a heavy curtain, blotting out her thoughts.

In the morning the first few minutes were like waking from sedation. Her body responded awkwardly, her mind wiped clean, like a sponged-off chalkboard. She had no memory of last night's anxieties, or of Ed coming to bed, just a visceral appreciation for the blank, restorative hours in-between. It was only in the shower, the water pelting her, that the world returned, and by the time she toweled off and got dressed she was at the mercy of circumstances again, her lips pinched. Downstairs in the laundry room, she spilled Cooper's food, one brick-colored nugget sinking to the bottom of his water dish. She stopped and sighed before fishing it out.

Lindsay was running late, and came down with wet hair and dark rings under her eyes, an erupted zit on one wing of her nose. Though it was the end of summer her skin was white as paste. Fran offered to make her eggs, but she just grabbed a Nutrigrain bar and stuck it in her backpack. If she noticed that Fran didn't have the TV on, she didn't say anything.

They kept the radio off while Lindsay drove. She was getting better, though Fran still watched the road as if she were at the wheel, alert to developments three or four cars ahead. As they neared the high school, they fell in line behind a bus, following along as it stopped to pick up her classmates, and only lost it when it swung into the circle by the front doors while they continued around back.

"Good job," Fran said, as Lindsay set the emergency brake and they both unbuckled. The drop-off was as chaotic as an airport loading zone. Ahead and behind them kids were piling out of SUVs and minivans. The one rule was to keep the line moving. By the time Fran got around to her door, Lindsay was already walking away. "Have a good day," Fran called after her. Lindsay flung a halfhearted wave over her shoulder and kept going.

In the car she was alone again, and though it had been her mission, as she drove home she thought it was wrong to feel relief at being rid of her. That was the exact opposite of what she wanted.

Ed was dressed and eating his cereal. He'd come to the same idea by himself: Should they go over there and wait?

She'd seen too many families keeping doomed vigils to think it would help, yet she was willing to go with him if he wanted. There was nothing that pressing here.

He sat back and covered his face, rubbing his eyebrows with his fingertips. "Let me call them first."

She stood watching him dial, thinking, illogically, that she should have been more protective of her, kept a better eye on her friends, asked more questions. She should have been home more. She should have talked with her instead of getting upset and yelling.

It was taking too long. He shook his head at her, then turned and left a message.

"They probably send their tests out," she said. "A place that small."

"I wish they'd tell us *some*thing."

They probably weren't allowed to—just as Records weren't allowed to give out patient information—but she said, "I know," and held him.

"What are we going to do?" he said.

They waited. They worked. She found the body online, in that morning's Geneva *Sentinel-Gazette*:

POLICE FIND BODY,
SAY DEATH SUSPICIOUS

A body was found behind the former Driftwood Inn Tuesday and police say they are treating the death as "suspicious." The state police Major Crime squad was aiding in the investigation.

Police said they were called to 96 Austinburg Road about 1 p.m. Tuesday. No information was available about the identity of the person or the cause of death.

Though it was no more than a police press release, she printed it out to show him.

"Well that's helpful," he said.

"I'm surprised the *Star-Beacon* hasn't called."

"You're giving them too much credit."

When the phone rang just after nine, she hoped it was them. She was closest, and picked up on the second ring.

"Hello?"

"Is this Mrs. Larsen?" a man asked.

"Yes it is."

"Mrs. Larsen, I'm Lieutenant Greer with the Geneva Police Department." He paused as if it were a question. Ed was beside her now, leaning in to read her face. She nodded at him. "Mrs. Larsen?"

"Yes, sorry. My husband's going to get on the other line."

"That's fine."

"Okay," Ed said from the living room.

"First off, I should let you know that right now I've got no news for you. At this point we're still waiting on the lab results. I can't give you a fix on when they'll have those, I'm hoping this morning. What I'd like to do is ask you a few questions, if that's all right."

She wanted to ask him where he was yesterday, and why he didn't have the decency to call them, but went along with it.

Her height, her weight, her hair and eyes, her birthdate. It seemed he was creating a whole new profile from scratch.

He asked about Kim's clothes, as if they weren't clearly listed on the flyer. Her shoes, her socks, her jeans, her underwear. His voice was flat and lulling, and as he slowly went over each item, her focus locked on a box of Fig Newtons in the basket on top of the microwave. He asked twice about her shirt, a baby blue Old Navy tee she'd bought for herself. Fran remembered saying she could buy a lifetime supply at Wal-Mart for that, and Kim giving her a put-upon look—sensible, out-of-touch Mom. Now, paralyzed by the Fig Newtons, she wondered if it was missing, or if she'd been strangled with it.

"Are you asking because your people have found something?" Ed asked.

"I'm just trying to verify the description."

He was just being thorough, she supposed, but when they got off she wondered if he was fishing for something else, the long, offhand interrogation designed to isolate a single detail they might not think was meaningful.

"What do you think?" she asked.

"He didn't ask about the jewelry."

"Is that good?"

"Logically metal's going to last longer than fabric."

"Why was he so interested in the shirt?"

"I don't know," he said. "Maybe it's all they've got."

Before she could block it, her mind flashed an image of Kim on the ground in just her shirt. Her hair covered her eyes, and her feet were dirty.

"I can't do this," she said.

"Maybe they've got a different shirt and want to make sure. That could explain it."

"Stop." He was trying to be hopeful for her. It only reminded her that for all of their research they knew nothing.

It was impossible to do any serious work, and she busied herself with laundry, sorting it from the hamper in their humid bedroom, aware of the phone on the night table and Ed downstairs in his office. Cooper nosed at the piles. When she came back up after starting the darks, he was splayed across the whites.

"I don't think so," she said, and then, when he didn't understand, stomped her foot and shouted "Get!" and he slunk away like a coyote.

She tried not to watch the clock, but there were so many in the house that she couldn't avoid them all, and anyway, there was no guarantee the results would be done by noon. Still, it felt like a countdown. Every second she expected the phone to ring, until she thought she would be relieved when it actually did.

She wasn't. She was in the middle of changing their sheets, and froze, looking up from tucking in a corner. It rang only once, meaning Ed had picked up. She waited, listening, as if she could hear through the floor.

The odds were that it was a false alarm—Connie or the *Star-Beacon* or Channel 12.

He was moving, headed for the front of the house. "Franny!" He sounded excited, and she thought that was good.

"What?" she called, playing dumb.

The stairs thundered. He was coming up fast—because he had to tell her face-to-face.

She didn't go to meet him, she just stood by the unmade bed. He came rushing down the hall with the phone in one hand. She didn't have to hear him say it. He was flushed and shaking his head as if he couldn't believe what he'd heard.

"It's not her."

"It's not her," she said, to make sure.

"It's not her."

He hugged her as if they'd won something.

"Thank God," she said.

He was still on the phone with the police. She let him go and sat down on the bed, her face in her hands, breathing in and out. The relief she felt was total, and though she knew that the body was someone else's daughter, and this reprieve was only temporary, for now she was grateful. She squeezed her hands under her chin, fingers interlaced, like a child. "Thank you," she said, ignoring Cooper's puzzled look.

Three weeks later they would do it all over again.

Immediate Occupancy

In October, after a last, perfect weekend, the weather turned. The days were bright but the light was thin, the sun lower in the sky, and gone by dinnertime. The nights were cold, the radio broadcasting frost warnings. As if it were a signal, Fran went back to work. Reluctantly, he followed.

When he walked into the office, Peggy seemed surprised to see him. She came around her desk and hugged him, patting his back. He reciprocated to let her know he was okay. Behind her, Jeri and Phil had made their way up the aisle, waiting for their turn. It was more ceremony than he wanted—inescapable, he supposed, and their condolences were heartfelt. They all knew Kim. He couldn't fault them for feeling sorry for him, even if he needed to resist it.

It was strange to be back at his desk after so long. The picture of the four of them on the boat from last Memorial Day stood prominently in the far corner, like an advertisement for the town. On the wall, neatly spaced, hung his softball teams. His Simpsons page-a-day calendar—a Christmas present from Lindsay—still displayed the date of Kim's disappearance, and as he tore off wads of gags he would never laugh at, he wondered if his colleagues still registered it in passing, or if it was just one small facet of his absence.

The office itself was quiet. He'd missed the tail end of the season, the last-minute flurry to nail down a place before the school year started. The listings were skimpy: shabby prefabs out in the boonies, summer cottages and high-end leftovers whose owners had been slow to lower their prices. Jeri and Phil had brought in a few new-to-market exclusives, and while they were fair game and he was eager to get back into the action, he'd been gone so long that he didn't want to straight vulture them. He needed to see what was out there and be patient.

That first day, he noticed everyone's phone was ringing but his. Peggy probably thought she was protecting him. "Hey," he said, sticking his head into the aisle. "I'm here too."

"It's like I'm the greenhorn," he told Fran that night.

"They're just worried about you."

"I'm not there for the therapy."

"The first day's the hardest," she said. "It'll get better."

It didn't. The market was daunting for someone trying to make a new start, and though they did their best to make him feel welcome, he wasn't fully there. He leaned toward the weekend and the promise of the next event, as if it might make a difference.

It was easier for Fran. Connie and Jocelyn had been part of the search from the beginning, and knew exactly where Fran was at. While he got along with everyone at his office, he didn't consider them friends. He might shoot a round of golf with Phil, or take Jeri to lunch at the diner, and they'd bitch and gossip and have a laugh, but he never shared his problems with them. They were colleagues bound by circumstance and the common ambition to make money, but he didn't know them, and they didn't know him. It was how he'd lived his life since he was a child—how everyone lived, he'd thought—showing the world only as much as he felt was safe and keeping the rest to himself. Even in his worst moments, he tried to project the illusion that everything was fine—impossible now, yet he went on smiling and shaking hands and joking, all the time knowing that people realized it was a front. He could no longer be that Ed Larsen, but, through a lack of imagination or just sheer exhaustion, he couldn't come up with a new one, and faked his way through the days like a bad actor, hardly believing himself.

Toward the end of a long afternoon during his second week, he was alone in the office when Peggy transferred a call. It was a woman in Pittsburgh whose mother had recently passed away: Anna DeMarco. Since he'd been back he regularly combed the death notices and probate cases, and he recognized the name. The daughter had grown up in the house and would have loved to keep it, but couldn't realistically. He offered his sympathies and signed her to a six-month exclusive.

The house was on Buffalo, one in a row of Dutch Colonials across the park from the Railroad Museum, convenient to everything. Like most of Kingsville's older neighborhoods, it dated from the steel boom of the twenties—cookie cutter houses on small lots for mill workers and their families. For all their charmless boxiness, the interiors had honest-to-God plaster walls and dark oak woodwork that builders couldn't duplicate today. They also had the original 60 amp service with aluminum wiring and screw-in fuses. He'd handled dozens over the years, in varying condition. Mrs. DeMarco had lived alone there since the mid-seventies. He expected obsolete floral wallpaper, avocado appliances and a colony of squirrels in the eaves.

It was too late to get the keys from her lawyer, but he stopped by the place anyway. The first thing he noticed, besides the wooden wheelbarrow planter on the lawn, was that the grass was shaggy. He needed to get the landscapers over there before he could take a picture.

The roof looked new, the gutters and downspouts vinyl, meaning they'd been replaced recently. Beige vinyl siding, which would put off anyone looking for something quaint or historic. And yes, once he came closer, vinyl windows. Like so many elderly homeowners, Mrs. De-Marco had paid to make her house as ugly and maintenance-free as possible. He'd helped his mother do the same thing, covering the cracked and knotty clapboards that leaked whenever it stormed, permanently solving the problem. He regretted it every time he visited.

In back there was a mossy patio, a concrete birdbath coated with dried black slime, and beside the cinderblock garage at the far end of the yard, a wilted garden fenced with chickenwire. Hung from nylon fishing line strung between the corner posts, foil pie pans twisted in the wind. As he surveyed the yards on both sides—toys in one, dogshit in the other—he caught a shrunken old woman with a broom two houses down watching him from her stoop. He waved to show he was no threat. She bent her head and went back to sweeping. Again he thought of his mother and her neighborhood, how quickly it had turned over—so fast that he no longer knew anyone on their street, when as a child he could name every family, their houses and yards an extension of them.

As a realtor he couldn't afford to be sentimental. For the sellers, for better or worse, the past was over. They were done here, gone, taking their possessions and memories, leaving behind a useful shell. What he was selling was the future. The question he wanted buyers to contemplate—not merely to guarantee a sale, but for their own sake—was: Do you think you'll be happy here? He didn't have to answer the question, though sometimes by reflex he did. Now, looking at the small world of Anna DeMarco's backyard, he thought a young family could be very happy here.

At home Fran greeted him with Lindsay's first progress report—all A's—and to match her good news he told her about the listing. He hadn't meant to, as if saying it aloud might jinx his chances.

"Why does that name sound familiar?" Fran asked.

He didn't know, and though she laid a hand to the side of her face and shook her head, she couldn't place it.

"*I* know," she said, brightening, over dinner. "If it's the same person. Short, white hair in a bun, kind of rotund?"

"I never met her."

"You did too. She used to work at the library. At the checkout. She used to call the girls Pete and Re-Pete."

"The one with the wrist thingy?"

"That's her—Mrs. DeMarco. Her husband worked for Crawford Container. Her daughter was the big piano prodigy."

"That's who I talked to."

"She went to the Eastman School—how many times did we hear that? I don't think she ever made it to Carnegie Hall."

"She's in Pittsburgh," he said, "if that means anything."

"What's her name? We can Google her."

Dolores Kern was her name, yet he hesitated, protective of his client, and she laughed. "I'm just kidding."

He wasn't sure that she was, if only because now he was curious too. He remembered seeing articles about the daughter in the *Star-Beacon* every time she won a competition—a gaunt, serious girl with lank dark hair—but that had been twenty years ago. The mystery of other people's children. He thought it was a good sign he was still interested.

He'd scheduled the landscapers for early the next day, but it rained. He went over to get his interior shots anyway, and noticed, as he pulled in, that the asphalt drive had a few cracks that needed patching. The drainage around the foundation wasn't great; he'd ask the landscapers to regrade it with a few strategically placed bags of topsoil. The porch was in good shape, though he would have preferred a nicer mailbox than the cheap black sheet metal one with two jutting tusks underneath for a rolled newspaper. Another little thing: The spring of the screendoor was rusted a powdery orange. He could take care of that himself, and made a note to swing by the Home Depot.

Even before he fit the key in the lock he had a number in mind—middling and realistic, acknowledging both the soft market and the seller's hopes—that none of these cosmetic defects could touch. The same held true for the interior. Paint, wallpaper, carpet, even bad pressboard cabinets weren't a problem, since the buyer would replace them anyway. What could knock down the price, without argument, were the guts of the house. The condition of the exterior was no guarantee. He'd seen antique Chrysler furnaces the size of truck cabs in perfectly maintained homes, their octopuslike ductwork sheathed in the original asbestos insulation. In this case, given his own mother's paranoia over her gas bills, he expected the heating system to be new. The wiring and plumbing would be the wild cards.

Inside, the air was heavy and stale with mildew. He'd have to open it up once the rain stopped. He turned on the lights as he went. The walls were bare, the rooms empty. No awful wallpaper, just plain eggshell that showed every flaw but set off the oak woodwork nicely. The baby blue carpeting was worn in paths, bright patches outlining where furniture had sat for decades (in a corner of the living room there was a rectangular space perfect for an upright piano). It was ugly, but underneath lay hardwood floors. The curtains were gone, exposing old blinds the color of manila envelopes, their pull-rings hanging like tiny wreaths. The fridge was propped open with its crisper drawer, a box of baking soda on the top shelf. Whoever had cleaned the place had done a good job. He was used to trespassing on the overflowing and intimate wreckage of lives suddenly disrupted, but there was almost no trace of Mrs. DeMarco, just a blaze orange sticker on the telephone in the kitchen with the numbers for the police and fire departments. He peeled it off as best as he could, rubbing at the stubborn adhesive with his thumb, making a note to bring some solvent for the last tacky smears.

The basement was his destination, there was no sense stalling. He found the door and swiped at the light switch and the bottom of the stairs appeared. As he descended, the air grew cooler, laden with the cavelike smell of mold. The walls were stone and mortar, the floor concrete, painted battleship gray. A bulbous and chromed old fridge stood in the near corner, and beside the brick chimney, attached to it by shiny galvanized ductwork, a hot water heater and modern two-stage furnace. On the front panel was the number of a good local HVAC contractor; from a chain depended a frosted plastic sleeve containing its service records. He was surprised to find it was fitted with central air—a luxury his mother protested she didn't need.

Central air meant at least 100 amp service, which he confirmed at the breaker box. He did a quick check of the pipes above him in the joists and found a typical mix of copper and PVC, proof of recent work. The mouse baits didn't bother him (he'd just chuck them) and the sump pump in the far corner was standard for homes of the era. He went upstairs thinking he might have lowballed himself on the price.

He moved from room to room, taking time to get the best pictures, given the gray light. In the master bath there were plastic grip bars beside the toilet and in the shower (he'd remove them before he showed the house), and the door in the hall bath was scratched badly below the knob by a dog that wanted out, but all in all the place was solid.

As much as he looked for one, there was no catch. He'd lucked out. It happened. There was no logic to it, and no irony, only this odd timing that kept him from being happy, or from showing the excitement he felt—the same charge he got when he was new to the game, the poker player's thrill at picking up his cards and fanning out a pat hand.

In the midst of this premature celebration, he almost forgot the garage. It hadn't been redone, and as he approached it, key in hand, he feared it would be stuffed with all the junk from the house. The sectioned door creaked up, resisting him, to reveal a pair of dented metal trash cans that could have been his mother's. They were far too heavy for an elderly woman to drag to the curb, but there was no wheeled caddy either, and again he flashed on her solitary life here, and his mother's in their old house, and Wozniak's grandmother while he was overseas, and wondered if it was inevitable that Fran would end up alone.

Back at the office they all wanted the lowdown. They weren't being patronizing, they were just bored. Things were slow, and like a losing team they needed to feed off every little success.

"It's not the Taj Mahal," he said, "but I think I can work with it."

At the end of the day he called the daughter and told her he'd looked over the place. With disinterest he ticked off the property's faults along with its selling points as if they were equal, and recapped the sorry state of the market. She waited, not once interrupting, interested only in the price. He recommended they start at 89,9—eight thousand higher than his original number.

"I was hoping for a hundred," she said. "I see on your website you've got houses on State Street listed for 124 and 119."

The internet made everyone an expert; it drove him crazy.

"Those are three-family apartment houses. The zoning and taxes are completely different. For a one-family three-bedroom, we're scraping the ceiling, mostly because of what great shape the place is in."

He was only being honest, but some proud part of him wanted to tweak her, and he had to disguise it behind an upbeat tone of voice. Over the years he'd learned to deliver unhappy facts as if they were good news.

"Let's start at 95 then," the woman said, as if that was a compromise.

"I'm not sure the market will support that."

"We can always lower the price."

"Eighty-nine nine we have an outside shot at. Ninety-five is pushing it. This isn't Pittsburgh."

"Believe me, Mr. Larsen, I understand that better than anybody. Let's try 95. If we have to lower the price, we lower the price."

It was hard if not impossible for sellers to understand they were in this together—that he now had a stake in their house and was doing everything in their combined best interest. It was the buyers who would end up paying, yet in the beginning it was the sellers who distrusted him, probably because they felt they were losing something valuable, and that he was profiting from it.

"My worry, Mrs. Kern, is that the market will do it for us, and that by then 89, 9 could be pushing it."

She thanked him for his concern as if it were misplaced and that any further argument would be futile. She was an only child, there were no other survivors he could appeal to. Beyond that, she was his client. Right or wrong, she would have her way.

"My wife reminded me the other day," he said when they'd finished their business. "We knew your mother from the library. She used to joke around with our girls."

"Thank you for remembering her."

"She was always so proud of you. Everyone in town was."

She laughed, just a stuck cough. "That was a long time ago."

"Do you still play, if you don't mind my asking?"

"I don't anymore, but it's kind of you to remember."

She'd indulged him, and he wanted to keep going and ask why she'd given it up—how, really, she could walk away from that talent. If they were riding in a car together to view a house, he would have found an offhand, joshing way to extract it from her, but the phone was too direct. He didn't want to be rude.

"I'm sorry about your daughter," she said.

"Thank you," he said, as he said to everyone, "I appreciate it."

"One of the last conversations I had with my mother was about her. She prayed for her, even when she was in the hospital."

"That was good of her."

"She was a good person. Better than I'll ever be."

She was the one being kind, trading this intimacy, but when he got off he thought it was unfair of her—as if he were still anonymous and not the object of mindless curiosity. Maybe that was why she no longer played: She hated being in the paper and having everyone treat her like a freak. He could have told her he knew how she felt.

The next day was sunny, one of those crisp October afternoons with a blue sky like summer. The landscapers came, and he got a nice shot for the website. Just before quitting time he officially posted it, and drove over on his way home to plant the Edgewater sign by the front walk. It was a part of the job he loved—like baiting a hook—though at 95 the place would sit for a while.

He wasn't surprised that the first few queries it drew were from other brokers, or that they were surprised to find him on the other end of the line. Everyone said they were glad he was back, as if he'd survived a lingering illness. He assured them that he was too, and that it was good to be working—not entirely a lie, because sometimes it was. He liked being in the office, doing nothing more than drinking his coffee and eating his bagel and filling in the morning's crossword, or choosing which listings to show clients from out of town. He was aware that his fleeting pleasure at these moments was disproportionate and fragile, based on a willed forgetfulness. In a larger sense, much of his daily life as he knew it no longer mattered, yet he clung to it.

His intuition proved true. No one was interested in Mrs. DeMarco's at 95, and as interest rates rose and the market softened further, the daughter refused to budge. Every Friday he sent the landscapers to rake the leaves and clean the gutters, figuring the weekends would bring out the Lookee-Lous.

The weekend before Halloween, after prolonged and frustrating deliberations with Mrs. Kern, he scheduled an open house for Sunday between one and three, as he would for any sluggish property, paying an extra twenty dollars for a featured ad in Thursday's insert. Almost immediately he was sorry. He could make church, but to get everything ready he'd have to skip coffee hour and the haunted hayride. Fran said that was fine, as if he didn't need her permission, but still it felt wrong. Since they'd been back at work, they dedicated their weekends to Kim, as if they might find her by looking part-time. Last weekend he'd spent half of Saturday taking the boat out of the water. This seemed like he was giving up completely.

If Fran had asked him not to—one word from her and he would have held off. Instead, Saturday night she made cookies for him to tempt the buyers, a ritual that dated back to the girls' early years. They loved open houses, chasing each other shrieking through the strange rooms, high on chocolate, while Fran helped him showcase a den or kitchen. He knew the business but relied on her eye for design. He still did: Anytime he rearranged a cluttered table or banished a lamp to a closet, he was exercising her taste. They were a team, and if she had any misgivings about tomorrow he would have agreed it was too soon and scrapped the whole thing. Now he'd have to go through with it.

In church he worried, but once he was there everything was fine. The OPEN HOUSE sign was in place, the yard free of leaves. He parked the Taurus by the garage, covering one of the worst cracks. The day was clear and cool, and he raised the blinds so light poured in the windows, then set the thermostat to seventy. He ran hot water in all the sinks, and in the tub and shower. He flushed both toilets, up and down, and listened to them refill. He was wearing his best suit as if it were a formal occasion—ridiculous, yet it felt right. Today he needed every advantage.

At five to one he did a last walkaround, pinching lint from the stair carpet. He made sure he had enough business cards and squared the pile of listings beside the plate of cookies. The specs were the least of it. He was ready for any question. By now it was no exaggeration to say he knew the house better than its owner, and he could honestly vouch that it was a good house. The price was too high, maybe, but someone would be very happy here. He stood in the front door, waiting for them.

The Advanced Stages

Sooner or later they'd find her. In a ditch. In a thicket. In a creekbed.

All fall Lindsay tracked the open cases online, watching as, one by one, they closed. The Alzheimer's patients and retarded adults, the little kids and alcoholics, the prostitutes and college students and runaways. The pretty girls like Kim.

The leaves were down, and it was easier. Hunters discovered them, hikers, horseback riders, early morning fishermen tromping through tall reeds to their favorite spots. Lindsay pictured their initial confusion and panic and then the long, drawn-out inconvenience, the whole day ruined, maybe flashbacks, nightmares. No one wanted to be part of that, even briefly.

At home it was inescapable, though they told her nothing. Her birthday was coming up, and her mother was bugging her about what kind of party she wanted. They could go bowling or roller-skating or they could just have something at home. How many people was she thinking? What kind of cake did she want? What did she want for presents? She needed to give them some lead time.

"I don't want anything," Lindsay said.

"It's your birthday. What do *you* want to do?"

"I don't know."

"Well, *think*," her mother said.

She wanted contact lenses. She wanted a job like Dana's at Quizno's so she'd have some money of her own. She wanted to be able to take the car without her mother acting like she'd never see her again. She wanted to go out on Friday nights with her friends. She wanted—if the right guy asked her—to go out on a date.

She asked for the contacts. Her mother warned her that they were expensive—they might be the only present she'd get. Her father asked what was wrong with her glasses.

"It's not about her eyesight," her mother said, though he was only joking.

It wasn't because of Kim and the way she made fun of her glasses (of her, really, except no one but Lindsay remembered *that* Kim). Last week in gym class she was under the basket, caught in a knot of more aggressive girls going for a rebound, when someone's arm knocked them off. When she put them back on (by then the action was shifting to the other end), she realized she was the only one in the whole class wearing them, and she wondered how long that had been true. In December she was finally getting her braces off, and she thought she might as well make a complete change—as if, once she shed her disguise, the world would discover she'd been beautiful all along.

Sometimes, leaning into the bathroom mirror, she could almost see the face she wished she had, and sometimes before taking a shower, turned in strict profile with her shoulders back and stomach sucked in, the body. She was going to be sixteen and no one had ever touched her.

Though she knew it was wrong, and complicated, for a short time she would have let J.P. Not anymore.

It was all boys thought of, according to her mother. She'd obviously never met the boys in Lindsay's class, who were obsessed with their XBoxes and PSPs and skateboarding and hockey and the Clash and their own disorganized punk bands and parties and smoking and drinking and dope and cars and zombie movies and hot sauce contests and Jack Black in *Saving Silverman* and getting the hell out of Kingsville like everyone else. They might pay attention to Cara Penrose's boobs when Cara passed by their lunch table, but Lindsay doubted they spent hours in serious contemplation of them—or not the way she'd wasted whole days and nights agonizing over J.P. Guys weren't like that, or not the guys she knew.

She didn't want a party. She didn't want a cake either, but her mother insisted, steering her toward the confetti one from last year. Lindsay didn't remember liking or not liking it, just the novelty of the colored dots inside the sponge cake, but went along to end the discussion.

"Did you want to invite Dana and Micah over, or do you want it to be just family?"

"Just family."

"I'm sorry it's not going to be nicer. It's supposed to be your day."

"I really don't care," Lindsay said, but she could see her mother didn't believe her.

Otherwise life had fallen into a dulling routine. Halloween was over, all the candy was gone except her father's nasty Paydays. After school there was a gap of an hour and a half before her mother got home. She couldn't be alone in the house, because it was possible Kim had been taken from there (they'd changed the locks), so she and Dana hung out in the Hedricks' basement, sprawled on their horrible aqua leather sectional, watching dumb VH-1 shows and trading the latest sophomore gossip. Three days a week Dana worked, and she watched by herself, Mrs. Hedrick checking on her every once in a while as if she might disappear.

Dinner was the hardest. Her mother had instituted a prayer for Kim before every meal, and it seemed to Lindsay that it was always her turn to say it. "And please help bring her back to us safely. Amen."

"Thank you," her mother said.

Though there was never a formal discussion, it was now Lindsay's job to do the dishes. She dedicated herself to it with the same concentration she gave her homework, making sure she got every spot off the stovetop.

Later, her mother went up first, her father watching TV from the far end of the couch with his eyes closed.

"Go to bed," Lindsay told him. "I'll close up."

"Okay, chief," he said, and then locked up anyway.

In her room she found the missing, or they found them for her. A deputy on routine patrol. A woman walking her dog. A DOT mowing crew. The leaders of Scout Troop 121.

She had her favorites, the little kids and teenagers she hoped had just run away. *In the company of adult male,* the FBI posters said, making her guess whether he was a kidnapper or a boyfriend or both.

Some had been missing for years but still had active sites. The first-grade teacher from the little town in Georgia who'd been a beauty queen. The college track star who went jogging at dawn in her upscale Dallas suburb. Lindsay wondered if someone who was plain would inspire the same devotion.

In the spillway of the lake. In the woods behind the ShopRite. In a field off of U.S. 41.

Burned under the overpass. Wrapped in plastic. Bound with ligatures.

In a chest-type freezer. In a foot locker. In a duffel bag. In an oil drum.

Dismembered. Decapitated. Partly skeletonized. In the advanced stages of decomposition.

There was never a mention of rape or torture, no matter how obvious the probability, as if by some unspoken agreement the reporters decided to leave out the most upsetting details. Those were the cases Lindsay took with her to bed, filling in the empty spaces as if these real-life nightmares could replace her own. What would it feel like to be stabbed or strangled or beaten to death? When would you pass out and stop feeling it? Was it just blackness then, and nothing after that? She had nothing to imagine it with besides sleep.

An irrigation worker in an orange grove. A Jet Ski rider by the marina. It was like a game of Clue without weapons or suspects.

She found herself looking at people strangely during the day. Ultimately everyone in her French class would die (Madame Cassada first), the question was when and where and who would find them. If they were lucky it would be in bed. A nurse would come, like at her grandmother's place. EMTs, people who knew what to do. On the bus home she sat with Dana and Micah, watching the sun flash through the newly bare trees, wondering if there was anyone out there waiting to be found.

Some of them turned up alive hundreds of miles away, identified in bus stations, but more often they were rotting in landfills and canals and ravines, in rockpits and flooded quarries. In abandoned cars. How many of them had sisters, and what were *they* supposed to do?

The idea occupied her as she sat alone on the Hedricks' sectional, watching "The 100 Best Toys of All Time," counting down the last half hour before her mother came home. Number 29 was Battleship, one of their favorite games—one that Kim usually won, though that never mattered. She remembered playing it on the floor of Kim's room one rainy day, both of them lying flat on the carpet so they couldn't cheat, the white pegs accumulating in diagonal patterns and then the short straight lines of red. She was eight or nine, an age when Kim agreeing to play with her was enough to make her happy.

Mrs. Hedrick chose that moment to come downstairs and check on her.

"Are you all right?" she asked, because Lindsay had turned away to hide her tears.

"Oh honey, it's okay," Mrs. Hedrick said, sitting next to her and patting her shoulder. "We all miss her."

Not like I do, Lindsay wanted to say.

"Here," Mrs. Hedrick said, "come help me make dinner. You shouldn't be down here by yourself."

She didn't want to, but did, and by the time her mother arrived she was mashing potatoes at the stove and feeling in control again. Mrs. Hedrick didn't say anything, as if it were their secret.

At home her mother said she needed to talk to her. She sounded serious, as if something major had changed. She sat Lindsay down at the kitchen table and looked at her, concerned.

Lindsay waited blankly, as if she was innocent.

"I know you don't want to talk about this, but we have to. Your birthday's less than a week away. What else do you want besides your contacts?"

The question was so far off the mark that she had no answer for it.

"You've got to tell me these things," her mother said. "Please. I can't read your mind."

Painesville

The dorm cleared out before the weekend. Talman took off after his last class on Friday, psyched to be driving cross-country with Hector. He'd never seen New York before. J.P. hadn't either.

"We've got room," Hector said at the car. "If you don't mind sleeping on the floor."

"Please, John, come with us," Talman said in his tortured boarding-school English, a challenge to his sense of adventure.

He'd have much rather gone with them, but his mom was expecting him. All week she called, asking what he wanted for meals, as if she'd forgotten his favorites. She was putting together her menus, checking with him to see if he agreed. The smallest turkey she could buy was a fourteen-pounder. Would he mind if she just made a nice turkey breast?

He could have left early like everyone else, but said he really needed to go to Chem lab Tuesday night. He was barely passing the class. Technically it wasn't a lie.

Over the weekend the stragglers gathered at parties that lasted until everything was gone. They dropped bottles down the stairwells, winged CDs out the windows, threw up noodles in the sinks. He remembered swaying over a bubbling toilet as he peed, blinking one eye and then the other closed so he could direct his stream. When the noise stopped, it meant he was missing.

Saturday he didn't wake up until the sun was going down. Sunday he came to in Michaela Albright's bed, surprised to find Michaela's bare back and freckled shoulders, the white blond wisps at the base of her neck. She wasn't a beauty or someone with a reputation, just a quiet, pixieish girl on his floor who'd had too much to drink. They both acted like it was a funny mistake, but hung out that night, talking till four in the morning. She was from Painesville, right down the lake from him, and wanted to be a doctor. "Thank you for not laughing at that," she said. Like everyone else she called him John, but in her mouth the name sounded familiar. He could sleep with her as long as all they did was sleep. Only an idiot would have turned her down, and only an idiot would have believed they'd just sleep, and the next morning they were even more confused. She had a boyfriend at home who was important to her. J.P. said he respected that, thinking it was a built-in way out.

"What about you?" she asked.

Instead of Kim, he thought of Nina.

"Yeah," he admitted. "Me too."

Because the dorms were empty, it was still their secret. They made a point not to be seen at the caf together, sneaking out for falafel and holing up in her room, staying naked most of the day. She didn't understand it—she was actually very shy.

She was leaving Monday after her Microbiology midterm, taking the bus back, which she hated. He hadn't gone home for fall break (or to Denison either, guiltily blowing off Nina and Elise), so he'd never taken the bus. "Are you ready?" Michaela said. "It's six hours." He could drive it in three, but because of the parking problem on campus, freshmen weren't allowed to have cars. He hadn't missed his until now. He thought he should drive her home, as if this was a date. He wanted to meet her parents. How could he explain, after the random way they hooked up, that he was serious?

He didn't know her at all, yet he was convinced, on the evidence of the last two days, that she had a good heart. After Kim and Nina, he needed a love that was simple, if there was such a thing.

He tried to persuade her to stay till Wednesday so they could together, as if with two more nights he could win her forever. He took it as a sign when she wouldn't change her plans. That was all right. Like the turkey breast, it wasn't what he wanted, but it made more sense.

She had to study Sunday night and then sleep so she'd be fresh for the test (she was on the Dean's List and said there was no reason he shouldn't be). Wide awake, in the shifting light of her screensaver, he watched her breathe, resisting the urge to kiss the thin skin of her neck. In sleep she seemed smaller, and he felt a rush of tenderness toward her, as if he were there to protect her instead of messing up her life.

After her midterm (she was pretty sure she'd aced it), he took the bus downtown with her to the station. As the line filed on, they lingered behind to kiss good-bye. To say he loved her would be unfair if not untrue, so he said he'd miss her. When she was gone he felt both abandoned and relieved. Walking along the dingy street outside of the station in his new coat, he shut his eyes and shook his head.

"What are you doing?" he said.

The dorms officially closed at noon on Wednesday. The halls were quiet, and he didn't have to wait forever for an elevator. He stayed till the end, and, leaving, envied the Nigerian grad student who manned the security booth.

The one o'clock bus was full, making him wait an unplanned hour for the two. A cold front had dipped down out of Canada, and by the time they were in Amish country it was dark and snow was falling, salting the stubbled fields. Cold seeped through the window, and he folded his coat inside-out like a blanket to insulate his shoulder. The interior stank of cigarettes, though each seatback sported a NO SMOKING sign and the ashtrays on the armrests had been welded shut. Muttered cellphone monologues bothered him, and the tinny beats of a dozen iPods. Across the aisle a soldier in desert camo slept with a stuffed Bugs Bunny in his arms, a prize from a fair, a present for a kid sister. As they rolled up 271 the driver suddenly braked, throwing them forward, pausing the one-sided conversations before they continued with even more force. There were no seatbelts, and as the snow flew thicker and night came down, J.P. imagined the bus sliding off the side of the road and rolling over, as if only another tragedy would absolve him.

Through the sprawling exurbs of Cleveland, past the exit for Geauga Lake, where they'd gone for their class picnic in eighth grade. Mile by mile he was going back in time, as if nothing of the last three months was real. In many ways it wasn't. He'd told no one about Kim, just as he'd told no one his real name, with the result that she was with him constantly, harping on him as she had in life, accusing him of being stupid and weak and a coward, and he had nothing with which to refute her. He drank and smoked himself senseless—at first on weekends and then whenever the opportunity arose—and slept through his classes, wasting money he wouldn't be able to repay for years. His GPA was below the minimum to keep his scholarship, meaning if he didn't turn things around he wouldn't be coming back next year. It wasn't that he didn't care—he was bitterly aware of letting down his mom, who'd stood by him through everything—but the more he dwelled on his problems, the more hopeless they seemed, and the more obviously of his own making. The truth was, the false person he'd become deserved to fail, and worse.

They dropped off passengers in Bath and Macedonia and Pepper Pike, places he'd never heard of, at stops outside convenience marts and doughnut shops. The snow was heavier toward the lake, blowing in rippling sheets beneath the high lights of cloverleafs. Police guarded cars that had spun off the road, their red and blue bars strobing over the median. On 90, near Mentor, traffic going the other way was backed up for miles. He wished they were, if only to postpone the inevitable.

"Painesville next," the driver announced over the fuzzy PA. "Next stop Painesville."

He could get off and call her and she'd have to come pick him up. Unless she was doing something with her boyfriend, or eating dinner with her family, in which case he'd be a jerk, and stuck there till the next bus.

As if she'd read his mind—as if she'd sensed his presence—his phone buzzed in his pocket. He levered himself off the seat to dig it out.

It was his mom, wondering where he was. She'd planned on serving him supper tonight. If that wasn't going to happen, it would be nice if he'd let her know.

"Sorry," he said, "it's snowing," and told her he'd call when the bus dropped him off.

"Be careful," she said, as if he was the one driving.

The soldier got off at Painesville, and he wondered, wildly, if the stuffed Bugs Bunny was for Michaela, if, with a doubletake worthy of a cartoon, he would see it next week, propped on her bed.

Perry, Geneva, finally Ashtabula, almost home. Erie was the last stop; the bus was nearly empty. "Kingsville next," the driver called.

They came in by Lake Road, skirting the bluffs and the summer camps boarded up for the winter, the wind pushing the snow sideways through the streetlights. Across from the gas pumps of Waite's Market, the town golf course was smooth and untouched, the greens and bunkers sculpted. He anticipated every landmark, every sign, his mind flying out ahead of the bus. Past the firehouse and the old grade school and the fenced substation and then down and back up the roller-coaster dip for the creek before they hit the town line and the highway turned into Grandview Avenue. They were coming up on the corner of Buffalo. The Larsens' was a mile away, walkable even in this weather, and he imagined rushing up the aisle with his bag and telling the driver to stop and let him off, then trudging through the drifts in his sneakers, climbing the stairs to their porch and ringing the bell and standing there until they let him in.

Silently he watched his chance go by. He was already late and his mom was holding supper. He'd go tomorrow, he promised himself. He didn't know what he'd say, but he'd go and apologize again, and if they turned him away that was fine, at least he would have tried.

He'd call Nina and see if she wanted to get together. She was the only one he could really talk to. They could walk on the beach and figure things out. With the snow they'd be the only ones there.

If he could do those two things he thought he'd be okay.

They made the light by the park, crossing Harbor, and rolled into downtown. The stores were closed, the churches dark blocks against the sky. They turned onto Superior and then Euclid, circling the courthouse, and slowed for Main. The interior lights came up, making people grumble. "This stop Kingsville," the driver said, braking, and J.P. hauled on his coat and gathered his bag. They pulled alongside the diner with its cluster of newspaper honor boxes out front, the neon clock above the grill shedding a lime green glow.

He was the only one who got off. He stood on the sidewalk in the cold as the bus pulled away from the curb and swung around the corner, leaving him facing the post office, its steps perfectly caked, tinted a pale copper by the streetlights. The night was quiet. With the snow falling, it seemed like a stage set he'd wandered onto after the movie was over. All he needed was for a church bell to ring.

Like an idiot—like a little kid—he hadn't brought a hat or gloves. There was nowhere to set his bag down, and he had to dig out his phone and open it with one hand.

"Hello?" his mom answered, as if it might be someone else.

"It's me," he said. "I'm here."

Halftime Entertainment

It was a tradition. Every Thanksgiving they played Conneaut, no matter how bad the weather was. She hadn't planned on going until her
mom told her about the ceremony for Kim. It was a good opportunity
to do something. The team was undefeated; everyone would be there.
She called Elise, thinking it would be easier for her to approach the Larsens. They'd always liked her better, the goody-goody of the three.
When J.P. called that morning, she thought it was too late to include
him, and risky, since—though none of it was his fault—they blamed
him the most.

"I'd really like to be part of it," he said.

"I know."

She wanted to tell him to call them himself, but felt guilty. All
along it had been Hinch's deal. She didn't know why she'd ever listened
to him.

"I'll ask Elise to ask them. The worst they can do is say no, right?"

He agreed, though, really, there were far worse things they could say.
She'd accused herself of them for months—alone or in dreams, waking
in the middle of Abnormal Psych or as she ladled out kung pao shrimp
to the realization that by leaving Kingsville she'd left Kim to die. On
the built-in bookshelf of her desk, at eye level, she kept her favorite picture of the three of them. It was from last summer, when they'd practically lived at the beach. They were wearing cheesy sunglasses they'd
bought at Wal-Mart and had their heads pressed together, beaming crazily, their hair stringy from swimming, the Three Seahags. As she was
writing a paper or e-mailing she'd look up from the screen and study
Kim's face—her smile, the lines of her eyebrows, the gold chain around

her neck, the yoke of her collarbones. While the picture was just an image—ink on glossy paper—Nina could still feel the living force of her personality. It seemed impossible that all of that energy was just gone.

At the same time she was aware that she herself had changed. Her roommate had her own set of friends, and without Kim or Elise to understand her, Nina hardly talked to anyone. As if in penance, she swore off partying, lying in bed nights and listening to the music thumping through the walls. On weekends she did laundry and signed up for blocks of time at her library carrel, and by her absence earned a reputation in her dorm as a humorless nerd, which she thought was funny. She didn't care if people thought she was weird, or proud, or stuck-up. Guys still hit on her, but now she could turn them down without explanation, as if she was sexless and chaste, preoccupied with higher things. Inwardly she laughed at her transformation into an uptight grind. Through solitude and hard work she'd become one of the girls she'd made fun of in high school. She'd become, essentially, Elise. She thought that when she was done mourning she would set this mask aside (it was like wearing black), but as the semester went on she stopped regarding her new incarnation as a conscious act and found she respected the responsible, self-possessed person she'd become more than the scheming, empty-headed teenager she used to be. The real wonder was that Kim and Elise had put up with her for so long.

Even over the phone her mom noticed the change and praised her for it, as if she'd been waiting for this new stage. She was happy Nina was finished with Hinch, and, looking back, Nina saw that all the guys she was with in high school were chosen not for any positive qualities of their own (Hinch was silly, an overgrown twelve-year-old) but for the not-so-hidden object of worrying her mother. Now, finally, she was the smart, thoughtful Nina her mom had always wanted, and the more her mom celebrated the breakthrough, the more Nina felt the urge to revert to her earlier self. Luckily she was only home for a week. Already she was dreading Christmas.

About an hour before game time, Elise reported back. The Larsens were okay with J.P. being part of the ceremony, with a few ground rules. He couldn't sit or stand with them, or talk to them or any reporters.

"Jesus," Nina said. "What about me? Can I breathe the same air?"

"We can stand with them."

"I can't talk to them."

"I'm just telling you what they said."

"Who did you talk to?"

"Mr. Larsen."

"So you're allowed to talk to them and I'm not?"

"He didn't say that."

"I'm just trying to get this straight."

"I just want to be there," Elise said. "That's what's important to me."

"It's important to me too, but..." She wanted to call them monstrous, heartless people. She wanted to say that she and J.P. didn't do anything, but that wasn't true either.

"Do you not want to go?" Elise asked.

"I want to go."

"Then tell J.P. what the deal is and let's go. It's going to be cold as shit out there."

"Thank you," Nina said.

"You can thank me when it's over," Elise said.

She called J.P. and explained the situation, listing the Larsens' demands, hoping he'd say they could go fuck themselves. Instead he said that was great, over and over, as if he was relieved.

"You don't mind that they won't let us stand next to them."

"That's okay."

"It is not okay," she said. "I think it's pretty shitty of them. You did more than anyone."

"You did too," he said. "It doesn't matter."

"I think it does."

"They could have said no."

"They wouldn't."

"They have," he said.

She'd admitted this was her fault, for narcing on Wooze, yet it never failed to silence her, as if she was powerless to console him.

"You need a ride?" he asked.

"I'm picking up Elise."

"I'll see you there then."

They spoke casually, as if they hadn't been apart for months. They'd e-mailed at the start of the semester, but soon he stopped, and while she was disappointed, she was also relieved, imagining he was busy. The last time she'd seen him, he seemed quiet and tired, as if everything was too much and he was shutting down. Maybe it was just her. The end of summer had been a mess. She'd just wanted to leave. Being back made her feel old and strange, as if she no longer had a place here. It wasn't like school, where she could get away with a disguise. The town was the same, not a single thing had changed. Obviously the problem was with her.

Outside, the sky was low and gray, and it was warm enough to snow, stray flakes swirling on the wind. Her mom had run out to the store earlier and warned her that the roads were bad, but now they were just slushy. It had been months since she'd driven, and as she swung onto Buffalo—plowed and salted down to the asphalt—a pleasant feeling of freedom came over her, as if, in the car, she could go anywhere and nothing could touch her. False, of course, since she was on her way to Elise's and then the game, where she would stand in front of the crowd like someone condemned, but for an instant, before everything settled onto her again, she felt what she suspected was normal. These moments had been more frequent lately. She didn't trust them, as if they were a kind of escape, and countered by consciously remembering Kim that last day, walking back to their cars. Her tattoo and her bathing suit. See ya there, Squinky Square. Like a cutter with her secret blade, the pain both released and returned her to herself. The most terrible thing in the world, she thought, was how easy it was to forget.

She slowed for the tracks, and as she crossed, looked down the infinite perspective to the west. The snow in the middle was untouched, the rails bare from last night's freights. She'd heard the one o'clock, but that was all.

Elise was watching for her from the door like a little kid and came out in a tassel cap and scarf in Kingsville's purple and gold.

"Go Vikings," Nina joked, and hugged her across the console.

"I figured if there's any day I can wear this stuff…"

"Why do you even have it?"

"Forensics."

"Oh God," Nina said.

"Fifth in states."

"It's true, you *are* the biggest sped ever."

"I missed you too."

"So what are we supposed to do for this thing?"

The ceremony, as far as Elise could tell, was to thank the community as a whole and the high school in particular for their support. They would gather in a circle at midfield and Kim's mom would make a speech. The band and the booster club had done a lot of fundraising; there was probably a big check involved.

"What do *we* do?" Nina asked.

"All we have to do is hold hands."

"Not with them."

"If it makes you feel better," Elise said, "you can hold my hand."

"Yeah, thanks," she said out of reflex, then, soberly, "I will."

"It's a deal."

"Dibs on J.P."

"You didn't have to call it," Elise said.

There was no traffic until they were a couple blocks from school, and then it was backed up solid, crawling. A straggly line of fans in purple and gold trudged through the slush beside them, huddled like refugees. The police were out, waving cars through stop signs. Her mom was right: Everybody was here. Nina couldn't remember it ever being like this.

"When's the last time we were undefeated?" Elise asked.

"Fucking never."

The lot was full, and volunteers in reflective vests were parking the overflow on the shoulder of the road. Among the cars, she recognized J.P.'s ruined hood and wondered if Hinch would be there.

She shouldn't have come. She should have stayed home and helped her mom make the stuffing and the turnips and the pea casserole. She should have found an excuse to stay at school, a friend who needed company, a project overdue. There was a place for her there—not the dorm but her carrel overlooking the quad far below, where her fellow students were just dots crisscrossing the walks. Safe in her perch behind the bird-proof glass, hour by hour she was turning herself into the responsible Nina she wanted to be. Here there was no refuge from the truth. Here people knew what she'd done.

She felt marked as she got out of the car, as if someone in the crowd had pointed her out. They joined the flow on the road, all of them headed the same way like cattle, toward the syncopated clatter of the marching band. It was so overcast that the field's giant light towers were on, the white clusters burning spots onto the surface of her eyes. They poured through the parking lot and bunched up at the gate, where two tables of booster girls wearing face paint were selling tickets, stashing the money in gray lockboxes. Behind them, wired to the fence beside a fussily illustrated CONQUER CONNEAUT poster with a Viking holding a downed Spartan at sword point, was a foam-board blowup of Kim's face.

Though she'd posted hundreds of flyers during the search, now it struck Nina as obscene, as if they were displaying her body like a martyr's. She wanted to take off her jacket and cover it so no one could look at her.

"Kim Kim Sal-a-bim," she whispered like a magic word, as if she could make it all disappear.

"She would hate this," Elise said.

"Except for your hat—she'd love that."

Getting in took forever, jammed up against everyone in their heavy coats, and then, immediately inside, they had to run a gauntlet of old classmates back for break, standing in circles and drinking hot chocolate near the concession stand. She kept moving, sticking close to Elise, using the herd as a screen, only to stop for a bottleneck at a table with another poster of Kim, this one with her smiling under a magic-markered rainbow. Two booster girls were doing a brisk business selling rainbow pins and ribbons and wristbands. She didn't know why she was irritated by this. Not merely because it was tacky. Maybe because it was falsely optimistic. Or maybe, she thought, because she no longer was.

Ahead, beyond the crush, by the base of the stands, J.P. leaned bareheaded against the fence with his hands in his pockets and his back to the track, searching for them. His hair was shaggy, and with his coat zipped to his throat he looked thin as a rock star. When he saw them, he pushed himself off the fence, giving them a nod and a smile that was more of a grimace.

He hugged her first. Up close he was bony, as if he was doing meth.

"I like the hair," he said, because she'd cut it short.

"I got sick of messing with it."

"Looks good."

He held Elise.

"So, are you ready for the Circle of Hope?"

"Is that what it's called?"

He pulled a rolled program from his back pocket and showed them a whole doublefold dedicated to Kim.

"They're over there, down front."

It took her a minute to find them. Kim's dad was wearing the same Vikings tassel cap as Elise, while Kim's mom held an oversized purple foam-rubber finger that said Kingsville was #1. Between them Lindsay sat with her head bowed as if she was their prisoner.

"Did you go over and say hi?" Nina asked. "You don't want to be rude."

"Stop," Elise said, and led them up the ringing stairs of the bleachers.

The center sections were packed all the way to the press box. They were lucky to find a spot in the corner against the back railing where they could simultaneously watch the game and the lines at the concession stand.

In the end zone the cheerleaders stretched tight a banner with Thor swinging his hammer, and their record, 9–0. The band launched into the fight song, and everyone stood to cheer as the team broke through the paper and streamed onto the field, gathering in a pack at the fifty to bounce and chant something unintelligible before taking the home sideline. To deep and universal booing, Conneaut ran to their bench, and Nina hoped they'd win.

Beyond her spite she had no interest in the game and spent most of the first half comparing her life at school to J.P.'s (it sounded like he was doing the same thing she was, keeping to himself, staying focused on work). She rose like everyone else when Kingsville scored, and again when Conneaut fumbled the kickoff, but didn't cheer every play like Elise, and grew tired of returning her gloved high-fives. With so many people crushed together the air was surprisingly warm, but the cold of the metal bench seeped through her jeans until her ass was numb. The drummers were relentless. "SPAR-tans SUCK, SPAR-tans SUCK!" the crowd chanted, and they were right. It was 17–0 when the Vikings returned a punt for a touchdown. There was no reason she should resent it, yet she did, just as she resented the booster girls sitting at their tables and her classmates socializing in little cliques behind the stands and Kim's mom waving her big finger whenever they scored. There was no reason she hated everyone.

"We have to go down around the two-minute warning," Elise said.

"Just make sure you're holding my hand."

"We need to restrain her so she doesn't bite anyone," Elise explained.

"That would be bad," J.P. said.

"We should have gotten drunk for this," Nina said.

"Even better," J.P. said.

"We should go out and get drunk after." She didn't mean it, but was helpless around them, dropping out of habit into her old shtick.

"Drunk on Thanksgiving," Elise said. "The Nina Tersigni Story."

At the two-minute mark the clock didn't stop. The band was filing in three distinct lines along the track, slowly massing in battalions behind the goalposts. A man in front of J.P. explained: There was no two-minute warning in high school.

"I was wondering," J.P. said.

"I swear that's what they told me," Elise said.

They started down, but with the score so lopsided the whole crowd was getting a jump on halftime, clogging the aisles and the walkway at the bottom. The seconds ticked off, less than a minute now. Twenty-five, twenty-four...Conneaut was resigned to just running out the clock. When it reached 0:00, the quarterback flipped the ball to the referee and the two squads jogged off to cheers.

The Larsens were already behind the bench with the Hedricks and Father John and Connie and a few girls Kim used to play softball with. A blinding light popped on—a TV camera, making people ahead of them on the stairs stop and gawk. It would be fitting, Nina thought, if they missed the ceremony because of this.

"Here," J.P. said, tapping her shoulder, and cut into an open row, heading cross-country for the center section. She and Elise followed, awkwardly stepping from bleacher to bleacher over people's blankets and coffee cups and smuggled-in bottles, all the way down to the bottom where there was a gate. They pushed through the mob on the walkway. Elise talked to the security guard, who let them onto the track.

In the glare of the spotlight Kim's mom was talking to a reporter. Nina hadn't seen her in months and was surprised at how good she looked—as if she'd had a total makeover. She was wearing lipstick, and she'd obviously lost weight. Nina had always thought of her as plain and dumpy, knocking around the house in sweatpants or Minnie Mouse scrubs from work, but here she was with a serious anchorwoman's hairstyle and a tailored suit. In her face Nina could divine the source of Kim's beauty. On her lapel was a rhinestone rainbow pin. She held herself straight, concentrating on the reporter's questions. Off-camera, Kim's dad held her coat, looking the same as ever, while Lindsay and Dana Hedrick hung back, leaning into each other, whispering.

Nina thought of herself and Kim, what they'd make of this bullshit. That was all they did at the Conoco, night by night honing their bitchiness to a fine edge. Angie and Sam, Sam and Angie. Tough-ass chicks. She had their shirts in her closet at home, preserved like relics in case they ever returned.

The light died and Kim's mom shrugged her coat on again. With both hands Kim's dad flipped her hair over her collar. The band was taking the field, tootling a Sousa warhorse. Nina kept her eyes on Kim's mom, waiting for her to look over. Would she just pretend they didn't exist? She turned away to say something to Father John and Connie, watching as the color guard passed, flags rippling. She was maybe ten feet away. Nothing was stopping Nina from walking over and declaring herself. If she were alone she would have in a second and ruined everything.

She didn't have a long speech, or a list of reasons why they were wrong. She didn't want to shame them. All she wanted was for them to know that the three of them had loved Kim, and missed her, and would do anything to have her back. These were things they should have already known, but for her peace of mind Nina needed the Larsens to acknowledge them.

The band finished with a flourish, poised in formation, and Kim's mom motioned for Lindsay to come stand between her and Kim's dad. Mr. Koskoff, the band director, and some girl who was president of the booster club joined them. They were the front line. Behind them came the Hedricks and Father John, then the girls from the softball team, and finally Nina and J.P. and Elise. Connie briefed them, flashing a printed diagram and pointing to the near hash mark. They'd stand there for the speech, then turn and hold hands in a big circle. The exit music would cue them to turn and walk straight off. Nothing fancy.

"I'm glad you guys could come," she said, and moved on.

"That was nice," Elise said, except it sounded like a question.

"Ladies and gentlemen," the PA said, expectant, as if they were the main act, "on this day of thanksgiving, we honor and remember one of Kingsville's own who couldn't be with us today. Please give a big Viking welcome to the parents of Kimberly Larsen—Ed and Fran Larsen."

All three of them looked at one another. Kimberly?

The band struck up a soaring brass version of "Somewhere Over the Rainbow," starting in motion as the Larsens walked out along the fifty-yard line. The cameraman hustled to stay ahead of them. The Vikings logo in the middle had been churned to purple mud, and they stopped short of that, turning to face the crowd. Group by group Connie sent the rest of them out like a director. Nina was between J.P. and Elise, and as she made her way onto the field she could see, beyond the Larsens, the six separate lines of the band intermeshing to describe, predictably, the arc of a rainbow. Instead of a pot of gold at either end, there were sequined baton twirlers.

The turf was slippery, and Elise took her hand. Of the Larsens only Lindsay visibly noted them, eyeing J.P. and trading glances with Dana. Kim's mom and dad gazed stoically over their heads, hurt yet bravely making the best of the situation. When Nina turned to face the stands, she saw why. They were nearly empty.

During the ceremony with the checks (regular-sized, accepted with handshakes held for the photographers), Kim's mom thanked everyone for their support. Thanks to the generosity of Kingsville High School, the reward for information leading to Kim's safe return was now over fifty thousand dollars. There was almost no applause, only a smattering picked up by her wireless mic. Nina wondered how many of the people left in the bleachers had kids in the band.

The Circle of Hope was even worse. Kim's mom invited the crowd to rise and join hands—pointless, since whole sections were empty. Nina turned toward the center and J.P. took her other hand. He wasn't wearing gloves, and she pulled hers off to warm his fingers. Across the circle Father John asked for a moment of silence. Kim's mom and dad bowed their heads; Lindsay waited an extra second before tipping hers. Nina studied them, feeling the urge to break free of J.P. and Elise and dash across the circle. Red Rover, Red Rover, we dare Nina to come over.

"SPARTANS SUCK!" some guy bellowed in the silence, sparking a laugh from the crowd. Kim's mom looked around as if she might find him.

You suck, Kim would have yelled back.

"Thank you," Father John finally said, and the music came up—"Somewhere Over the Rainbow" again—and they all let go and walked off like they were supposed to.

They waited for the Larsens, who came off last, stalked by photographers. The school paper wanted shots of them with Mr. Koskoff and the booster girl, and then a different TV reporter pulled them aside. While the cameraman fussed with his setup, the band played their versions of "It's a Beautiful Day" and "Another One Bites the Dust."

"Okay," the security guard said, pointing toward the gate, "we've got to clear this area."

There was no arguing with him. A pair of cops was waving people off the track. The team was coming back out, the manager rolling two Gatorade coolers on a cart. Everyone but the Larsens had to go.

The crowd was swarming the walkway, heading back to their seats, armed with popcorn and nachos and hot dogs. The score was 27–0, and whatever Nina wanted, whatever the Larsens were withholding—not forgiveness, not exactly—she wasn't going to get it. The bleachers were filling, cutting off J.P.'s escape route. She took a last look back. Kim's mom was still being interviewed with her coat off, Kim's dad and Lindsay standing to one side.

"You guys can stay if you want to," Nina said. "I'm out."

"You want to go somewhere?" Elise asked.

"Yeah," she said. "The hell away from here."

"My house?"

"Are we allowed?"

"Don't be like that."

"Sure," J.P. said.

They had to fight the tide, sidling along the edge of the crush, brushing against puffy, swaddled bodies.

"You're going the wrong way," someone's mother with a tray of hot chocolates told them, and Nina thought of splashing them in her face.

Once they were free of the walkway, it was easy. The rainbow girls only had a few customers, while the lines at the concessions and restrooms were huge. The same classmates were still chatting in little groups as they passed. Like the Larsens, they pretended not to recognize them.

"You know you can't come back in," an older guard at the entrance warned.

"We know," Elise said.

There was no one outside the fence. The cops were gone. Cars were parked on both shoulders at crazy angles, as if abandoned in the last seconds before some terrible disaster. The wind was bitter, skimming snow from the drifts. They went on for blocks without seeing anyone, salt crunching underfoot, seagulls fighting over tailgaters' trash the only sign of life. Nina swore she'd parked closer than this, but everything looked different, weirdly motionless. She'd always thought of Kingsville as a ghost town, now here it was, literally depopulated, as if only she and J.P. and Elise had survived. And while that was wishful, the exact opposite of what had actually happened, she was glad to be with them. Here, as nowhere else, she was free to be herself in all her contradictions. Without having to say a word, they understood.

Behind them a roar went up, long and drawn out, then dying mildly, probably the kickoff. None of them looked back. They walked down the middle of the road, silent and purposeful, like the last three people on Earth.

The next day she went to the river.

Wish List

The holidays settled on them like a spell, like the frigid weather forcing them indoors. The days were too short. At work Fran was part of the crew that hung the decorations, festooning the waiting room and the ER with green and gold tinsel, refilling the dish of miniature candy canes outside of their sliding window. Her doctor had taken her off Ambien after she woke up in the kitchen at three a.m., eating leftover macaroni and cheese with her fingers. The new prescription left her tired all the time, and she couldn't drink. Cheerless herself, spreading the spirit of the season seemed even more important.

The songs bombarded her—at the office and in the car going home, in the grocery store and on TV—corny and reassuring, a link to her childhood. They nested in her head until she whistled despite herself. *What a bright time, it's the right time, to rock the night away. One seems to hear, words of good cheer, from everywhere, filling the air.* In her distraction she sifted the lyrics for solace or inspiration and discovered they were hearty nonsense. You had to be happy to agree with them.

Around Halloween she'd foreseen the possibility of Christmas without Kim, and decided, with no hesitation whatsoever, that they needed to include her. Now when she told Ed they should go ahead and buy her presents, he paused as if giving her time to rethink the idea.

"Would you rather just not get her anything?" she asked.

"No."

Then why did he act like it was bizarre, and wrong? She bought all of their gifts anyway. He didn't have to lift a finger.

"What about stockings?" he asked.

That night she ventured into Lindsay's room to deliver the news. She sat on the edge of her bed as Lindsay turned from her draft on the causes of World War I, tolerating this latest interruption as if she couldn't spare a second. Like her father, she greeted the idea with silence, making Fran explain that Kim was still a part of the family. Now more than ever they needed to keep her in their thoughts.

"I *do*," Lindsay said, flaring, and though she finally agreed, Fran knew she was alone in this hope.

It wasn't the first time. She'd always been the one in the family who loved Christmas the most, or any occasion. She was the planner of parties, the arranger of vacations. Ed would have been satisfied staying home all summer, coaching the team and going out on his boat. She was the one who unfurled the map of the West on the dining room table and measured out the legs of the trip—not because she had some extravagant urge but because that was what families did. She'd grown accustomed to the role of motivator and organizer, as they had, surrendering to her, sometimes, as in this case, grudgingly. Afterward they might thank her ("That was fun," Ed would admit, giving her a kiss), but now, at the beginning, they withheld themselves as if she was misguided and demanding.

Normally she just absorbed the slight and led them by exaggerated example, but between work and home and Kim, she hardly had time to shop. Saturday was dedicated to cutting and decorating a tree, a task that, at their best, tested their patience. Sunday they didn't get back from coffee hour until one, and then she had to address all of their Christmas cards (they were using a picture from graduation, the four of them tall and smiling on the worn grass of the baseball field, meaning for the first time in a decade Cooper wouldn't be in it). While she went through the stack from last year, Ed lay on the couch, watching the Browns. Lindsay, as always, was hibernating upstairs.

She promised herself she wouldn't bug them too much, since they'd made it her personal crusade, but things slipped out. At dinner or before bed, over breakfast. "I still don't have a clue about your mother," she fretted, because Grace was impossible to buy for. "I'll ask her," he said. Twice, three times. It wasn't conscious. She was prodding herself more than anyone else.

She didn't know what she'd get for Kim. It wouldn't be hard, once she started. When Kim had just discovered clothes, they'd go to the mall together, eating lunch at the food court, spending whole afternoons comparing their tastes. It gave Fran an opportunity to buy the nice younger stuff she couldn't wear. It was almost like shopping for herself, a perfectly vicarious thrill. She took a mother's pride in how good Kim looked, tall as a model at thirteen, with her own mother's cheekbones. That was sheer happiness, finding something they both liked, but there was the fear too, watching the older girls cruising in catty packs, that these easy moments of closeness wouldn't last.

Looking back, Fran was sure she'd spoiled her, as sure as she'd short-changed her later, her disappointment turning them into unflinching enemies. It was just a phase—she'd outgrown her own teenaged disdain and found her mother was a smart, competent woman people relied on. And yet it saddened her. She could see the same change happening in Lindsay, and felt helpless and overwhelmed, already stretched too thin. When Fran invited her to the mall, Lindsay turned her down, using her own all-purpose excuse: She didn't have time right now.

No one did. On the radio they were counting down the days, and Fran still had gaps in her lists. Connie and Jocelyn were easy enough, but she had no clue about Rich or Carrie or any of the cousins. She was done badgering Ed for suggestions and went online to order a replacement for Grace's L.L. Bean robe, paying an extra twenty dollars for guaranteed delivery, and though she could cross off another name, the whole process was unsatisfying. A gift was supposed to be surprising yet perfect, an indication of how well you knew the other person, and though Grace would never complain, Fran was ashamed when she recalled all the thoughtful gifts Grace had come up with over the years, especially for the girls, who grew harder and harder to please. A robe was the adult equivalent of underwear, utterly generic. Fran wanted to blame the situation but couldn't entirely. In the past she'd always found a way to make Christmas nice for them.

Ultimately she had no choice. She was too busy during the week, and so many of her coworkers had donated their sick days to keep her on the payroll when she was out that she didn't feel right taking one now. When she told Ed she was going to the mall on Saturday, he froze, as if she expected him to come with her. He seemed relieved when she asked if he minded watching Lindsay. Though normally he argued the con side of that debate (she was sixteen, she didn't need a babysitter), he snatched at the chance.

"It's going to be a nightmare out there."

"You forget," she said, "I do this every year."

The night before, she set the alarm for six. In the morning she dried her hair downstairs so she wouldn't wake them. She gathered her lists and left the house while it was still dark, her breath like fog in the car, reminding her of when she used to smoke. Both of them did, two packs of Marlboros a day, lighting the first one with their coffees and stubbing the last out in the ashtray on their nightstand. She quit when she was pregnant, and while it had been twenty years, now, driving west out of town ahead of the dawn, it seemed another unexpected way Kim had changed their lives.

The four lanes of 20 were empty. The Premix plant was running third shift, lit like a prison, its loading dock lined with trucks. The streetlights showed her the gates of Greenlawn Cemetery, but the graves and the garish aluminum-siding cross were mercifully lost in the dark. Against her will, the blank face of North Kingsville Elementary stirred her memory. She fought it off, focusing on the road. Across a field, a giant star made of colored lights shone beneath the prefab steeple of the Living Water Baptist Church, the crusted snow holding smears of red and yellow and green. It must have been on all night, a shepherd standing watch over its flock. The idea pleased her. Wasn't that what the season was about—heavenly signs and news of miracles?

Over the Ashtabula line, one by one, other cars joined her, all of them headed in the same direction, some passing her and pulling away as if it were a race. She'd thought of stopping at Happy's Donuts for a large coffee to get her going, but scrapped that plan, needing to keep up. As she turned into the mall the lot was already filling, early birds taking the spaces by the main entrance. The car in front of her split off, and she followed it around the side, counting it as an advantage.

The doors wouldn't open for another fifteen minutes and it was too cold to stand outside, so they sat in their cars with their lights off and their heaters running while the sky lightened, the day breaking gray and drab. She went over her lists, envisioning her route and the major stops she'd make. As eight o'clock neared, the first few shoppers crossed the plaza. They were all women, alone or in pairs, none of them young. Rather than viewing them as her competition, Fran saw a sisterhood, wives and mothers, aunts and grandmas, providing for their families. She turned her car off, got out and walked over to wait with them.

She wasn't dismayed that a few of them knew her from TV. As she told the small audience, it was heartening to know someone out there was listening. From habit she was wearing her pin and had a few extras in her bag that she passed around.

"I'd wish you a Merry Christmas," one woman said, "but..."

"Please," Fran said, "we need all the good wishes we can get."

"God bless you," a bundled, cronelike older woman said, clutching her hand, and Fran thanked her. This was the elusive community the news always talked about—people she would have never met except for Kim.

Once the doors opened she saw them only in passing, all of them off on their separate quests, but throughout the day, no matter where she went, her reception was the same. At any second, waiting to pay or navigating the chaotic halls with her bags, she could become the center of attention. Cashiers and shoppers alike waylaid her to convey their sympathy and share their own stories of loss as if she would naturally understand. She found herself nodding, offering her condolences, and would have had no problem with it except that they took so much time. She was already behind.

She was okay when she focused on shopping, but just walking along she was hostage to every teenager, every girl, every mother and daughter. The main atrium was done up in cotton batting like the North Pole, complete with a waving elf driving a scale-model train. She'd stood with Kim in this same line of toddlers waiting to see Santa. They came every year. Lindsay had cried her first time, wary of the stranger behind the beard, where Kim never hesitated, taking Lindsay's hand and leading her like a guide. In family lore the story served as proof of their contrary natures, but now, out of fairness, Fran resisted reading too much into it.

She couldn't stop for lunch—the food court was a zoo anyway. She dropped her first set of bags at the car and grabbed a coffee at the Starbucks (served by a girl Kim's age who looked familiar) and started improvising on top of the list. She found a cute shrug for Lindsay at Fashion Bug, and some fun earrings at Claire's, and at Radio Shack a speaker station for her iPod and a keychain with a digital picture frame she could fill with her favorite shots (she almost bought three of these, but held off). The back of Sears was quiet and had golfballs for Rich, and, in their auto center, for the family, emergency kits for both cars. The Discovery Store took care of the cousins, though the line for the checkout stretched into the shelves. Carrie she drew a blank on, but if she came up empty she could always do a gift certificate to J. Jill—and then she saw the Fiestaware pitcher at Pottery Barn. Her arms were full again, and so far she'd gotten nothing for Kim.

The danger with going out to the car was that she knew she couldn't leave. It was past three and the light was fading, making her think of dinner.

Inside, the carols pursued her from store to store. She should have eaten lunch; she was dragging and had a headache, her attention scattered. At Old Navy she saw an embroidered skirt that was a possibility but finally not right for Kim. She stalked the housewares aisles at Kmart, hoping to find something for her dorm room, and realized she had no clue what Kim might need, though she did pick up a new laundry basket for Lindsay, which she then had to lug around.

By then she'd almost completed her circuit of the mall. She'd put a serious dent in her list, though there were still things she'd have to make special trips for, like Ed's fish finder, which only Dick's sold, or a new googly-eyed steak for Cooper at Petco. The stocking stuffers she could grab at the CVS after work; that was easy. She had tons of stuff for Lindsay but not a big gift, and as every year when she needed something special, she naturally gravitated to the jewelry counter at Penney's.

They were reliable, and cheaper than Kay's or Zales. She could always find something for the girls. She'd bought their first pearls here, and Kim's good watch, and her butterfly, which she never took off, not even to shower.

The pendant was one of a dozen charms in a designer line. Fran had chosen it over the others with hardly a thought. It just fit Kim at sixteen. Now, leaning over the display case, she tried to pick one for Lindsay but nothing jumped out. The ladybug was too childish, the angel too pious. Gull, seahorse, shell, sand dollar—all wrong. It had to be something simple. Not the clover or the rose. In the end she was left with the moon, the star and the heart.

The heart was the one she would have liked to give her. The star actually fit Kim better, her bright, fiery personality. To be true to Lindsay—the distant, changeable night owl—she had to go with the moon.

Her mind was made up, yet she lingered over the butterfly, desirous, as if she could replace the original. She'd never burden Lindsay with it, and to buy it for Kim again made no sense. She herself wouldn't wear it, since it wasn't hers, and yet she wanted it.

How could she explain it to Ed? She'd have to hide it, sneaking the velvet box out of her dresser in solitary moments, opening the lid to admire it like a talisman, as if it had the power to recover its wearer.

"Can I help you with something?" the salesgirl asked—in her twenties, plain but well-dressed, with the unfortunate name of Crystal. Fran was grateful she didn't recognize her.

"I was looking at the moon." She pointed through the glass.

"I like that one too. That's solid twenty-four karat, not gold plate." She reached in and pinched the crescent out, holding it on her flattened palm.

Fran turned it as if inspecting the workmanship and read the price off the tiny tag. She didn't remember Kim's being so expensive.

"We have some nice chains for it over here."

Fran had already noted that they had the right one, a box weave, but made a show of looking through them, ignoring the girl's pitch. The chain itself cost fifty dollars. When she doubled the price, she couldn't justify it.

"Do you need some time to think it over?" the girl asked, because she had customers on the other side and couldn't let her keep the moon.

"Thanks," Fran said, and then stood there empty-handed, staring at the display, cross with herself. It was late and her feet hurt and she was far from done. She had nothing for dinner, and Ed wouldn't take it upon himself to order out. They'd be waiting for her, housebound and helpless as shut-ins after she'd battled the crowds all day.

All she wanted was this one thing. Like a child denied, she argued with the universe. It wasn't fair. She'd been so good. She wasn't asking for that much.

When the girl came over to check on her she asked to see the butterfly, as if holding it in her hands might be enough. It was thin as a razor blade, and she thought of the gold against Kim's skin.

"I'll take both of them," she said.

She put them on her Penney's card so Ed wouldn't see the bill, and was glad she did, because at Williams-Sonoma, as she was paying for Connie's and Jocelyn's hand-painted dessert plates, her MasterCard bounced. She covered it with her Visa, but didn't dare risk anything else.

On the way home, passing the star and the school and the cemetery gates in the dark, she puzzled over how she could buy herself something so expensive when she didn't get anything for Kim. Finally, maybe, it came down to the fact that she was here and Kim wasn't. All along, she thought, the gifts she'd wanted to give Kim were never for her, but, like the butterfly, for herself.

Later, when she told Ed she'd changed her mind, he paused as if waiting for an explanation.

"Don't get me anything either," she said. "I already have everything I need."

But of course, being a good husband, he didn't listen to her.

America's Most Wanted

He hated the phone, the ring waking him from his thoughts like an alarm. He didn't want to talk to anyone; it could only be bad news. He kept the machine on, letting the message kick in, straining despite himself to hear the foreign voice emitting from the kitchen.

In the living room, Fran picked up—a mistake. He cocked his head, trying to gauge her tone, bright but measured, endlessly reasonable. "Yes," she said, pacing by the doorway, "that would be fine."

He turned back to the game. A minute later she was standing behind him with the calendar.

For their end-of-the-year recap, the *Star-Beacon* had picked Kim as their top story. She seemed pleased by this. Saturday they wanted to send a reporter out to interview them, and a photographer to take pictures.

Why did she have to ask when she'd already said yes?

"Pictures of what?" Because, ridiculous as it sounded, he didn't want them in Kim's room.

"I don't know. What kind of pictures do they usually take?"

"Sure," he said.

"You don't have to be in them if you don't want to."

"I didn't say that."

"You didn't have to," she said, as if somehow he was at fault. Hadn't he just said he would?

She acted like she'd read his mind, but, really, who wanted to stand out in the snow and pose while the neighbors peered at them from their windows? Lindsay didn't either, but that Saturday, like Ed, jacketless and squinting into the sun, she did. Anything for Kim.

"Thank you," Fran told them when the photographer was gone, as if they'd done her a great favor, then sped off to be a guest on a cable-access show in Erie.

Her latest crusade was getting Kim on *Dateline* or *America's Most Wanted*, using local TV as a stepping stone. According to her chat group, after Natalee Holloway the networks were hungry for missing girl stories. She'd put together a new DVD and mailed copies to every station from here to Toledo. He admired her energy, even if he didn't understand it.

New Year's Eve they stayed in. Fran was online most of the night and then went to bed at her regular time, and Lindsay kept to her room, so he watched Dick Clark by himself, yawning. As the seconds ticked off and the ball dropped, he thought this had been the worst year of his life, and that the best was long gone. On TV everyone was dancing, celebrating to Kool & the Gang. He switched it off and went through the house, killing the lights.

The year turning was supposed to be hopeful, a new beginning, but he was stuck in last summer. The market was stalled and his desk wasn't busy enough to hold him. He escaped, driving the white streets as if he had a client, ending up by the picnic pavilion on the bluffs. He smoked with his window open and the heater blowing. As winter locked in, that last unfinished day came back, the lake crowded with boats, Queen Anne's lace rampant by the highway, heat shimmering like gas above the tracks, while outside, unreal and temporary, snow fell on the lighthouse and the jetties and the ice shingling the harbor. On the fourteenth it would be six months.

They marked the anniversary with a well-attended prayer vigil led by Father John, and music by the combined choir and high school glee club. All four network affiliates from Erie carried it. Later, getting ready for bed, Fran complained that Lindsay hadn't sung a note.

"You know she hates those things."

"No one *likes* them," she said. "Some things you just have to do. That's life."

He wanted to defend Lindsay, but it was true. He had to wake up and go to work. He had to eat and sleep and know what was coming up on the calendar, though he no longer looked forward to anything. Pretending to be interested took a constant effort. When he was by himself he went slack, and then he remembered he had to fix the light in the closet or refill the cars with wiper fluid or buy more ice melter. He had to explain to the bursar's office that Kim wouldn't be attending school this semester either.

Some of it was money. He'd sold a small industrial site in November, but nothing since. Wednesdays the *Star-Beacon* was full of foreclosure notices. Ten years ago they would have seemed an opportunity (false, it turned out, the start of his downfall). He skipped their estimated tax payment and cashed in another mutual fund to hold them over. The bills came in waves. He'd fought them off for months, but that couldn't last. All of their money was in the house, and the longer they held on to it, the less it was worth. He could imagine their address listed for the whole town to see. As a father, he wanted to hang on until Lindsay was through with school. As a professional, his advice to himself was to get out now.

The day of the Super Bowl his mother had another ministroke. They moved her to a skilled-care wing, where she shared a room with a tiny Greek woman who'd lost her feet to diabetes. The woman seemed pleasant enough (all she did was knit and watch TV), but his mother was used to her privacy and didn't like her. "She talks. All day long, 'blucka blucka blucka,' like I know what she's saying." She missed her dining-room friends. She could walk with a walker, the doctors said, but the physical therapist was nasty to her and she refused to go anymore. After speaking with the staff, he doubted the charge, but arranged to have her see a second therapist. That lasted one day and led to several meetings. Ultimately he and Fran had to sit down with her and lay it out plainly: She needed to do her rehab.

"I don't want to," she said fiercely, tearing up. "It hurts me."

"You're not going to get better if you don't," he said.

"I'm too old to go through this again."

Inwardly he agreed—he didn't want her to suffer—but Fran was unmoved. "I know it's hard, but if you stop walking you're never going to get out of this bed. That's not what you want, believe me."

The idea frightened her into action. Now her daily routine included a walk to the sunroom at the far end of the hall after lunch. When he visited he accompanied her on the long journey, stepping and then halting beside her as she inched the walker forward, puffing with effort. Every time he left he was overcome by her determination and ashamed of his own flatness, and vowed to take Fran's advice.

As a coach he was a practiced motivator, a preacher of mental toughness, but much of what he felt was out of his control. He had a dream in which Kim fell from the upper deck of a stadium. For some unknown reason he was in a luxury box on the other side of the field. He saw her stumble on the concrete stairs and pitch over the railing in slow motion. He reached out his arms as if to catch her, and then, magically, he was directly above her, watching her fall toward the seats below. While she was in the air, he wished that somehow she would fly or float down (he was aware it was a nightmare, and not entirely subject to gravity). He didn't see her hit, just the crowd flinching at impact, clearing a space around her. Police were pushing through the aisles. He didn't tell Fran about the dream, knowing she'd hold it against him. He only had it once, but pieces came to him during the day, flashing like clips in a movie trailer. The question that bothered him was why she was sitting over there alone. He should have been with her.

He had trouble thinking at any length, and to occupy his mind he watched TV. The problem was, anything emotional made him well up. One night he was watching *The Shawshank Redemption*, an old favorite. "Hope is a good thing," Morgan Freeman said, and he had to turn it off and breathe deeply, blinking, not wanting anyone to see him.

He hadn't given up on Kim, as Fran sometimes implied. He still met with the detective and called Perry once a week, though whatever friendship they'd had was over. As he had all fall, he lobbied for a thorough search of Wozniak's property. They made it sound like an impossibility. He thought seriously of going over there himself. He thought of buying a gun, except Fran would think he was crazy.

The problem was, he was painfully sane. He realized that he was depressed and angry, but in his position it made sense. After six months he was merely being realistic. He didn't see what Fran hoped to accomplish, waking early and updating the website, running all over the place chasing after TV coverage. He was afraid that eventually she would exhaust herself and end up in the same place he was.

He did what he had to. He manned the grill in a KISS THE COOK apron at the church pancake supper and scooped popcorn at the high school basketball games. He handed out buttons and balloons and pens and Koosh balls and key chains. He stood behind Fran in his best suit as she drove home the D.A.R.E. speech she'd practiced on him, and shook hands in the receiving line after the program, listening to how impressed people were with her. While he suspected she was deluded, he was proud of her too. He'd always known she was capable and strong—it was partly what attracted him to her—but she'd gone beyond anything he could have imagined. The transformation was total: hair, makeup, clothes. Since she'd quit drinking she'd lost so much weight that her face had changed. Sometimes when she was at the mic, under the lights, it was like watching someone he didn't know.

For Valentine's Day, he wasn't sure how much they should celebrate. He planned on getting her roses and chocolates, as always, but not champagne. He was hoping they could have a nice dinner at home.

"You're *not* serious," she said. "It's Valentine's Day. The only thing this chick is making is reservations."

To atone he took her to Biscotti's in Conneaut, where she told him about the panel she'd been invited to join (he was welcome too, though most of them were mothers), and the conference in Albany next month, and the cookbook she and Connie were putting together, and the possibility of meeting with the governor. April 9th was National Missing Persons Day—it was a perfect opportunity to get the word out. She'd cheated and had a glass of wine, and she was excited, craning over her place setting as she spoke.

"Wow," he said. "You've been busy."

"I know I haven't been around much. I'm sorry. Not that anyone misses me."

"I miss you."

"No you don't. You just miss me making your dinner."

"That too," he admitted. "Lindsay misses you."

"Now I know you're lying."

"She's been bugging me about a job."

"Quizno's," she said, as if it were a problem. What she meant was that the shop was a lonely outpost on the wrong side of the railroad underpass from downtown. It shared the same cracked plaza—former home of a 7-Eleven—with the Broad Street Mini Mart, which sold liquor, cigarettes and lottery tickets. It was a corner he tried not to drive his clients by.

"She'd be with Dana, and there'd be a manager there the whole time."

"How's she going to get there?" Because, though Lindsay and Dana both had their licenses, they couldn't have passengers other than family.

"I'll talk to Grant and Helen, maybe we can do a tag team. I just want to get her out of her room and off the damn computer."

"I'm with you on that."

"We can't keep her locked up."

"I know," she conceded, sitting back. "It couldn't be someplace easy."

"I don't think there is such a place."

"It's not going to get in the way of her flute lessons?"

"That's one day a week. Her grades are great."

"Her grades *are* great, I've got no problem with her grades. Did she ask you to ask me?"

"Why?"

"It's like you're trying to sell me on the idea."

"I think it's great that she wants to work. I mean, we wouldn't even be having this conversation if things were normal."

He'd finished the thought in his head before the words left his mouth, and regretted them immediately.

"You're right," she finally said. "I'm sure it's just me."

"It's not just you. I've got the same worries you do."

"Let's talk about something else," she said, looking around at the other couples. "We're supposed to be having a romantic evening."

They tried. She had a second glass of wine, though she wasn't supposed to, and a third, and then dessert and espresso. They both ate too much, they agreed on the drive home, and, groaning, went straight to bed, where, to his surprise, she reached for him and climbed on top. She was noisy, where she usually worried about Lindsay hearing them. He could feel her ribs through her skin, each of them distinct, and the bones of her shoulders. She arched and then flung herself down on him, her hair in his face. Her mouth tasted of wine, and he wondered if she only wanted him because she was half drunk.

"It's been a long time," she said in the dark afterward.

He hadn't thought so, but then he tried to remember the last time, and, oddly, couldn't.

"Too long," he said.

Later, listening to her snore, he couldn't recall that ever happening before, and took it as a bad sign. The next time he'd know how long it had been, to the day.

Being the Cup

Her weeks now were measured out in shifts. Monday-Wednesday-Friday, after school till close, plus Saturday lunch. Her mother said she couldn't work more than twenty hours and that she'd have to quit if her grades suffered. It was already March. They were nearly done with the third marking period and she had straight A's, so basically that was impossible, but her mother said it like a threat. Her father trusted she wouldn't abuse this privilege. To Lindsay it sounded like they were talking to a convict. Dropping her and Dana off in their matching black shirts, her father told them not to work too hard and then waited until they were inside to leave.

They couldn't have been safer. At night when the weather turned mild a few bikers might hang around the minimart before racketing off, but two of the guys on their crew, Tyler Stafford and Jared Hamilton, were on the football team, and Mr. Candele, the manager, was bigger than either of them. The only time she and Dana were alone was on break, squatting on milk crates and smoking right outside the backdoor. She knew her mother imagined her being dragged into a car (she'd imagined it herself, being yanked by the wrist through an open window), but the chances of that actually happening were ridiculous. At home she liked to say the most dangerous part of working there was the smell.

Her first week she was the Meat. It was a rite they'd all gone through. "Meat, go get me some olives." "Tell the Meat she doesn't have to nuke the meatballs five thousand times." "Yo, Meat, what part of 'no tomato' don't you understand?" Dana rode her harder than anyone. At school their crowd was several rungs below (and opposed to) Tyler and Jared's, and it was weird to see her joking with them.

Dana had warned her that the job was mindless—cleaning lettuce, slicing cheese, wiping tables. Lindsay figured a little drudgery was the price of independence. What she hadn't counted on was how embarrassing it was. Along with the logo shirts, they had to wear gay baseball caps and black aprons, which, as the shift went on, gathered mustard and mayo stains, and floury handprints from the rolls. The menu was loaded with trademarked names like Trippin' Turkey and Cabo Chicken and Yin-Yang Salad. When she repeated the orders of people from school—guys especially—she couldn't look them in the eye. She knew the prompts by heart, but the words came out muddled. "What kind of bread would you like on that?" The plastic gloves they wore came in three sizes, none of which fit her. In the middle of building a sub, one slipped off and she had to fetch another pair. She forgot what people wanted and had to ask again. Just being there made her dumb.

She was tired all the time. Except for break Mr. Candele never let them sit down, even when they were all caught up and the place was empty. "If you're leanin', you're cleanin'," he said, so much that they used it on one another.

As the Meat she drew the shit jobs. They made her clean the bathrooms and take out the trash. They gave her whole bags of onions to cut. They saved the baked-on broccoli cheese vat for her, and watched like judges as she scrubbed at it with a gummy green pad, the white scum packed under her fingernails. They made her be the Cup.

Friday and Saturday, no matter what the weather was like, the Cup walked up and down Broad Street, waving at cars. The costume was awesomely stupid, eight feet tall with googly eyes and a dippy grin and a red straw poking from the top. A built-in fan at her hip kept it inflated, buzzing so it was hard to hear. Despite the constant rush of air, the interior held the vinegary stink of curdled sweat, like a guys' locker room, though after a few minutes the space filled with her own stale cigarette breath. The light through the white fabric and the claustrophobic closeness reminded her of reading underneath the covers. She could only see straight ahead through a mesh window in the big Q on the Cup's midsection. Because of its circumference her arms poked out like flippers.

Dana said it was tough getting up if you fell down. She told Lindsay horror stories about gangs jumping out of cars and beating up Cups, using their cellphones to shoot video that ended up on the net. Here they just threw stuff. Cups, cans, sometimes pennies. They didn't hurt because of the padding, but it was pretty degrading. You didn't want to stand too close to the road. Back when Dana started, Lindsay had driven by just to give her shit for being the Cup. Now Dana helped her into the costume and walked her across the lot like a sacrifice.

"Good luck."

"Yeah, thanks," Lindsay said through the mesh.

It was Friday rush hour, and she was posted by the light at Broad and 16th to entice people into bringing sandwiches home for dinner. She ambled back and forth along the line of stopped cars at a safe distance, waggling her arms, throwing in a few clumsy poses ("Superstar!") to stave off the boredom, all the while waiting for the first bottle to come flying toward her face.

Instead, people pointed and smiled, shaking their heads. Drivers honked. Kids waved to her, even some adults, and Lindsay naturally waved back. After months of dreading every public event, it felt strange. They didn't know who she was, they just liked her for giving them something to look at, and she liked them for being kind. Dana hadn't warned her about this. The goofiness of the costume had rubbed off on her. All of a sudden she was like the Bubble Boy. Everyone was rooting for her.

She liked being in disguise, and putting on a show. In real life she couldn't dance at all, but now she tried out Pee Wee's big shoe dance, and the Macarena, and as much of the Electric Slide as she remembered from second grade. She did William Hung's "She Bangs" and practiced kung fu moves on a sign until she broke a sweat. Dana was crazy. This was way better than working.

The only thing anyone threw at her was a balled-up Dairy Queen bag, which she saw coming and which fell short, rolling nearly to her feet. "What's up with that?" she asked, arms wide, taunting the car—a blue Camaro—then, as the driver took off, shook her fist at it, still in character. "You better run, bitches! I'll cup you good."

She was pretending to hitchhike when something thumped against her back.

It was Dana, coming to her rescue. Lindsay couldn't believe it had been a full hour already.

"So, what'd they get you with?" Dana asked, looking the costume up and down for damage.

"Just that."

"That's nothing."

"It really wasn't bad."

"Yeah, no, you don't want to say that too loud. Just wait till summer, it's brutal inside that thing."

"It was kind of fun, actually."

"Okay," Dana said, "now you're scaring me."

Inside, Tyler and Jared greeted her with laughter, miming karate chops.

"Go ahead, Lindsay Lohan!" Jared said.

"Best, Cup, ever," Tyler said.

"A-thank you, a-thank you," Lindsay said, trying to bow without falling over.

The next morning when she was doing her routine she felt something small bounce off her. On the sidewalk lay a smoldering cigarette, a Newport by the green bands around the filter. Whoever flicked it was through the light and gone, and really, it hadn't hurt.

The half-full coffee that splashed across her sneakers was something else ("Okay, that's fucked-up"), but still she kept on clowning, waving to the kids and the silly adults. Some woman in a two-tone van even took her picture. Looking out at the world through the mesh, Lindsay thought that you either got the Cup or you didn't. She was glad she did, no matter what Dana said.

Later there would be other, more serious initiations, like the first time she cut herself slicing bread, the first time she burned herself on the oven, the first time Mr. Candele let her be the Finisher, but the Cup was the big one. From then on they treated her like an equal, all of them united against the customers who said, "Mmm...toasty" after the first bite.

By May she'd earned her first raise and developed a crush on Jared, which Dana immediately picked up on, ragging her mercilessly. Though it was hopeless, she looked forward to going in just to be with him. It was her place now, more so than home. Here she could be bitchy and silly, and when she was working side-by-side with Jared, happy, every second ripe with possibility. The right touch, the right look, and the whole world was hers. At dusk, when the dinner rush was kicking their asses and the headlights of passing cars reached in the window, sometimes she'd glance up from the sandwich she was making and catch a glimpse of the pigeons that lived beneath the underpass wheeling in front of the dark downtown, showing the white undersides of their stubby wings, and wonder if Kim ever felt like this.

Last Summer

After everything, she couldn't go back to the Conoco. She hadn't wanted to come home at all, and did only because her mom asked her. It would be cheaper, her mom said, as if she had to rationalize it somehow. Nina could save more money this way. Nina agreed, but told her this would probably be the last time.

"That's fine," her mom said. "I just need you here right now."

Elise got her on at Sal's, where the older crowd ate. After working food service at school she wasn't shocked at how disgusting the kitchen was, or how much of the menu came straight out of cans. The customers loved it. She smiled and made great tips, proving her mom right.

She and Elise and J.P. were a unit. The Giant Eagle had closed, and he was working at the Golden Dawn downtown. He hadn't bothered to fix his car; he said it looked better this way. They sunned by the river before shift and drank at the beach after. Hinch and Marnie were still at the DQ but didn't hang out like they used to. The weather was forest-fire dry, the empty streets wavering in the heat. Some days it seemed like it could be last summer, that any second Kim would come walking out of the trees and across the rocks with her beach bag. It seemed impossible that it had been a year.

At the service marking the anniversary, the three of them sat together near the front. Lindsay had come back special from camp to read the lesson. Tall and tan, with her hair cut short, she looked more like Kim than ever. Kim's mom had lost too much weight; her eyes were sunken, her cheeks creased. On his way out Kim's dad nodded to J.P., they all saw it. They could only hope it was a start.

Later that night, in their jeans and sweatshirts, they sat around the fire and remembered how strong she was, how wild. Stubborn. Smart. Competitive. Elise admitted she was a little intimidated by her.

"Why?" Nina asked, though she knew exactly what she meant.

"I was," J.P. confessed.

"You didn't want to get on her bad side," Elise said.

"No you didn't," J.P. agreed.

"It wasn't like it was premeditated," Nina said. "I've got a temper too."

"And we still love you," Elise said. "Remember the time she kicked that guy's truck at White Turkey?"

"I thought she was going to kick his ass."

"He asked for it," Nina said. "He stole her spot."

They drank to her, clinking the necks of their beers together, then sat listening to the waves folding over themselves. Out on the end of the jetty, the lighthouse swept its beam across the water. Above them, beyond the stars, the Milky Way flowed, ghostly. Despite all of their memories, every night they came to a place where there was nothing to say. There were still some beers left, but it was time to go home. Nina thought that Kim would have hated knowing she was the reason they were sober.

In bed she listened to the one o'clock moving through and imagined herself lost in the dark woods, trying to orient herself by the echoes. A short blast and then a long flaring one like a warning. There were pockets of marsh back in there, stands of cattails and black pools teeming with mosquitoes. One of her worst fears from childhood was stepping off the path and being sucked under the mud. What had happened to Kim was something else, but the result was the same, and in the drowsy, dreamy interlude before sleep she had a hard time keeping the two of them separate. In the morning she would recall this confusion and see it as wishful, as if she could save Kim by becoming her. Or maybe, she thought, she missed Kim so much that she wanted to be with her.

Elise had been having dreams too. In one the three of them hiked out the tracks west of town to the bridge like when they were kids, except when they got there a fire was burning in the middle of the trestle. Kim wanted to walk out and douse it with her Girl Scout canteen, and they had to stop her.

"What do you think it means?"

"We should go out there," Nina said.

She expected Elise to protest, but the idea had been in her head longer than Nina's.

"Should we take J.P.?" Elise asked.

No, they needed to do this alone.

When Nina told him their plan, he said he understood, but she could see he wanted to come. He told her to be careful, as if it was dangerous.

Wednesday at nine in the morning he dropped them off with their backpacks at the crossing by Crawford Container, then stood there waving good-bye over the roof of his car. She was afraid he was going to watch them all the way around the bend, and was relieved when she looked back and he was gone.

The right-of-way was raised and uneven, a mound of loose stones that clashed with every step. They each chose a track and soon fell into rhythm, walking side-by-side over the oil-darkened ties. A sign advised them that they were trespassing on Conrail property. The trees were still, the sky cloudless. Sun glinted off the rails.

"What are you going to do about him?" Elise asked.

"What?"

"What what. You know what."

"Nothing," Nina said.

"Probably smart."

"I don't think it would be good, with everything."

"You should tell him that."

"Why?"

"Because it's seriously painful to watch."

"And this would make it better how ...?"

"At least he'd know then."

"Sometimes it's better not to know." She didn't mean about Kim, it just came out that way. Everything was about her now. It was why Nina hadn't wanted to come back, and why anything with J.P. seemed sketchy. "Why don't *you* tell him if you're so worried?"

"I will if you want me to."

"Don't you dare."

"Uh-oh."

"Just let it go, okay?"

"Okay," Elise said, holding both hands in front of her like she was afraid.

They walked on, not talking. There was no shade. They were wearing their swimsuits under their cutoffs, and Nina was beginning to sweat. The rails lay straight on ahead, vanishing a mile away in a white haze. Their pilgrimage had seemed like a good idea—as if by retracing their steps they might recover something—but now she wasn't sure. There was nothing out here but the daisies and weeds on both sides, simmering with insects. They passed a neat stack of ties soaked black with creosote, and, later, a dead fire with a scattering of cracked red keg cups. From the woods came the razzing of a dirt bike, so close it was threatening, then gradually moving away, still hidden. She could see how for kids this would have been an adventure. She would have never been brave enough to come out here by herself. Like all of their boldest exploits, the idea had been Kim's.

After a while they stopped beneath a tall signal showing two green lights. Elise had brought water, and they passed the bottle back and forth.

"I've got no problem with it," Elise said. "If that's what you're worried about."

"Thanks for your permission."

"You're welcome."

"Jesus, that's all I need right now."

"You know what scares me?" Elise said. "We're turning into a couple of old maids."

"I'm just taking a break."

"Right, me too."

"It's not like it's going to be forever."

"I hope not. I'm getting weirder every day. The other night I was actually thinking of giving Sam a call."

"You should have. Sam's harmless."

"Exactly," Elise said.

The signal above them clunked and turned red.

Nina checked her watch. "The ten thirty's early."

Elise offered her the bottle a last time, then zipped her pack closed, and they set off again.

Nina measured her stride to fit the ties. Though she didn't show it, what Elise said bothered her. Since Kim disappeared she'd become cautious about guys. It only made sense. It wasn't like she decided to feel that way, she just did. Where she'd been living, her paranoia was justified. There had been three rapes in the neighborhood right next to campus, and the security in her dorm was a joke. At night, walking back from the library, she stayed in sight of the blue lights of the emergency phones, her room key protruding from one fist like a blade.

They hadn't gone far when the drumming of diesels overtook them. The sound seemed to be coming from everywhere, though behind them there was no sign of a train. In the distance the headlight appeared. Nina's rails began to sing, a metallic lashing that ran through the steel like a current until it was drowned out by the engines. They crossed the stony right-of-way and stopped shy of the weeds and stood there as the train hurtled past. Elise waved, and the engineer tipped his cap.

The train was a deadheading freight hauling dozens of empty silver-sided autoracks. They flashed by, rocking on their springs. Elise clamped both hands over her ears until the last car passed—an autorack, not a caboose, and Nina felt cheated.

They checked both ways before getting back on the tracks. The rails were singing again, long shivery filaments that lingered well after the train was gone. Soon there was nothing but the birds and insects and their own footsteps.

Up ahead the tracks curved.

"How far is it?" Elise asked.

"Not far. A half hour?"

When they were in middle school, going out and back took all day. They packed sandwiches and Goldfish and Kool-Aid Koolers they'd frozen overnight, and Kim brought her dad's old transistor radio so they'd have music. They had their cellphones in case something happened, a safeguard that now seemed ridiculous. How could their parents have ever let them go alone?

Beyond the curve they came upon an old spur Nina remembered, a single pair of bedless tracks veering off into saplings and weeds. Somewhere back in there was a flooded gravel pit where people had bonfires. The river ran right behind it.

"We must be close," she told Elise.

"Good."

Minutes later she could hear the rush of water like far-off traffic and held out an arm to stop her.

"What?"

"Listen."

As they walked, the noise grew until finally the trees gave on open space, the land dropping away sharply. The bridge straddled a low falls where the river pinched in. With the dry spell the channel was narrow, shoals of stones along each bank. Upstream the water was dark as oil, and smooth, undulating in waves before it entered the chute, pouring over boulders, breaking white around the pilings and swirling in turbid pools on the far side. That was where they'd jump.

The drop was at least thirty feet.

"I don't know," Elise said.

"I don't know either."

There was no choice. They tugged off their clothes and shoved them in their packs, folded their sunglasses and pulled their hair back, double-knotted their beat-up sneakers. As if in tribute, they were both wearing their suits from last summer.

Just walking out onto the trestle was a test. There was no railing, and you could see through the ties to the hillside sloping away below. Nina went first, hunched over her feet, arms out for balance. A light breeze was sweeping down the river, and she imagined herself sailing off the side like a kite. She paused before a gap in the ties to get both feet into position and lost all momentum. They hadn't even reached the river yet. Beneath her the treetops rose like spikes. If she fell, at the very least she'd break a leg—her spine, more likely. Elise would have to climb down and get her, and they were miles from the nearest road. They'd have to bring in the Life Flight, except there was nowhere to land.

"You okay?" Elise asked, right behind her.

"I'm good," she said, but she had to wait a few seconds before she could step over the hole.

"You want me to go first?"

"I'm good," Nina said, then, after her legs balked again, "Yeah, why don't you."

Elise didn't have any trouble, while she shuffled across, stopping often. Elise waited for her, talking to give her something to focus on. "I can't believe we used to think this was fun. A train's not going to come while we're out here, right?"

"No," Nina said. She could barely speak. She needed all her concentration to stay upright.

As they crossed above the riverbank they stopped to toss their packs over the side. She wouldn't let Elise help her slip out of hers. It landed on the rocks, raising a puff of dust.

"Is it easier without it?"

"No."

They were over the water when she got stuck again.

"Want to turn around?"

"No."

"All right. This one's not that big."

"Fuck! Why can't I do this?"

"You *are* doing this," Elise said. "Come on, we're almost there."

It was a lie designed to keep her moving, and it worked. She knew how far they'd come. There was no way she was going back.

Once they'd made it and were centered above the pool, Elise helped her sit down. Even with her bottom solidly planted, she was afraid she'd slip between the ties. Below, the dark water swelled. It was impossible to tell how deep it was, and they sat for a while in the sun, resting, looking off over the river and the trees, still as a picture. High up, a hawk was turning circles, and she thought that if Kim's spirit was anywhere, it was here.

"Three Amigos," she said, pressing the Boy Scout salute to her heart, meeting Elise's outstretched fingertips, then touching her chest again.

"Three Amigos," Elise said. "We should have brought a bottle of champagne or something."

"Or at least some Kool-Aid Koolers."

"The blue ones."

"The green ones," Nina said. "Sorry I'm being such a chicken."

"That's okay, I'm one too."

"No, you saved me. I never used to be afraid. It sucks."

"Maybe it's temporary," Elise said.

"I hope so."

"Let's find out."

She pushed herself up and offered Nina a hand.

"Can't we just stay here?"

"You can if you want to."

There was no point in stalling. It was the whole reason they came. She knew she couldn't do it alone, and she didn't want to be stuck up here by herself. Still she couldn't move.

"Come on. For Kim."

"Not fair."

"Okay," Elise said, and swung her arms like she was going to jump.

"Wait."

She reached out and Elise helped her to her feet. She crouched, knees bent, as if she wanted to sit down. Elise steadied her and got her to walk. They baby-stepped toward the edge. Far below, the water rolled in a slow boil.

"Oh shit," she said.

"Ready?"

"No."

"For Kim," Elise said, and together, screaming, they jumped.

Once they were in the water, she was fine, and could laugh at herself. Doing it was easy. It was the anticipation that was nerve-racking. All she needed was the courage to make up her mind. Later she would think it was the same with J.P. After she kissed him, the rest just happened naturally.

Catch and Release

With Lindsay away at camp they were alone, and the days slowed. Cooper moped around the house, searching for her. After dinner he snuck upstairs and sacked out under her bed, and they had to wake him up to go pee.

Apparently she had a boyfriend named Chris who taught archery, though over the phone she wouldn't commit to how serious it was. "He's a really nice guy," she said, whatever that meant. Fran wanted to trust her judgment. She had Cabin 15, the eleven- and twelve-year-olds, a tough age, lots of drama. Their nightly devotions focused on how they could treat one another better.

She sounded happy and busy—she always seemed to call when she was doing her laundry—and Fran didn't ruin the mood by bringing up Kim. Camp was supposed to be a vacation from the real world.

She couldn't help but tell her to be careful.

"I *am*," Lindsay said defensively.

"Want to talk to your dad?"

"Sure."

Fran handed him the phone and then listened in. He kidded her about Chris and told her, joking, that things were mighty quiet around here without her. He was getting out on the boat a little—"Somebody has to feed the fish." He brightened while he was talking with her, laughing as if everything was funny, a side of him Fran hadn't glimpsed in months. He checked with her to see if there was anything else, and when there wasn't, said, "Okay, I love you, Linds. 'Bye," and went back to the couch, where he sat, blankly watching the game.

She worried about him now. He was smoking, though she'd asked him not to. She'd hoped he would go back to coaching, but he said it was too soon. Instead he went fishing, taking the boat out after work and on Saturdays, calling from the lake to say he'd be late for dinner, or not to bother, he'd grab something at the marina. She reheated leftovers in the toaster oven, or just had yogurt. The bat bag sat in the garage, gathering cobwebs along with Kim's car. Sunday was reserved for church and visiting his mother, who was struggling. Fran understood that he was grieving; what made her impatient was the way he withdrew into himself. At her most uncharitable, she thought he actually enjoyed wallowing. Secretly she was afraid he'd given up.

She could have used his support. While she still organized local events for Kim, she'd taken on the CUE Center's crusade for a national database of missing adult children. Like the Amber Alert system, it would have the ability to instantly notify the public. The biggest roadblock they'd run into wasn't official but practical: police mistakenly upholding an eighteen- or nineteen-year-old's right to disappear, in violation of Suzanne's Law. When she spoke to groups, she said, "That's exactly what happened to us," because, in retrospect, it was. The police hadn't believed them, and wasted crucial hours. People came up to her afterward and said they ought to sue, an idea she dismissed with little thought. Money wasn't the point. If she could spare one family what they'd been through, it would be worth it.

She couldn't completely blame him for not wanting to come with her to these speaking engagements. He'd heard her spiel before, and often her audiences were small—members of the Lions or the Rotary, the blue-haired regulars at backwater libraries—but she tired of having to explain his absence. Driving home cross-country after a poorly attended event, she wondered if they were still in this together, and then when she pulled in, his car was gone.

It was partly her fault. In the spring he'd been so miserable, and she couldn't be there every weekend. She encouraged him to take the boat out, thinking it would be good for him. Now she wanted to hold him liable for following her advice.

Connie thought it was his way of removing himself from the situation so he wouldn't have to deal with it, and Fran mostly agreed. When threatened by anything unpleasant, he retreated, whether that meant into silence or his hobbies or just another room.

When she confided with some of the other mothers online, instead of confirming what she was feeling, they told her to let it go. Everyone has their own schedule, they said, everyone needs their own space. Be patient. There were worse things he could be doing.

Go with him, one woman from Missouri said—advice Fran took as a challenge, impractical as it sounded. His trips lasted for hours, and she had so much to do, but what better way to get close to him? On the boat he couldn't run from her.

Friday at breakfast she asked if he was going out tomorrow.

He nodded over his cereal.

"Want some company?"

His hesitation was deliberate, quizzical. He shrugged. "Sure."

"What time do we have to get up?"

"Four thirty if you want to catch anything."

"I can do four thirty."

"The weather's not supposed to be so great."

"That's okay."

"We won't be back till after lunch."

"I'll make some sandwiches."

"You're going to get up at four thirty on a Saturday," he asked.

"I'm up at five fifteen every morning."

She liked that she'd surprised him, she just wished he didn't act like it was a bluff. That night he gave her another chance to back out, shaking his head and smiling as if she didn't know what she'd gotten herself into, until she wondered if it was a bad idea. She had a vision of the two of them trapped on a tiny raft surrounded by miles of open water. It would be a kind of test, like surviving on a desert island—but that's what a marriage was, wasn't it? They would have to help each other or die.

In the morning the clouds blotted out the stars. The forecast was for scattered showers, winds five to ten miles an hour, waves three to five feet. "That's from last night," he said. "They're just guessing." He stood in the driveway, trying to read the sky like a farmer. "Hope you don't mind getting wet."

"Good fishing weather." She'd heard him say it a million times.

"I like your attitude."

As they came down the long hill through the park she could barely see the lighthouse, a white blip in the mist. Fog hung low over the ball-fields and the parking lot—soaked though it hadn't rained, the middle ranked with custom pickups and empty trailers. The marina was lit and busy with fishermen, most of them his age, wearing the same uniform of jeans and windbreakers and baseball caps, paired up or solo, a few with grown sons. "Could be ugly," he called to them. "We'll find out, won't we?" They all knew him, waving or tipping their chins in recognition as they readied their gear, then pausing to watch her pass as if she was bad luck. Except for a heavyset teenager in a Browns hoodie and olive barn boots, she was the only female there.

He was so practiced at unsnapping and then folding the cover that she felt like she was in the way. She handed him the rods and his tackle box across the gunwale, then stood on the dock feeling useless while he rearranged the cockpit. He turned the key and the gauge cluster glowed a radium green. She'd gotten him the fish finder for Christmas. It was the first time she'd seen it out of the box.

"We should have enough gas. We're not going way, way out."

Because of her? No, she wanted to say, let's go as far as we can.

She waited while he primed the engine. It caught on the first try, idling deeply, lug-a-lug-a-lug.

"Okay, cast off the lines. Aft first."

"Got it."

She didn't need him to remind her. When the girls were little they were here every weekend. She undid the lines and hopped onto the bow, scissoring around the windshield as he backed into the inlet and joined the slow file of boats heading out, their running lights gemlike in the dark. He stood to steer, the wheel at his waist, guiding them by the blinking NO WAKE buoys. There was no wind and the air smelled fishy.

She could feel the resistance of the water beneath them. It made her impatient, as if they were late.

They cleared the mouth of the inlet. Across the harbor, in the murk, an ore boat sat at port, black as a whale, a spotlight shining on its flag. The water was choppier here, pitching them about, and he eased the throttle forward so the bow rode higher. As they glided by the lighthouse she saw puffed-up gulls sleeping on the rocks, and then, without a word, he gunned it and they were beyond the breakwater and dashing across the lake in the dark, smacking the waves, the spray stinging her face. The engine was deafening and the wind made her squint. She ducked down and hung on to the grab bar, bracing herself, struggling to see ahead of them. He wasn't doing it to scare her—she was sure he drove even faster when he was alone—he was just giving her a taste of what it was like. When he looked over she smiled to show she was having fun.

They motored out for a while. With the fog and the darkness there were no landmarks, just the navchart on-screen she couldn't read. She thought he was losing the others, that he was trying to find a quiet place where they wouldn't be disturbed. Her image of him fishing involved solitude and calm, almost like meditation, the lake an empty space he could fill with his thoughts, but here he was—"There you go!" he hollered—stabbing at a green blob on the fish finder and racing off to intercept it.

A raft of boats was already parked over the spot. He slowed, their wake pushing them from behind, and dropped it into neutral, claiming a space on the edge of the pack. The sun must have risen; the gray surrounding them was brighter now. From across the water came the gurgle of an outboard. She thought they were too close, as if they were intruding.

"Let's get you set up," he said, leaving the wheel unattended.

The swells rocked them. He was used to it, moving easily, while she kept a hand on the seat back to stay upright. According to the finder the fish were between fifteen and twenty-five feet down. He measured out her line and tied on her lure, which was tapered and silver and speckled to look like another fish, with oversized eyes and three grappling-style hooks. He showed her the button to free the reel, trapping the line against the rod, then hauled back and let fly, lifting his thumb as he cast. The lure rose in an arc, floating high and dropping into the water with a plop. He pushed the button so she could reel in and try it herself.

Hers flopped off to the right, not half as far.

"That'll work," he said.

Years ago she'd known how—she actually hadn't been bad—and she was pleased she could still do it, if stiffly. She had to coach herself through the individual steps: Button, thumb, reach back, cast and let go at the same time. He did it with an offhand ease, whipping his straight and far, letting it sink a long time before reeling in, deftly jerking the rod left and right to imitate a smaller fish darting away.

"Looks like Tommy's on 'em," he said, as a guy in a blaze orange hat a couple of boats over netted something big. What were they—perch, bass? She had no idea, but now she wanted one, if only to prove she belonged here.

She was getting better, even if she wasn't catching anything. Occasionally she put the lure where she wanted to, though never as far out as his. It began to mist, droplets coating her face so she had to wipe them away. He had an extra slicker for her, several sizes too big, with a billed hood he cinched tight with a drawstring. It was only after he'd put his on—the yellow cuffs cracked and dirty—that she realized he'd given her his new one. She couldn't decide if it was kind of him or condescending, treating her like a guest.

"Got one on," he said a minute later, his reel whizzing as the line paid out. The fish ran sideways and then astern, zigzagging, bending the tip of his rod. "Hook feels like it's set pretty good. I'll just let him tire himself out."

"Want me to get the net?"

"I think that's a fine idea."

It didn't take long. As he reeled in the last twenty feet, the fish flashed just under the surface. She dipped the net in and hauled it up, unexpectedly heavy, its gills still flexing.

"It's not going to win any prizes, but it's a nice little smallmouth." He pinned it against the lid of the cooler to work the hook out with a pair of pliers, then slipped it overboard. It lolled in the water, stunned, then swam off.

He caught another that looked like it might be the same one, then another. "Why don't you come over here and try."

They switched places. On her fifth or sixth cast, she felt a tug on the line, but when she jerked her rod to set the hook she lost it. "Shit, I had something."

"Hit 'em again."

Her arms were getting tired. She rushed and let go too early and her lure sliced off to the right, crossing his line. "Sorry."

"No problem."

She dropped her next cast exactly where she wanted it.

"Nicely done," he said, but then nothing happened.

"Why am I not getting any bites?"

He shrugged and pointed to the water. "Ask them."

The mist accelerated to a sprinkle and then a steady rain that tapped at her hood. Most of the other boats left, but a couple stayed. A drop hung from the tip of her nose. She had to continually rub it off with a knuckle.

"You okay there?" he asked.

"Just frustrated. I can see why this is addictive. It's like gambling."

"Except all you win is fish."

"And you don't even keep them."

"It's catching them that's the thrill."

"I'm trying."

"You're doing good," he said. "I'm amazed you came out at all."

"I figured it was the best way to spend some time with you. I haven't seen much of you lately."

"I know."

"So what's going on?"

"Just fishing."

"I noticed."

"Not every day."

"Pretty much."

He looked at her as if she was being cruel by making him explain. "It relaxes me. When I'm out here, I don't think about anything but fishing."

"That's great, just don't forget about the rest of us, okay?"

"I don't."

"I don't know, sometimes it feels like you're avoiding me."

"I'm not."

"What am I supposed to think when you don't come home all week, Ed? The only time I see you is at breakfast."

"I'm sorry."

The mood was broken. She'd promised herself not to bitch at him, and now there he stood, scolded, rain dripping off his chin.

"Don't be sorry, just talk to me. Maybe I'd like to go fishing after work too. Not every day, but... Just keep me part of it, whatever you're doing."

"The same here."

It took her a second to interpret this. Her first reaction was to argue that there was no comparison between her work on the database and him fishing, but, standing in the pouring rain, a mile offshore, it seemed like a fine point.

"That's fair," she said.

They sealed it with a peck and a wet hug, apologetically declaring their love for each other. The rain made a frying sound on the water. Only one other boat remained, and it had a cabin.

"Ready to head in?" he asked, as if this was all she'd wanted.

"Forget that," she said. "I'm gonna catch something."

A Break

It was how they told time. By the fall they'd picked up the awkward yardstick used by new parents—sixteen months, seventeen. They counted backwards, snagged on that last day, which grew less and less present as week by working week the rest of the world surged ahead.

The semester swept Nina along, reading assignments and papers occupying her evenings. The leaves changed and the weather turned. In the morning frost coated the inside of her window. For break, she and J.P. visited Elise and slept on the floor of her dorm room. They'd spent so much of the summer together that it wasn't weird. The bond between her and Elise had never been stronger. It was only after J.P. dropped her off that she missed Kim, as if she'd been there with them.

Back in Columbus, instead of missing Kim, J.P. missed Nina.

Lindsay was a junior, and starting to think about colleges. Her grades were unnatural—she was first in her class. She was leaning toward Northwestern and the University of Chicago, partly because she wanted to live in the city, which they'd visited just once, when she was ten. The idea terrified Fran and Ed, but they promised each other not to discourage her. A larger problem was the money. Their hope was that she might qualify for some merit-based scholarships.

Lindsay was aware that they wanted her to go somewhere cheaper and closer to home. She'd already started preparing for that battle. It wasn't just Chicago they didn't like. Case Western was in Cleveland, Carnegie-Mellon in Pittsburgh. Anywhere she went would be expensive. She was planning on taking out student loans and working to pay her own way.

She was still at Quizno's, saving for a car. For her birthday her father said he'd match whatever she put up, but he wanted to help pick it out.

The next few weekends they rode around the county, test-driving tired Hondas and rickety Neons. The one car they could agree on—a black Paseo—had a leaky transmission, and they widened the search to include Eric, the two of them printing out possibles from cars.com.

Fran envied their afternoons together. Lindsay could still be sweet, running to the market for her, or spontaneously making cobbler for dessert, but like Kim before her, she spent more and more time away from the house, working and hanging out with friends, too many of whom were new. She and Dana were still inseparable, but Fran hadn't seen Micah since school started, and Lindsay couldn't give her a reason for it, other than they were both busy. She also had a brand-new boyfriend, Matt, who took her out every Friday and Saturday, dropping her off right at midnight. Lean and shaggy, he was on the cross-country team and played the bass in the jazz band. His father was an ex-cop from Rochester who worked at the new prison and was a big Cubs fan. Other than that they knew little about him. When Ed came back from a day of car-hunting with Lindsay, Fran pumped him for details, but he didn't know anything—proof that she should have gone with her.

Ultimately they bought a pale green Ford Escort, Ed spending a little more to make sure Lindsay had something reliable, and getting out of the driveway was a puzzle again. They'd just been through this with Kim—the job, the car, the boyfriends, the whole college process—and their familiarity made it all feel strangely secondhand. They agreed that Lindsay was easier, more reasonable, more mature.

"Some of that's her nature," Fran said, "but it's also because she's had to be. She's grown up a lot in the last year and a half."

They'd all changed, Ed could have said. Whether for better or worse he wasn't sure. He still had moments when everything that was wrong with his life settled on him at once, inescapable and rigidly interconnected, and he clenched his fists to bleed off the urge to kill whoever had taken her. They passed, yet he feared at heart he'd become vengeful and bitter. Sundays he prayed for forgiveness. The rest of the week he believed the feeling was justified.

The investigation remained open, though the term was misleading. In

November, thanks to the department's mishandling of the case (or so he liked to believe), Perry failed to win reelection. Whatever satisfaction Ed took from his defeat was hollow. The new sheriff, Jim Trucks, immediately cleaned house. The next week the detective called to let them know he was retiring, but that he'd briefed his replacement and made sure the files were in order. He wished he'd been able to do more for her.

"I know," Ed said. What he should have said was "We do too."

The new man made a point of coming to the house, shaking their hands like a politician. Detective Braden was young, and short, which made him seem even younger. He'd driven a patrol car in Akron for seven years before making the grade, he said, as if to prove he was old enough. He'd been involved with several missing persons. In his experience they were all different. Once he had his office squared away, he planned to revisit the case from the beginning, with no assumptions. There was a lot of material to digest. He knew he was coming into the situation late, so he hoped they didn't mind if he called them from time to time with questions they may have already answered. He gave them his card and shook their hands again, but after he'd left, Fran said what Ed was thinking: "It's like we're starting all over again."

Ed used the opportunity to push for a new search of Wozniak's property, and in a perfect example of how the system worked, in early December Jim Trucks went to the district judge, who happened to be an old hunting buddy, and procured a warrant.

Wozniak was back in Iraq with his unit, so they served his grandmother and occupied the farm for three days, tramping the woods and dragging the ponds, sifting the ashen bed of the fire pit. The state police assisted with their ground sonar, a black-clad team creeping through the withered orchard like minesweepers. From the house they removed sheets and pillowcases and items of women's clothing, samples of a rug that had recently been washed and a piece of floorboard beneath it, a toolbox and assorted hand tools, a computer hard drive, two digital cameras and their memory cards, a video camera and tripod and assorted tapes, a DVD player and assorted disks, two rifles, a shotgun, two handguns, and approximately a thousand rounds of ammunition, several hunting knives, a

samurai sword and ceremonial dagger, pornographic magazines, videotapes and DVDs, working handcuffs, dildos and other assorted sex toys,
a large cache of fireworks, butane torches, glassine envelopes, a triple-
beam scale, and approximately three thousand dollars in cash.

The TV trucks reappeared on Lakewood, reporters in overcoats and
gloves doing their stand-ups from the sidewalk. To fend them off Fran
took down the wreath she'd bought at church and hung a sign that said:
THE LARSEN FAMILY ASKS THE MEDIA TO PLEASE RESPECT OUR
PRIVACY. THANK YOU. On the news the cameras zoomed on it.

For two weeks they waited while the police went through everything.
In the end the only thing the police could charge him with was posses-
sion of illegal fireworks. Ed wasn't surprised—he'd had forever to clean
the place.

There were pictures of Kim.

"You don't want to see them," the detective said. "They're private."

It was the last they spoke of it, but the idea haunted Ed. While he was
proud of her beauty, from the time she started to develop, the attention men
paid her worried him. As her father it was his job to protect her. He imagined the detective looking through the pictures, and Wozniak. What about
her privacy? If she was gone, he thought, no one should have them.

After the search he was even more certain that Wozniak was guilty.
Just the fact that he hadn't come forward was enough. Ed was sickened
that Kim would be with someone like him. It was the drugs, that had to
be the answer, and blamed himself for not realizing she was in trouble.

Christmas passed, and New Year's, like reminders. His whole focus
now was on convincing Braden to bring in Wozniak for questioning,
though he was overseas and protected by the whole balky bureaucracy
of the Marines, so it was a surprise when the detective called him at
work one snowy afternoon in late January to say there'd been a break in
the case. Nothing was official yet, but he wanted to give them a heads-
up. The Indiana State Police had just called. They had a suspect in custody they'd linked to at least three other murders along I-90. From what
he'd told them, they were pretty sure he was their guy.

The Killer Next Door

On the way home, they were subdued. With the radio off, the only sound was the heater, and the wipers slapping away snowflakes. Outside, Kingsville slid by, drab and overcast. They'd had false alarms before, but this was different.

"What do you think?" Ed said, to break the silence.

"I don't know," Fran said. "He's obviously crazy. Who knows how much of what he's saying is made up."

"Braden sounded pretty sure."

"What do *you* think?" Fran asked.

"I think it would help if they had some evidence. I know for sure there was no gas can in the car."

"If she ran out of gas, she would have just called someone."

"And what happened to the car?" Ed seconded. "He doesn't even try to explain that."

"That's the big thing."

His name was James Wade. He was sixty-seven and divorced and lived in a suburb of Elkhart, Indiana, right off I-90, as if that proved anything. The police seemed to think he was serious. He'd been arrested for trying to abduct a college student. He was bipolar, and a convicted sex offender. In custody, he claimed he'd killed more than thirty women, beginning when he was a teenager. He'd drawn maps to show where he'd buried some of his victims—not Kim, of course—though so far the police had found nothing.

"I don't know," Ed said.

"I don't know either." She sounded tired, as if the news had sapped her. "I noticed Perry was there."

"Yeah, nice, right? Thanks for showing up."

At least Braden had held off telling the media, for now. There were no TV trucks lurking outside the house.

"Nice and quiet," Ed said.

"That won't last."

"We'll have to say something."

"*I'll* have to say something. You'll just stand there."

"We need to tell Lindsay."

"You need to tell your mother."

"Fuck," Fran said, closing her eyes. "I was having a really good day at work."

Inside, Cooper pranced at her feet, asking to be let out. "Mr. Frantic," she said.

She hoped Ed would stick close, but he retreated to his office. She listened to him clacking at his keyboard. She couldn't help but feel skeptical about the news, partly because it was all happening at a distance, and partly because it was unimaginable. After not knowing for so long, she couldn't believe the answer was so simple, and so remote, as if it had nothing to do with them. She hoped James Wade was lying, yet at the same time she was impatient for their waiting to be over, one way or another. She wanted to go and make Wade tell them where Kim was—by torture, if necessary.

Even now it was hard to admit she was dead. Wade said he'd forced her into his car and drove her to a deserted self-storage place. Telling it, Braden had edited himself, and now each time her mind called up the scene, Fran shied back from picturing Kim in his car, let alone Wade raping and murdering her, though these were details—unlike the gas can, or the car—that she couldn't factually refute. It was like a blind spot right in front of her face.

As always, she had to come up with a statement. She cannibalized one from last month, cutting and pasting. She'd grown so lazy. In the beginning, she'd been if not hopeful at least conscientious, as if Kim's return depended on her. At some point she'd stopped believing that, though she still prayed every day.

She was mulling what she should put on the website, cleaning up some old fundraising stuff, when Ed came in for a cup of coffee.

"They're starting to roll in," he said.

"How many?"

"Just one."

"Looking for a scoop."

"You're not going to give it to them."

"Hell no."

School was letting out. She called Lindsay to warn her, but got her voicemail.

"Uh-oh," Ed said, peeking through the drapes. "We've got Cleveland."

She tried Lindsay again, and again a couple minutes later. "I'm not getting through," she told Ed. "You better keep an eye out for her."

He dug in the front hall closet and found the sign asking the media to respect their privacy. When he opened the door, one reporter waved as if Ed might join him for a friendly chat on the sidewalk. Ed waved and closed the door.

"You know what," Fran said, and jabbed at the calendar on the fridge. "She's working today."

"Good. Let her work."

But already she was calling.

"No," Fran told her, "you can stay there. I just wanted to let you know what's going on. And be careful when you come home. You might want to park at the Hedricks'."

Ed was surprised. He'd been ready to take Lindsay's side.

"There's no point in her being here," Fran explained. "You agree?"

"Yes."

"They can call me a crappy mother. I'm going to work tomorrow."

"No one's going to call you a crappy mother."

"Ed," she said, "I'm not stupid."

"You're a good mother."

"It's okay," she said. "I know what I am. I'm tired of this shit."

"We all are," he said, though he didn't really see an alternative.

At the press conference they learned that a former babysitter for the Wades had come forward and said he'd molested her. They tried not to show surprise, knowing the cameras were rolling. "We've been asked not to comment on the investigation," Fran said. "That's all we can say right now."

"Jesus," she said when they were back inside, "it would have been nice to know that."

Braden apologized. He was out of the loop on that one too. Indiana had released the information without telling them.

"Why did I think he'd be different?" Fran said when they got off.

"Are we still going to work tomorrow?"

"I don't know."

They watched the news together. In the video, Wade was balding and dull-eyed, slumped over a sack of a gut. He shuffled in his jumpsuit as if drugged, and maybe he was. To Fran he seemed sloppy, not dangerous, but she knew it was impossible to tell. Anyone could be a monster.

The coverage wasn't about Kim or any of his other supposed victims, but an amazed appreciation of his double life, as if he were fiendishly clever, duping his family and coworkers (he had no friends, Ed noted). So far there was no proof, but the botched kidnapping may have been intentional, one expert said. Wade was suffering from stomach cancer. Worried about his own mortality, he wanted credit for his life's work.

There was nothing they could do. It felt like they were back at the beginning, at the mercy of the same dizzying possibilities, except she no longer had the strength for it. They'd been through enough.

"I can't do this anymore," she said, and wept while Ed held her.

They both stayed up until Lindsay came home.

"How are you doing?" Fran asked.

"Okay," Lindsay said, as if nothing had happened.

"It's up to you if you want to go to school tomorrow."

"I have to. I've got a test in AP Bio."

"That's fine. Your father and I may be staying home, we're not sure. Everything's kind of up in the air."

It seemed like her mother wanted an answer to this, so Lindsay said, "I can make it up if I have to."

"No, that's fine. We just wanted to give you the option."

"Thanks."

Upstairs, safely in bed, Lindsay listened to Cooper breathing fitfully. For more than a year, while she'd lived with the probability that Kim was dead, she'd also cultivated a fantasy in which she'd run away and was living anonymously in some city, working during the day and going out at night with friends, reading in her warm apartment—the life Lindsay herself had begun to dream of, away from Kingsville and the shadow of Kim. Now she hated herself for ever being so stupid. To rid herself of it, she pictured Kim under the snow and the dead leaves and the dirt where James Wade had buried her. She thought she should be able to hear her thoughts, as if they shared a telepathy just because they were sisters, except they never had before, and all she could think of was the snow and the darkness.

Ed, likewise, in the long, empty moments before sleep, decided that James Wade had killed her. Only Fran refused to accept it, out of reflex more than any honest consideration. She needed Kim's death to mean something, and Wade was a total unknown. There was no way she could have foreseen him. It was easier to believe that Wozniak had killed her. Once again, she felt cheated by the world's incoherence.

In the morning, the TV trucks dieseled in the dark, and Ed had to escort Lindsay out the back and across the frozen yard to her car. Wade was on the front page, along with a tiny picture of Kim, the same photo they'd used for the poster. Even if they wanted to go in to work, they couldn't. For the time being, the world was closed to them.

Braden had news. Unable to corroborate Wade's stories, Indiana pressed him for exact locations of the bodies. The state assumed he was using them as leverage, as if Wade had designed every step of his endgame. To show good faith, his lawyer had gotten him to comply in the most recent case. Armed with his directions, search teams were combing a county park outside of Valparaiso.

Ed wanted Wade dead, if it was true, but wanted Kim home more. Braden asked Fran if she could describe Kim's jewelry.

"Why?" she asked, giving Ed a look. "You already have all that."

"Would you have any pictures of it?"

"We've been through this." She didn't have any of the cameo ring or the friendship bracelet Nina had given Kim, but she'd been wearing the butterfly in her prom picture.

"You'd tell us if they found her," she asked.

"They haven't found her," Braden said. "They're for the FBI. They want everything. Can you e-mail it to me?"

Minutes after Fran sent the picture, Braden called back with the reason they needed it. He apologized—he'd just gotten the news himself. Around noon the FBI would be making an official statement. This morning they'd opened two safety deposit boxes Wade kept under an alias in Michigan. They were full of jewelry.

"I don't like it," she said when they'd hung up. "Everything's going too fast."

"We've never had the FBI working for us."

"Obviously we should have."

Ed didn't say it, but if this was the end, he wanted it to be quick, and then, an hour later, when the phone rang again, rescinded his wish.

Neither of them moved to get it. Fran pointed to him.

"You get the next one," he said.

He reached for the receiver, feeling lightheaded. He thought, ridiculously, that it might be a wrong number, or Connie.

It was Braden, and Ed turned to Fran.

"I'm telling you this unofficially," the detective said, "so I have to ask you not to talk to the media. Mr. Larsen?"

"Yes." He beckoned her with his free hand.

"They found the woman in the park."

"They found the woman," he told Fran, at his side now, stock-still. "What does that mean to us?"

"It's not a hopeful sign. I'm sorry."

Ed meant to thank him for letting them know, but Braden was gone.

He set the phone in its cradle and Fran held him. His instinct was to make a saving joke—he wished they'd gone in to work. He vetoed it, angry with himself, and wondered why he'd even thought of that. Was he really such a shallow person? He wanted to think he was just overwhelmed. They both were. And yet, rubbing her back, he felt hollow and heartless.

"I need to lie down," Fran said.

He went up with her to their bedroom. They took off their shoes and spooned on top of the covers, Fran dabbing her eyes with a ragged tissue. The room was too bright to sleep, yet they did easily, deeply, as if, after so many months of hoping, they could finally rest.

The phone in his pocket woke him. The room was gray and his mouth was dry.

"Who is it?" Fran asked, still facing away.

It was Braden. Ed thought that he'd talked with him enough for one day.

"Mr. Larsen, I'm so sorry. I've got some bad news."

Ed sat up, steeling himself to hear that they knew where Kim was. He needed to be there to take her home, so did Fran. Maybe then this endless waiting would be over.

"They just found Wade in his cell. I'm sorry. He killed himself."

Article L02-37

Fran identified the butterfly from a digital picture the FBI sent. It was a formality—the agent had told them the pendant was among the effects—yet it was a shock to see it isolated like a specimen with a ruler below to show the scale. She was hoping they'd made a mistake, and even then her mind seized on the possibility that it might be some other girl's. Penney's probably sold thousands of them every year.

There was no trace of Grace's cameo ring or Nina's bracelet. The page they sent her showed fifteen different gold chains, none of which was the box weave, and she imagined the other mothers clicking on the windows and leaning into the screen. She was supposed to sign an affidavit stating that the pendant was Kim's, have it notarized and include any documentation of ownership, then wait until they were finished with their testing. After the first month she realized it might be a while.

The state police were closing their investigation, leaving only the nonprofit K9 teams to pursue Wade's clues. As Fran went on the air to appeal to the public one more time, she had the feeling he was still preying on their hopes. She made a new page for the website, including a transcript of his confession and a map of the I-90 corridor from Erie to Toledo. The area in question was massive. Ed had already started checking out self-storage facilities, every weekend inching his way west. She didn't have his faith or his energy, and envisioned quitting, as if she was beaten.

The weather was bad, and because they were looking for a body, the new search lacked the urgency to attract volunteers. After a while he was out there by himself. When she could she went with him, cruising the county roads off of each successive exit. There was nothing but truckstops and farmland, and when they did locate a self-storage it was invariably ringed by a cyclone fence and the ground was covered with snow.

They debated Grace's suggestion of hiring a private detective, or just someone who could dedicate himself to the case full-time. In the end they spent five thousand dollars on a retired cop who submitted a beautiful three-inch-thick report that said he couldn't find her.

Over spring break they took Lindsay on a tour of the nearby colleges on her shortlist, stopping in Ann Arbor and Chicago, awkwardly sharing a motel room. Lindsay liked Northwestern, right on the lake, and riding the L into town, but the city scared Fran, the sprawl of it, the rundown neighborhoods. Driving out and back on 90 she couldn't help but think that at any second they might be passing Kim and never know it.

They celebrated her at every occasion. For Arbor Day they dedicated a tulip tree in the circular turnaround of the high school. The branches were cluttered with yellow ribbons, a fundraiser for the booster club.

In May, after much discussion, they held a memorial service on what would have been her twentieth birthday. Father John and Ken Wilber, the choir director, helped plan it. The hardest part was seeing Kim's headstone for the first time. They'd picked out the white granite together, and spent hours tweaking the design and the inscription (BELOVED DAUGHTER in Anglia cursive), but to see the span of her life set in stone was too much, and Fran had to turn away. Holding her, Ed assured the owner it was what they wanted.

So many people came that they couldn't all fit—the first time that had happened, Father John said. Blown-up photos of Kim at every age leaned on easels along the communion rail. Across the aisle, Nina and Elise and J.P. sat together, and Ed asked if it was all right if he invited them back to the house after. She thought they had nothing to apologize for, but said it was all right, and in front of everyone he walked over to their pew and hugged Elise and then Nina and then J.P. In the receiving line he embraced them again and nodded tearily, while Fran shook their hands, thanked them for coming and passed them on to Lindsay.

"I'm sorry," she said that night, after everyone was gone. "I can't just turn my emotions on a dime like that."

"You knew they'd come."

"It would have been nice if you'd told me ahead of time you were going to do that. That's what threw me."

"It wasn't their fault."

"They lied," she said. "Maybe I'm a bad person for holding that against them."

"It had nothing to do with what happened, we know that now."

"We *didn't* know that, and it could have, but they didn't care, they were more concerned about themselves. That's what makes me so mad."

"I think they understand that. Did you talk to them?"

"I talked to Elise. You know Nina and J.P. are dating? That's a little odd."

"Maybe," he said.

"You don't think that's odd?"

"Think about what they've got in common."

Like us, she might have replied.

Publicly the service succeeded, providing the illusion of finality, an ending to the story. Privately whatever peace it brought them was temporary.

The stone was permanent, and so close. Though there was nothing buried under it, Fran stopped by after work, bringing leftover flowers from the gift shop and taking away the old ones. Kim's friends left unopened packs of Newports and full bottles of beer, which Fran dropped in the garbage bag with the flowers. Once, on her way to lunch, she saw a pickup with a Marine Corps decal parked by her plot, and a goateed dude she suspected was Dennis Wozniak paying his respects. She pulled into the lot of the Dairy Queen and sat there like she was eating, waiting for him to leave. On top of the stone he'd placed a Big KitKat, Kim's favorite. Ed went with her on weekends, but confessed that sometimes he came by himself as well. He'd seen Wozniak too, and the KitKat. While Fran didn't care for Wozniak, she was glad Kim had her regulars. As far as she knew, Lindsay hadn't been back since the service.

And then, before Fran was prepared for it, Lindsay was off to camp, taking her car, which didn't seem to bother Ed. He said it was still too early to go back to coaching, but helped Jerry once a week, throwing batting practice and hitting fungoes to the girls. On weekends he had projects around the house. She was attempting to resurrect her garden. Sundays they visited Grace, who was doing better. They worked and fished and went out to dinner, but she found herself drawn to the cemetery more and more, as if Kim was really there.

In her dreams Kim appeared, completely fine. Fran asked her where she'd been.

"I was right here," Kim said, like Fran was making a big deal of it.

She spent too much time alone in the house. Cooper was going deaf, and every once in a while he jerked his head up, alert, turning as he tracked a sound only he could hear, as if someone was creeping down the hall.

"Who is it?" she asked him.

They used to joke that they had ghosts. Now she wished they did.

She missed Kim, but she also missed keeping vigil. Often when she was trying to lose herself in weeding or watching TV she felt an inner spur, as if she needed to stop wasting time and go look for her. That obstinate hope had sustained them for so long. It was impossible to just switch it off.

She used the second anniversary as an opportunity to do good, staging a walkathon for autism. She went on the radio and asked for everyone's help bringing Kim home, but with no expectations.

She thought she'd resigned herself to this limbo when, one Friday at the beginning of August, she came home and found a pink receipt on the front door saying a package was being held for her at the post office. She didn't bother to go inside. She took the rest of the mail with her— catalogs and all—and drove downtown. She got there with five minutes to spare, along with everyone else. Standing in line, she found herself wishing for the impossible—that she'd been wrong, the butterfly wasn't Kim's.

The package was in the back. When the clerk returned with a slim padded envelope, it seemed too small to Fran. Though Sandy knew her, she showed her ID before she signed.

She didn't open it there, where people could see. She drove home with it on the seat beside her like a bomb. Ed was due any minute, but she brushed off the thought of waiting for him. She carried the package upstairs to Kim's room and closed the door, took the scissors from the wire cup on her desk and sat on the edge of her bed with the sun falling on her lap and neatly cut off one end of the envelope.

The paperwork cushioned a flattened cocoon of bubble wrap, through which she could see the curve of one wing. It took her several tries to slide the point of the scissors under the strapping tape, and then the plastic pulled open easily.

The pendant was bent, the thin gold noticeably bowed. The sun flashed off the finish as Fran tilted it in her hand, and she wondered if they'd polished away any fingerprints. The delicate eyes at the tips of the wings where the chain attached were still intact. After a while she stood and pressed it against the top of her dresser with her palm to see if she could fix it. When she saw that she couldn't, she slid it off, pressed it to her chest—it was cold on her skin—then brought it to her lips and kissed it. She held it there a moment with her eyes closed, as if making a wish.

The Grateful Parents

In the end it took a stranger to save them. In the fall of 2008, nearly a year and a half after James Wade killed himself, Braden called Ed at work. They'd heard nothing for so long that for a second he didn't believe it.

There was no mistake. The FBI had confirmed the ID.

A woman in Mentor, a civilian searching with her own dog and a GPS. She was known to the local cops, a sparky, always phoning in complaints and tips on cases. A lonely older lady. Apparently she'd made it her crusade. They'd gotten lucky. Sometimes that's how it went with these cases.

"But I'll let you go," Braden said. "You probably want to call your wife."

"They're sure?" Fran asked, worried, as if this good news could be taken away.

He told her they were.

"It's a miracle," she said.

The word seemed too strong to him, but he didn't contradict her. "It sounds like this woman was obsessed."

"Thank God she was," Fran said.

She would meet him at home. She was leaving right now. "I knew we'd find her," she said. "I love you."

"I love you too," he said, though once he'd signed off, he felt let down. The news had drained him, too sudden and strange, too final. It registered, he just needed some time to accept it. They'd lived so long with the prospect of never finding Kim that he'd almost convinced himself it didn't matter. Fran was happy, that's what was important. He thought he should be too, though essentially, he couldn't help but remind himself, nothing had changed. He was glad this phase was over, that was all.

At home, once they'd told Lindsay and his mother, Fran kicked into her old spokesperson role. She took the calendar off the fridge, grabbed a yellow pad and started a list. They needed to book Lindsay's flight right now. Did he want her to order a wreath in his mother's name? What should it say? Should they go with the long or the short service? They'd have to find out when Father John was available, because they definitely wanted him. She was thinking they could do the reception here; it would be less expensive and more intimate. She could do the baking herself. She had to run every detail of her plans by him, as if he might object. He hadn't seen her like this in a long time, totally energized, and wished he felt the same. In the face of all these arrangements, his mind was shutting down, along with his body. He tried to help, but she was moving too fast for him. All he wanted to do was sleep.

Technically the reward was still in effect. At last count it was fifty thousand. Fran wanted to meet the woman and present her with a check. It was the least they could do. He agreed, though the idea of standing in front of the cameras again depressed him.

The feeling stayed with him through the busy days that followed. When friends stopped in, he fielded their congratulations with a feigned relief, while Fran gushed. He didn't know how to explain it, this disconnect. Everyone was happy for them. As Fran said, it was the best news they could have hoped for. Ed knew this to be true—how many times had he wished for some unexpected deliverance—yet now that it had actually happened, he felt as helpless as he did at the beginning, at the mercy, once again, of unseen forces. All along it had seemed wrong to him that his fate was out of his control. This was just further proof. He didn't see it as something to celebrate.

Part of his resistance was selfish. With Lindsay gone, their life had been quiet. All summer Fran had worried that they would drive each other crazy, cooped up in the empty house. Instead they discovered—as if it were a surprise—that they liked each other's company. They spent more time together, bringing almost formal attention to their conversations. They had wine every night, and ate off the good china. It was like a courtship, or a honeymoon, and he was heartened to find that if she was all he had, finally, that was enough. He had come to rely on their quiet evenings, their weekends a cocoon the two of them shared, separate from the rest of the world. They still grieved, but privately, without headlines or reporters peeking in the windows.

Now not only were they no longer invisible, their story had become this crazy woman's. Her name was Mimi Knapp, and the press was fascinated with her. The idea that she'd taken on this impossible quest and succeeded was irresistible. She was a regular visitor to the website, one of their many armchair detectives, except she'd gone far beyond that. She'd left messages in the guestbook from one mother to another, pledging to find Kim, and plastered a room of her rental place with topographic maps. Like Wade, she lived alone, a mystery to her neighbors. She was a cashier at a Bi-Lo; in every picture she was in uniform, as if they were the only clothes she owned. She had a Dutchboy haircut, though she was easily in her sixties. Her German shepherd's name was Ollie. In retrospect, her son joked about her dedication to the search. They fought about it constantly. Many times he'd pleaded with her to stop. He'd seriously thought she was disturbed.

Fran called her colorful, as if her bizarreness was fun. Ed just thought she was odd. The first time they spoke on the phone, she put the dog on so they could say hello to it. "He's the real hero," she said, "Ollie-Ollie Olson Free-o."

Ed thanked her and then sat there while she and Fran chatted like old friends.

She said she couldn't accept the money, that's not why she did it. "If my baby was missing, I'd want everyone out there looking." When Fran insisted, she said she'd donate it to the Humane Society, if that was all right.

They set a date for the one gap in their schedule—late Thursday morning, so they could make the noon news. When Fran said they were looking forward to meeting her, she responded that Ollie was looking forward to meeting Cooper.

"She is different," Fran admitted.

For some reason, Ed wasn't amused. He knew he was being ungracious, possibly even jealous, but it bothered him that Fran would let an outsider intrude on them when they had so much to do. They were making this into a production, and while they'd done the big check thing a hundred times in the past, every time he thought of posing with the woman, he felt queasy and short of breath, as if he couldn't do it.

Strangely, he was more at ease dealing with the funeral home. Choosing Kim's coffin and vault should have upset him, but there, at least, the mood was properly somber. He and Fran were subdued as they followed Mason Radkoff through the showroom, calmed by the stately vases of white lilies and cream walls with their tasteful sconces, nodding as he gently went over the benefits of each model. While Ed knew his pitch was false, he could agree with the pretense of comfort and eternal rest. He tried not to think of the expense. This ceremony was necessary, and dignified, and right.

"I never want to do that again," Fran said in the lot, as if she'd forgotten his mother.

The preparations were endless, ridiculous. He wished they could skip straight to the funeral, but even that was turning into a circus, with the reception afterward. Fran had enlisted Connie and Jocelyn. They'd taken over the dining room table, papering it with guest lists and recipes. Ed steered clear of them, hiding out in his office with Cooper, flinching whenever Fran laughed at something. He knew he should be glad for her. Instead he tried to imagine himself laughing, and couldn't.

What puzzled him most was that just last week he'd been happy, or happier than this. Since the news, the world had turned sour. He wasn't able to concentrate, and gave up before he could form his thoughts. Nothing seemed worthwhile, not even old reliables like the Indians. It was all noise, pointless. The one thing he was looking forward to was seeing Lindsay, and she'd only be there for the weekend, and would probably spend most of it with her friends.

For the event on Thursday, Jocelyn wanted to use the backyard, thinking of the dogs, and the space they'd need for all the media. Connie thought it would be neat if they made dog biscuits for Ollie. Fran sent him to the Foodland for cookie cutters and a five-pound bag of whole wheat flour, and Wednesday night they filled the kitchen with smoke. Cooper was their official taster, leaving Ed to watch TV by himself. The Indians weren't close to making the playoffs, and the game didn't hold his attention. He kept picturing tomorrow, the reporters lined up on the sidewalk, and his thoughts started to circle on him. When he tried to swallow, his throat caught, a web of saliva stuck halfway. His gut was rumbling, and though it was only ten o'clock, he told Fran he was going up to bed.

"Take some Gaviscon, that'll help."

It didn't, as he knew it wouldn't, just as he knew he would feel the same way in the morning.

He was resigned to the invasion, yet even at his most dour he hadn't foreseen the scope of it. At dawn Lakewood was an unbroken wall of satellite trucks. Fran said she expected some of them were national. He shaved and showered and tied his tie, his head spinning as if he were hungover.

He stayed inside, watching from the living room as Jocelyn took charge, lining up the media in the drive, checking their credentials before letting them into the backyard. A dozen techs paid out cables along the gutters, duct-taping them across the sidewalk. It was like they were making a movie. By nine there was a bank of lights and tripods aimed at the back deck like a firing line.

Out front a crowd gathered, some neighbors, some people he'd never seen before, many of them children, though it was a school day. A police car rolled up. With a twinge, he realized the patrolman waving them off the street was Perry.

The woman was late, and it was almost time. Jocelyn had arranged for Fran to do an exclusive with Channel 12 from Erie, a reward for being the first station to cover them. Ed wasn't needed, and he retreated to his office, closing the door. He sat sideways at his computer, swiveling in his chair and absently scratching Cooper's ears. Cooper panted, confused by all the excitement. Ed closed his eyes and tried to control his own breathing, but it was no use. He smoothed Cooper's fur, fingering the hard lumps under his skin—fatty deposits or tumors, the vets weren't sure. He wouldn't be with them much longer, and Ed would miss him. Soon he would lose his mother too, a fact he could barely grasp.

"Yes," he said, leaning in close to his nose, "you're a good boy."

From the front came a wave of cheering, making Cooper turn toward the door. A minute later, Fran looked in.

"You ready, Freddy?"

She had the check under one arm like a prop, and she was smiling. Her face had been made up for her interview so she looked younger, almost rosy, like the teenager she'd been, and he thought that though he might never reconcile himself with Kim's death, he could not deprive her of this.

"Ready as I'll ever be," he said, and, taking her hand, went out to face his public.

When the moment came, he stood beside her. Mimi Knapp was a character, wearing a beat-up jean jacket and a black POW/MIA hat. Her dog's bandana was an American flag. She was taller than he'd expected, and overwrought, tearily holding on to Fran, then clinging to him as if they'd been reunited. She'd found Kim, that was the only reason she was here. He'd wanted to be the one, as if that mattered. As he held her, he thought that the unforgivable thing, ultimately, wasn't the randomness of the discovery, but that she'd kept looking long after he'd stopped.

The presentation was staged. Jocelyn set them on their marks and stood back.

"Okay, everybody," she said, raising her arms wide like a conductor. "Big smile."

There's No Place Like Home

At the check-in she had to prove who she was. To get the discount, she needed to give the ticket agent the name and address of the funeral home. She could submit a copy of the death certificate on her way back. To Lindsay it seemed like too much just to save a hundred bucks, but she wasn't paying for it. Her father had e-mailed her with the information as soon as they knew, then called again last night to remind her, as if she might forget to bring it. Like her mother, she organized her important papers in a folder so they'd be handy.

"What relation are you?" the woman asked gently.

"I'm her sister."

"I'm so sorry."

"Thank you," Lindsay said, equally soft, and slid the folder into her backpack.

"Just the one bag?"

At school it had taken her a while to shed the feeling of being singled out. Now it returned, an intimation of what was to come. Until then she'd been enjoying her anonymity, listening to Holly Golightly on her iPod as she moved with the swarm of passengers across the tram platform and up the escalators to the noisy concourse and into the shuffling, switchbacked lines. It was the answer to a Trivial Pursuit question: What airport is the busiest in the U. S.? The chaos was intimidating and thrilling. Tonight, on a weeknight, there were more people here, she estimated— and more interesting people—than in all of Kingsville.

The irony was that this was her first time flying by herself. She literally couldn't have done it without Kim.

Security was another crush of people, and once she'd unzipped her laptop and ducked through the metal detector and put her shoes on again, she had to navigate a maze of food courts and flashy retail galleries until she found the correct terminal. She stood on the moving walkway, passing gates with more enticing destinations. She imagined joining the line filing into the jetway for San Francisco and calling her father from the plane, saying she'd made a mistake. It's okay, she'd say, you can go ahead without me.

The few people waiting for her flight looked like they came from Erie, and were being sent back. A woman her grandmother's age wore a black and gold letter jacket listing all of the Steelers' Super Bowl wins. A badly tattooed guy wore a flannel, baggy acid-washed jeans and Timberlands. Lindsay took a seat by the floor-to-ceiling windows and listened to Cat Power, gazing out at the Tron-like landscape—nothing but darkness and the sapphire runway lights. The emptiness made her think of space, and whether there was a heaven. She was nineteen, older than Kim had ever been, yet she would always be her baby sister. Little Larsen. How long had it been since anyone called her that? She'd outgrown it, like everything else.

The flight was on time and mostly empty. They rose out of the city, headed west, then banked around, crossing north of the skyscrapers downtown, climbing over the vast absence that was the lake. The lights describing the far shore slowly approached, twinkling, then fell away behind them, and the farmland of Indiana, cut by I-90—cloverleafs and rest areas bathed a dull orange. Did they really need to go so fast? The train would have taken nine hours, but the flight attendants barely had time to serve them pretzels and a beverage before they prepared for landing. She secured her tray table and Cleveland slipped beneath the wing. The wind buffeted them as they descended. Somewhere down there was the spot where Kim had been found, and camp, and her highschool, and their house, in which, right now, her mother would be setting out their best china for the reception tomorrow, refusing Aunt Carrie's help and fretting that she wouldn't have time to get everything done.

Once they were on the ground, she realized she'd forgotten the time change. She didn't mind losing the hour. What was strange was turning her watch ahead when she felt like she was going backwards.

They must have been the last flight of the night. There were only two gates, both deserted. The seating area was dark, the newsstand locked behind a steel grille. A janitor's cart sat in the middle of the hall.

Her father was waiting at the baggage claim in his old down vest and a beat-up Sea Wolves cap he wore to cover his receding hair. His face was windburnt from being out on the boat so much. He looked, she had to admit, like someone from Kingsville. When she hugged him, he reeked of cigarettes. He took her backpack and asked how the flight was.

"Good," she said.

"Any problems picking up the ticket?"

"Nope."

"How's life in the big city? Working hard?"

He saw her bag come out and grabbed it.

"I can take it," she said, but he waved her off.

The parking lot was smaller than her dorm's, and poorly lit. He'd brought the Taurus, and set her bags in the back, on top of a pile of FOR SALE signs.

"I thought you might bring the Escort."

"You know, I didn't even think."

"How's it doing?"

"Okay. I take it down to the marina, so it smells like bait. I'm just kidding, it's fine."

She waited until they were on the highway to ask how things were.

"Good. Remember the Kizers? I just closed on their old house."

"How's Mom doing?"

"A little frazzled, with everything. She's afraid it's going to rain."

"Is it supposed to?"

"You know her, she wants everything to be perfect. I told her that's why they have the tent."

"The tent?"

"It's not a tent like you go into. It's more like a covering. You'll see."

"Okay."

Her legs were jumpy from sitting for so long, and she rubbed her face and watched the signs sail by.

Her father drove the limit, trucks highballing past as they crossed the state line. WELCOME TO OHIO, THE HEART OF IT ALL.

All night she'd been going east, now she was going west. It was like she was circling the town, spiraling in as if she couldn't face it head-on.

There was no avoiding the Conoco, shining bright at the top of the exit, and then the long dark stretch of Route 7 and the dip over the bridge. Though it was barely eleven, the light at State and Harbor had gone blinking yellow. The Dairy Queen was closed, and the gates of the cemetery.

"What's the plan for tomorrow?" she asked, though she knew most of it. She just didn't want to be ambushed by anything.

She'd only been gone two months, and she'd come back for fall break, so why did she expect the house to look different, faded or decayed, the lawn gone wild? Everything was the same—the coachlight and the pillared porch, her mother's Subaru in its spot by the garage. It wasn't until her father stopped before the door to fit the key in that she realized the yellow ribbons were missing. They were done waiting.

Cooper waddled up the hall, barking.

"Oh, Mr. Ferocious," Lindsay said, and knelt down. He wriggled in her arms, trying to lick her face. "Yes, I missed you too."

"Look who it is," her mother said, and hugged her extra, like she'd never let go. "Your timing's perfect. I just finished putting the living room together. Come see."

"She's been working on it all day," her father said.

"There," her mother said. "Aren't you glad you didn't have to help?"

It was more than a day's work. The walls were lined with pictures of Kim. She'd recycled the blowups from the memorial service. Between them, as if to fill any gaps in the timeline, hung huge collages of snapshots, from Kim as a red-faced newborn all the way up through that last summer. Lindsay was in some of them, cropped or off to the side. Her mother's computer was set up in one corner, running a slide show. On the coffee table, as if part of some ritual, sat five black leatherbound albums.

"Wow."

"I told you she's been busy."

"I had extras made, so there's a whole set for you."

At school the only picture Lindsay had was hidden deep in her desk, along with her shots of Jared and Matt and Eric. Her suitemates were under the impression that her grandmother had died.

"I don't have room right now, but thanks."

"You can take a CD, can't you?"

"Sure. So, how are Uncle Rich and Aunt Carrie?"

"Already bitching about the Days Inn," her mother said. "Surprise, surprise."

They were glad she was home, but it was late, and they had a big day tomorrow. Cooper tagged after her, claiming his spot at the foot of her bed as if she'd never left. She'd forgotten her nightshirt and had to wear an old pair of pajamas, making her feel like even more of a guest. On her way to the bathroom she passed Kim's dry-erase board, wiped clean. Brushing her teeth, she stepped out and stood in front of the empty board. She wondered if her mother would ever get rid of it, or any of Kim's stuff. The medicine cabinet was full of long-expired prescriptions and contact solution.

Lying in bed, still moving from the plane, she recognized that her room was a museum too. From the custard yellow walls with her Cowboy Bebop and Inuyasha posters to her sticker-fringed monitor on the child-sized desk, it all belonged to another person, a clueless girl she loved and felt sorry for ditching.

The day after they found Kim she received an e-mail from J.P. asking if he and Nina and Elise might be allowed to attend the funeral. She kept his request in her inbox, meaning to forward it to her father so he could be the one to tell him the service was family only, but every time the subject line came up she grew more and more annoyed. It was the first time she'd heard from him in years. Finally she deleted it, then deleted it from her deleted folder. He'd probably searched the university directory for her address. The girl who'd lived in her old bedroom would have been flattered and happy.

She didn't remember Cooper jumping up on the bed, but in the morning he was stretched out beside her. The room was dim and gray and smelled warmly of pumpkin pie. She was surprised to find it was 9:30. Knowing she was on Central Time, they'd let her sleep in. She could hear her mother banging around the kitchen and decided she'd better get up. Outside, the sky over the woods was a quilt of clouds. Standing at the window, she recalled all the times she'd selfishly prayed for rain. Please, she thought, not today.

Downstairs her mother had all four burners going and the sink piled with mixing bowls.

"Those can wait," her mother said. "What you can do is start putting together the pasta salad."

Her father breezed through in his down vest. He was going to pick up Grandma. Did they need anything while he was out?

"Vanilla extract," her mother said. "But by the time you get back it'll be too late. I'll just grab some from Sunny."

After the pumpkin pie there was a Dutch apple, then a cheesecake, and a quiche. The basement fridge was stocked with a case of white wine. It was like preparing for a holiday, except Lindsay noticed the dishes were all Kim's favorites, as if this was the last time her mother would ever make them.

"Did Dad tell you about meeting the crazy lady?"

"No."

"Actually I shouldn't say that, she was very nice. I don't know. You know how sometimes you can look into a person's eyes and tell they're not right? She was like that. Very pleasant to talk to, and obviously we owe her everything, but… We had a chance to talk in private before we did the photo op, and she said—she actually said this— finding her was the only reason she was still alive. She started crying, and we're in this little room by ourselves. I didn't know what to say."

"That's weird."

"I hugged her and told her how much it meant to us, and she was fine. I just wondered, what's she going to do now?"

"Find someone else."

"Well," she said doubtfully. "I suppose we all have to find ways to go on. Anyway, that was interesting."

The moral was for her, Lindsay sensed, and meant to be encouraging. She could have told her mother it was needless. She had no intention of letting Kim destroy her. Somehow she'd make it through today, and tomorrow she'd return to her new life at school, where no one could see her sister's ghost hovering over her.

Everything was done except the quiche. When she finished doing the dishes, her mother told her to go take her shower. They had to leave no later than one fifteen.

"If you need anything ironed," her mother called up the stairs, "just hang it over the railing."

In the bathroom Lindsay calculated how many hours she had to endure until her flight left. As the spray warmed her front she caught her eyes in the tiny mirror of Kim's waterproof CD player and held them a few seconds, accusing herself. Was that all this was to her—an interruption?

A knock on the door stopped her. Her father had called. There was some sort of problem with Grandma's heart monitor. They'd have to bring his suit and meet them at the funeral home. That meant they needed to leave in forty minutes. Could she do that?

She could, but her mother couldn't. They were late, and in the rush her mother forgot his belt. She had Lindsay call ahead to let him know.

"At least it's not raining," Lindsay said.

"For now, knock wood."

Her father's car was in the lot. They parked beside it and hurried in.

He was standing in the lobby, talking softly with Uncle Rich and Aunt Carrie, dressed like lawyers in matching black. Almost hidden behind him was her grandmother, hunched over in her heavy camel-hair coat. She carried a tripod-footed cane and hung on his arm. Lindsay hadn't seen her out of the nursing home in so long that it was a shock. She'd had her hair done and was wearing lipstick. "Don't you look nice," she said, taking Lindsay's arm so her father could get dressed.

She'd been told the service was going to be family only, but Connie and Jocelyn were there, chatting with Mr. and Mrs. Hedrick. She thought of J.P. and Nina and Elise, and wished she'd forwarded his e-mail. They knew Kim better than anyone here.

In minutes her father returned, buttoning his collar. Father John had solved the problem. No one would know he was beltless under his robes.

Outside, the limo was waiting. She helped her father with her grandmother, sitting her in the middle. Behind them came Uncle Rich and Aunt Carrie in their white Escalade, the Hedricks' Volvo and Connie's Pontiac. Lindsay wondered why they bothered with a procession. The drive to the cemetery was less than a mile, and the casket was already there. As they crawled across Harbor an old man standing on the corner removed his hat.

No one spoke until her father said, "I hope she doesn't mind us being late."

"She won't," her mother said, patting his leg.

Lindsay thought it was Kim who was late, though she knew to keep the joke to herself. Today was supposed to make them feel better, and she had her own fantasies of Kim looking down from above. As they passed the Dairy Queen and slowed for the turn she pictured them doing the drive-thru as a tribute, sitting in the far corner and eating fries as Father John delivered the eulogy.

They rolled through the gates, making oncoming traffic wait. Among the headstones stood a blue tent with the casket and two rows of folding chairs. Father John had gone ahead and was crossing the lawn as the line of cars parked.

The smell of burgers grilling warmed the air. The funeral director ushered her mother to the front row while Lindsay and her father led her grandmother. There were four chairs set out for them by the nap of an astroturf mat. On each lay a single red rose.

For their safety the florist had removed the thorns, leaving the stems defenseless. As Father John asked them to bow their heads, Lindsay dug a thumbnail into one of the empty nubs, gouging a wet crescent.

I am the resurrection and the life, saith the Lord; he that believeth in me, though he were dead, yet shall he live.

Her mother and father held hands through the prayers. Her grandmother lifted her glasses and dabbed at her eyes with a tissue, her lips quivering. The polished finish of the casket reflected the front row, and Lindsay found herself in it, a bloated, faceless shape. Though no one had told her, she knew the only thing left of Kim was bones. It was impossible and true at the same time. Her hair and eyes and smile were gone, like those long gray afternoons playing Battleship. A day like today, she thought. That would never happen again, or anything else between them, only in her memories. Whatever grudges she held against her, she had to let them go. She looked past the casket to the trees where sparrows flitted in the branches, oblivious. She didn't believe in the forgiveness of sins or the life everlasting. She didn't even know if she wanted to. She thought she should, for Kim.

"Amen," everyone said, and Father John closed his prayer book on the silk ribbon. Deliberately, in stagy slow motion, he padded over to the casket and laid a hand on the lid as if he were blessing it. He turned to them and held up his hand.

"We're not here to say good-bye to Kim," he said, and dropped it. "Today we're here to remember her, and celebrate her, and hold her that much closer to us. Because we love Kim, we need to keep her alive in our hearts, and carry her wherever we go, just as we carry God's love with us."

He went on for a while about the difference between being lost and being found, and the idea of people searching for what they think they're missing. Lindsay scratched at the stem of her rose, opening a green wound. She thought she should be feeling more, but she just wanted it to be over. She didn't need him to tell her about carrying Kim around.

When he was done he hugged her mother and father. There was another set of prayers, and then—she should have predicted it—the funeral director cued a boom box and played the song Lindsay hated. She hated it because it was fake and because, though she wished she were immune, it made her cry every time. Her father, thinking she was sad, patted her back.

As the song played they were supposed to place their roses, one by one, on top of the casket. When it was her turn she wiped her eyes and stepped onto the astroturf mat. She looked down at the lid and pictured Kim that last day at the Dairy Queen, saying she'd miss her. Good-bye, she thought, and carefully set hers next to her mother's.

She thought they would lower the casket, but no, a final prayer committing her to God's mercy and that was it. The service seemed too short, somehow incomplete. She wanted to do it over, as if this time she'd get it right.

They all hugged beside the casket, thanked Father John and the funeral director and headed for the limo, leaving Kim and the roses behind.

"I'm glad we got to do that," her mother said on the ride back.

The rain held off until they were almost home, providing a popular topic of conversation, as if Kim or God had intervened, depending on who was talking. The Bonners were there, and the Naismiths, and the Finnegans. Her parents had invited the whole neighborhood and all of their friends from church. Lindsay had no idea what to say to them. They asked about her classes and how she liked the city, more out of politeness than any real interest. They were fascinated with the pictures of Kim, and all the work her mother had done. Aunt Carrie pointed out a shot of the two of them in which Lindsay looked exactly like Kim in this other picture. She ferried people across the room to compare them, and Lindsay retreated to the kitchen, content to help Connie and Jocelyn with dessert.

"You're not mingling," her mother said.

"I don't feel like mingling."

"Another hour, hour-and-a-half, tops."

The promise only made it seem longer. Uncle Rich had had too much to drink and was loudly badmouthing the Democrats to Father John. Her father and Mr. Bonner were discussing the zoning of waterfront condos. She sat with her grandmother at the computer, watching the slide show. What surprised her was how intimately she knew Kim's wardrobe.

"Is that you?" her grandmother asked, pointing.

"That's Elise."

"She looks like you."

"Not really."

"You'll have to forgive me, dear. I don't see so well anymore."

"That's all right."

"This is you."

"That's Nina."

Lindsay stayed with her until the party broke up, then helped her father walk her to his car. She clutched Lindsay's hand through the window, letting in the rain. She'd see her again at Thanksgiving but said good-bye as if this might be the last time.

Over their objections, her mother sent Connie and Jocelyn home, saying she and Lindsay could handle things. Once they'd taken off, she sat down on the couch with her glass of wine and confessed that she just wanted everyone out of the house.

"So, kiddo," she asked the graduation picture of Kim behind Lindsay, "how'd we do?"

"I should let Cooper out," Lindsay said.

"Excellent idea."

The good dishes had to be done by hand. Her mother sipped steadily as they worked. She fumbled a knife into the rinse water, chipping a coffee cup. "Come on, Franny," she scolded herself. "Pay attention."

It was past nine when they finished, and by then all Lindsay wanted to do was go to bed. Her mother thanked her and kissed her cheek, then sat back on the couch, surrounded by Kim.

"I'm just going to rest here a while, if that's all right."

In bed, with Cooper snoring beside her, Lindsay listened for her father's car. She kept returning to the service—the limousine and the trees and Father John placing his hand on the casket like a healer. After all these years she hadn't expected the funeral to make a difference, so why did it bother her? As she had so many times, she remembered that last day, driving around with Kim in her old car. It was sunny, and they stopped to park by the high school. She retraced their route through town, past the cornfields and nursing homes and the golf course, over the tracks, splitting off at some point to swing down to the park and the softball fields and the harbor, where they hadn't been at all, and then suddenly she was the Cup, except when she looked out of the mesh square she realized she was dancing in the middle of the highway.

In the morning her mother woke her. She had to leave for work and wanted to say good-bye. After last night her recovery seemed superhuman. Lindsay was weak with sleep, and echoed her, saying she loved her.

"You be careful," her mother said. "Please. I don't want to lose you too."

"You won't," Lindsay said, but, after she was gone, thought it was probably too late for that.

Her flight was at nine. She was dressed and ready by seven. It was done raining but gray, the tree trunks blackened. At school she'd thought of taking the puzzle box or some other treasure from Kim's dresser. In the end she didn't even open her door. She had her own roomful of crap she was trying to escape.

Her father drove her to the airport in the Escort, passing the Conoco on their way out, timing Erie's minor-league rush hour perfectly. At the ticket counter he gave the agent an envelope to spare Lindsay from having to touch the death certificate. She showed her ID and signed a paper to make it official.

She kissed him good-bye at security.

"Fly carefully," he said.

She dismissed the idea. "I'll see you in two weeks."

He stood there while she went through the metal detector, then waved to her all the way down the hall to her gate.

The other passengers were businessmen, busy with their laptops and their phones. No one was interested in her. She handed the gate agent her boarding pass, got on and took a window seat, grateful to be alone.

In the air she changed her watch, gaining back the lost hour. The pilot said they were fighting a headwind but he'd try to get them in on time. Beneath the wing, I-90 snaked through the brown panes of Indiana. The shore appeared, a dividing line, and smoky Gary, and then, after miles of sunstruck water, the towers of the Loop. They banked down, shuddering through tufts of clouds, the gear clunking beneath her feet. Below, in miniature, stretched the city where she lived, the unknown neighborhoods and boulevards and parks. As they taxied to the gate, the pilot apologized: They weren't on time—they were early. At the ping she stood and took down her backpack. Slowly the rows ahead emptied, and then she was hustling up the aisle and ducking through the door, free and striding to keep pace. The gate was seething with people. She came out of the jetway and turned left with everyone else, joined the horde streaming for the concourse and disappeared into the crowd.

Acknowledgments

Special thanks to the Conneaut and Ashtabula, Ohio, Chambers of
Commerce and Visitor's Bureaus for their invaluable help.
To Sheldon Calvary Camp for always giving me a place to stay.
And to Pizzi's for torps and Covered Bridge for stromboli.

As always, constant thanks to my faithful readers:

Paul Cody
Lamar Herrin
Liz Holmes
Stephen King
Dennis Lehane
Lowry Pei
Alice Pentz
Susan Straight
Luis Urrea

Deepest thanks to Trudy, Caitlin and Stephen
for dealing with this nightmare come true.
My apologies for the scare.

And finally, grateful thanks to David Gernert, Stephanie Cabot,
Courtney Hammer and Erika Storella at the Gernert Company;
And to Josh Kendall, Sonya Cheuse, Clare Ferraro, Liz Parker,
Paul Slovak, Molly Stern and Veronica Windholz at Viking.